"DO NOT TRY TO INTIMIDATE ME."

"By the look of you, I'd say you are intimidated without my even trying." Damon grazed her cheek with the back of his hand, letting her have the full effect of his devil's eyes.

"Really, my lady, before you seek to cross swords with the devil, you should know that he can be very dangerous . . ."

His hand moved up, pushing her hat aside and off, dragging the stray gold curl down from her coiffure. He ran the silky tress between thumb and forefinger, twirled it around the latter, and holding her thus ensnared, pulled her close . . .

"Very dangerous, indeed . . ."

His mouth came down on hers, and Gwyneth felt the ruthless force behind it, caught the dark, sensual taste of him. The kiss was hot, male, and it immediately turned her bones to water. Oh, God, yes, she had every reason to fear him, every reason to defend herself before it was too late—

Other **AVON ROMANCES**

WICKED AT HEART

DANELLE HARMON

AVON BOOKS ◆ NEW YORK

WICKED AT HEART is an original publication of Avon Books. This work has never before appeared in book form. This work is a novel. Any similarity to actual persons or events is purely coincidental.

AVON BOOKS
A division of
The Hearst Corporation
1350 Avenue of the Americas
New York, New York 10019

Copyright © 1996 by Danelle F. Colson
Inside cover author photo by Thomas Keegan
Published by arrangement with the author
Library of Congress Catalog Card Number: 96-96027
ISBN: 0-380-78004-6

First Avon Books Printing: August 1996

AVON TRADEMARK REG. U.S. PAT. OFF. AND IN OTHER COUNTRIES, MARCA REGISTRADA, HECHO EN U.S.A.

Printed in the U.S.A.

RA   10   9   8   7   6   5   4   3   2   1

To Chris—
beloved husband and wise friend,
who gives me so much more than
words can express.
I love you.

Prologue

May 1802

The sex was great.

But that was about all the University of Oxford offered Damon Andrew Phillip deWolfe, the sixth Marquess of Morninghall, fourth Earl of deWolfe, and heir to one of the richest estates in England.

He'd mastered both Greek and Latin before he'd seen his tenth summer; he yawned through Aristophanes, Euripides, and even Thucydides, whose supposedly difficult works on the Peloponnesian War offered him no stimulus or challenge; he knew more than his Oxford dons, despised his rooms in Peckwater Quadrangle, and made no secret of the fact that he was bored out of his brilliant, young mind.

For Lord Morninghall was only fifteen years old and, in the several months he'd been here, had found nothing at Oxford's ancient Christ Church College to interest him.

Except the dean's pretty, young niece.

Three years his senior, she lay beside him in the darkness, golden hair tangled in a pillow of grass and skirts sliding up her legs with no small degree of help from young Morninghall's eager hand. She was oblivious to the magnificence of the Great Quadrangle which surrounded them, the brilliance of Wolsey and the architecture of Wren, oblivious to the perfume of

1

the night air, the echoing vastness of the courtyard, and the music the fountain made as it bubbled and splashed beneath the quiet stars. And now Great Tom, that noble old bell in the imposing central tower, began tolling out the curfew, 101 solemn strokes ringing through the night.

Bong . . . Bong . . . Bong. . . .

The students were supposed to be in.

Bong . . . Bong . . . Bong. . . .

A twinge of warning spread through Damon, but he ignored it, and soon the bell's summons had faded into the haze of passion his mind had become, heard but soon forgotten, no more a claimant to his attention now than the damp coolness of the earth beneath him, the musky scent of the grass, or the star-shot beauty of the velvet night above his head. There was only this strange but exquisite being beside, now beneath him, only the feel of frothy lace and satin as he anxiously pushed up her skirts, only the softness of inner thigh and the flimsy barrier of silk stockings as he hooked a finger atop first one, then the other, and slowly peeled the filmy garments down each leg. She urged him on with mouth and hands and breathy moans, and his heart began to pound with wild abandon. He buried his face in the curve of her neck, drowning in the rosy scent of her hair, the musky perfume of her skin. Her soft gasps of pleasure feathered the hair at his ear, and her hands roved encouragingly over his shoulders, his back, his bottom. He had a last coherent thought, a terrible vision of his peers spying on him from a darkened room overlooking the Quad above, but then his searching fingers found the silken nest of curls at the junction of the girl's thighs, and he could think of nothing else.

The area was soft, slick, hot, wet. He cupped the mound of springy hair with his palm, his fingers sliding into the warm and honeyed center of her.

She gasped and arched against him.

Good God, I hope I am doing it correctly.

He must have been, for as he stroked and thumbed her cleft, the girl moaned and shut her eyes, her nails digging like cat's claws into his back. Her flesh was liquid heat, and as Damon eagerly explored these alien folds of damp femininity, she began squirming and gasping and making little kitteny sobs deep in her throat. Gaining confidence, he kissed her neck and the warm, fragrant skin of her bosom while his fingers caressed her slick petals; then, tentatively, he slid his middle finger into her, all the way up to the knuckle, and caressed the hard little bud of her passion with his thumb.

"Oh . . . Damon," she gasped, seizing his head and yanking it down to hers. She was frantic, writhing, splaying her fingers through his hair as her lips wildly sought his. "Yes. . . . Touch me . . . *there.*"

Her mouth was hot and sweet, her tongue bold and thrusting. He felt his own body growing hot and savagely feverish. Yes, he was definitely doing it correctly. To hell with the classics, with Greek and Latin, with all that university sought to teach him; such pursuits were worthless compared to the education Miss Sarah Cherwell was giving him. Oh, this was good; no, it was better than good. *Oh, God bless you, Oxford.*

He broke the kiss, taking in great gulps of air. "Am I—hurting you?" he murmured, barely trusting himself to speak. How embarrassing it would be if his voice, still in transition from boy's to man's, decided to crack right now.

"Oh, no. Oh yes, my lord. Oh! *Oh!* Yes! . . . There. Rub me. Stroke me. . . ."

Confusion and impatience warred with instinct. Was he or wasn't he hurting her? "This way?"

"Harder. *Deeper,* Damon . . . oh, yes, look at me, I need to see your face—" She grasped his jaw, took it in both hands, hauled his head down to hers, and began kissing him hotly, greedily, feverishly. "Oh, those *eyes* of yours, they set my blood afire. . . ."

He slid his finger in deeper, his thumb caressing the moist petals of flesh, finding and rubbing that curious little bud of hardness until she was sobbing and

gasping and moaning his name. Her reaction excited
him and ignited his blood, made his rod swell and
strain and want, and soon the breath was roaring
through his lungs, mingling with the damp heat of her
skin and releasing the scent of roses from her hair, her
skin, her clothes. How different the female body was
from his own, how delicious the sensations just touching it evoked. His fingers were bathed in her love
juices now, his cock hard and pushing against his
trousers. And now, finally, Miss Sarah was reaching
for him, her butterfly-fingers unfastening his trousers
with quick and skillful surety and pushing them over
his bottom, down his legs.

Cool air swept over his backside. And then she
reached for him.

Damon froze, suddenly unsure.

But she persisted, wrapping her fingers around him,
squeezing gently and lightly stroking him until a hot
wash of feeling made him groan and push himself
against her, into her hand. Sweet agony. Blissful
anguish. She pulled him closer, her fingers and voice
guiding him, encouraging him, reassuring him.

"Come, my Lord Lover," she breathed, "let me
pleasure *you*."

Under her skillful ministrations, Damon felt as if
he were dying and late for an appointment with
heaven. He surrendered to her clever fingers, her
caressing hand, and with a harsh groan, moved over
her, completely covering her writhing form and pressing her down into the spongy, manicured grass with
the adolescent impatience of his passion. Her pale
hair haloed her head, and he buried his face in the
silky tresses, then the curve of her neck, heatedly
kissing, licking, and tonguing her tiny, shell-shaped
ear, her arched throat, her swollen, hungry lips. She
moaned softly, urging him on, and now her thumb
and fingers were swirling around the tip of his erection, bringing on savage bolts of sensation that made
the sweat break out all over his body, made all human
reason flee his head, made him think of nothing but—

but—*oh God, I cannot hold on like this, oh God, oh God*. And now she was guiding him toward that hot junction between her legs, spreading them and arcing her body so as better to accept him, her hands fluttering along his back, over his bottom, positioning him where she wanted him and initiating him into this age-old act with deft and knowing skill.

Bunched up skirts and tangled, frothy petticoats were lumped beneath his torso, but Damon knew the moment he was inside that forbidden, dark center of her, knew the moment when all was lost. With a groan, he sank into her, feeling himself sliding inch by glorious inch into that deliciously wet, deliciously hot cavern his fingers had just sampled. Her hands cupped his straining buttocks, urging him in deeper, further; her body writhed beneath his, inciting him to begin that violent, bucking motion he'd witnessed countless times in species other than his own, heard about from the ribald tales of his peers but had never experienced himself. Her hands were in his hair, her mouth pushing against his, her tongue thrusting between his teeth, her body a wild, hot thing that sought to be tamed. His elbows dug into the grass, but he cared not that stains would blemish his fine shirt, cared not that she was all but shredding it with her nails, cared not for anything, for all that was in his world was grassy earth, silky hair, the pungent scent of sexual musk, and her, her, *her*—

He felt the rushing maelstrom of his first release before he actually cried out with the violent force of it, pounding and pumping and driving his hot seed into her. Her nails dug into his back, her face split in a grimace of anguished ecstacy, her body arched, and then she too was bucking and crying out beneath him, her inner muscles squeezing and contracting and draining the last of his strength, the last of the juices from him.

It was over. Damon's arms tightened around her, and he dropped his sweating brow into the cool grass behind her shoulder, his breath coming in panting, labored gasps as he sought to make sense of all that had just happened to him.

"Oh, Sarah. . . ."

"Lovely, wasn't it? You did admirably well for your first time."

He was beaming, knew he was grinning like a fool. "You—it—was brilliant. Positively brilliant."

She giggled. He ran his hand along her jaw and turned her head so he could kiss her. Already, his rod was stirring again, and he wondered, vaguely, if, once activated, it ever stopped. He dragged his hand through her hair, anticipating a repeat of what they'd just done and silently thanking Lords Wycombe and Evesham for provoking him to commit this act as his initiation into The Circle. Not only was he a *man* now, but for the first time in his life, he had friends. Good friends, too—

A shoe came down on his back, squarely between his shoulder blades.

"If it isn't young Morninghall. Enjoying a new *curriculum,* my lord?"

Damon froze, and the world swung into sharp clarity. In the space of a heartbeat, he felt the summer breeze on his bare arse, the girl stiffening beneath him; he knew the dreadful silence of the night, the horrible taste of fear, and the sickening plunge of the stomach when one has just been caught doing something dreadfully, unforgivably wrong.

Whooping laughter erupted from one of the darkened rooms above, echoing over and over again through the vast, darkened courtyard.

Wycombe, Evesham, and The Circle. Laughing at him, every one of them.

He'd been set up. Betrayed. Deep, crushing hurt had barely reared its head before it was smothered by rage and, then, humiliation and embarrassment that must, like everything else, be concealed properly behind a mask of cool indifference, for he was the Marquess of Morninghall and there was no room for dread, no room for excuses, no room for being only fifteen years old when you've just been initiated into the act of maturity and now must pay the consequences for it.

Slowly, he raised his head and found himself looking up into the enraged face of the dean.

"Get up."

The voice was harsh, stone cold, and awful.

Miss Sarah, recognizing the owner of that voice, let out a shriek, threw Damon off, and scrambled to her feet. "You beast! You savage, rutting *beast,* have you no respect for a woman's virtue? To attack an innocent woman, to pull her from her chambers and seduce her! Have you no honor? Have you no *shame?*" She yanked her skirts down and began screaming at him like a woman gone mad, leaving Damon to stare at her in numbed shock. What babble was this? *Attacked and seduced her?!* His brows rose and he drew himself up, but before he could deliver his own scathing defense, she slapped him full across the face and flung herself into her uncle's arms, letting loose with a convincing display of tears that would have brought the level of the Atlantic up by at least a foot.

And still that awful laughter, echoing out over the courtyard from the window above.

Damon's well-bred dignity was the only thing that kept him from fleeing. With as much disdain as he could muster, he jerked on his trousers and buttoned them, though only he knew that his fingers tangled with each other and his heart was pounding wildly. And all he could hear was that terrible laughter bubbling out of the window above his head, going on and on and on . . .

And Miss Sarah's shrill voice.

"He attacked me, Uncle! He forced me into this horrible, shameful act, I swear it. I am the victim here, please understand! He overpowered me! He raped me! He—he—oh-h-h-h . . ."

Cradling the girl to his chest, the dean fixed Damon with a furious stare. "Is that so, Morninghall?"

It wasn't so at all. Damn far from it, in fact. And suddenly the rage swept in on a tide of hurt, rage that was deep and raw and black, for Damon had been betrayed by not just The Circle but by Miss Sarah herself, and he was not in the mood to feel gallant. He raised his head, looked the dean straight in the eye, and hoped his voice would not betray the maelstrom of emotion that fisted his heart.

"I did not attack your niece, sir." And then, so full of anger and hurt that he was unable to help himself, he added disdainfully, "In fact, the 'virtuous' Miss Sarah was the one who wanted to do it right here in the Quad. Personally, I would have preferred a proper bed, but I'm afraid that *she* was most adamant—"

The resultant crack of a hand across his face nearly broke Damon's aristocratic nose. Stars spun before his eyes, and he felt the ground come up hard against his hip, his shoulder, as he went down. It took him a moment to realize the dean had actually hit him, and gingerly fingering his nose and lip, he looked dazedly up into the man's thunderous face.

The dean gave him no time to recover. Snaring Damon by the front of his shirt, he yanked him to his feet with a forcefulness that nearly choked him. "I knew when you came here you'd be nothing but trouble," he seethed, glaring into Damon's impassive face and viciously twisting the shirt until Damon couldn't draw breath. "Knew it the moment I laid eyes on you! Too damned young! Too damned smart! Too damned spoiled!"

Damon stumbled, gasping, as the dean shoved him violently backward. He lost his balance, landing hard on his backside. More laughter burst from the windows above. He felt his eyes beginning to burn with tears of humiliation, and knew he was fast losing his grip on aristocratic indifference.

"Supreme intelligence has always been your curse instead of a blessing, hasn't it? How very unfortunate that you couldn't have put that wonderful brain of yours toward the pursuit of self and science, instead of letting yourself be governed by what lies inside your trousers! What a loss to humankind that you're ruled by the devil you so resemble, instead of by the God you've chosen to ignore! What's that, Sarah? Yes, of course, dearest, I know. There, there, darling. It's all right, that beast shall not go near you again." The dean cradled his niece's head against his chest and, glaring at Damon, shook a finger to emphasize his point. "And don't think your money will buy you out of this one either, Morninghall. Spoiled, titled, and rich you may be, but I don't give a bloody damn. No wonder the dons abhor you. No wonder you've abandoned your studies in favor of carnal pursuits. No wonder your very own *mother* thinks you're the devil, wicked, filthy fiend that you are! Now pack your things and get your spoiled little carcass out of my sight!"

Damon finally found his voice, but it was little more than a pitiful whisper. "Pack my things? But sir, I don't understand—"

"Understand *this!* From this moment on, you are no longer welcome at Oxford, and I never want to see your face around here again! Your studies here are *finished,* do you hear me? *Finished!* I'm sending you back to your mother, where you damn well belong!"

Sending you back to your mother . . .

Damon went deathly pale. The world began to rush in on him, like a constricting tunnel from which there was no escape. Then the facade of aristocratic aloofness he'd tried so hard to maintain cracked right down the middle, leaving him raw and exposed and vulnerable.

He whirled and fled into the night, the laughter of The Circle's members floating out over the vast courtyard behind him.

Lord Morninghall's final night at Oxford was nothing short of hell. It was a long time before he finally dropped off, and when slumber finally overcame him, it was broken by dreams of his mother's cruel hand against his flesh, his mother's wine bottle crashing against his shoulderblades as he fled, his mother's tormented ravings about his devil's eyes, his devil's doings, his devil's deeds. . . .

Now, in the sane light of early morning, Damon was bleary-eyed and depressed, his movements wooden as he tossed his few things into a satchel and set it down in a chair. Outside, dawn's light was just touching the magnificent carved spires that soared above the city, softening the forbidding stone and toasting the ancient buildings in peachy washes of pink and gold. Below his window the carefully groomed lawn of Peckwater Quad was a misty green; doves cooed from the elegant courtyard, and sunlight slashed against the stately Corinthian columns of the library opposite.

Oxford. It would be the last time he'd look upon its noble, ancient beauty, the last time he'd behold its quiet magnificence. He set his jaw. He didn't care. He hadn't learned a damn thing here, anyhow—except how to make a girl moan and sob in the throes of passion.

He sat down and put on his shoes.

I don't care.

But he *did* care. Despite everything, life at Oxford was still better than life at Morninghall ever had been, and the thought of returning to his ancestral home chilled his bones and made his heart accelerate with sudden anxiety.

I won't go back there, he vowed, bending over and yanking on his other shoe. *Mama will scream at me. She'll call Reverend Croyden in and make him exorcise the devil in me. And after he leaves, she'll take to the bottle and beat me. Again and again and again . . .*

At Morninghall there was no place to escape. Not in the library, where he had once been able to lose himself in books while hiding from his mother's heavy hand. Not in the huge bedchamber, which, with its gloomy, ancient furnishings, heraldic crests, and magnificent carved four-poster, had always frightened him, for it had belonged to five other marquesses before him and was still—he used to think when he woke up, trembling, in the dead of night—haunted by their wandering spirits. Not in the house, not in the stables, not even in the fact that he was heir to the title and the vast Cotswolds estates that went with it.

For at Morninghall there was nothing to protect him from his mother's madness. Nor, when she learned he'd been sent down from Oxford, her wrath.

The young marquess finished with his shoes and, without straightening up in his chair, put his head in his hands. It would be as it always had been. Damon the Devil. Damon the Beast. Damon, born on the sixth day of the sixth month in the sixth year of the decade. Oh, God help him. . . .

His hands began to shake, his palms to perspire against his equally hot brow. He could see it now. The wailing would start, then the screaming, the sobbing, the drinking, the beatings . . .

Clawing his hands over his face, he rose, gathering his resolve and trying to put the inevitable out of his mind.

The sun was higher now, burning the mist off the manicured courtyard, turning the honey-colored stone of the library lemon and gold and sparkling off its beautiful Venetian windows. A blackbird sang from somewhere near, and already Damon could smell the scent of food from the hall's kitchens, could hear laughter in the adjoining room. The great university was awakening. It was best to leave now, before everyone found out what had happened—if they hadn't already. He had been humiliated enough.

He tied his cravat, pulled on a sober, elegantly fitted jacket, then, picking up his hat and satchel, turned his back on his room—and Oxford. Head high, mouth carved in stone, he left the stately Palladian building in Peckwater Quad that he'd called home these past few months, passed the library, skirted the vast, magnificent Great Quadrangle, and exited Christ Church via the Gateway, above which the seven-ton bell, Great Tom, had tolled out his impending demise the night before. He made his way south down Fish Street, hoping no one would recognize him, hoping someone would, and all the while wishing with all his heart that the dean would come running out of nowhere to call him back.

But no one recognized him. No one paid him any attention. And the dean did not come to call him back.

He clenched his satchel, his fingers trembling. He kept walking, his face devoid of all emotion, his eyes staring straight ahead, his brain numbing itself to the fate that awaited him at Morninghall.

It was some time before the sounds finally penetrated his misery. Church bells pealing gloriously. Barking dogs. The distant sound of music, singing, cheering. And it was coming closer.

For one brief moment Damon had a fantasy that it was all on his behalf, that the noise he heard was a crowd of people coming to drag him back to university. But that wish was quickly dispelled as the cheering grew louder and louder and people began to run past him, bumping into him, knocking him aside, and yelling at him to get out of the way. The crowd thickened. Someone's elbow caught him a glancing blow in the ribs; a dog and a pack of small boys shot past, heels flying. Windows scraped open above his head, and all around, on both sides of the street, people leaned out, waving brightly colored handkerchiefs and cheering wildly. Others came streaming out of buildings, out of the colleges themselves, and, in a mass exodus, went running down the street.

Thankful for an excuse, any excuse, to delay his return to Morninghall, Damon straightened his hat and followed them.

The crowds were several feet thick by the time he reached their epicenter. He shouldered his way through, eliciting outraged looks and curses he pointedly ignored. Fortunately he was tall enough to peer over the heads of those nearest the street, and was thus able to see the object of all the attention.

It was a carriage drawn by a nervous team of gray horses which had all they could do to get the vehicle through the overwhelming, cheering crowds. Trying to see, Damon stood on tiptoe, his view distorted by hands waving before his face, his ears ringing with the wild cheering, his ribs squeezed among a mass of hot, perspiring bodies which were all pressing, shoving, pushing, and struggling as they fought for viewing room closest to the street. A gap opened in the sea of heads in front of him, and it was then that Damon caught a glimpse of the one whom all the bell ringing, all the cheering, all the shouting, calling, singing, and celebrating was for.

It was only a glimpse, but it was enough to change the Marquess of Morninghall's life forever. A glimpse of a handsome man, his blue-and-white naval uniform sparkling with gold trim and military magnificence, his hair gleaming like a pharaoh's gold in the bright morning sunlight. A glimpse—of a hero.

That hero leaned out of the carriage, gallantly catching a young woman's hand and raising it to his lips, laughing as the movement of the carriage dragged him free and she, crying his name and pressing her handkerchief to her sobbing mouth, ran to catch up. Courage stamped itself in every plane of his face, humor turned up the corners of his firm mouth, and a hint of reckless bravado shone in cool, gray eyes which swept the crowd, seeing all, seeing no one, as he waved to the throngs of people who had poured into the streets just to pay homage to him.

"Commodore Lord! Commodore Julian Lord! Oxford welcomes you! Welcome to Oxford, Commodore Lord!"

Unreasonably angry and unable to explain why, Damon fought for air and turned to a woman who was squashed in the throng beside him. Her gaze flew open when she saw his eyes, and with a gasp, she tried to step back, one hand going to her heart.

The customary reaction only fueled his irritation. "Dare I ask what a national hero is doing in Oxford?" he drawled, wishing she wouldn't stare at him so.

"H-he's come here t' receive an hon'ry doctorate from the university," she said hurriedly, pressing against the mass of bodies in her desire to be away from him. "If ye'll excuse me, please . . ."

Dismissing her, he turned to watch the carriage until it was finally swallowed up by the crowds that ran to keep up with it. The celebration, the clamoring, the cheering went with it. In its wake a lonely wind followed, as though it too worshiped Commodore Lord and had no wish to be left behind. Damon stood there on the pavement, a few last people running past, until he was all alone once again, a few bits of paper skittering past his feet, the sounds of the celebration fading off as the procession made its way toward the Star Inn.

Commodore Julian Lord. Loved by everyone, respected, admired, revered, and adored. Damon had never been loved. He had never been respected, admired, revered, or adored.

And he, standing there on the pavement and clenching his fists with the force of his envy, knew there was nothing in this world he desired more.

If Julian Lord could be a hero, then so could he. If Julian Lord could glean the love of an entire nation just by sinking a few French ships, then so could he. He would run away, then, and join the navy. He too would become a great naval hero. He too would beat the Frogs and win the undying admiration of his countrymen. Then everyone would love him, just as they loved Julian Lord.

So be it.

Lifting his chin, Lord Morninghall kicked his way through the litter blowing mournfully around his feet and headed south.

Toward the sea.

Men sensual and hardened by pleasures! You who in full Parliament outrage your victims and declare that the prisoners are happy! Would you know the full horror of their condition, come without giving notice beforehand; dare to descend before daylight into the tombs in which you bury living creatures who are human beings like yourselves; try to breathe for one minute the sepulchral vapour which these unfortunates breathe for many years, and which sometimes suffocates them; see them tossing in their hammocks, assailed by thousands of insects, and wooing in vain the sleep which could soften for one moment their sufferings!

French prisoner of war Colonel Lebertre

Chapter 1

❦

A decade had passed since that fateful day Lord Morninghall had been sent down from Oxford, and during that time Britain had managed to plunge herself into yet another war, this one with her former colonies across the Atlantic.

Again.

The war of 1812 was mainly a result of British arrogance, for His Majesty's vessels were wont to stop neutral-trading American ships for "inspection" and steal the very seamen from them, claiming they were—rightly or wrongly—British deserters. Naturally the fledgling United States took offense, because not all of the men taken from its vessels were, in fact, deserters. Nor, for that matter, British.

The ongoing war with France, and now the one with the United States, made Britain's ports a beehive of activity. Battered warships limped into their dry-docks for repair and were quickly sent back out; new vessels constantly were taking shape on the slips, craft of every size and description hustled supplies about the busy harbors, and seaside taverns were filled with smart officers clad in blue and white, the elite of the finest navy in the world. But it was easy, while reading about yet another British victory in some distant place, or watching a great man-of-war getting underway and feeling the swell of pride that was inevitable in even the least romantic of hearts at such a glorious sight, to forget about the more squalid, shameful side

17

of war. The side about which no one wanted to think. Tough seamen now blind, missing limbs, or insane, reduced to crying piteously for coins in the streets and along the beach. Widows left alone, helpless and destitute. Orphaned children.

And the navy's prison hulks.

Nasty, horrible things they were, floating gaols with conditions fit only for rats. Shorn of their masts, rigging, and sails, deformed by ugly superstructures and painted in the dingy smoke of their own galley chimneys, the once-proud men-of-war were now home—and hell—to thousands of French, American, and other prisoners of war, who spent their miserable existences hoping for either escape or death. Anchored in every major British port, prison hulks were the most ignoble command glory-seeking officers in His Majesty's Royal Navy could glean.

And in Portsmouth, on a spring day in 1813, just such a command was that of the sixth Marquess of Morninghall, fourth Earl of deWolfe.

It was not a happy situation.

"My lord? About this visitor?"

So absorbed was he in his reading that Damon hadn't even heard Midshipman Danny Foyle slip into his cabin. "Visitor?" he asked absently, not bothering to look up as he slowly ran his forefinger down a paragraph of text.

"Er, the uh, woman, sir . . ."

"Ah, yes, the indefatigable, abominable, venerable Lady Gwyneth Evans Simms." Damon shut the book and turned his unsettling gaze on the midshipman, nailing him to the bulkhead with a stare that could penetrate steel. "As if a visit from Admiral Bolton, the stabbing of the purser, and now the escape of three more prisoners weren't enough for one bloody week—"

"Surely, sir, last night's escape wasn't *our* fault," Foyle whined. "Everyone's saying it's the work of the Black Wolf—"

"Black Wolf, my arse. This *Black Wolf* character is naught but that insufferable American captain who escaped from our ship *last* week—what was his name?—Matson? Morgan? Yes, Morgan something-or-other—"

"Merrick, sir. Connor Merrick, that is—"

"Morgan, Merrick, whatever. Why everyone thinks this Black Wolf fellow is the ghost of some dead prisoner, come back to get his revenge, is beyond me. It doesn't take a genius to figure out that this mythical moron—who, *incidentally,* started vexing us directly following Merrick's escape—is the American himself. And now he's targeting *my* ship just to get his revenge on me. 'Tis enough to plague a man right into the grave, the whole bloody lot of it." With a curse, he shoved the book aside and stalked to the stern windows, his commanding height making the deckhead seem to drop several feet.

"Christ, I need *air,*" he swore, flinging a window open.

Foyle gripped his hands behind his back, hard, to still their trembling. He was afraid of Lord Morninghall. *All* of them were, right down to John Radley, the heavy-handed lieutenant who commanded the *Surrey*'s complement of Royal Marines. And now His Lordship was in one of his black tempers, though Foyle figured he certainly could not be blamed for it. It was damned humiliating that the American prisoners had escaped, and even more humiliating that the whole of Portsmouth—thanks to the newspapers, which picked up on everything in this busy naval port—knew about it. Foyle bit his lip and risked a glance at the big book His Lordship had been reading. It was a copy of *Peterson's Index of Illnesses, Complaints, and Physicks.*

"Are you ill, my lord?"

The marquess shot him a threatening glare. "Do I *look* ill, Foyle?"

"You look . . . uh, fatigued, sir!"

"Fatigued. Well, yes, of course." The captain turned toward the open window, his head bent as he absently inspected his thumbnail. He was a picture of calm, but Foyle was not fooled; Morninghall was very adept at hiding his emotions beneath an unimpassioned cloak of ice. "So, what does the old harridan want, anyhow?"

"Old harridan?"

"This infernal Welshwoman, damn you."

"Oh. Yes. Well, as you know, sir, the, er, *old harridan* has decided to take up the plight of prison ships as her latest cause and crusade, and wishes to start with ours."

"I see."

Still toying with his thumbnail, the marquess stared hard across the glittering waters of the harbor. Sunlight reflected off the waves below and radiated over his diabolical countenance. Foyle thought the flames of hell must look like that, reflected in the face of the devil who surveyed them, and the very thought made his throat go dry.

"One must wonder why she doesn't attack the civilian convict hulks instead. . . ." the marquess mused, his low, silky voice doing little to banish Foyle's uneasiness.

"I don't know, sir. Her husband, the late Lord Simms, had a passion for naval affairs; perhaps that has something to do with it."

"Doubtless."

Foyle's nervousness ran away with him, and he began to babble. "Still, my lord, one must wonder why the Transport Board has granted Lady Simms permission to come aboard. You know how they usually are, unwilling to let anyone come aboard the hulks because they're so afraid someone will think that conditions are much worse than they really are. It would be easy to draw the wrong conclusions, and declare that the prisoners are being abused, maltreated, neglected, when *we* know, of course, that such is not the case. Surely she must have got permission from her brother-in-law, the new Lord Simms—I mean, he *is* highly placed in the Transport Office—"

"Mr. Foyle . . ."

"Well, it's true, sir, how else would she be able—"

"Mr. *Foyle*."

The midshipman's jaws snapped shut and paling, he took a wary step backward.

Morninghall glared at him, then turned to lean against the bulkhead, his hand absently splaying over his chest, his thick lashes drifting shut over intense, coldly dispassionate eyes. His dark hair was swept elegantly off his high, intelligent forehead, and Foyle noted that, against it, his face looked suddenly pale and drawn. He also noted the tightened lips, the fingers curled around the back of one chair, the light film of perspiration that gleamed on that noble, aristocratic brow.

"My lord, are you well?"

"Of course I'm well," the marquess snapped, firing another glare at his hapless subordinate. He closed his eyes once more. "Just . . . never mind."

"I could fetch the ship's doctor, if you wish—"

"I believe the chaplain might serve me better, as I am beyond the help of that butcher who calls himself a surgeon. But don't bother, Foyle." He pulled out a handkerchief and dabbed at his brow, then regarded the midshipman with angry impatience. "Just . . . leave me alone. I don't wish for company at the moment."

"And the, er, visitor, sir?"

"Ah, yes. She who seeks to make my life hell. Champion of orphan and pensioner alike, widow of the most nauseatingly eloquent bastard ever to sit in the House of Lords, defender of the oppressed, and now training her guns on *my* command as her goddamned Cause of the Month." The marquess straightened up and again turned to look out the window. "Tell the old bat she may come aboard at eight bells."

"Er . . . she's waiting on the pier now, sir, and requests permission to come aboard immediately."

"She will come aboard when I say so, and not a moment before."

"But—"

"I *said,* Foyle, *make her wait.*" Damon said coldly, leveling his hard stare on the youth. "Do I make myself clear?"

Foyle nodded. "Yes, sir. I . . . shall make her do just that."

"Good. And mind that you close the door after you this time. I'm in no mood to suffer the stench coming up from below."

Lady Gwyneth Evans Simms sat primly in the boat, trying in vain to keep her skirts free of the puddle that sloshed at her feet and wrinkling her nose at the horrendous smells drifting toward them from the prison ship. HMS *Surrey* had once been a fierce warrior of the sea, but looking at her now, it was hard to believe she had once ruled the waves under a great cloud of sail, hard to believe she had ever been anything but the disgraceful atrocity she had become. Shed-like structures enclosed what had been her forecastle and waist, and clotheslines, their garments billowing in the wind, were strung between masts that were now nothing but mere stubs. The hulk lay atop the harbor like a black, cancerous sore, and Gwyneth had no trouble envisioning the living hell she must be for the hapless prisoners of war contained within her. Eyes watering, she pulled out a handkerchief scented with rosewater and pressed it to her nose, her violet eyes dark and angry above the fragile white square of linen.

She was thankful for her anger. People told her she had a sweet face, and sweet faces were a liability when one was trying to command respect, attention, and results. But today there was no need to force her heart-shaped countenance into one of sharpness and severity, for Lady Gwyneth Evans Simms had every reason to be not only angry but downright furious.

It was bad enough that this Lord Morninghall character thought to keep her waiting, but anticipating the insufferable, intolerable conditions in which he kept fellow living beings was enough to stir the warrior in Gwyneth. Well, she had a thing or two to say to the loathsome beast when she came face to face with him!

Her gaze snapped from the prison hulk to the tar who rowed the little boat steadily toward it. He was staring at the swell of Gwyneth's high breasts, a dreamy little smile turning up one corner of his mouth, a faint smear of perspiration glistening on his brow. Well accustomed to lecherous gaping and bawdy comments, Gwyneth fixed him with a bullet-eyed stare and asked icily, "Do you find something to interest you, sailor?"

Surprised by such rancor in one so lovely and fair, the tar colored and grinned. "Beggin' yer pardon, ma'am—"

"That's Lady Simms, if you please."

"Aye, beggin' yer pardon, but I was just thinkin' ye look a sight different than we was all expectin' ye to look. His Lordship's gonna be none too pleased when we brings ye aboard."

"And does that worry you? I cannot help but notice that you are not rowing with equal stroke or vigor. Keep in mind, sailor, that I am not a person who likes to be kept waiting."

"Yes, m'lady."

Grinning, the seaman put his back into the task. The oars dipped into the sparkling waters of the harbor, rising, dripping, plunging back down again. The little boat sliced through the waves, carrying Gwyneth ever closer to the prison ship.

She pressed the handkerchief against her nose once again. The smell of the thing was overwhelming.

Of all the causes into which she had thrown her heart and soul—and there had been many—this one was surely going to present the greatest challenge. Not that she minded challenges; in fact, she thrived on them. But this was the first cause she was taking on without the backing and political muscle of her deceased husband, who had succumbed to pneumonia thirteen months before. Dear old William. He had been a powerful man in the House of Lords, and a good friend too. She still missed his companionship, his wise counsel, dearly. She almost wished he were here to see her now, taking on this wicked blackguard who commanded HMS *Surrey,* prison hulk.

She'd done her homework well enough. Damon Andrew Phillip deWolfe, sixth Marquess of Morninghall, fourth Earl of deWolfe, born 1786, sent down from Oxford in 1802, entered the navy that same summer. She reached into her reticule, took out a tiny notebook, and read over her notes, though she had already memorized the facts and such an action was merely a token one. Commended for bravery at Trafalgar in 1805. Promoted to lieutenant in 1806 and captain in 1810. Court-martialed in 1811 for threatening bodily harm to another officer after a dispute of unknown origin, and subsequently put at the bottom of the seniority list within his rank. And there, her last entry in the chronology of Lord Morninghall's naval life: he'd made the newspapers a month before for dueling with—and killing—the son of Admiral Edmund Bolton, an act she suspected was the catalyst behind his swift and merciless transfer to the prison hulk he now commanded.

A *prison hulk.* And he a marquess, besides!

She closed the notebook and tapped a finger against its cover, gazing at the approaching bulk of that very ship. Surely such ugly stains upon what otherwise might have been a glorious career would have made Morninghall bitter, a fact she would have to keep in mind during her dealings with him. She envisioned him as small, cocky, and mean. Or perhaps bloated and self-important, a swine weighing in at twenty stone with a nose gone scarlet from drink. Either way, he'd be a thoroughly miserable character. And, no doubt, the sensational news sweeping Portsmouth— that the mysterious man calling himself the Black Wolf had raided Morninghall's ship the night before and made off with several American prisoners—

would add no sugar to a temper that was probably already worse than bad.

Normally, Gwyneth's dealings with such a fellow would be conducted with patience and pity. But this man, with his high-handed dictate about allowing her to come aboard when he damn well felt like it—

Well, Gwyneth was not inclined to be patient, pitying, *or* understanding.

The raucous yelling and catcalls of the men imprisoned within the hulk invaded her thoughts at the same time she noticed that the sunlight had fallen off, throwing her ice-blue skirts into shadow. Looking up, she saw the immense, smoky bulk of the ship looming above her like a mighty fortress of death, and then the sailor was maneuvering the boat against the rickety-looking stairs built against its filthy, curved hull.

Not even the gulls dared venture near this floating hell. Indeed, even the water that surrounded it seemed to be as still and dead as the River Styx.

"Ye sure ye wanna be goin' aboard her, m'lady?" the tar challenged, grinning as he fought to be heard over the prisoners' yelling.

"You sure you don't want a refreshing swim in the harbor?" Gwyneth yelled back, shoving her notebook back into her reticule. "Help me up, if you please."

Hundreds of waving, clawing arms covered with filth thrust through the barred gunports, and the clamor grew deafening.

Gwyneth stuck out her hand toward the seaman, waiting.

He stared at her for a moment, then he shrugged and took her gloved hand. Moments later she was standing on the little platform at the bottom of the stairs. Alone.

Morninghall had sent no one to meet her.

With one hand steadying her blue velvet hat, Gwyneth marched up the damp steps, and every voice on the ship went silent.

Chapter 2

Gwyneth was met by a young midshipman on deck.

"I am Midshipman Foyle," he said grandly, taking her gloved hand and puffing out his chest with self-importance. "Welcome to HMS *Surrey.*"

"Indeed."

Her sharp tone did not faze him, nor did the offensive stench coming up from below. Pressing her handkerchief against her nose, Gwyneth declined his offered elbow and instead swept up her skirts with her free hand. As she followed him aft, she was all too aware of the stares of the seamen, the hushed comments, the snickers and elbow-jostling that surrounded her. Someone let out a long, low whistle.

Gwyneth never paused, though her eyes narrowed and spots of angry color bloomed in her cheeks.

"Pay no attention to this lot," Foyle said, his voice high and whiny, not unlike a colicky child's. "The sea is no place to learn manners, I'm afraid."

"As your very *gentlemanly* captain has already proven," Gwyneth remarked acidly, still seething over the appalling conditions that surrounded her and growing more furious by the moment. To think that decent human beings were forced to live in this floating hell, their only crime being that they had fought on the enemy side! "But no matter. I already dislike what I see here, and by the time I am through with him, Lord Morninghall will rue the day he ever met me."

The midshipman only raised a skeptical brow and looked away, but not before Gwyneth caught his private smirk. Of course it was easy for him to be so blithe, *he* was not the one forced to live in the conditions she could only imagine below! And Gwyneth knew from experience that men in Foyle's position usually harbored no pity in their hearts for others, but found self-importance and satisfaction in the bullying of the weak, the unfortunate, the helpless. Foyle was of that mold; she saw it in the spoiled set of his mouth, in the swagger of his stride. And she could see him smiling, as though he'd found her remark amusing. Did he think Morninghall would send her running with her tail between her legs? Well, the both of them had another thing coming if they thought she was some quaking ninny. Gwyneth was about to open her mouth to say as much when Foyle suddenly seized her elbow, steering her around a group of filthy, vacant-eyed prisoners just coming up from the black mouth of a hatch.

The sight was enough to stop Gwyneth dead in her tracks.

The prisoners, their once-yellow clothes tattered and filthy, blinked in the sudden light, knuckling their eyes and groaning before another midshipman angrily urged them on. Chains dragged from their ankles, making a horrible, rattling noise as they scraped across the deck. Their faces were bearded and encrusted with grime, their backs were rounded and hunched, and some had advanced signs of scurvy.

"Dear God," Gwyneth breathed, paling with horror as the group approached.

"Come, m'lady, you shouldn't have to look at these wretches."

"They're in chains," she murmured. "Why?"

"One of their number escaped last night and drowned in the marshes, the stupid sod. They're being taken off the ship so that they might bury the wretch—hence the chains. Come, let us move on."

Despite the bile that welled up in her throat, the sudden pity that tightened her chest, Gwyneth resisted the midshipman's efforts to draw her forward, instead forcing herself to watch in growing horror as each prisoner was led past. One young man paused, stretching a pathetically skeletal hand toward her as though she were a vision he needed to touch in order to believe, before the midshipman cursed and swung his musket hard across the back of the man's legs. The prisoner went down, smashing his chin on the grimy deck. Wordlessly, he picked himself up with what shreds of pride he had left, the threadbare yellow shirt issued by the Transport Office and stamped with the letters "T.O." revealing raw, bare patches of sore-ridden skin. Gwyneth stood frozen, her fist against her mouth, the back of her throat aching with unshed tears. But the man was now too ashamed to look at her. He hung his head and, now limping, shuffled off with his companions. Gwyneth swallowed hard, determined not to let Foyle see how much the sight had affected her. She needed her wits, and her rage, if she was going to do any good here.

"Begging your pardon, m'lady, but as prison ships go, this is one of the *good* ones—"

"*Good* ones?" she said angrily, his sniveling voice snapping her out of her shock. "I see nothing at all that is *good* about this—this *atrocity,* and I suspect that by the time I've finished touring the down-stairs—"

"Belowdecks, ma'am," he corrected, sheepishly.

"*Belowdecks* I'll find enough information to condemn the lot of you. I've seen *pigs* kept in better conditions than this!"

A breeze, ripe with the stench of the nearby mud-flats, came up, whipping the laundry strung above Gwyneth's head and tugging a long, blond curl from the severe bun into which she had scraped her hair. She shoved it back beneath her hat, trying to calm her shaken nerves. With a sharp jerk of her head, she bade the youth to move on.

They passed a hatch, a gateway into the stinking bowels of the ship. Gwyneth paused, despite Foyle's urging, and hesitantly took the handkerchief away from her nose. Hidden beneath the noxious fumes, the stench of sickness, imprisonment, excretions, and death, was the faint scent of—

"That's vinegar you're smelling," Foyle said importantly, as she wrinkled her nose. "The captain orders the ship fumigated every night."

"Obsessed with cleanliness, is he?" Gwyneth drawled, with cutting sarcasm.

"He does his best, m'lady. And we set the sails to direct a breeze down there too. Sorry if you find the vinegar offensive. It's not *our* fault that—"

"The scent of vinegar is not what I'm objecting to," she said. "Where are the prisoners kept?"

"Belowdecks."

"Take me there, please."

"Oh, I can't do that, m'lady. No one's allowed below, and besides, it's no place for a gentlewoman, I'm afraid." He led her beneath the poop deck and stopped at a large door sporting a bright coat of red paint. "Anyhow, here we are. I'm sure that His Lordship will be . . . delighted to meet you."

With that, Foyle knocked once on the door and, with sudden terror animating his face, hesitantly pushed it open.

Gwyneth, prepared to do battle, sailed in. And halted in her tracks.

There, before the stern windows, stood a high-backed swivel chair upholstered in wine-red velvet. The back of the chair was toward her, and above it she could just see the crown of a dark head.

Foyle found his voice, which came out as a thready squeak. "Your Lordship? Lady Gwyneth Evans Simms to see you."

A lengthy pause, then a deep-timbred voice.

"I know."

A moment passed. The silence grew uncomfortable. Then, slowly, the chair began to rotate.

First an ear. Then a ruthless, aristocratic profile.

Then the face of the devil himself.

Gwyneth's breath caught in her throat, and she stepped back involuntarily.

"Do come in, my dear," His Lordship drawled, with an imperious sweep of his hand. He had one long, tautly muscled leg thrown casually over the other, and his snowy shirt was open at the throat to reveal a broad wedge of tanned skin whorled with hair. He did not bother to rise, he did not bother to take and lift her hand, he did not bother to honor her presence at all, as any man of his breeding ought. Instead, he merely raised his brows and said with arrogant self-confidence, "How stunned you look— but, ah, I seem to have a similar effect on all the woman I meet."

Effect wasn't the word.

Danger, she thought. It was there in his lean, powerful body; in his relaxed, watchful pose; in the very way he looked at her—as though he were going to rise out of that chair at any moment and ravish her, right there. His face was strikingly chiseled, angelic yet demonic, beautiful, wicked, arresting. But it was his eyes that were so unnerving. They were cold eyes, almost iridescent, thawed by a hot, underlying sexuality simmering just beneath the surface, glowing with cunning intelligence yet veiled by thick lashes which lent him an expression of boredom and challenge. They were piercing, those eyes, expressive, pure as a Siberian glacier and devastatingly lethal.

Devil's eyes, she thought, swallowing hard, *and he knows just how to use them.*

"You may leave now, Mr. Foyle," the marquess murmured, never taking that malevolent stare off her.

Gwyneth waited until the youth had made his swift exit. "And what *effect* is that, Lord Morninghall?" she challenged.

The marquess looked at her. Something shifted in

those eyes, moving subtly across them, humor that came and went as quickly as a wisp of cloud over a darkening sun, before they became chillingly cold and hard once again.

"Do you know," he murmured faintly, leaning forward to pour himself a glass of brandy and purposely neglecting to offer her one, "my own mother thought me the devil." His voice was deep, elegant, and cultured, as polished as heirloom silver, both hard and soft at the same time and oozing a dark and unexpected sensuality. Hard and soft. Angelic yet demonic. The man was a study in paradox. "She ended her days in a London asylum, where she took great delight in informing her equally mad audience that she had birthed the Antichrist." He raked her with that frozen stare. "You are younger than I expected, a mere chit. What do you want?"

The swift change of thought, the quick move from pleasantry back to cutting rudeness, was enough to bring Gwyneth's head up and her color right along with it. She fixed him with what she hoped was her most militant glare.

"What I *want*, Lord Morninghall, is a tour of your ship, with the intention of condemning it to the hell you so proudly proclaim yourself to have crawled out of. Shall I entrust you to accompany me, or your more affable midshipman?"

"Frankly, my lady, I am not inclined to give you a tour, and Mr. Foyle has other, more important duties to occupy him. You may leave anytime you wish. For that, I would be most happy to *escort* you."

Booted leg crossed casually over his knee, he let that icy-hot gaze of his slide heatedly over her bosom, leaving Gwyneth feeling as though he'd just stripped her naked and ravished her without laying a hand on her suddenly warm flesh. Then, as though the sight failed to interest him, he let out a bored sigh, rose, and went to the window, where he stood gazing out over Portsmouth Harbor with his back to her.

And a broad, beautifully shaped and tapered back it

was, too—the kind usually possessed by princes, warriors, *kings.*

Gwyneth stared at him. "You are unforgivably rude, sir," she said, clutching the strings of her reticule and trying to keep her voice even.

"So I have been told."

"You are also vain beyond tolerance."

"Yes, I've been made aware of that, as well. Pray, tell me something I *don't* know."

She clenched her fists, gritted her teeth, and privately cursed him, but he did not turn around. All the while she noted that his hair was dark and glossy, swept back off his forehead and curling against his white collar, and that she had a sudden, insane wish to run her fingers through it.

"Very well, then," she said stiffly. "Address the wall if you wish, as I'm sure it's the only thing you *will* have an effect on. I, for one, am going to seek out your second in command and get some answers from *him.*"

That brought him around, as she knew it would, and in his face she saw a quick impression of sensitivity crushed by something dark and malevolent running just beneath the surface. But that sensitivity was just a fleeting impression, so fleeting she wasn't even sure she'd seen it; it was all too apparent that this man had absorbed hard lessons in life, or maybe no lessons at all, for within that angel-devil's demeanor lurked a dark carnality which made her want to back away from it, as a winter traveler moves close to a warm fire and suddenly finds it too hot.

Very slowly, he put down his glass, impaling her with those diabolical eyes.

"And do I have an effect on *you,* Lady Simms?"

"A most disagreeable one," she snapped, chin high as she unflinchingly met that glittering stare. But she could not hold it, and a hot flush stole over her cheeks almost immediately. She jerked her gaze away and moved across the cabin, running a gloved finger over the back of a chair so that he wouldn't notice her deteriorating composure. Not that he could fail to.

She paused, looking disdainfully at the carved bed with its maroon-and-gold curtains, the freshly painted deckhead, the plush rugs which softened the deck planking. "Your rudeness aside, I find it most upsetting to see that you live in such splendor compared to what those poor wretches beneath your feet are forced to endure."

"You expect me to endure those same conditions, do you?"

"I expect you to improve the conditions those prisoners are kept in. How you live your own life is not my concern, nor interest."

"Pity, Lady Simms. I'm sure you would find my life quite fascinating," he murmured, but there was an undercurrent of sarcasm and bitterness beneath the elegant, silky words.

"Yes, as a matter of fact, I would. For example," she said, drawing herself up, "why do you, a peer of the realm, continue to serve in the navy when you have political duties and responsibilities to your government to fulfill?" She tried raking him with her own stare, but it had no effect on him whatsoever, only raising a slight, infuriating smile and his dark, wicked brows, as though he knew quite well what she was up to. "After all, you are a *marquess,* for heaven's sake."

"Perhaps I like my post," he said faintly, lifting his glass and carefully watching her over the top of it.

"You're a peer of the realm. Don't tell me you enjoy the shame of being relegated to a job normally reserved for the lowliest of lieutenants."

"I don't. In fact, I loathe the navy, and I curse to hell the day I ever entered it."

"An obvious fact, given your recent record." He darkened with anger, but Gwyneth ignored him, refusing to be cowed. She picked up a book that rested on the table, a thick, well-worn volume about medicine and health complaints. She thumbed idly through it, tossed it contemptuously aside, and gazed at the marquess, only to find him regarding her with thunderous fury. "So why don't you get out of the navy, then, if you hate it so much?"

He did not answer, but merely let fire come into those cold, ruthless eyes.

Gwyneth was persistent. "And why aren't you at sea?"

"What is this, question-and-answer time?"

"I see I've struck a nerve," she said, refusing to back down.

"Indeed you have. I happened to kill my admiral's son in a duel. The admiral returned the favor by assigning me to this *noble* command. A fitting reward, wouldn't you say?"

"Only if said admiral's son was less vile than his killer."

"I can assure you that he was. A mere cockerel strutting around the barnyard of the navy, pink-cheeked, idiotic, and irritating. He should have known better than to have challenged me."

"And you should have known better than to get on the bad side of your superiors. But then, that seems to be your style, is it not? And the reason why you find yourself in charge of a mere prison hulk when others of your rank are out commanding dashing frigates and bringing glory and honor to Britain's bosom."

"If Britain's bosom wants glory and honor, it would be wise to attach someone other than myself to its tits."

She gasped. "You ought to be ashamed of yourself, *sir!*"

"And you, madam, ought to be minding your own damned business."

Gwyneth's nostrils flared with rage. For a moment she wished William were here; but no, she could handle this wicked demon without any help from anyone.

"Lord Morninghall," she said smoothly, lifting her chin and regarding him with a coolness she didn't feel, "I hope you know that I can make your life very, very difficult. It would behoove you to treat me with a little respect."

"I treat people with as much respect as they deserve. You, my dear, quite imperiously demand to come aboard, you threaten me, and now you stand here insulting me. Personally, I see no reason why you deserve any of this respect with which you wish to be treated. But go ahead, wave your magic wand, bring the entire admiralty down on my head if you so wish. I can't sink much lower than this, now, can I?"

"You'd be surprised," she said, with steel in her voice.

"Indeed I would. Now if you'll kindly remove yourself from my quarters, madam, I would be *ever* so obliged."

"And if *you* would kindly hear me out and then provide me with a personal tour of the prisoners' cells, *I* would be ever so obliged."

He put the wineglass down. Then he moved toward his bed and leaned suggestively against one carved post, legs crossed at the ankle, arms folded over his broad chest. One hand came up, cradling his chin, the forefinger and thumb absently bracketing his mouth and making those eyes the focus of his face as he stood gazing at her.

Assessing her.

Gwyneth felt an involuntary tremor beneath that malevolent scrutiny.

"You really are the venerable shrew they say you are, aren't you?"

Gwyneth smiled.

"I mean, I thought you'd be older," the marquess mused, absently rubbing his chin and mocking her with his faint smile. "You don't look a day over one and twenty years. Are you certain you're *the* Lady Simms, the same one who married an old goat for his money, lobbied Parliament for prison reform, and upset all of England with your endless squalling about the fate of miners' orphans?"

"I am. And are you really *the* Lord Morninghall?" she countered, holding up the lorgnette that hung suspended from her neck and studying him through the circles of glass. "The one who was sent down from Oxford, court-martialed for insubordination, and what was it?—oh, yes, last night—" she let the lorgnette drop to her breast, "*visited* by that gallant rescuer, the Black Wolf? A marvelous escape he effected, rescuing those Americans right out from under your nose. . . ."

Lord Morninghall lowered his hand and straightened up to his full height. A blood vessel throbbed in his temple.

Undaunted, Gwyneth raised her chin and looked airily out the window. "I think I should dearly like to meet this Black Wolf, as I'm sure we could entertain a very nice partnership. Why, between my efforts at reform and his at rescuing hapless prisoners of war, we'll have every poor sufferer off this boat in no time, won't we?"

The marquess loomed over her, tall, angry, and threatening. "I think you had better leave . . . if you know what is good for you."

"Oh, I intend to leave, my lord, just as soon as I have this tour that I've promised myself. I can assure you, I find both being aboard your ship and being in your presence equally odious."

"I said, *get out.*"

"What, are you one of these superstitious captains who objects to a female on your ship? Really, Morninghall, such foolishness—"

"Oh, I don't object to females in the least," he murmured, beginning to move forward. Gwyneth's heart flipped over and began to pound out a frantic warning, but she stood her ground. He came right up to her, until his handsome, malevolently beautiful face loomed inches above her own and she was leaning backward in her effort to retreat without giving up an inch. "In fact, I *enjoy* them quite a bit."

"Do not try to intimidate me," she said, defiantly meeting his gaze.

"By the look of you, I'd say you are intimidated without my even trying." He grazed her cheek with the back of his hand, letting her have the full effect of those devil's eyes; up close, she could see that the irises were a clear, transparent blue-gray, ringed by a darker circle of slate; up close, she could just see the gold that radiated around each pupil, as though his maker had tried to interject a bit of godliness in him and, failing, given him up to a darker force. She jerked her head back, staring at his still-upraised hand.

"You *are* intimidated, aren't you, my dear?"

"Never!" But Gwyneth stepped back—and felt the bulkhead against her spine.

His head moved closer, and there was nowhere left to go. His hand cupped her nape, his thumb dragged sensuously down over throat. She caught the scent of sandalwood, of male heat and male power, and her knees went weak beneath the touch of those adroit hands, the power of that cunning smile. Gwyneth did not slap him. She did not say a word, merely holding his gaze and feeling fury rising up in her breast.

"Really, my lady," the marquess said, letting his voice drop to a smoky murmur as his lips neared hers, "before you seek to cross swords with the devil, you should know that he can be very dangerous. . . ."

The hand moved up, pushing her hat aside and off, dragging the stray gold curl down from her coiffure. He ran the silky tress between thumb and forefinger, twirled it around the latter, and holding her thus ensnared, pulled her close.

"Very dangerous, indeed . . ."

His mouth came down on hers, and Gwyneth felt the ruthless force behind it, caught the dark, sensual taste of him. The kiss was hot, male, and it immediately turned her bones to water. Oh, God, yes, she had every reason to fear him, every reason to defend herself before it was too late—

She acted.

In a single brutal motion, her knee jerked up, and several layers of skirts and petticoats were not enough to blunt its force against the marquess's groin. Cursing savagely, he stumbled and fell, clutching a leg of the table for support, the breath rasping through his lungs as he fought for air.

He looked up at her, his eyes burning with something worse than fury.

And Gwyneth stood gazing down at him, a triumphant, haughty little smile playing across her face.

"I would beg you, Lord Lucifer, to remember just *who* is the dangerous one here," she said smoothly. "And by the way, don't bother escorting me off the ship; I can see to it myself."

She picked up her hat. Then, leaving him to his agony, she sailed to the door and slammed it in his face.

Chapter 3

He hadn't expected her to be so young. He hadn't expected her to be so dauntless.

And he hadn't expected her to be so damned *beautiful*.

He shouldn't have been fooled by the sweetness of that heart-shaped face: behind those wide, violet eyes was a hellcat. And that gown of frosty blue satin threaded with silvery embroidery had displayed the kind of figure that turned his blood to steam: high breasts, narrow waist, and flat, gently flared hips. Damon could still taste her on his lips, could still smell her peach soap, could still feel the throbbing ache in his groin where she'd kneed him. Medusa had no right to be such a beauty. Medusa was supposed to have snakes as her crowning glory, not thick piles of shimmering gold hair, the fragile, wispy curls kissing her nape, framing her ears. Medusa wasn't supposed to have a neck like a swan's, gracefully arched and just as white. Medusa wasn't supposed to have skin so deliciously fair that even a freckle would've looked foreign on it, rosy soft lips, and flashing, violet eyes which had not quailed with fear even under the devil's most deliberate intimidation.

He hated her.

He wanted her.

He—

The attack hit just as he was hauling himself back to his feet via the aid of the table leg. Pain slammed into his chest. It was no ordinary pain, but a horrible, constricting sensation, like a giant fist squeezing his heart, tight, tighter, now so tightly that he couldn't breathe. Gasping, he half fell into the chair and over the table, his body breaking out in a cold sweat, his hands shaking, his vision narrowing until it was merely a scope through a gray and shrinking tunnel. He grabbed for the *Peterson's,* curling it under his chest as he sank down over it, the heavy book pushing against his heart.

He closed his eyes, feeling himself detaching from his body, leaving it.

I'm dying. This time it's for certain. Oh, God, help me, I don't want to die as I have lived—

Alone.

"Milford." His knuckles turned white as he gripped the *Peterson's* and he heard his heart racing like a galloping horse. *"Milford!"*

Silence. Stillness. Lazy footsteps on the deck above. Gasping, the sweat rolling down his temples, Damon raised his head and tore open the medical encyclopedia, desperately searching for the correct entry, the subtitles growing foggy beneath the encroaching gray clouds of the constricting tunnel.

A fluttering wavered in his chest.

He couldn't think, couldn't concentrate. He had to read the entry four times before its meaning sank into his dizzy brain. He found his symptoms and read the words next to it.

"A sharp and incessant pain in the chest can be the result of overwork, worry, or impending death—"

"Milford!" Damon shouted, hoarsely.

Further on, *"or a stomach colic caused by an excitement of nerves."*

He lunged to his feet, the book crashing to the floor. This wasn't the stomach, the stomach was much lower than where this pain was, the stomach didn't flutter erratically beneath the sternum. No, this time he was truly dying because his heart was pulsing, stumbling, that gray tunnel was collapsing in on itself, and now he couldn't think, couldn't breathe, couldn't see, couldn't get enough air—

Damon dove forward, clawing at his throat, fighting desperately to breathe.

Air!

The tunnel collapsed.

The next thing he knew, he was lying on the floor, staring dazedly up at the bulkhead and the Reverend Peter Milford's worried face.

"Damon?"

He took a deep, tentative breath. The pain was gone, as though it had never been. Stillness, silence engulfed him.

"Are you all right?"

"Christ, I'm dead."

"I'm not Christ, and no, you're not dead." Stretching out a hand, the young chaplain helped Damon sit up and then pressed a glass of brandy to his lips. "Another fit, my friend?"

"It wasn't a fit, I don't have *fits*. It was an attack." He raked the hair off his damp brow. "A heart attack."

"I see," the chaplain said patiently, his hazel eyes kind and concerned beneath his rumpled blond curls. "Shall I send for the surgeon?"

"No, he'll merely look at me as though he thinks I'm imagining it all, as though it's all in my head, same thing the miserable old wretch tells me every time I summon him." Damon lunged to his feet and, leaning against the table's edge, mopped his brow with a handkerchief. At least the pain and feelings of suffocation were gone, as was the horrible, paralyzing panic that went with it. "What does *he* know, anyhow, the worthless butcher, *he's* not the one suffering these blasted things!"

"Perhaps the surgeon is correct," Milford mused, unflinching as Damon shot him an angry, threatening glare. "I mean, you *do* tend to let your imagination get carried away. . . ."

"My father died three years short of his fourth decade, and my mother ended her days in a London asylum. Don't tell me my illnesses are all in my head!"

"Your father died in a duel with Lord Aylesbury, Damon, with a bullet in his chest. And your mother, from all accounts, was strung more tightly than an overtuned violin. Something snapped. As it will with you if you do not find some measure of calmness and serenity. Now sit down, for pity's sake, and tell me about this lovely creature who nearly ran me over in the corridor outside."

That brought Damon's mind immediately away from his health, as the clever young chaplain intended it should.

"Lovely creature? Is *that* what you think of that confounded Jezebel?"

Peter gave an infuriating smile. "I see our opinions differ. As always."

"That 'lovely creature' could've led the British Army to victory at Austerlitz," Damon snarled, staring out the window with a gaze that threatened to burn a hole through the smoky glass. "As it was, the cursed witch nearly unmanned me. 'Twill be a bloody wonder if I'm ever able to father a child now."

"Yes, well, since you've no intention of ever marrying and producing an heir, I don't see why it should matter," Peter quipped, ignoring Damon's furious glare. He reached down, picked the *Peterson's* up off the floor, and with a disapproving frown, placed it on the table. "By the way, who was she?"

"Lady Gwyneth Evans Simms."

The chaplain paused, then nodded once. "Ah."

"Does that explain it?"

"Quite aptly, I'm afraid."

Damon refilled his glass and began to pace slowly back and forth. "She has apparently decided that prison ships are a blight upon humanity, and has taken it upon herself to reform them, starting with ours."

"Can't say as though I blame her. I have long held the belief that the British practice of imprisoning people on foul and stinking ships is something God must weep over daily."

"I know it is. Why do you think I have taken steps to put matters aright?"

"Taken *steps?!*" The chaplain, incredulous, shook his head. "Be honest with yourself, Damon. And with me. Your so-called actions have nothing to do with any pretended concern and compassion for those prisoners, and everything to do with getting revenge on Bolton and a navy you think has betrayed you."

"The navy *has* betrayed me. And as for the prisoners and my actions, the end result is the same, regardless of my incentives. That's what *really* matters."

"Rubbish, Damon, and you know it."

"Look, if I wanted guilt, I would have become a Catholic. Spare me the damned sermon, Peter. It isn't even Sunday."

"I see I'm getting too close to your fiercely guarded heart."

"You know me well enough by now to know I lack such an organ."

"I daresay. Perhaps, then, a stroll belowdeck among those who suffer worse than you will plant one in that unfeeling chest of yours. But no. Such a garden is too stony for a heart seed to germinate, let alone flourish. Forgive me for even suggesting it." Peter moved to the door, his face tight with suppressed anger. "May God have mercy on you, Damon—"

"Wait."

The chaplain paused, his hand on the door latch.

"I just don't want that meddling witch interfering on my ship," Damon muttered, keeping his sullen gaze on the contents of his glass.

Peter turned and leaned back against the door, silently watching Damon as the latter agitatedly rubbed his thumb around the rim of the glass, his mouth growing harder by the second. "I see."

Damon glanced at him, eyes mutinous. "Is that all you have to say?"

"Actually, it isn't. But what I *do* have to say is something you'll have no wish to hear."

"That's never stopped you in the past."

"Indeed." Peter's mouth turned up in the barest of smiles. "You tell me that you have no desire for that 'meddling witch' to interfere on your ship. Well, I think the only *interference* Lady Simms will provide will be on your heart."

"I know that. What do you think nearly did me in a damned minute ago?"

"No." The chaplain smiled, a teasing light in his eye. "I'm talking romantically."

The marquess looked up. Peter Milford had met many men in his life, but he had yet to encounter one who could convey such emotion as Morninghall just by altering the shadows and expressions in his eyes. Now he saw irritation move across the slate-blue irises, before the studied, terminally bored look swept in to mask everything.

"I would never fancy a woman like that. I prefer dainty, well-bred, mild-mannered—"

"Tarts."

"Damn you, Peter. If you weren't a man of the cloth, I'd tell you right where to go."

"Right. And if you weren't a stubborn marquess, I'd tell *you* where to go. Never mind, I'll tell you anyhow."

"I don't want to hear it. Besides, it is not that Welshwoman's quest that I disapprove of, but her high-handedness. A meager command I may have, but it is *my* command and I quite object to anyone coming in and telling me what to do."

"Damon." The chaplain fixed him with a sad smile. "When are you ever going to realize that God did not make you for the service? You would be far happier, I think, if you left the navy, found yourself a wife, and took up your duties at Morninghall."

"I'm not leaving the navy. I have a score to settle

with these bastards. Besides, I'm hardly marriage material, and Morninghall is the last place on earth I wish to go."

"I stand by my feelings," Peter said, as though Damon had never even spoken. "Admiral Bolton hates you for killing his son in that duel, and will not let up until he has broken you. Furthermore, you have never been able to take an order with humility and obedience, were never meant to submit to anyone's authority but your own, and thus, you can never hope to get anywhere in the navy. For mercy's sake, Damon, you are the Marquess of Morninghall. Go home. You don't belong in this environment."

Damon turned to look out the window, his hands clenched tightly behind his back. "Why do I think I've heard all this before?" he soliloquized.

"Forgive me if it bores you."

"If I go home, I'll be even *more* bored. Out of my bloody skull, I daresay."

"If you go home, you can put that intelligence of yours to better use than what you're doing with it here."

"I've just heard a similar load of bollocks from Lady Simms. I don't need to hear it from you."

"Ah, so you're back to Lady Simms again. On your mind quite a bit now, isn't she?"

"I'm warning you, Peter, my mood is black enough. Don't push me."

"Fine. Maybe you'll find this of more interest instead." The chaplain picked up the newspaper he'd thrown onto the table at his hasty entrance and held it out to Damon, who eyed it uncertainly. "Go ahead, read it. Headlines, first page."

Damon shot him a suspicious look. Then he took the paper, his expressive, dark brows coming together in a frown, his eyes moving rapidly beneath their veil of sable lashes as he read.

"'Masked Avenger Takes HMS *Surrey* by Surprise.'" He lowered the paper, his expression cold. "Ah, I understand. You brought me this to annoy me all the more, didn't you? Shame on you, Peter. I thought you were my friend."

"You have no friends, by your own admission. Read on."

Damon shot him an irate glance, then returned his attention to the paper. "'Naval authorities in Portsmouth believe that the mysterious masked man who effected the escape of several prisoners of war from the prison hulk HMS *Surrey* is none other than the escaped American prisoner Captain Connor Merrick. . . .'" He returned the paper to Milford with a casual flick of his wrist. "I don't want to hear about it, know about it, *think* about it. I have enough problems."

Peter sighed, and rolling up the paper, tucked it beneath his arm. "Of course, Damon." He turned to go. "Now, if your demise is no longer immediate, I have other duties to attend to."

"Yes, go. I'll summon you next time I see death coming for me with a collection basket. Though I suspect its angel won't be garbed in white."

"You're too hard on yourself, my friend. You may hate yourself, but I can assure you that God does not."

The marquess's expression went bleak, and silently, he turned to gaze out over the harbor once more, his fingers curling and uncurling.

"Oh, and by the way, Damon. You should know that Midshipman Owens is getting a little rough with the prisoners. I would speak to him, but . . ."

Damon shut his eyes. "Yes, Peter. I'll take care of it."

Lady Gwyneth Evans Simms rapped sharply on the roof of the carriage, and the vehicle came to a stop in front of the small house she and her sister, Rhiannon, were renting in Portsmouth.

She was still boiling with rage at the effrontery of that insufferable Lord Morninghall, and his rude treatment, his cutting remarks, and worse, his touch, were all fresh in her mind. She could still feel that hot, practiced hand skimming over her flesh, could still taste that searing kiss, could still smell the spicy scent of sandalwood, could still see those eyes.

Those eyes!

The footman helped her down from the carriage, and skirts in hand and lorgnette swinging from her neck, Gwyneth stormed past the neat beds of daffodils and manicured hedges into the house.

Rhiannon was sitting in the parlor, a book in her lap and Mattie curled at her feet. Both she and the old dog looked up as Gwyneth sailed in.

"Well?"

"I need a drink, Rhiannon. Something strong."

"That bad, was it?"

"The man was an insufferable boor!"

"Really, Gwyn, how could you have expected him to be anything else? I mean, he runs a prison hulk, for heaven's sake. We are the company we keep."

"Lord Morninghall's company is something you couldn't pay me enough money to *keep*," Gwyneth spat, as their maid, Sophie, brought in a tray holding a bottle of whisky and two glasses. "He was positively odious. Awful."

"I hear he's devilishly handsome."

"He's a vain, rude, arrogant *beast!*"

Gwyneth picked up a glass and, hands shaking with rage, splashed some of the whisky into it. She collapsed onto the sofa, letting the liquid fire burn its way down her throat. Out of the corner of her eye she could see Rhiannon, head slightly tilted, ginger curls cascading from their loose coil, green eyes bright and amused.

"So, what does he look like?"

"*You* would ask."

"Well?"

Gwyneth's sigh was long and bracing, the sort one makes when the task ahead is known to be grueling. "His hair is the color of black coffee, thick and gleaming, with just enough curl in it to give it some interest. He wears it swept back off his forehead, rakishly cut, longer than is fashionable, but on him the effect is altogether . . ."

"Appealing?"

Gwyneth stared hopelessly, unseeingly into the fireplace. "He is magnificent, Rhiannon."

Rhiannon sat up. "Go on!"

"His shoulders are broad and proud, his physique a Greek statue with life breathed into it. But no warmth. He is like animated stone."

"Oooh . . . a dangerous man, then!"

"Yes, dangerous. His hands are elegant, his nails clean, his fingers—" *masterful*—"his fingers long and sensitive. Rather like a musician's, or an artist's."

"Oh, do go on, Gwyn!"

"He is tall. At least six feet. I had to tilt my head back to meet his eyes."

"And his mouth?"

"Sensual."

"His nose?"

"Every inch an aristocrat's."

"His temper?"

"Horrible." Gwyneth leaned her brow into her hand. "But his eyes, Rhiannon, they are without contest his most arresting and memorable feature. When he looked at me, I sensed that he could read every one of my thoughts, could even see inside my head and know just what kind of effect he was having on me. He made my knees weak with just one look from those eyes. . . . I felt like he was the charmer and I was the snake. It was altogether chilling. Fascinating. *Scintillating.*" She shuddered and looked straight at her sister. "They are devil's eyes, Rhia."

Silence, with only the ticking of the clock, went on for a long moment.

"He frightens me, Rhia. I am not used to feeling frightened. I—I am not quite sure how to deal with this emotion, or with Morninghall himself."

"Well." Rhiannon pursed her lips and frowned, but behind her sympathetic concern her eyes were gleaming with excitement. Impulsively, she reached out and touched Gwyneth's knee. "Think of it this way, Gwyn. You *have* been moaning that you haven't had a challenge since William died."

Gwyneth sipped the whisky, and stared hopelessly into the fireplace.

"He kissed me, Rhiannon."

Rhiannon sat straight up in her chair. *"Oh?"*

"He employed all of the predictable male methods of getting rid of a woman: first rudeness, then intimidation, and failing their success, unwelcome advances."

"Surely you didn't let him get away with it!"

"Of course not!"

Rhiannon leaned forward, elbows on her knees, face bright with excitement. It was all too obvious that she hoped Gwyneth *had* let him get away with it. Even Mattie raised his noble head, his brown eyes inquisitive. "So, what did you do?"

"I kneed him in the groin," Gwyneth replied, airily. Then she looked at her sister and both burst into laughter.

"You didn't!"

"I did!" Gwyneth put down her glass before she could spill its contents. "Oh, Rhiannon . . . how right you are. I mean, my life *has* become so very pointless and boring since William died, and perhaps this is just what I need to give me an interest in things once again. I can't think of a better cause than reforming the conditions on those horrid hulks and driving Lord Morninghall mad in the bargain."

"If anyone can drive a man mad, Gwyneth, *you* can."

"You don't do so badly yourself, sis."

The two giggled once more.

"And so what are you planning to do to His Lordship?" Rhiannon ventured, watching her sister over the top of her glass.

"I plan on making his life hell. And this, dear Rhiannon, is how I am going to do it. . . ."

Chapter 4

⟨ ─⟨◦⟩─ ⟩

The following morning found the Marquess of Morninghall standing before a mirror, just finishing shaving, when his new cabin boy, Billy, walked in carrying a tray. On it were Damon's breakfast and a vase containing three daffodils over which the boy's too-eager-to-please eyes were peering. He stopped at the sight of Damon, smiling hopefully.

"Your breakfast, my lord."

Damon angled his neck and, keeping his gaze intent on his reflection, pulled the razor over the side of his Adam's apple. "I know, you damned fool. You don't have to announce it as though you're a butler in the finest house in all of England. Just set the bloody tray on the table and take your grand aspirations elsewhere."

Tilting his head to reach a hollow better, he made three more quick, precise flicks with the razor, trying not to look at the brat in the mirror. But the boy didn't move. Damon's cold gaze slid sideways in the mirror to fasten on the small figure's reflected eyes. Billy's smile had crashed, his throat was working, and his eyes, so wide that they seemed to dominate his narrow, freckled little face, were filling with tears.

A quick stab of guilt, then anger, roared though Damon, and he whirled, gesturing with the razor.

"Damn you, get out of here!"

The tray crashed to the table and Billy fled, the daffodils quivering in their vase, their heads bobbing

50

madly with the jolt of impact. Damon stared at them, the razor clenched in his fist. Damned brat! Sniveling, pitiful little wretch! Always trying to do something nice, always trying to bring something beautiful into his world when there could be nothing beautiful about it, nothing at all, and it was no use trying—

Still fuming, Damon swung his attention back to his reflection and finished shaving. Then he yanked the thick towel from around his neck, wiped his face and throat, and flung the thing into a basin while he carefully fingered the several small, inevitable nicks. Lack of sleep was no excuse for his bad temper—he spent every morning in a bad temper because the days that followed them were never anything to look forward to—but it was a better excuse than none at all, and he needed an excuse, any excuse, so the brat's wounded eyes wouldn't haunt what was left of his conscience for the rest of the whole bloody day.

Yet even as he tried to drive that hurt little face from his mind, he knew it wasn't Billy who deserved his bad temper.

It was that contemptible bitch, Lady Gwyneth Evans Simms.

Already, she was trying to make his life hell.

His finger paused on a tiny gouge just above his Adam's apple, and in the mirror he saw ice chips beginning to glitter in the flat glaciers of his eyes. The hellcat had not been content to torment him with her very unwelcome visit yesterday. She had not been content to anger him with a promise to make his life difficult. She had not been content to insult and enrage him with her constant reminders of how much of a failure he was, nor was she content to be the catalyst behind one of his attacks. Oh, no, she had to rub salt in the wounds, coming to him in the most erotic dreams he had ever experienced, tempting and taunting him with that rosy mouth, those flashing eyes, that body he wanted to possess with every raging demon that ruled his black and tortured soul, until in a fit of lustful rage he had thrown her down on the deck, right there in the dream, right there on the rug behind where he now stood, driving himself into her until she was broken and begging, subdued, mastered, repressed. His blood began to pound at even the thought of it—the prim and elegant Lady Simms laid out on his rug like some common tart, screaming her defiance even while she begged him to take her. . . .

And she would, too.

Beg.

He slowly let his fingers fall away from his throat. In the mirror his eyes remained unfeeling and soulless, only a slight heightening of their natural iridescence betraying the rising fury of his emotions. His dark brows remained unmoving. His forehead showed not the slightest trace of a crease; his mouth seemed carved from ice. The man who looked back at him was impenetrable, polished, cold. Emotionless and lacking both soul and conscience. He raised his chin and fingered a small shaving nick, still holding his own gaze. Ah, what the mind harbored, what the face could conceal. *And what he wouldn't give for a chance to put that militaristic virago in her place.*

His eyes glowed with unholy light.

Right here, right now.

He felt the rage starting, a hungry spill of red-hot lava devouring everything in its path and making him burn as if with fever. His hands curled into fists and he caught a glimpse of his eyes, fanatical, fiery, and now blazing with the devil's own fury. Unable to gaze upon that malevolent face in the mirror any longer, he spun on his heel and yanked out a chair, trembling. The red haze followed him, burning in his chest, his throat, his head, inescapable and growing hotter by the second. Scenes flashed before his eyes: Commodore Julian Lord engulfed in the glory and admiration that he, Damon, had found briefly but lost; his tyrannical first captain, whipping him over the breech of a gun until he overcame his fear of heights and climbed the mainmast; and there, puncturing these visions like bolts of lightning, his rival, Adam Bolton, getting promoted over him because he was the son of an admiral, the bastard rubbing his nose in it until he'd incited the fight with Damon that had been building for as long as the two had known each other; the court-martial, the public insults, the duel, and Bolton's father, avenging his son's death by putting Damon in charge of this reeking sewer, pulling the rug out from under him and destroying his naval career. His mother hurling a wine bottle at him, Oxford and humiliation, Morninghall and terror, and over it all the mocking taunts of Lady Gwyneth Evans Simms—

Damon pressed the heels of his hands into his temples and stared down at his breakfast—*be calm, be calm*—seeing the toast stacked with military precision in a little metal rack, the pats of butter on a tiny plate, the knife, fork, and spoon rolled up in a crisp square of white linen, the strong black coffee in its porcelain cup, the small, delicately enameled pots of marmalade and jam, dainty, exquisite, *God help me, I want to smash them,* like the frail shell of a songbird's egg, *God help me, God help me,* and over everything the nauseating stench of death and disease snaking its way in from the rest of the ship—

Something inside him exploded. With an inhuman howl of rage, he crashed his fist down on the table, sweeping everything off the tray with one violent slash of his arm. The stupidly pretty little jam pot, the lovely little coffee cup, the little rack of toast, and, yes, even the daffodils, sweet, mocking, sunny when all the world was black—all went flying. China crashed to the deck, shattering in a thousand pieces. Coffee ran everywhere, toast went skidding, and the daffodils lay quivering on the rug, broken, tragic, accusing, before giving a final tremor and falling still.

Damon put his elbows on the table and drove his knuckles into his forehead, into the bone, willing the rage to subside.

Then, as Billy rushed in and stared in dismay at the

carnage, he leaped to his feet, crushed the flowers beneath his heel, and strode out of the cabin.

At the very moment Lord Morninghall's fist was falling upon his table with the force of a dropped mortar, the man widely believed to be the Black Wolf was taking his schooner out of a hidden cove and slipping out to sea.

If ever there was a fellow who needed a war to keep him out of trouble, Connor Merrick was that man.

He had come from a family that thrived in unrest. His father, Captain Brendan Jay Merrick, had been a legendary privateer during the American War of Independence and now owned a successful Newburyport shipyard in partnership with Connor's uncle Matthew Ashton, a hothead if ever there was one. Connor's mother, who now ran Mira Merrick's School of Fine Seamanship, had been an uncontrollable hoyden during that same war, garbing herself as a boy and becoming the finest gunner on the schooner *Kestrel*. Connor's grandfather Ephraim had been a crusty shipbuilder of unpredictable temper, and Connor's sister, Maeve, had run away from home when she was sixteen, spending seven years terrorizing the West Indies as the Pirate Queen of the Caribbean until a cunning British admiral by the name of Falconer had fallen in love with her and put paid to her nefarious activities by means of a wedding ring.

What goes around, comes around. Nearly fifteen years ago Maeve had stolen the *Kestrel* from their father, and now Connor, recently escaped from the prison hulk *Surrey*, had stolen it from Maeve.

On this fine spring morning he stood at the tiller, watching the southern coast of England moving away off the larboard beam. He waited until the schooner's sails were drawing and she was well underway; then, giving the helm to one of his crew, he leaned against a gun carriage, raised a cup of cold coffee to his lips, and reread the note from the Reverend Peter Milford, his contact aboard the prison hulk *Surrey*. His green

eyes scanned the paper; finally he crumpled the note,
tossed it carelessly over his shoulder into the sea, and
whistling, watched his crew as they busily set the
topgallants.

His lieutenant, pretending to be engrossed in coil-
ing a line, observed him from several feet away. Orla
O'Shaughnessy was a petite Irishwoman with dark,
windblown hair and soulful blue eyes, and she had
served the Merrick family well. In her youth she had
been Maeve's maid; later, when Maeve ran away and
became the pirate queen, Orla had been the most
trusted member of her crew of lady pirates. And now
here she was, swept up into another adventure by yet
another Merrick. She knew both Connor and Maeve
well. She also knew that Connor thought of her as
nothing more than a friend, but that did nothing to
calm her heart whenever he was near.

Tall and lanky like his handsome father, with the
same easy smile and natural charm, Connor was
enough to melt any woman's heart. Several months of
hell aboard the prison hulk *Surrey* had not claimed
his winsome grin, and dressed in a billowy, white
shirt open at the throat, his long legs painted with a
bit of black fabric that passed for trousers, it was easy
to believe that his bones held more flesh than starva-
tion and abuse had afforded them.

Heaven help her, she thought, overcome by a hot
flush. Thinking of his body did her no good either.

She forced herself to look away, her gaze settling
upon the crumpled note, now no more than a white
dot as it bounced and bobbed in the *Kestrel*'s wake,
retreating further and further astern before finally
sinking out of sight. It was no use. Connor was
heading for the hatch, his stride jaunty and confident
as he approached, and she had no choice but to look
up at him.

"Another rescue, Con?" she ventured, straightening
up and leaving the line neatly coiled on the deck.

He stopped and leaned against the gunwale beside
her, dangerously, temptingly, close. He was pale and

gaunt from his recent stay aboard the prison hulk, and hell-bent on rescuing his compatriots still incarcerated there, but the experience had not left him bitter as it might have left a lesser man, nor had it broken him. But, then, he was a Merrick, she thought, with wry admiration. Merricks didn't break—they merely bent, like saplings in a storm, making the best of situations and growing stronger in spite of their adversities.

"Another rescue indeed. Tomorrow at midnight the Black Wolf strikes again." He closed his eyes and turned his face skyward, smiling as he relished the joyous thrum of the wind through stays and shrouds, the leap and pulse of the ship beneath him. The empty mug dangled lazily from one finger, and the breeze played havoc with his curling auburn hair. "My God, I cannot tell you how damned *good* this feels, to be out in the sunlight, with the breeze on my face once again. I thought I'd never get off that confounded hulk."

"Had your sister known you were on it, I'm sure you would've been off it much sooner."

"How could she know, being off in the Caribbean as she was with her admiral husband? I'm only glad that he's back here in England on leave. I was ever so fortunate to escape from that damned hulk and find none other than our own little *Kestrel* sitting pretty-as-you-please in Portsmouth Harbor right next to his flagship!"

"This little schooner holds fond memories for you."

"Aye, she sure does, Orla." He gazed blissfully up at the taut mainsail which caught the wind above his head. "Remember when we were all tiny, and my father used to take us out on her, teaching us how to sail? I used to sit right there, on that very gun, when it was Maeve's turn at the tiller."

"How could I forget?"

He ran a hand affectionately along the gunwale. "Five and thirty years is this old lady, yet she's still as sound as a spring filly, and just as frisky, God love her. You'd think she's bloody immortal!"

"Sir Graham made sure she enjoyed every dockyard benefit that his own ships did," Orla explained. "New sails, new rigging, carpentry work, a fresh coat of paint—whatever she needed, the admiral saw that she got it."

"Yes, but you can't overlook Grandpa Ephraim's influence on her either. She was his masterpiece—and no one could build a ship the way he could."

"No one," Orla agreed, a bit sadly.

Waves broke and hissed along the *Kestrel*'s bow and hull.

"Poor Grandpa is probably cackling with glee in his grave, knowing his life's masterpiece is pitted once more against the British. . . ."

They were both silent, only the sounds of wind and sea intruding upon their thoughts as they remembered old Ephraim Merrick. Blustery, eccentric, and cantankerous 'til the end, he had made light of the illness that steadily had been eating away at his insides, until one day he had gone missing—and so had the tiny sailboat he'd kept moored in the river's mouth. Maybe he hadn't known about the nor'easter that had howled in over the coast that night; in all likelihood he had. Five days later a few pieces of his little boat had washed up on a deserted Plum Island beach, and no one ever had seen the old man again.

Orla looked down, her dark hair blowing about her face.

Connor cleared his throat.

"Well!" he finally said, mustering a note of cheer. "Are you ready for that rescue then?"

"Aye," she replied, her smile wan. "Child's play, Con. At midnight, I take it?"

"Midnight. Though what we're supposed to do with ourselves in the interim, the devil only knows."

"Are you bored?" she teased with a little smile.

"That, my dear Orla, is an understatement. A salmon trapped in a bucket couldn't be more *bored*."

"I suppose that once the admiral learns who stole his wife's ship, you'll have excitement enough to keep you busy."

"His wife's ship, you say! Never forget, Orla, that Maeve stole her from our father, and while the rest of us all love our sister, she was never granted exclusive rights to the *Kestrel*. She had her turn with her; now it's mine. Besides, my father designed the *Kestrel* as a warship, not a training vessel for Maeve's children." He slanted her an inquisitive look, and his teasing smile made her heart jump. "Surely you're not having second thoughts about leaving Maeve and coming along with me, are you?"

"Be serious, Connor." She laughed and kicked idly at a deck seam, hoping he hadn't seen the desire in her eyes. "While I'm quite happy that your sister and Admiral Falconer have managed to sustain their newly wedded bliss, I must admit that my own life has not seen this much excitement since he forced us to give up piracy. I have not felt this—this *alive* in years."

"Doubtless, neither has our lovely *Kestrel*." Connor straightened up. "Well, I'm off," he said and, still swinging his coffee cup, headed below. "Holler if you need me."

Orla watched his dark head disappear beneath the coaming and her smile faded, as weighty as her heart. Maybe if he hadn't known her for so long, things would be different. Maybe if she hadn't had such a notorious past, he might show some interest in her. Maybe if those tiny wrinkles weren't starting to frame her eyes, and those scattered strands of gray to thread her hair, he might find her lovely. But she was in her third decade now, well past her first blush, and Orla knew in her heart of hearts that Connor Merrick was not apt to pay her any more notice than would any other decent, God-fearing man.

A despairing thought, when she considered that all she really wanted was a husband who loved her, fine children, and a home of her own.

The same things Maeve had.

The same things all of the ex-pirates of the *Kestrel*'s crew now had.

There had been that brief thing with Maeve's English cousin Captain Colin Lord, but the shipwreck had changed all that, and there had been no one since. And so, for the past eight years, Orla had made her home with the Falconers, remaining by her friend's side as one year led into another. Maybe she'd stayed because many had predicted that the fiery pirate queen wouldn't last a year with Sir Graham, and Orla had wanted to make sure that everything worked out all right between them. But Maeve had made a commendable, if not formidable, admiral's wife, obviously channeling her piratical ways to the bedroom—a fact evidenced by the admiral's excitable and precocious brood of three. The years had passed, but while Maeve had taken well to settling down, life had become meaningless and dull for Orla. She had begun to yearn for the days when she and the *Kestrel*'s crew of lady pirates had ruled the Caribbean. She had begun to ache inside whenever she saw a young couple in love, holding hands and gazing deeply into each other's eyes, and to ache even more if they had a child tagging along with them.

Life had to contain more than it did.

She began to pray, something she hadn't done in a long, long, time, for something.

Anything.

And then Sir Graham had announced he had business in London, and that it was time to leave the West Indies and go home for a while. The ocean crossing had been dull, as had the weather. The days had stretched into tedious regularity, and when the great flagship, accompanied by Maeve's schooner, the *Kestrel,* had finally put into Portsmouth, Orla had decided that she simply could not bear to be dragged from one place to the next, meeting Falconer relatives who meant nothing to her and putting on a smile when she was miserable inside. She would stay aboard the *Kestrel* while the family was away. Portsmouth had to be more interesting.

And it was.

She had been quietly pacing the darkened deck the night the four escapees from the prison hulk *Surrey* had come up over the side like boarding pirates. Her instincts were as sharp as they'd ever been, and as they'd burst onto the deck, they'd found themselves staring into the mouth of her blunderbuss. Even now she smiled in amazement. Who could've known that, of all people, the man at the other end of her gun would be her old childhood friend Connor Merrick?

Oh, her prayers had been answered all right. She'd wanted excitement, and mother of God, she was going to get it.

Orla looked out to sea, sighing. Maeve was going to be furious at finding her ship gone. Her husband, the admiral, would no doubt put to sea immediately in hopes of retrieving the vessel before his wife saw to it herself.

And Connor Merrick, hot-blooded and passionate, would have no intention of giving that vessel back.

Orla straightened up and headed for the hatch, the galley, and her own breakfast. Wise move or not, one thing was certain: life with the Merricks would never be boring.

Lady Gwyneth Evans Simms had no shortage of ideas on just how to make Lord Morninghall's life hell, and she wasted no time at all in putting those ideas into action.

The day after her confrontation with that prince of darkness, she rose at dawn and, with Mattie slumbering at her feet and the sunlight streaming in over her desk, went to work. She spent the morning composing a letter to her brother-in-law, the new Lord Simms, in the Transport Office, skillfully playing upon his own inflated sense of importance in order to further her desires: a second, more invasive visit to the prison ship *Surrey*. By noon she'd written to one of William's friends in Parliament, sent a note off to another in the Admiralty, and penned a third to Maeve, Lady Falconer, whom she had met and befriended two years before when Maeve's husband, Sir Graham, had come to London on official business. Hopefully the American woman's seafaring past—not to mention her high-ranking admiral of a husband—would be of help to Gwyneth in her efforts. By teatime she was describing the conditions she'd glimpsed aboard the hulk to a circle of genteel and horrified acquaintances who promptly declared themselves the Ladies' Committee on Prisoner Welfare, and by seven o'clock she was rewarding herself for her hard work with a well-deserved immersion in her favorite hobby, gardening, wishing that each head she chopped from the fading daffodils was Lord Morninghall's own.

I'll show that diabolical scoundrel I mean business, she vowed, hurling the wilted blossoms into a bucket. By tomorrow all hell was going to break loose.

So involved was she in her thoughts, her work, that she never realized twilight had fallen, and Rhiannon, standing in the doorway holding a book, had to call her twice.

Gwyneth's head jerked up and she looked around, rubbing the small of her back. Dear lord, it had certainly grown late; the blackbirds were calling, as if to usher in the coming night, and the sky was fading fast from mauve to indigo. She looked at her sister, silhouetted in the doorway, and smiled guiltily. "Forgive me, Rhia. I didn't hear you."

"Thinking of Lord Lucifer again, sis?"

She grinned. "I am plotting his destruction."

"Lady Covington told me he is devilishly handsome."

"Oh, he's devilish all right. The devil incarnate."

"I still want to know what it felt like when he kissed you. What his lips were like, and whether you really *do* see fireworks when a devastatingly gorgeous man ravishes you."

"I told you, silly, he did not *ravish* me."

"His kiss, then. What was it like?"

"Rhia . . ."

Her sister giggled and, clutching the book, folded her arms across her bosom and eyed her with high humor. A blackbird skimmed over Gwyneth's head and landed in a clipped conifer, causing the fringed branches to bounce and swing. How she loved their musical warbles, their bright-eyed stare—

"Well?" Rhiannon repeated, her eyes mischievous.

"You are ever the romantic, Rhiannon. Stop reading those silly novels and dreaming about knights in shining armor, will you?"

"It is healthy to dream, Gwyn. You should try it yourself some time."

"I am too busy to dream, and if I did, it would not be about knights in shining armor. And especially not Lord Morninghall."

"Appearances can be deceiving, Gwyn. He may not be all bad."

"For God's sake, Rhiannon, he's in charge of a *prison hulk.* You are most welcome to accompany me on the morrow, to see for yourself what hideous places that ship and others like her are. A disgrace to Britain, if you ask me, a living hell for those whose only crime was to be caught fighting on the opposite side."

As Gwyneth returned her attention to her daffodils, Rhiannon tapped a finger against the book's spine and watched her older sister shrewdly. Gwyneth did her best to present a militaristic and severe demeanor to the rest of the world, but she had never been able to fool Rhiannon. *Be strong,* Gwyn often advised; *even if you don't feel strong, at least deceive the world into believing that you are, and it will be yours on a platter.*

Well, Gwyneth had surely learned her lessons well.

If nothing else, their impoverished upbringing—not to mention old Lord Simms's tutelage—had made sure of it.

Gwyneth was back to kneeling in the dirt, spade in

hand, bucket at her elbow. "Another five minutes," she said, fussing with her daffodils. "Please, Rhia, don't wait for me, your tea will get cold."

But Rhiannon stood unmoving, watching her sister quietly, her eyes thoughtful, her mind remembering. . . . Remembering Gwyneth, the eldest of the three, taking a job in the local public house all those years ago after Mama and Papa died, so that Rhia and little Morganna would have food in their bellies. Gwyneth, never complaining about the slave-like conditions and never shying from the hard work. Gwyneth, always enduring the patrons' endless groping and lewd suggestions with a brave face, but retreating to her tiny room after closing time to suffer in silence. Even now Rhiannon's heart filled with guilt as she thought of Gwyneth, dividing the food on her plate between her sisters as she blithely pled a sour stomach. They had taken her complaints at face value and wolfed down the food, but how many nights had poor Gwyneth gone to bed without any supper so that her little sisters would not go hungry? Swallowing a sudden lump in her throat, Rhiannon watched the weeds thumping into the wooden bucket, the movements of Gwyn's delicate shoulders. No wonder Gwyneth felt the sufferings of the poor and the unfortunate so keenly. Their own hard beginnings were not so easily forgotten.

And then Lord Simms had come into their lives.

The elderly but kind-hearted widower had been en route to visiting a friend in Cardiff when he and his small entourage had stopped at the public house for the midday meal. It had been only natural that he should notice the lovely, fair-haired Gwyneth, only natural that he, as most males who'd set foot in the tavern, would become immediately fascinated with such a model of sophistication and beauty in the midst of such country commonness. The earl had remained in the area, and then the offers of marriage had come—repeatedly—until the day the pub burned down after a chimney fire, and Gwyneth, as head of the family, had had no recourse but to accept his hand in order to keep her sisters fed and clothed.

Rhiannon alone knew the sacrifice that Gwyneth had made.

Rhiannon alone knew the tears that Gwyneth had cried behind her closed door the night she finally decided to marry the old man.

And she alone knew that old Lord Simms had never laid a finger on his wife, who was still as pure as she was the day she married him.

Now Rhiannon watched as her sister bent down to her flowers once more, her simple frock pooling in the dirt around her knees. Even with her hands stained with earth, her hair falling down about her swan-like neck, Gwyneth still managed to appear regal. Lord Simms might not have made a woman out of her, but he had managed to turn a clever country girl into a lady. And Gwyneth, who had loved the old man in her own way, had done him proud.

The last blackbird called out a farewell, and the dimming garden was quiet save for the rhythmic scraping of Gwyneth's spade. Leaving her sister to her flowers, Rhiannon quietly went back inside.

Chapter 5

Deep in another part of the prison hulk *Surrey,* one that did not receive the morning sunlight, fresh breezes off the harbor, or even the cry of seagulls, two people sat together in the foul and wretched gloom.

Nathan Ashton and his little brother Toby were Americans whose only mistake had been to be in the wrong place at the wrong time. As a lieutenant and a midshipman, respectively, aboard Captain Connor Merrick's Newburyport-built, forty-four-gun frigate *Merrimack,* the two had enjoyed a salty, swashbuckling adventure at sea until finally falling to the British. Outmanned and outgunned, the *Merrimack* had fought bravely, sinking before the British could take her into their own navy, but her people had not fared so well. Given the choice of joining the Royal Navy or being incarcerated in one of the prison hulks, what remained of the American crew had patriotically chosen the latter.

Patriotic, they had been. And naive.

Now, three months later, their patriotism was stronger than ever, but naiveté had died the day they'd set foot on the prison hulk.

And a hellish three months it had been, too, thirty-year-old Nathan thought, as he sat in near darkness and, by the light of a cotton wick set in an oyster shell and propped in fat saved from their rationed meat, worked steadily on the hole he was boring in the ship's hull. It was impossible to hear the desperate grinding of his tiny knife, due to the loud, incessant racket made by the prisoners on the deck above as they scraped and rubbed it with sand, but then, he had planned it that way. Nine inches deep the hole was, but Nathan had just managed to saw through to the other side, and now a shaft of daylight rewarded him for his efforts.

He put his nose to the coin-size airhole and then motioned for his little brother to do the same.

Frail and suffering badly from malnutrition and cold, Toby scrambled to the hole, put his face against it, and sucked in huge gulps of the chilly air. His eyes closed and tears began to course down his freckled face, pooling in the lower corners of his cracked spectacles and tracing paths through the grime on his hollow cheeks.

"Oh, Nathan, I've not felt anything this sweet since before the *Merrimack* went down." He pulled back, his brown eyes full of emotion in his gaunt and sickly face.

Nathan swallowed hard. The youngest of the Ashton brothers and born very late in their mother's childbearing years, little Toby had never been strong and hearty like the rest of them. He had wanted to become a lawyer or physician, and had signed on to their cousin Connor's ship only because he was a New Englander and their father had been a patriot in the first war, and he had considered sea service to be his prescribed duty. But seafaring life had taken its toll on the thirteen-year-old, and life aboard this wretched prison ship was wasting him away to nothing.

Nathan reached out and put his hand on Toby's bony shoulder. "Don't you worry none, little brother. We'll get out of here soon enough and back home."

"I'm cold, Nathan."

"I know. I am too."

"And hungry."

Pressing his face against the hole and digging sawdust out of the edges, Nathan jerked his elbow at the tin plate behind them. "Then eat, Toby. I know it ain't fit for a dog, but they ain't going to feed us anything better, and if ye don't eat, you're gonna come down sick."

Still sniffling, trying bravely to stop, Toby pulled the plate toward him. On it were a chunk of rock-hard bread and a piece of maggot-infested beef that looked as though it had been dragged through the mudflats and smelled no better. His head bent, his greasy ginger hair clumping on his brow, the boy methodically began picking out the maggots, laying them in a squirming row on the deck beside him.

"I'm gonna die here," he said quietly.

"Jeez, Toby, don't talk like that, you're scaring me."

"They guard us more closely than they do the Frenchmen," the boy mumbled, turning the bread over and poking a broken nail into it to extract a wriggling maggot. "Why is that, Nathan?"

"Because we're American, little brother. If you watch those Frenchies, you'll see they're content to spend their time gambling, gaming, and fighting; stay away from 'em, lest they suck you into their vices. But you don't see any of us Yanks wasting the contents of our purses on stuff like that, do you? Nay, *we* put our energy into tryin' to escape. *That,* Toby, is why the British guard us more closely."

"I wish we could've got off when Connor did."

"He'll be back for us, Toby. He won't desert us, I can promise you. But we'll have to be ready for him when the time comes."

Toby was quiet for a long moment, thinking of their brave, likable cousin who, even during the bone-chilling, brutal months of the English winter, had always found a way to make him laugh. It had been Connor who had showed him how to make friends with the rats; it had been Connor, grimacing, who had shut his eyes, held his nose, and choked down the weevily bread, joking as he did so about the "extra meat"; Connor who had paid a whopping forty-four shillings per month for the *Statesman*, just so they would have news of the outside world; Connor who had kept their memories and spirits alive with stories about home. Connor had been the one to make them think about tomorrow, and Connor had been the one who, on those wretched nights of bitter cold and rotten herring for supper, reminded them that God had not forgotten them.

Hard to believe, but then Connor had never led them astray.

Toby cupped his hand around the squirming maggots and pushed them into a small pile. Once he had been unable even to touch the things. Now the sight of them no longer made him want to wretch, but he still couldn't eat the bread as long as they infested it. *Connor.* He loved his pragmatic, solid-tempered brother, but he missed his cousin. How bleak life had become since Connor had made his escape. . . .

Connor had been one of the lucky ones. One night a month ago, right before the new captain had taken over the hulk, a prisoner had managed to overpower a guard and leap overboard, musket fire following him down into the cold, black harbor. The following morning his bloated body was discovered on the mudflats, where he'd been caught by the tide and drowned. Connor and Nathan had tried to prevent Toby from seeing the fellow, but under the captain's orders Lieutenant Radley of the Royal Marines had marched all 460 prisoners up on deck and made them look at the poor fellow. Crows had been tearing at the dead flesh, and Toby had been violently sick over the rail. For two days the body had been allowed to lay there, until several angry and disgusted prisoners had petitioned the captain to be allowed ashore to bury their poor comrade.

It was the last permission that captain had ever granted. Upon their return a mutiny had developed over the treatment of the dead man, and in the ensuing fracas the captain had been knifed in the back by one of the Frenchmen.

Lord Morninghall, the new commander, had arrived to take over a week later.

Toby idly moved the clump of wriggling maggots with his knife, training them into a large letter C. Five feet away a rat—this one christened Polly by Connor himself—lifted its nose, whiskers quivering as it crept toward Toby's neglected piece of meat.

He looked up, watching it with disinterest. "The Black Wolf's gonna rescue us, ain't he?"

"The Black Wolf won't stop until he's either caught or there's no one left on this hulk to rescue. Relight that wick, will you? The damned stench has snuffed it out again."

With a trembling hand, Toby put down the knife and got the wick going once again. Then, drawing the filth-encrusted tatters of his yellow Transport Office clothes around his skeletal body, he huddled against the damp hull. His brother looked around at him in impatience.

"Eat, Toby. For God's sake."

"I can't. Not that."

Nathan closed his eyes on a silent prayer. Above his head the deck cleaning suddenly stopped. His hand froze with it, so the sawing sounds would not betray him.

"If Morninghall finds out about what you're doing, he's gonna put you in the Black Hole, Nathan," the boy murmured, watching with lifeless eyes as his older brother pushed his finger into the opening and dug out more sawdust. "You don't want to spend another ten days down there like you 'n' Connor did before, do you?"

"Morninghall is not going to find out. Have you even looked upon his face since he took over command of this thing? 'Tis Radley that I'm worried about, the infernal son of a bitch."

Above, the scraping sounds started up again, accompanied by the sloshing of buckets of water being thrown across the deck. Nathan immediately turned his attention back to the hole.

"I can get two fingers through here now, Toby. By the week's end we ought to be able to grease ourselves up like pigs and slide right on through."

"I'll never survive the swim, Nathan. You go."

"I'm not going without you, and you damn well know it."

"Then I'll wait until I'm stronger and I can make the swim too."

"You ain't gonna get any stronger if you don't eat."

"I can't eat," the boy whispered, pitifully. "And so I guess I'll just have to wait for the Black Wolf to come and get me." He pressed his nose against his tattered sleeve to strain the foul air, and as one fat, hopeless tear ran down his cheek, he watched the rat as it made off with the meat.

The maggots remained on the dark planking.

No matter. By dark the rats would have found them too.

That night Gwyneth found sleep elusive. She lay in her big bed, gazing up at the ceiling through the canopy of foamy lace, the shelf clock gently ticking away the hour. She was thinking about Morninghall, about deadly grace and a demon's face, about hands that fanned fire and lips that had wanted far, far more than just one stolen kiss. She sighed and flipped over. Still she saw that face, felt those hands. Frustrated and despairing with insomnia, she got up and went to the window. She sat on the velvet-cushioned seat, hair unbound, feet curled beneath her nightgown, arms wrapped around her legs, and chin propped atop her knees as she gazed out over Portsmouth's harbor, where the lights of the many ships anchored there were like stars strewn across a midnight sky.

She dreaded what she would find when she went aboard the prison hulk on the morrow. That she would go aboard it, she had no doubt; William's brother, Richard, had grudgingly granted her permission, despite the fact that the Transport Office had no desire for anyone to know what *really* went on aboard the old hulks. But she knew how to handle Richard, and she suspected she could handle the Transport Office.

It was Lord Morninghall who worried her, fascinated her.

And, if truth be told, frightened her. For never before had she felt the utter devastation of the senses she'd experienced during that brief moment in his arms, and she didn't quite know what to do about it.

Wearily, she pushed her hair off her brow. The ticking of the clock began to grow maddening. Unable to stand it any longer, Gwyneth shed her nightgown and went to her wardrobe, pulling out a simple dress of blue muslin and an indigo mantle trimmed in sable. She was not afraid to go out at night; she had Mattie and the lady's pistol William had given her for her twentieth birthday. Both would go far to discourage the attentions of any particularly unpleasant characters. She loaded the tiny weapon, tucked it in her reticule, and, pulling on a dark cloak, crept slowly down the stairs.

As though he'd already anticipated her intentions, Mattie lay against the door, waiting for her and thumping his tail against the rug. She leaned down to pat him.

"Walkies, Mattie?"

The dog was up like a shot. He shook himself, long ears flapping against his head and making a racket in the stillness of the house. His leash hung from a coat hook, and hoping that the sound hadn't woken her sister, Gwyneth clipped it onto his collar, unlatched the door, and slipped out into the night.

The sea air was chilly and bracing, carrying the scent of salt, the tidal flats, and the tangy smoke from Portsmouth's many chimneys. Gwyneth pulled her hood up, shivering. Above her head the branches of a chestnut tree whispered in the wind, and the moon floated high in a sea of silver cloud, sheening the waxy hedges that lined the street, glowing upon iron stair railings, stone-tiled rooftops, and cold panes of window glass. The street was narrow, deserted, the houses appearing to hold up the night sky. From somewhere off in the distance a dog barked, and if she strained her ears, Gwyneth could just hear the last sounds of drunken revelry coming from one of the many cheap taverns that competed for space along the waterfront.

She pulled the dog close to her and moved down the quiet street, her breath pluming the air, her body slowly warming as she walked faster. She had hoped the exercise would clear her head and afford her some sleep, and never intended to go to the waterfront—but that was where she ended up, staring thoughtfully out at the coffin-like mass of the prison hulk *Surrey* from the edge of a deserted pier and listening to the sea suck and lap against the old wooden piles beneath her.

The night was deadly still, even the taverns closed now.

Gwyneth hugged her arms to herself, shivering a little. Mattie sat beside her feet and yawned. She reached down to rub his ears, and it was then that she saw a boat moving silently across the harbor.

She went perfectly still, straining her eyes in the darkness. The craft blended into the darkness of the harbor so perfectly that Gwyneth wasn't even sure she'd seen it, but beside her Mattie had sat up and taken a step closer to the pier's edge, nose lifted to the thready breeze and nostrils quivering.

He whined softly.

Sure enough, there it was, moving like a phantom, no splashing, no creaking of oarlocks, nothing. Gwyneth suddenly felt very exposed on the open pier, and decided she'd seen enough. She tugged on Mattie's leash.

"Come on, Matt. Time to go."

But the dog planted his feet, tail stiff and rigid, eyes

fixed on the moving shape. The craft weaved between the big frigates and men-of-war, the anchored lighters and scrubby fishing boats, silent, unobserved, stealthy. On it was a solitary figure, his clothes as dark as the water that surrounded him.

Gwyneth lifted her brows. The boat was headed straight for the prison hulk.

The Black Wolf? Surely not . . .

The boat coasted to a halt some fifty feet from the old hulk's stern, a black wedge against the silvery harbor. There was a silent commotion of movement aboard the prison ship; then soft splashes sounded in the night and moments later Gwyneth saw three heads moving through the water, long wakes of ripples trailing behind them. One by one the figure on the boat dragged the swimmers out of the water and into the tiny craft, pushing them down to its bottom and hastily throwing a blanket over the lot of them. Then the boat moved off, quickly threading its way through the anchored ships before finally disappearing into the night.

Mattie turned his head to look behind them, but Gwyneth was still gazing out over the harbor. She laid a nervous hand atop the dog's head and gave a little laugh.

"Call me a hopeless romantic, Mattie, but I think we have just seen the Black Wolf in action."

She turned—and stifled a scream.

A tall figure of a man, dressed entirely in black, stood motionless at the end of the pier, preventing her escape.

Then he began to move slowly toward them.

Mattie's hackles went up, and he issued a low, warning growl which trembled all the way up the leash. Gwyneth stood frozen. The apparition kept coming, black cloak swirling around his booted ankles, hat pulled low over his masked face, the glint of a smile beneath. Mattie lunged forward against the end of the leash, his growls now rising to a frenzied, snapping snarl. Still the figure approached, growing larger and larger out of the darkness, not pausing until it stood a mere ten feet away.

Teeth bared, snarling, Mattie pressed close to Gwyneth's legs.

"Quiet," the figure whispered.

The dog went immediately still.

Gwyneth looked up into that dark and shadowed face and took an involuntary step back.

"Really, my lady, the war has enough spies without the feminine ranks deciding to join them." The voice was little more than a deep whisper.

Gwyneth kept her hand anchored around the dog's collar like a lifeline. "Who are you?"

"Why, you said it yourself, my dear. The Black Wolf. Who did you think I was?"

"The Black—" She stared off over the harbor, but the small boat was gone. "Then who . . ."

"One of my compatriots," the tall figure murmured easily. "I cannot perform a rescue all by myself, you know."

He moved closer. Mattie edged close to Gwyneth's legs, staring up at him and growling softly. Gwyneth retreated a step, keenly aware of the silent harbor behind her.

"Really, pretty lady," the Wolf whispered, his voice sending shivers through Gwyneth's blood, "if you insist on retreating, I do hope you can swim. Because, you see, I'm not dressed to effect your rescue, and I should hate to see you drown."

She stared at him, overcome with awe, terror, curiosity.

He reached out, palm turned upward and fingers cupped, offering to draw her away from the edge. She stared at that black-gloved hand, afraid.

"No? Perhaps, then, you can tell me what brings you here at such an hour. I do not like surprises. Or spies."

It was not an invitation. It was a threat, and Gwyneth knew it.

She backed up, away from that out thrust hand.
"I—I couldn't sleep."

"Why not?"

*Because there's a diabolical marquess named Morn-
inghall who has set my blood afire, that's why.*

"I'm afraid that is none of your affair, sir."

He smiled. "Of course it isn't. And I doubt I shall
sleep either . . . after glimpsing such a beauty as you."
His rogue's smile gleamed in the darkness, and he
took another step closer, his hand still outstretched.
Gwyneth stood her ground, her heart pounding
wildly, Mattie pressing against her legs.

The Black Wolf reached for her.

She stepped back—and felt empty space beneath
and behind her right foot.

"Don't—" he warned, and quick as a striking
snake, he seized her wrist.

Gwyneth felt the heat of his body through his glove,
the lethal strength of him. Then he was slowly drawing her forward, toward him, eyes locked with hers,
her hand still lifted, until the back of it was against his
lips and his dark head was bending low over it with all
the chivalry of a practiced gallant.

Those shadowy eyes held hers, and Gwyneth's
heart beat even more wildly, but not with fear.

As he slowly straightened up and lowered her hand,
his fingers warm through the gloves and his gaze still
holding hers, he drew her close . . . closer . . . so close
that her breasts were crushed against his chest, her
heart pounding crazily against his, and she had to
crane her head back to stare up into his masked face.
He smiled, a faint thread of white in the darkness.

"I don't think—"

He silenced her with his mouth. She resisted—at
first—then gave herself up to the kiss, her head
swimming madly, the blood thundering through her
ears, as his hand followed the curve of her spine,
shaped the swell of her bottom, and molded her hard
against his loins. A coil of heat started in her breasts,
in her femininity, and she clutched at a fold of his

coat, thinking she was going to swoon and hoping to God she would not. Still he kissed her, his tongue plunging into her mouth and tasting of her own until finally his hand grazed her jaw, caressing the silken flesh there for a long, agonizing moment before he slowly pulled away.

"Ah, lady. Would that my every rescue be rewarded thus!" He brushed her cheek with the back of his fingers, making her shiver uncontrollably. *"Au revoir, ma cherie."* Then he turned and melted back into the darkness from which he had come—leaving Gwyneth dazed and shaken while Mattie trembled at her feet.

The following morning the papers were ablaze with the latest news, the headlines screaming out their message for all to see:

PRISON SHIP SURREY RAIDED BY MASKED AVENGER! BLACK WOLF MAKES OFF WITH THREE MORE AMERICAN LAMBS! ROYAL NAVY IN DISGRACE! And so on and so forth, ad nauseam.

The papers already tossed out the stern windows to educate the fish, Damon sat staring down at the *Peterson's.* It lay open to the appropriate section, headaches, and diagnosed Damon's as being anything from a brain tumor to an overload of the stresses of current life.

It had to be the latter—of course.

A very irate Admiral Bolton had already come and gone, nearly five hundred prisoners were cheering loudly enough to split the very ship in two, Radley was outside yelling for order in the uproar, and through it all carpenters were hard at work, hammers banging as they patched up the compromised hull, voices shouting back and forth as they fought to hear each other over the din. One of them had come in earlier to report another hole, already as big as a man's fist, this one several inches beneath the sentry's walk running around the hull just above the waterline. Radley had gone off to try to find the culprit, and as Damon had sat in his swivel chair, fingers pressed against his pounding temples, Radley had marched back in, a defiant American by the name of Nathan Ashton in tow, the enraged clamor of the prisoners beyond the door and on the decks below making hearing all but impossible. "Ten days Black Hole, Captain, he doesn't deserve any less!" Radley had thundered, to which Ashton had started hollering protests, Radley had begun yelling for fourteen days instead, and Damon had calmly rotated the chair around, shutting himself off from all of it until Radley had finally dragged the fellow back out, his enraged promises of eternal escape attempts still ringing in Damon's aching head.

It was obvious to anyone how the escapees had got past the seven night sentries who continually paced the open-floored gallery. Five of the guards had lumps the size of hen's eggs on their heads, and the other two—liars who couldn't be trusted as far as one could hurl a brick—had no doubt been bribed by the prisoners themselves.

The wild uproar continued outside. Damon hoped to hell that the night's events, along with the punishment of Nathan Ashton, wouldn't bring a mutiny down on his head. Radley had told him all about what the prisoners had done to the last captain.

Massaging his temples, he stared out the stern windows. There was a boat putting out from shore, and in it was Lady Gwyneth Evans Simms.

His head began to pound even harder.

Soon enough the commotion rose in pitch and he knew she was aboard. He calmly poured himself a glass of brandy and then swiveled the chair around to face the door, legs spread before him and his moody gaze directed on the unforgiving wood. Sure enough, a fist began to rap against it.

"Enter," he drawled, glass dangling negligently from his hand.

Foyle showed the woman inside. And then he fled.

And Damon forgot his headache.

Her hair was scraped up and back from her high

cheekbones, plaited and wrapped atop her head with a pair of pearl-encrusted combs to anchor it. A cossack-style hat of purple velvet, also sporting pearls and several plum-colored feathers, was perched neatly atop this elegant coiffure, giving her a smart look of militant efficiency. A pearl choker ringed her swan-like throat, a bodice of plush lavender velvet showed off the swell of her breasts to maddening temptation, and pale lilac skirts shot with silver thread only added to her regal hauteur. She had a parasol, and the way she was looking at him, he wondered if she were going to smash him across the head with it. But despite the picture she presented, he knew there was a passionate being beneath all the ice. He could see it in the flush that moved across her cheeks at his deliberately rude stare; he could see it in the sudden confusion and, yes, anger that darkened her violet eyes when he merely sat there, looking at her. At last he raised his glass in a mocking salute and smiled.

"Ah, such passion you exhibit for your so-called *causes,* Lady Simms. One must wonder if that passion extends to the bedroom as well."

She reached into her reticule and withdrew a small pistol, pointing it dead center at his chest. His brows rose.

"I'll have no more nonsense from you, Morning-hall. What you did the other day was unforgivable."

"My memory fails me," he murmured, eyes gleaming, though he knew very well what he had done and had only to look at her rosy lips, the tempting swell of her white bosom, to experience that heady pleasure all over again.

"Mine does not. Get up."

He sipped his brandy, pointedly ignoring the pistol. "I must say, this *is* a surprise. I knew you were dangerous, but armed besides?"

"I want a tour of this ship. *Now.*"

"Do you?" He waved the glass, not spilling a drop. "Well, I want command of a frigate, my abilities glowingly reported to my superiors, and an end to what has just become a throbbing headache. *Now*. But as I do not expect to have any of my wishes granted within the next several moments, I shall have to make do without them—and so, my dear vixen, shall you." He rose to his feet and slowly, deliberately, moved toward her, seizing her wrist and easily forcing the pistol toward the deckhead. Alarm flashed in her eyes, then anger. Holding her so, he leaned down into her face until her eyes were not three inches from his own and her nostrils flared with fear. "Do not threaten me, Lady Simms. I can promise you, you'll live to regret it."

And then, to add to her humiliation, he let her go.

For a moment she merely stood there, cheeks dark with anger, back stiff as a ramrod, as she massaged her wrist and glared at him. He could see the pulse beating wildly at her throat, the venom and fire in her stare.

She put the pistol back in her reticule and moved past him, the scent of peaches following her. She went straight to the chair he had just vacated and sat, her parasol stabbing into the decking before her as she leaned over it and fearlessly met his gaze.

"You amaze me with your conceit and arrogance, my lord. Do you honestly think you have an effect on me? That you frighten me?"

The glass still dangling from his hand, he leaned negligently against the bedpost. "I do not frighten you, but you desire me."

"Like I desire the devil, whose company, I must admit, would be immensely preferable to your own. But I did not come here to compare your *devastating charm* to that of Satan, the wealthiest London blade, nor even that of the Black Wolf. After all, there is really no comparison."

"I hardly think that you are in a position to make that judgment, madam."

"Really? Well it just so happens that I met that worthy hero last night, on that pier you can see just over there," she replied, airily gesturing toward the

window. "He was quite dashing. Magnificent, in fact.
I can see why every female in Portsmouth must be
dreaming of being swept away by him. God help me, *I*
certainly was!"

She saw the deliberate shot to his male pride hit
home. His mouth went flat and hard, and fire began to
glitter in those eminently fascinating, mesmerizing,
frightening eyes. For the briefest of moments, he
allowed humor to move across the cool irises, as
though granting her points for the well-aimed hit;
then they became cold once more, the gaze of the
dispassionate aristocrat. He gazed flatly at her for a
long, unpleasant moment, until he had her nerves
squirming, her heart beating wildly; then he let his
gaze move slowly down her face, her neck . . . her
breasts.

Gwyneth's insides caught on fire. She regretted
putting the pistol away, but there was no way to
retrieve it without losing face.

Morninghall remained staring at her, weight slung
suggestively against the bedpost. Not moving. Just
. . . looking.

She met his stare, refusing to be intimidated.

At last he straightened up and moved toward her.
Gwyneth's stomach flipped over. He came right up to
the chair, looking down at her with a malevolent little
smile on his lips for a long, terrible moment. Then,
his fingertips dragging across the polished wood of its
arm, he moved with a sinister, stalking grace around
the chair, in what could only be a deliberate attempt
to unnerve her. Gwyneth didn't move. He was behind
her now, his fingers whispering over the top of the
chair, just above her nape. She sat frozen. He came
around the other side, still looking down at her,
silently mocking her fear, before finally pausing dead
in front of her and putting his hands on both arms of
the chair.

He leaned close, trapping her where she sat, those
diabolical eyes very, very close to her own.

"A tour, you want."

She stared fearlessly into those wicked depths. "Yes. I cannot see why that is so much to ask."

His nose came closer. "I do not concern myself with the workings of this ship, nor with what goes on outside that door. That's Foyle's job. Perhaps he will oblige you."

"Perhaps he will. But I'd rather *you* escort me, my lord."

He straightened up a little, the sunlight catching in the rich waves of his hair, that same terrifying smile still on his lips. She could feel the heat of him, the banked fury, and her feet longed to take flight. She dug them into the planking, anchoring herself by gripping the handle of her parasol.

He noted her fear, and the smile became downright malicious. "And why is that?" he murmured silkily, looming over her.

"You said yourself that you do not concern yourself with the workings of this ship. Perhaps it is time you viewed firsthand, the horrors those imprisoned here are forced to endure."

The devil eyes glittered. "I do not care what they are forced to endure. They made their beds, they shall lie in them."

"You would condemn a man simply because he fought for another side and was unfortunate enough to end up in the *gentle hands* of the Royal Navy?" she returned angrily.

He leaned so close she could feel his hot breath on her face, the heat that emanated from his powerful body. "I did not ask to be put in command of a prison ship. I do not *like* being in command of a prison ship. And I do not like *you,* Lady Simms. In fact, at the present moment, I cannot think of anything that appeals to me more"—he was so close she could feel his brow just touching hers—"than the idea of tossing you down on that bed and having my way with you. Persist in annoying me, and you may very well see a side of this beast you will wish you hadn't."

The back of her head pressed against the chair. "Do

you always resort to intimidation and empty threats to get what you want, Morninghall?"

"I can assure you, my dear, that they are not empty. And I would be more than delighted to prove it."

Malevolent eyes glittering with warning, he straightened up at last, the master of the moment, triumphant.

"And I would be more than delighted to shoot you where you stand, should you even try," Gwyneth murmured weakly. He gave her only a disdainful look, and she thanked God he couldn't hear the wild thumping of her heart. Her hand shaking, she reached into her reticule and extracted the tiny pistol, pretending to examine its fine finish before looking up at him. She smiled sweetly. "The tour, please."

He merely stared at her. Not a nuance of emotion passed over that dispassionate face.

She cocked the pistol, the faint click sounding very loud in the cabin, and pointed it at his chest. *"Now."*

His beautiful, sensuous mouth curved in the faintest of smiles, and somehow that slight movement made him all the more sinister, all the more terrible.

He turned his back on her, in blatant disregard for the weapon now trembling in her hand, and moved to the door.

"Very well, then," he murmured, opening it with a mocking flourish, his smile alive with malice. "Come along with me. But do leave the pistol here, my dear."

It was damp within her trembling hand. "And why is that?"

"Because I shouldn't want to have to use it on one of these poor wretches you seek to help when they turn on you."

She stared at him for a moment, uncomprehending. Then her gaze dropped, and she slowly put the weapon down on the table. Her legs barely able to support her, she got to her feet, following his back and quelling the impulse to drive her parasol straight between those lordly shoulders.

Chapter 6

She had bested him, damn her to hell. She had not backed down, had not given in, and now here she was, walking along just behind him, triumphant, victorious, smug.

Damon saw red.

She wanted a tour, did she? She wanted to see firsthand what horror the prisoners had to endure. Oh, he'd show her all right. He'd show her just what a miserable command that bastard Bolton had given him; he'd show her to just what kind of glory he'd come; he'd show her sights that would make her hair curl, her skin turn green, and the sweat pop out on her fine and lovely brow.

He strode out onto the quarterdeck, not bothering to shorten his stride so she could keep up; his eyes blazing, the expression on his face sent people running out of his path. The deafening clamor made by several hundred bored and miserable wretches came to a slow, screeching stop at the sight of her. Someone gave a long, low whistle; another a mocking bow; and yet another hollered a taunt in broken English that she was going to get her fine gown as filthy as the grave. Then one of the Americans, on hands and knees as he scrubbed the deck, caught sight of Damon. Elbowing his mates, he pointed and began to call out insults. Damon kept his face coldly expressionless, determined to ignore the man and his chanting mates, knowing the humiliation was only going to get worse as they went below.

"I need to know what happens to new arrivals when they're first brought aboard the ship," Lady Simms was saying in a clinical, no-nonsense tone, raising her voice to be heard above the noise.

He walked ahead, not bothering to turn around. "They're given a bath."

"Warm water or cold?"

"Ice water, straight out of the damned harbor. They're prisoners, they don't deserve any better."

He heard her enraged intake of breath, and the fact that he'd gotten to her filled him with gratification and pleasure. *Good.* But her footsteps had stopped, and when he turned he saw her extract a small notebook and pencil from her reticule and begin to scribble madly.

"Bath . . . ice water . . . must make note of this to—"

"Come along," he snapped nastily. "I haven't got all bloody day."

She shot him a look that could've melted iron, refusing to move, her brow knit and her pencil moving over the page, the wind ruffling the feathers of her hat, rippling the fine lilac silk of her skirts.

He seized her elbow and yanked her forward. "I said, 'Come along,' damn it!"

"Take your hands off me, you scoundrel!" She jerked free of him and held her elbow protectively close to her body, her eyes spitting sparks. "I want to know what clothes they're issued, what they're fed, if they're allowed visitors—"

"They're issued clothes by the Transport Office, and they're fed as well as the seamen aboard His Majesty's ships. They have nothing to complain about, damn it, so come along before I lose what little goddamn patience I have left." He saw two marines anxiously watching him move toward the ladder. It was not safe for him to go below unescorted, even less safe for the lady. He jerked his head and they immediately fell into place behind her, tense, watchful, their weapons at the ready and their eyes alert for possible trouble.

The hatch to the lower deck awaited him like a hangman's noose, a black hole of stench and noise below. Heat rose from it as from a furnace. Fumes pushed out of it, ripe with the eye-watering stink of urine, excrement, sweat, and vomit. Already Damon could hear the prisoners down there, yelling and shouting, already he could see their dim shapes clustering around the base of the ladder, pale faces turned upward—waiting for him like hungry demons in the pit of hell. He had a flashback of Oxford, his tormentors leaning out of the windows above his head, laughing, mocking, taunting him as he fled, sobbing, across the lawn. He did not want to go down there. God help him, he didn't. He clenched his fists, steeling himself. *They're just prisoners, for God's sake, they mean nothing, nothing!* He was keenly aware of *her,* still behind him, she who was about to witness his further humiliation, she who would probably laugh right along with them, and he felt his pulse begin to throb in time to his headache. He turned and stared coldly at her, hoping to put her off. She was wrinkling her nose and frowning as she peered down into the hatch, but she did not go for her handkerchief.

He had to give her credit. She must be made of strong stuff indeed. "I see that the heat and stench alone are affecting you. You'd be wise to abandon this idea, now."

"On the contrary, my lord. We have barely scratched the surface of this problem. After you."

Needles of hatred stabbed through him, and at that moment Damon had never loathed anyone as much as he did Lady Gwyneth Evans Simms. But he would not let her triumph, would not let her see his fury, and so he nodded, allowing his expression to set in its familiar mask of cold dispassion. Then, silently vowing revenge for what she was putting him through, he descended through the hatch, going down first.

Gwyneth's first sight of the lower deck was something that would remain with her for the rest of her life. As she crept down the ladder into a hot, acrid darkness, illuminated by nothing but mean stabs of daylight sifting through narrow, iron-grated scuttles, all noise suddenly stopped, the sounds echoing on the heavy air like the repeating echo of a gun. In the murky, malodorous gloom she saw hundreds of gaunt faces staring at her, frozen with curiosity, interest, awe. She felt the overwhelming despair, misery, and anguish that infected every inch of this horrific place as keenly as though it were the plague. Already the heat was intense, making her gown cling to her skin; the overpowering stench caused her eyes to water and the bile to rise in her throat. As she stepped down onto a deck that was slick with grime, she saw the marquess standing stiffly by the companionway, where the only headroom was to be had, making a big pretense out of studying his watch. His features were rigid, his eyes shuttered.

"Seen enough?" he asked sharply, looking up.

She could only stand there, crouched beneath the low overhead deck as she stared about her, too shocked to answer, even to record in her notebook what her nightmares could not have begun to imagine.

Men, some half-naked, some wearing nothing more than the grime that covered them, reposed on benches or stood idly about, caught in the act of playing dice, conversing, making ship's models out of bits of wood. They stared at her. Lice crawled in their hair. Flies drank from the sweat trails that cut rivers down their filthy faces. Scabs dotted their skeletal legs, their bony arms, the patches of skin that showed through the remnants of their clothing. Some of them had hard, feral eyes and starved smiles; others looked at her with sad gazes devoid of hope. Still others just stared, corpse-like, right through her, their minds already dead and waiting for their bodies to follow. Hammocks—some stowed, some hung, some lying in the damp filth that carpeted the deck—were everywhere, and the deck overhead was, at five feet, so low that nobody could stand up, the result being that those prisoners who were on their feet were round-backed and hulking, adding to their frightening, monstrous effect all the more.

And then the noise started.

"Aaah, look at the fancy Englishwoman! Come to stare at us like animals in the zoo, come to gawk! Bah, you go, leave us! Go now, no humiliate!"

Movement, violent shoving. "No, let her stay! We never get to see pretty ladies. Let her stay!"

"Hey, *Capitaine,* you got yourself *une belle femme?* You share her with hungry Frenchmen, no?"

"Come here to my hammock, *ma coeur!* Let me show how a *real* man pleasure you!"

The insults and abuse grew deafening, fists flew, and a wave of threat and hostility began to push the crowd forward. Gwyneth looked nervously at Lord Morninghall. He shoved his watch into his pocket, his eyes blazing, and turned to one of the marines who stood on the ladder just behind them. "Shut these wretches up!" he snapped, seizing Gwyneth's arm and hauling her quickly toward the next hatch.

But not fast enough. She saw two men eating a dead rat, another grinning madly as he exposed himself to her, another urinating against the hull and watching, fascinated, as the urine streamed down the blackened wood. Filthy hands reached for her, and she gasped when someone snatched the hat from her head with a shout of triumph, pulling her hair, pulling tears of pain to her eyes, flinging the hat out into the masses like a trophy. She pressed close to Morninghall, suddenly terrified of becoming separated from him.

"English pig! How dare you bring your woman aboard to flaunt her in our faces!" An American voice, that one.

And more French: "You wait. Black Wolf rescue us! Black Wolf make you laughingstock, *aristo!*"

The clamor grew louder, angrier, and behind her she could hear the marines yelling angrily for order.

Morninghall had released her arm and was just going
down the ladder now, his shoulders set and rigid, his
hair gleaming in the dim lantern light.

"Why aren't these men dressed better than they
are?" Gwyneth asked, yelling down to him over the
din. She grasped the coaming and yanked her hand
away in disgust at the grime that soiled her glove. "I
thought you said the Transport Office issues them
clothing—"

"They do. These men, *madam,* are the very lowest
of the low, the *Raffalés,*" he responded, without
bothering to turn around. "You will find the officers,
the gentlemen, and the Americans in a more acceptable state of clothing, breeding, and manner."

"Surely being of a low social class should not mean
they have to go about freezing and half-naked!" she
cried over the noise.

He looked up at her over his shoulder. "If they are
freezing and half-naked, it's their own damned fault.
They gamble away their clothing, their hammocks,
even their food, going hungry during the day then
slinking around like rats at night and devouring the
crumbs left on the deck. What do you want me to do
about it, forbid the gaming? Christ, I'd have a
damned mutiny on my hands."

Gwyneth's jaw snapped shut, for she had no answer
to that. And the stench was starting to suffocate her.
She continued down the hatch, terrified of losing
Morninghall, each step bringing her into hotter air,
louder noise, more terrible smells. It was all she could
do not to draw her handkerchief and press it to her
nose. She took tiny breaths, each one an anguish in
itself.

She reached the bottom of the ladder and found
herself on another deck. Sweat was now trickling
down her brow and the curve of her spine, and the air
was unbreathable. Instinctively she reached for her
handkerchief; then, coughing, she crumpled it in her
fist. If these poor people could endure such air—for

months, sometimes years, on end—she, who had to
suffer it for only a brief time, would not make them
feel even more wretched, more humiliated, by refusing to share their plight. Determined to ignore her
discomfort, she peered through the gloom, the shifting wall of unwashed, skeletal bodies, and saw a small
group of prisoners sitting on a little bench, one of
them, finer dressed than the others, holding a book.

"What are they doing?" Gwyneth asked.

"Damned if I know," the marquess retorted, giving
her a look that dared her to challenge him.

Her temper began to boil; she clenched her teeth in
frustration. Behind her one of the marines was just
coming down the hatch, his boots gleaming dully in
the lantern light. "The gentleman's an officer," he
offered, hearing her question. "He's teaching the
others English."

The gentleman in question looked up and inclined
his head at Gwyneth, this pitiful attempt at gallantry
tearing at her heart.

"Don't look so upset, ma'am. These men, they
make their own beds, just as His Lordship says. The
Raffalés, they don't care about anything. They gamble
away the clothes right off their backs, the food right
out of their stomachs. But the rest, they all have their
own little trades and professions, teaching dancing,
fencing, drawing and painting, and the like to the
others—for a small fee, of course. They make ship
models out of the beef bones or the bread, sell it to the
masses, hold little auctions and such. I know it looks
like hell here, ma'am, but the prisoners, they adapt.
Why, the Americans even elect their own officers to
govern them, just as they do in their own government;
make their own laws, define crimes, and mete out
punishments. Cleanest of the lot, though, those
Yanks, real fussy about their persons. . . ."

His words blended into a soup of incomprehensible
excuses as Gwyneth, feeling faint, fanned herself with
her notebook. "Then why is the stench so bad down

here? Are the latrines never emptied? Are the decks never washed? Are these men never allowed to bathe?"

Lord Morninghall was waiting, watching. Flickering shadows of lantern light painted his face in tongues of orange, making it appear diabolic, savage even, the devil surveying the flames of hell with eyes that glittered coolly. "Those things, and others, are *supposed* to come about," he muttered darkly, almost to himself. "But it would appear that sometimes the very people one assigns to oversee such tasks find more *interesting* things to do."

The marine flushed, visibly distressed. Seeing that Gwyneth had noted his captain's cryptic words and was now studying him keenly, he gave a lame smile, trying to defuse the tension-filled moment. "We don't like to wash the decks too much, ma'am, especially not in the cooler months. More damp, it just brings on sickness and such—"

"What about bathing?"

"Well, er, yes, some of 'em bathe . . . sometimes . . ."

"Aren't they given *soap?*"

"Soap isn't something the authorities issue, ma'am. I mean, this isn't a fancy manor house or anythin'. . . ."

"So I see," she murmured coldly. She entered this too in her notebook, but as she bent her head, the sweat ran down her brow and into her eyes, and the smell pushed its way into her nose, the back of her throat, even her head. She had a sudden, very real fear she was going to faint.

She saw Morninghall regarding her, coolly disdainful yet meditative, as though he knew her plight and was reveling in it. She shot him a look of pure loathing and took a few hesitant steps away from the ladder.

Down here the air was so heavy, so thick with the scent of excrement, urine, vomit, and sweat, that the few lanterns that penetrated the gloom did so with the same effect of a ship's light in a heavy fog, making it appear fuzzy, hazy, dim. Gwyneth, gagging, could take in only desperate, pinched gasps of it. Each tiny breath brought her near to retching. The fumes of ammonia and excrement stung her eyes, making them water. Her nose burned, her stomach began to roil, and the heat, emanating from hundreds of sweating, unwashed bodies crammed into such a small space, pressed against her senses, her clothes, making her hair go damp and cling at her temples. A fly buzzed around her eyes and she batted at it, only to have it come back; she batted at it again, harder this time, feeling hysteria and a mad urge to flee this hell of hells beginning to overpower her. She tried to stand up, bumping her head on the low deck overhead, and as she instantly recoiled, near to sobbing, she saw a dead rat underneath a bench and more flies crawling across it, some of them rising to move lazily through the humid, unmoving air.

And still those devil's eyes of Morninghall's, watching her.

The fly came back, and with a little cry she swatted at it, backing up to where the marquess waited.

"Seen enough?" he asked harshly.

She shot him a look of pure disgust that he could let things be so bad down here, and saw the shame, the embarrassment in his gaze before he turned his face away, his jaw hard.

"No, my lord," she replied, her voice trembling with anger and determination. "I feel as though I'm going to be ill, my head is dizzy, and I am near to swooning for lack of air—but no, I'm not ready to leave. I would ask, however, that since this wretchedness does not appear to be affecting you as it is me that you be gentlemanly enough to stay close to me, perhaps take my arm, in case I become unsteady on my feet and finally succumb to that which I see and smell around me."

Damon stared at her, momentarily disarmed and struck dumb. The woman was as pale as a sheet, perspiring, swaying dizzily—yet she was not about to

abandon her quest. She had nothing to gain personally from doing this, yet she was still able to put aside
her own physical discomfort for the common good of
something greater than herself, able to overcome her
disgust and fear and find compassion for these filthy
men who had taunted and insulted her. It was total
selflessness, and in contrast he felt small, mean,
unworthy. Something hurt inside of him, as though a
crack had split the frozen ice of his heart, and a wave
of admiration for this plucky little woman's spirit and
courage swept through him in a startling, overwhelming wave. He reached out, as she had humbly asked
him to do, and steadied her elbow. "Very well, then. If
you wish to see more then you might as well see the
Black Hole as well."

She choked on another breath. "The Black Hole?"

The marine piped up. "Where the prisoners are
punished, madam. We keep 'em down there for ten
days at a stretch when they're behaving particularly
bad."

Her face went gray. "Yes, yes, of course. Just lead
the way."

With Morninghall's hand firmly supporting her
elbow, Gwyneth thrust herself toward yet another
hatch, this one so dark and forbidding that it yawned
out of the gloom like an empty grave at midnight.
Morninghall went down first. Slowly, his shoulders,
his head, disappeared into that black rectangle.

The marines waited behind her. Lightheaded, nau-
seous, and growing more and more distressed, Gwyneth followed the marquess.

Down into the hold they went, into stygian darkness and stenches that made the upper decks smell
like a rose garden in comparison. There were no
prisoners here and it might've been faintly cooler, but
the stench—of bodily wastes that had filtered down
from the decks above, of dead and decaying vermin,
stagnant water, ammonia, reeking mold, and rotting
wood—was enough to steal the last of Gwyneth's
already meager breath. She paused, unable to breathe,

to see, in the darkness. Behind her, a guard lit a tiny lantern which sputtered and went out in the airless gloom. Swearing and dashing the rivulets of sweat from his brow, he got it lit once more.

Morninghall was standing a little distance away, feet braced on a huge rib that curved out of the keel, hands clasped behind his back as he stared sightlessly into the gloom. He looked as though he were in pain. "Show her the Hole," he ordered, hoarsely.

Her head swimming, her teeth clenched to hold back a rising and horrible urge to vomit, Gwyneth picked her way over the ship's great ribs in the wake of the guard. For a moment she heard no sound behind her; then there were splashes as Morninghall caught up, quickly closing the distance between them. Moisture seeped through her kid slippers as she sloshed through the oily, stinking water. She had to hold her skirts up to keep them from dragging through filth and decay, and her pearls, slimy now with perspiration, felt as though they were choking her. She slipped and Morninghall caught her elbow. As he pulled her up, she saw shapes rearing out of the gloom, rodents scurrying near her feet and along the beams high overhead. Sweat was running freely down her brow, her temples, the curve of her upper lip, and she was fast losing the ability to breathe.

Dizzily, she heard Morninghall's deep voice somewhere near her ear. "You all right?"

She nodded gamely. "Yes, thank you. Show me this thing, please."

Morninghall nodded to the marine, who, breathing through a filthy handkerchief pressed to his face, thrust the lantern toward a structure built into the curve of the hull.

"The Black Hole."

Leaning heavily against Morninghall's arm, her vision reeling and her hair wilting against her dripping brow, Gwyneth stared through the gloom. There it was, a box six feet by six feet, looming out of the darkness like a coffin.

Clutching her notebook, eyes watering, she stumbled toward it, this unspeakable prison tucked down here in this grave of a ship, abandoned, forgotten, forlorn. She saw tiny holes no larger than her little finger for ventilation in its side; she felt the utter misery, terror, and despair oozing from it before she even got to the thing and placed a shaky hand against its door, leaning against it lest she faint.

As she did so, she heard movement behind it, felt the pitiful scratch of fingers on the other side.

There was someone actually in there.

The full horror of it all overcame her at last. Heat, shock, and the noxious fumes finally permeated her brain, and darkness began to come down over her vision. She felt the notebook slipping from her hand, felt her knees collapsing, had a vague sense of falling backward. . . .

And then nothing.

Chapter 7

⎯⎯⎯⎯⎯⎯⎯⎯⎯⎯⎯⎯

$\mathbf{T}$he Marquess of Morninghall, cursing, stepped forward and caught her.

For a moment he stood there, the oily bilge oozing about his shoes, his adversary's body—warm, soft, and buried within a tumble of pale silk skirts and frothy petticoats—filling his arms. For a moment he could look only at her, stunned as he was from the horrors he had just seen, her golden head dangling over his elbow and exposing the throat like a pale offering, the combs falling from her hair and dragging soft, uneven clumps of it down with them. Her lips were parted, her lashes weighty and long against her flushed cheeks, and as the damp heat of her body rose, he caught the scent of peaches. Delicious, sweet, ripe peaches—

A host of feelings smashed the brittle veneer of Lord Morninghall's black heart.

"Er . . . Uh . . ."

He looked up to see the marine staring at him.

"Best get her topside," the man finished sheepishly at Damon's glare. "Fresh air's the best thing to revive a lady from a swoon."

"Well, lead the way then. You have the damned light."

Easily cradling his burden in one arm, Damon paused to retrieve her notebook from where it had fallen, picking it up with two fingers, shaking the water off, and shoving the thing into his pocket. He was so angry he was shaking inside: partly with Lady Simms for forcing him down here; partly with himself for not taking any responsibility for it; and mostly with Foyle and Radley, whom he had entrusted to keep this place clean. Foyle had made daily reports, assuring Damon that things were not this bad, but these conditions were appallingly wretched, criminal even, and it was obvious the cheeky little wretch had been lying to him all along.

Heads were going to roll, Damon thought savagely. Foyle and Radley were not going to escape the full fury of his shame and rage.

Just ahead the marine was trudging up the ladder now, one hand gripping his musket, the other holding the lantern behind him to light his captain's way. Lady Simms weighed less than a bundle of feathers, but Damon still found it no easy task to carry her up the steep, narrow ladder without knocking her dangling legs against the grimy wood, harder still to ignore the noisy flood of jeering laughter that met him without losing his carefully controlled composure.

"Ah, look at the fancy lady! Guess she must've seen a mousey, eh?"

"Or taken a good look at *le capitaine!*"

Damon walked straight through them, his arms rigid around his burden, his face devoid of all emotion.

"Naw, 'twas Ronny's pissing against the bulkhead that did it! Probably ain't never seen a cock that long!"

"Well, what d'ye expect? She's an English *lady,* ain't she? Probably ain't *used* to seein' cocks the size of Ronny's rod!"

"Aye, well, she ain't seen *mine,* then!"

Guffaws, shouts, and laughter roared around them. Filthy bodies pressed close, staring, laughing, leering.

"Hey, Cap'n, ye show her yers?"

Damon kept his impassive gaze straight ahead and shoved his way through them as he started toward the next ladder.

A hand grasped his sleeve and a dirty, grinning face filled his vision, blasting him with its sour breath. "Ye hear me, Cap'n? I asked ye if ye'd showed her—"

He turned then, impaling the wretch with the full effect of his blazing gaze. *"Sod off,"* he snarled, his low, dangerous voice and murderous eyes instantly shutting the heckler up.

Immediately the entire deck went silent.

The prisoner gulped, spread his hands, and backed up. "Hey, look, Cap'n, I didn't mean nothin' by it—"

"Get out of my way."

"Really, I—"

"Move."

The prisoner retreated, and without sparing him another glance, Damon crossed the spot where he had stood and resumed his journey to the deck above, the silence following him all the way topside.

There: clean, blessed, healthy air at last. He filled his lungs with it, wanting to inhale until his chest burst, wanting to forget the nightmare he'd just left, but already prisoners were pressing and shoving to get a glimpse of his lovely armful and the guards were clearing a path through them to the door of his cabin.

Midshipman Foyle came running. "Shall I fetch the ship's doctor, sir?"

Damon turned on him, trembling with fury. "I will see *you* in my cabin in one hour. Be late, and so help me God, I'll have you whipped so severely you won't be able to sit or shit for a week, *do you understand?!*"

Foyle paled, his mouth dropping open. He backed away, eyes suddenly wary. "R-right."

Damon strode into the cabin, kicked the door shut behind him, and leaving damp footprints across his clean rug, deposited Lady Gwyneth Evans Simms atop his bed.

His heart was pounding. The blood was screaming through his temples. His head felt ready to explode.

He pressed his fingers to the sides of his brow and shut his eyes, trying to block out the things he had just seen. He changed his shirt, washed his face and neck, threw open the windows, and leaning out over the harbor, inhaled great, greedy breaths of cool air. *Don't think about what you saw down there. There isn't a damned thing you can do right now anyhow. Don't think about it, and don't think about* her.

But if it weren't for her, he wouldn't be thinking about it.

It was her fault: hers for showing it to him, Foyle's and Radley's for letting it get that way. But no, he should've gone down there before this. He was as much to blame as the others, if not more. Guilt, anger, hatred, lust; all conspired to wring and twist his insides into a seething knot of anguish.

He shut his eyes on a deep, steadying breath, tried to get control of himself but couldn't.

Unable to help himself, he stormed over to the bed and stood looking down at the catalyst of this storm of emotion. He clenched his hands with impotent rage and swallowed, hard. Then he knelt before her, stripped away her dirty gloves, and chafed her wrists. No response. Annoyed now, he splashed some water on a cloth and mopped her face and neck. Such ministrations only fueled his lust, his wish to conquer this woman who had been the cause of such anguish. She had humbled and excited him with her courage, and now—as his gaze took in her smooth forehead, the delicate wing of one eyebrow, the narrow nose and the high cheekbones, cut from alabaster and lightly blushed with a pink so delicate it should've been saved for a rose—he felt that lust beginning to burn out of control. His breathing sharpened, growing heavier, deeper, hotter. His fingers were lingering on the warmth of her neck now, whispering over the choker of pearls, the dewy white skin, toward those tempting, luscious breasts, separated from his touch by nothing but a scrap of velvet. . . .

Peaches. He wanted to throw her in a bowl and sprinkle sugar and cream over her, gorge himself on her delicious sweetness and lick her clean. *Peaches.* He wanted *her.* Here, now. His fingers pulled at her bodice, began to tremble. He felt the blood beating in his ears and pressed two fingers into his brow, terrified of what he was capable of, knowing he was beyond help.

Look at her, Damon! Seduce her, don't rape her, for God's sake!

God help him, she looked soft, delicate, lovely, sweet. Even fragile.

Fragile, like the daffodils, the porcelain, the pretty cups he had smashed to bits beneath his rage. *Sweet,* like the scent of peaches clinging to her. His head began to pound violently. He hated fragility and he hated sweetness, because if you were fragile you were weak, and if you were weak you were worthless. He wanted to crush both fragility and sweetness right out of existence, annihilate them, destroy them, conquer them.

Conquer her. *Now.*

He made a fist and drove it into his throbbing brow, his erection like a granite pole shoving against his breeches.

Take her, damn it!

He spied a half-empty bottle of brandy on the table and, with shaking hands, grabbed it and poured himself a glass, somehow managing to avoid spilling the entire lot. And still, she lay behind him, across his bed like a sweet offering.

It was no use. He started to move toward her—and with a savage curse spun and fired the goblet across the cabin with all the strength of his rage. It exploded against the bulkhead with a splintering crash.

A moan issued from the bed. His hand still outstretched, Damon froze. And looked.

She lay where he'd left her, head pillowed on a fan of disheveled golden hair, lilac skirts draping a deliciously curvaceous hip and one hand resting childishly near her temple. Her eyes were open and staring hazily at him.

"Why did you just destroy your goblet, Morninghall?"

He felt like a child who'd been caught in the act of doing something naughty. Blood heated his face; his heartbeat quickened. He snapped upright and moved threateningly toward her, fists clenched.

"Because I like *breaking* things," he snarled, defiantly.

"Why?"

"Because it *feels* good!"

"I see."

"You don't see a damned thing, and now that you're awake you can just get the hell off my ship before I break something else."

He glared down at her, and Gwyneth, who was just recovering the full use of her blurry senses, had no illusion as to what he wanted to *break* next. And the sight of him—looming over her in a black fury she could not understand, hands clenched at his sides, face dark as a thunderhead, and those soulless, devil's eyes blazing with a hellish fire—was not exactly one she found benign. Dangerous, yes; magnificent, yes; but far from benign. A thrill shot through her, and tingles went racing over her skin.

Anger, however, got the better of her.

Propping herself up on one elbow, she smiled sweetly, mockingly, up at him. "Why, you look shaken, my lord. Upset even. Dare I suspect you actually had a concern for my welfare? Better yet, perhaps the wretchedness of the conditions beneath your feet has finally penetrated that granite tomb containing the remains of your heart."

"I don't have a heart."

"Oh, but you do. A very black one though, isn't it? Cold as the grave and just as rotten."

The fury was going out of his face, leaving it a stone effigy. Only the eyes were alive—glittering, malevolent, dangerous. He turned away. "Impressive. You should have been a poet."

"And *you* should be ashamed of yourself, Morninghall. *I* am ashamed to think I share the same species with you, so embarrassed and disgusted am I over the things my eyes have just witnessed!"

He poured himself a glass of brandy.

"Doesn't the sight even *affect* you?!"

"As you said, my heart is a black one."

"For God's sake, how can you calmly stand there with absolutely no feeling, no concern, no caring for the people who are suffering and starving beneath your feet?! *How can you?*"

He turned then, and she saw the shame, the fresh anger in his eyes. "I didn't know it was so bad."

"You mean to tell me you've never been *down there?*"

"As a matter of fact, no, I haven't. Foyle was supposed to be handling things. I trusted him to do a task, and he failed me. Lied to me. Damn you, don't look at me like that. I told you I have no wish to be on this sodding ship, I never *wanted* to be on this sodding ship, and I would like nothing better than to be out of this sodding *navy*—"

"Then get out of it!" Furious, Gwyneth shot to her feet and faced him squarely. "Let other men who are nobler than you serve it! You are a vile and wretched beast who is so far gone in self-pity you can't even *see* the plight of those whose sufferings far eclipse your own petty troubles! And you know what makes that even more unforgivable? It's that you do not care!" She stalked around the swivel chair and jabbed her finger into his chest to emphasize her point. "You don't *care* what those poor men have to endure," *jab,* "you don't *care* what they have to eat, drink, or sleep in," *jab,* "you care only for your own ambitions, desires, and comforts—"

He snared first one of her wrists, then the other, yanking them high above her head; then, putting the brandy down, he drew her threateningly up against the wall of his chest until her angry eyes were just inches from his own. "Those men brought their sufferings on themselves," he growled, his face so close to hers that she could see the fury pounding in his brow. "They're wretched, they're prisoners, they're the *enemy,* damn it, they're—"

"Human beings!" she spat, fighting to jerk free. "And they deserve to be treated as such!"

"They will be treated as their behavior warrants."

"No behavior warrants the treatment they are receiving!"

"Your behavior warrants a treatment all its own, and if you don't stop your damned struggling, I can assure you you're going to get it."

She froze, twin spots of mortified color blooming in her cheeks as she looked down and saw what he had seen. In her struggle one rosy nipple had popped free of her décolletage.

She gasped, her face aflame. She tried to yank her wrists free, but his grip might as well have been an iron manacle, so tight, so fiercely unrelenting was it. She backed up, her thighs coming up against the edge of the bed. "Unhand me this instant, Morninghall."

He cocked a eyebrow and smiled, thinly. Then she was no longer pressing against the bed of her own accord.

He was pushing her.

"I said, 'Let me *go!*'"

"Gladly," he murmured, his deep, low voice sending a warning screaming up her spine. "For a price."

As he shoved her backward, they fell crosswise over the bed in a rustle of silk, her wrists still caught in his grip.

She glared up at him, her arms trapped above her head, her every instinct screaming at her to run for her life, but there was no escape. He loomed over her, dwarfing her, his body cutting off the light from the window, his face now in devilish shadow. She tried to get her knee up, but realized it was pinned between his hard thigh and the bed. His gaze dropped to her exposed nipple, and she saw his diabolical eyes beginning to gleam and sparkle with an inner light, a savage hunger. Her nipples fired with response, thrusting toward him, and she felt a swirl of heat between her thighs. Oh! Let her body betray her; her mind was strong! She would not let him know he was frightening her, and she would *not* play his game!

"A price, you say," she managed with a little laugh, pretending not to understand his blatant insinuation. "I assume that *price* is to leave you alone and go torment some other prison ship?"

He leaned close, *far* too close, his darkly malevolent face and broad shoulders filling the space above her head. "*Au contraire,* madam. I have no wish for you to leave me alone. You have been a married woman; don't feign ignorance where my *intentions* are concerned." She froze as he dragged a finger down the wildly beating pulse at her throat. "You know that I want you. And I will have you begging and screaming for me to take you before this hour is out."

"I see that self-confidence is one of the few qualities you seem to possess. However, I fear your so-called *intentions* are sadly wasted on me."

He leaned closer, eyes just inches from her own, burning with fury and fire beneath lashes blacker than sin. "Dare you challenge me?"

"I am not so foolish. Nor insane."

"Ah, but if you consider the challenge foolish or insane, then it can be only because you know you will lose. Were you truly convinced that you could resist me, you would merely laugh at the notion and tell me to give it my best shot, if only to ridicule me for my failure afterward." His voice lowered in pitch. "I don't see you laughing, Lady Simms."

"Your arrogance is beyond belief."

He smiled, knowingly. "You desire me."

"You—you do nothing for me, Morninghall. Nothing!"

"I think I will prove you wrong."

Dark lashes came down to hood glittering eyes. His thumb stroked the sensitive underside of her wrist, and she tensed as he lowered his head, his breath whispering over her brow, his lips grazing the soft hair at her temple. Gwyneth shivered involuntarily. His spicy scent—sandalwood, soap, and hot, aroused maleness—filled her senses.

"*Shall* I prove you wrong, then, my lady? Or are you too much of a coward to allow me try?"

As if she had a choice! The clever, conniving blackguard had her backed right into a corner. She could either refuse the challenge and run away like a coward, thus proving her lack of faith in her own body and losing any respect she might otherwise have gleaned from him, or she could recklessly accept the challenge and try to harden herself against his virility—no easy feat, as already evidenced by the tingling fire that swept through her at the very idea of it. But she *must* show strength; she must not let him frighten her!

To hell with him then! Let him do to her as he would; she would put her mind elsewhere and humiliate him with her lack of response to what he so arrogantly assumed was his devastating attraction. *And he* is *attractive, isn't he, Gwyn?* her conscience whispered, excitedly. *You* want *him to touch you. You hate him fiercely, but you cannot deny that you find him dangerously exciting, forbidden, wicked. . . .*

She shut her mind to such foolishness and, steeling herself, worked on pulling every shred of rage up from the very depths of her soul.

He nuzzled her temple, drew little circles in her palm, and she felt her limbs going weak. "Your answer, Lady Simms. I grow impatient."

"You leave me little choice," she declared, with more bravado than she felt. "Do your best, Morninghall, and I'll be the one laughing when this ridiculous fiasco is over."

"You *are* a fool, Lady Simms. But I shall enjoy this, truly I will. And so, I daresay—" his lashes lifted and she saw the glittering fire in his eyes once again— "will you."

She shrank down into the mattress, away from

those eyes, from the tiny flecks of gold embedded in the slate that ringed his blacker-than-Hades pupils. He smiled, knowing he'd won the game long before he'd started it, and touched her face.

He pulled the remaining comb from her tumbling hair, then caught a long ribbon of it and dragged it through his fingers, his smile growing all the more wicked as he felt her involuntary shiver. "See? You're enjoying this already, aren't you, my dear?"

"I'll enjoy it when hell freezes over."

"Hell will never freeze over—" he smiled and trailed his knuckles down the side of her throat—"as long as I am in it."

"Would that I had my pistol then, sir, for I would be glad to put you there."

"Your pistol, dear lady, is on the table where you left it. I invite you to retrieve it and carry out your threat."

She tried to sit up but felt his hand—his hot, very strong hand—hard against her bosom, preventing her escape.

"That's enough, Morninghall. Let me go."

He merely raised his brows.

Sudden dread shot through her. This was no silly challenge to save her pride. She was playing with hellfire itself, and she was going to get burned—badly. Now his fingers were whispering over the delicate rise of her collarbone, grazing the pearls at her throat, feathering lightly over the swell of her breasts, brushing across the exposed—and mortifyingly hard—nipple. Angrily Gwyneth tore one of her arms free and caught his wrist. She felt the unforgivably hard knit of sinew, bone, and muscle beneath his clean, white cuff, the frightening power that arm wielded, and knew he could smash her as easily as he had that goblet.

And just as quickly.

He smiled, white teeth against a face dark with malice.

"Do you know the signs a woman's body shows when she craves a man's touch?" he murmured, oblivious to her hand wrapped around his wrist, dragging it right along with his own as if it weren't even there. Such strength terrified her, excited her. "It shows the signs yours does, my dear. If only you could see yourself as I do: the color in your cheeks, the faint glaze in your eyes, the hunger in your parted lips, the quickening throb of your pulse beneath my fingers." He pulled at the velvety top of her bodice, gently teasing it aside. "And, ah, yes . . . I see that this sweet little berry is blushing as rosily as its twin."

Gwyneth let go of his wrist and wrapped her fingers around his hand, pushing futilely. It would've been easier to move rock. Blind panic shot through her.

"Afraid, sweetheart? You disappoint me."

"No!" But she was, and they both knew it.

"You have only to tell me to stop."

"I *have* told you to stop."

"Your sharp tongue has told me, but your body asks me to continue. When *it* commands me to stop, then I shall."

"This is not the challenge I had in mind, Morninghall. Release me this instant or I shall scream."

"Oh, you'll scream all right," he murmured with a sly little grin, "that I promise."

Then, as easily as if her strength were a child's, he pulled her hand back up over her head and pinned it there on the mattress with its mate. She struggled but was no match for his strength. His fingers slipped beneath her bodice, stroked the side of her breast until she gasped. "For you see, madam, I know how to melt you like butter beneath my tongue, how to have you wailing in the throes of ecstasy." He hooked his thumb over her décolletage, gently teasing it down until her other nipple sprang free. "Such lovely breasts you have . . . high and firm and whiter than fresh cream. Do you know what I am going to do with this sweet offering, Lady Simms?" He smiled and, cupping the breast, popped it free of the plush plum velvet. "Do you know how you will moan and writhe beneath me when I take this hard little fruit into my mouth, how your head will thrash on the pillow, how your legs will open and your mind will go to mush when my lips and teeth and tongue make love to it?"

Fire radiated from that nipple, pooling in the center of her thighs.

"You are . . . *despicable*," she said, uttering this last word as though it were a rat that had found its way into her mouth.

"Despicable? Because I cause your body to blush and weep with desire, my little vixen?"

"Because you . . . " *Heaven help her, she had to make him stop.* "Because you live aboard this ship yet still turn a blind eye to the horrors endured by those poor unfortunates whose fate you preside over."

"Ah, so we are back to that again," he murmured, bending his head to watch, with a mesmerized, fascinated expression, the actions of his fingers. His hair fell in rakish waves over his brow; his long lashes swept down to veil wicked, glittering eyes. "Forget that for now, Lady Simms, and watch what I am doing to you. Your reactions are well worth observing. Watch your body begging me to continue, even while your attempts at rage fall short of the mark."

Unable to help herself, Gwyneth looked down to see his thumb circling one rosy aureole, the hard teardrop in the center of that blushing disk swelling and pouting. Heat pulsed through her breast.

She moaned but tried to pull free. "Release me, Morninghall. The game is over."

He smiled dangerously, then caught the nipple between thumb and forefinger and pinched it gently, watching in triumph and satisfaction as her breathing became uncontrollably labored.

"I said, 'Release me.' *Now*."

Watching her from beneath his lashes, he lowered his dark head toward her breast.

The first touch of that faintly bristled jaw against her skin sent a violent shock through every nerve in

Gwyneth's body. She twisted and cried out, trying desperately to free her arms from his grip, to thrash herself onto her stomach, to knee him in the groin, all to no avail. He laughed darkly and, leaning down over her, stretched her arms even higher above her head and held them fast, exposing both breasts to his gaze, his relentless attentions. The mattress sank as it took his weight, and she bit her lip as he ran his faintly bristled chin up the inside of one arm, causing goose bumps to rise all along the sensitive flesh. His lips brushed her wrist, his tongue touched the inside of her palm. She caught her breath at the feel of the wet, intimate little kisses, squirmed madly, and hated him all the more. And now those kisses were dragging along her wrist, back down her inner arm, inside her elbow, over her sleeve, and lingering atop one breast.

"Admit you desire me, Lady Simms," he murmured, his breath hot against the curve of her breast. "Your body has already done so."

"Damn you, Morninghall, the only thing I *desire* is that you do something about those prisoners!"

"You lie, madam." His jaw rasped against her flesh as he cupped her breast and lifted it toward his mouth. "You are not thinking of those prisoners. Not now. You are thinking of what you would like me to do to you." His fingers shaped and massaged her breast, her nipple, rolling it and pushing it slowly toward his mouth. "You want me to rip this annoying scrap of velvet off of you and put my hot tongue against this sweet, tasty little berry that even now calls me closer. . . ."

His mouth whispered over her areola now, his lips softly grazing the nipple, while his thumb teased and flicked over the burning, aching crest.

"I w-want you to begin taking steps to improve conditions on this ship. *Now.*"

His lips closed around one thrusting peak, and with a tiny cry Gwyneth convulsed upward, even as her flesh swelled in his hand and filled his hot and hungry mouth. She felt the bristles of his jaw scraping the softness of her breast, felt his breath flowing warmly over her skin, and she could do nothing but writhe in sweet anguish as his tongue circled the pink button of her areola.

"Please . . ."

He lifted his head, just fractionally. "Please what, madam?"

"Please stop it. I beg of you."

"Your body is not begging me to stop, my lady. Oh, no, your body is hot for me. You don't want me to stop, do you?"

"I—I don't—I . . ."

"Do you?"

He fastened his mouth around her nipple once more, pulling it fully into his mouth, his cheeks drawing in and out as he began to suckle her, hard. Gwyneth's senses exploded and the spot between her legs went up in a burst of flame, a flood of moisture, a hot pit of aching, craving need. She fought, trying to free her wrists, still pinned above her head against the mattress. She heard small suckling noises coming from his mouth, felt his palm cupping her breast, and then cool, sweet ecstacy as his tongue, warm, wet . . . *oh, God, I'm going to die* . . . fastened on her nipple and pressed, licked, and laved it.

Gwyneth arched up once more, her lips drawing back from her teeth in a soundless cry, feet kicking and fists driving into the pillow high above her head.

"You like this, don't you, my enchanting little enemy? How delicious you taste. How delicious I'll bet the rest of you tastes as well. . . ."

He gently nipped her nipple, and fire shot out of her breast, through her belly, and straight into the pit of heat between her thighs. She moaned and tried to yank her wrists from his hand, but she was no match for his strength. Through half-opened eyes, she gazed deliriously down at his dark head, the loose, rakish hair tickling the swell of her other breast even as his free hand teased and tweaked its waiting nipple. Then he drew that engorged bud into his mouth, flicking his

tongue over it, suckling it, and laving it until she
thought she would scream.

"Damn you, get off me!" she cried, even as her body
arced upward to meet him and the back of her legs
dug into the edge of the mattress. She struggled to free
her wrists. "I'll kill you for this, Morninghall, I'll see
you *finished*—"

He laughed and his hand left her breast, smoothing
down over her velvet stomacher, down over the skirts
that were bunched atop her legs, reaching down to
pick up her hem.

She felt cool air against her ankles.

His fingers were grazing her calf . . . coming back
up her leg, dragging the hem up with them.

"Please, Morninghall!"

He only chuckled against her breast, carrying the
hem in his fingers and burning a slow, torturous path
up the inside of her calf, over her knee and toward
that aching, burning part of her that wept with
wanting. Past the top of her garters, past the highly
sensitive inner flesh of her thighs, still higher—

Whimpering, she tried to clamp her legs shut, only
to find the hard pillar of his leg; she tried to jerk her
wrists free, but they were hopelessly pinned beneath
his hand. And still his fingers dragged the hem up
higher. . . .

And higher—

He shoved her legs apart with the blade of his hand.

"No!"

"Yes."

She cried out, bucking and writhing as his fingers
slipped into that embarrassingly wet, private place.
She felt her skirts falling back down over her legs, felt
the bed springing up as he rose, only to scoop up one
thigh while still imprisoning her wrists and drag her
body around so that she lay at an angle to the
mattress, her head crammed against the bulkhead,
her hips poised at the edge of the bed, her slippered
feet hanging several inches off the floor.

"Tell me you want me to leave you alone *now*,

madam," he growled, leaning over her. He seized her hem and threw the thick pile of skirts and petticoats up over her belly in a rustle, his hand shoving her thighs apart once more, seeking her dampness. Her head rolled against the hard wood, and the deckhead above blurred into a spinning whirl of light. Again his mouth fell against her breast, greedily suckling, nibbling, devouring its tender, pink flesh. Again his weight—heavy, hot, and male—pressed against her stomach, driving her down into the mattress as his fingers plunged into her dampness and his palm ground against her, shamefully rubbing the throbbing flesh.

"Go ahead, madam, make me stop. Make me stop, I dare you!"

"I cannot," she gasped, mindless now with want. "Please—"

"Please what, my lady? Squeeze you?" His thumb found something down there in that hot wetness and pressed down on it . . . hard.

Gwyneth choked back a scream.

"You make me *burn,* Lady Simms," he snarled, his angry eyes close to hers. "I shall enjoy making you do the same. Burn. Burn until you can no longer take the air into your lungs!"

"Please, I beg of you—"

Seizing her by both hips, he yanked her toward him so that she lay flat on the mattress, her knees bent and feet hanging, his leg bracing her thighs apart. She felt his thumb driving against that tiny, weeping bud of her femininity, pressing circles against it, fluttering it from side to side, teasing, tickling, pinching, toying with it until mindless, keening noises were bursting from her throat. Gwyneth sobbed, tried to sit up, but fell back behind the onslaught of his mouth as it crashed against hers, his tongue plunging between her teeth and filling her senses with the taste of brandy, male heat, and male fury. She beat futilely at his shoulders, found she was clawing at them in frenzied want instead. He rubbed and rolled that burning spot, kneading it, until a great rush of white heat began to build deep within her, stealing her very breath away—

"That's it, darling. Weep for me, come for me, let it go. Flow over my hand, and scream your delight."

Bastard, I'll see you dead for this!

His kissed her once more, savagely.

Oh, God, don't stop!

His mouth left hers then, his lips moving down her throat. His hands came up to shape her body as though it were a sculpture, the finest art, tracing the outline of her ribs, her waist, her hips, her legs, barely touching the thick pile of skirts that lay atop her belly. She gazed up at him, drugged with passion; he stared down at her, triumphant. And then he began to sink out of her sight. Weakly, Gwyneth raised her head, saw him kneeling between her legs, his intense, burning eyes watching her face from behind a mountain of bunched-up purple skirts, silver netting, and frothy white petticoats.

He put his hard, hot hands on the insides of her thighs, easily forcing them apart as she struggled to hold them together. His eyes gleamed with a wicked light, and too late, she knew what he was about to do.

Where his mouth was headed.

What he intended to suckle next.

"No!"

He laughed, bent his head so that only his tousled, dark hair met her view, and bracing her thighs wide apart with his hands, fastened his mouth against that hot, weeping place between them. And Gwyneth did scream, her lips stretching back from clenched teeth, a thousand lights exploding before her eyes. She felt his tongue, darting out to press and lick and stab the juicy spot where his fingers had just been, and then his teeth were there, nibbling, nipping, biting, grazing. She fought to get her legs together, but she was no match for his superior strength.

"Ah, madam, you are sweeter than this honey I lick

from you. My God . . . I want you . . . all of you . . .
now."

His mouth clamped onto that hard bud of sensation
in which all feeling was centered, his lips stretching
over his teeth to protect it from his bite as he drew it
deeply into his mouth and suckled her madly.

Gwyneth screamed, convulsed, and beat her fist
against the mattress.

He drew harder on her, his hands hot against the
inside of her thighs, his thumbs spreading her feminine lips, his tongue lancing against her pulsing bud,
flicking it, laving it, licking it, suckling it.

"God damn you, Morninghall!"

She climaxed then against his mouth, a fierce,
gripping explosion of pleasure so excruciatingly intense that it spun her out over the edge and left her
adrift on the very brink of consciousness. She drove
her hands against his skull, her fingers tangling in his
hair as she pushed at him and sobbed in sweet agony,
her body exploding with wave after wave of hot,
liquid fire.

And still his mouth clung there, licking and sucking
every last drop of sweetness from her.

"Say it, madam," he growled. "Ask me to make you
mine!"

"Never!"

"Say it!"

*"Damn you to hell for the devil you are, Morning-
hall. NO!"*

With an angry roar, he lurched to his feet, yanked
her skirts down over her knees, and swung away from
her. She caught a glimpse of the huge swelling at his
groin. His chest was heaving, his eyes ablaze with
fury, his face violent and thunderous.

Gwyneth stared up at him, the last wave of climax
fading and a numbness tingling between her legs. He
had ravished her, made her beg and cry and scream as
he had said he would—but she had not taken him
inside her.

She had not let him put his seed into her.

And he was furious.

His insolent, contemptuous gaze swept over her naked bosom, her tingly nipples, and it was then that the red haze of wrath stole over her as she realized that he had not taken her as he had wanted, but that he had humiliated her all the same.

He had reduced her to a wanton strumpet.

"You put on a stunning show," he said, sneering as she jerked her bodice up, "but I admit, I've had better."

Then he made the mistake of turning his back on her.

Blind rage and mortification seized her, and before she could stop herself, Gwyneth grabbed the small brass telescope that rested on a table beside the bed and, with all of her strength, flung it at his proud shoulders.

He turned at that moment, saw the missile—and ducked. The edge of the instrument caught him just above the ear, and he fell sideways against the swivel chair, sending it crashing into the bulkhead as he went down with a heavy, sickening thud.

For one paralyzed moment, Gwyneth could only stare at that dangerous, powerful body, sprawled atop the decking, the telescope rolling across the floor away from it. If she was lucky, she had dashed his brains out. If she was not—

She wasted no time. Without a second's more hesitation, she jumped from the bed, sidestepped the marquess even as he began to stir, and ran for the door.

Chapter 8

Gwyneth ran straight from the frying pan into the fire, which proved to be two guards waiting just outside the cabin on the quarterdeck.

Shoving her hair off her brow with a trembling hand, she mentally composed herself and went straight for the nearest one, too distraught to notice his lecherous leer, his hungry eyes, never realizing he and his companion had been listening just outside the door and that her passionate cries had roused their own animal appetites to a fever pitch.

"Excuse me, but I beg you to see me off this ship immediately."

The sailor leaned on the stock of his musket and regarded her lazily. "Is there a problem, ma'am?"

She glanced nervously behind her. "No problem at all. Please, I must leave. Now."

Her heart was thundering in her breast, pulsing against the pearl choker at her throat, banging in her ears. She must look a sight, but at the moment all she could think about was self-preservation, escape— and Morninghall. Any moment now that enraged prince of darkness was going to come storming out of his cabin and drag her right back into the Hades he ruled.

"Right this way then, ma'am," the guard said, smoothly, taking her elbow in one massive hand.

Thank God, thank God, thank God. . . . Relief swept through her, and it was all she could do not to succumb to the tears hovering just beneath the surface. Gratefully she allowed him to guide her away from the cabin, his companion trailing just behind, their boots thudding hollowly on the deck. Her hem swished around her legs with every stride, reminding her of how *he*'d seized it and dragged it up her thighs. *Oh, I'm so very mortified!* She forced her head up, straightened her spine, kept her gaze straight ahead. Inside, though, she was shaking, confused, burning with shame and the horrific realization that Morninghall had just made love to her, for God's sake, raped her with tongue and mouth and hands, and she had actually . . .

Oh, God, she had actually *enjoyed* it!

She closed her eyes on a silent moan of horror, opened them, and saw that the guard was escorting her toward the stairs that led off the ship.

And then past them.

She paused, his blunt fingers biting into her elbow. "Excuse me, but I would like to leave," she protested, trying to wrench her arm free.

"You can leave when 'is Lordship says ye can." The guard hauled her forward, his fingers hard against her flesh. "Meanwhile we gots to put you in a holdin' area."

"Aye, a holding area," aped the second guard, who pushed himself so close to Gwyneth's backside that she could feel his bulging stomach and erect manhood pressing against her, could smell his pungent, unwashed body over the acrid odors snaking up through the hatches.

Alarm shot through her. She looked around for help. The deck was cleared of prisoners for the coming night, and only a few guards, all pretending to ignore her plight, were about. Panic iced her spine and she began to struggle with sudden foreboding.

"I *said,* 'I wish to leave this ship immediately!' " she said angrily, trying to appear braver than she felt.

"Oh, we'll let ye go. Just as soon as the cap'n gives

us permission," said the first. "Meanwhile, ye'll be quite comfortable in the holdin' area. Spacious accommodations. Complete with a *bed*."

Gwyneth dug both heels into the deck as he tried to pull her forward, her slippers scraping across the weathered old wood. Oh, damn her haste in fleeing Morninghall, for had she been composed, she wouldn't have forgotten her pistol! "I demand that you release me this moment, or I shall scream for help!"

"We wouldn't like that none, ma'am. Wouldn't like it at all." Then, without warning, the first guard yanked her against his chest, slapped a palm that smelled of sweat and gunmetal across her mouth, and dragged her, kicking and struggling, toward an ominous, ramshackle deckhouse garbed in peeling paint and smoky grime, through which someone had drawn an obscene network of graffiti.

Gwyneth fought madly, ineffectually kicking out at the guard with one slippered foot. Her hand was wrenched cruelly behind her back, and the guard, laughing, hauled her toward the sagging door of the deckhouse. Didn't anyone *see* her? What was happening?

Help! Her voice was a muffled cry against the guard's palm. *Somebody help me!*

Several other guards lounged against the deckhouse and railing, not saying a word, some pretending interest in the harbor front, others merely grinning and watching with high amusement. One of them yanked open the door, sending it banging back against the wall, and Gwyneth's captor hauled her inside.

The door slammed shut behind them.

"You can stop yer strugglin', ma'am," the first guard said, still keeping his hand over her mouth. "We won't hurt ye."

"Aye, we already knows what she likes, don't we, Ralph?"

"A little kissin' to start with. Look at me, girlie."

Ralph dug cruel fingers into her jaw and spun her around, nearly snapping her neck and instantly catching her around the waist before sealing her mouth up once more. "Ye fit me like a glove, ye do," he murmured huskily, brushing his lips over her brow and leaving her choking on the stench of a breath as foul as anything she had inhaled below.

"She'll fit me better," the other whined, grabbing Gwyneth's other wrist and yanking her away from Ralph. "Come on, let's have a go."

"Take your hands off me this instant, you bumbling oafs!" Gwyneth cried on her first lungful of air, making a mad lunge toward the door. It was in vain. Ralph, losing his patience, caught her, flinging her toward a filthy gray mattress, his hands already going for his trousers as he dove after her. The mattress shot to the side as Gwyneth fell; she hit the deck hard, her shoulders smashing into a filthy wall, her teeth nicking the inside of her lip. The guard's sweating, stinking body landed just inches from her own. Then his hands were groping at her bodice, his massive weight pinning her to the deck, his thick, sloppy lips dropping wet kisses on her throat, her collarbone, her bosom, as she screamed and struggled and tried to twist out from beneath him.

"Oh, Ralph, ye're making her put on a fine show. Tweak her nipples and she'll dance even nicer for ye!"

"Get off of me, you wretched *beast!*"

"Shut up, bitch," Ralph snarled, and then her air was cut off as his huge hand clamped around her throat and pushed downward, choking her.

Blind panic shot through her. Her fists flailed against his shoulder, and she sank her teeth into her lip to keep from fainting.

"Like that, don't ye?" the guard panted, his calloused fingers cruelly pinching one nipple through her bodice, his great, moist lips buried in the hair at her ear. "Cry and wail for Ralphie here as ye did for *him*," he growled, his other hand already going for her skirts. "Thrash yerself about like the vixen yer eyes tell me ye are. Go ahead, twist and wriggle, oh yes, that's it, sweetheart—"

Gwyneth let out a gurgling scream, her nails ripping at the guard's neck in her panic.

He flung her skirts up—and the door crashed open, a thunderclap from the gods.

"Bloody hell!" the smaller guard screeched as Ralph, one fist around Gwyneth's skirts, the other still crushing her throat, raised his head and violently sucked in his breath.

It was the marquess.

There he stood, tall, lethal, and silhouetted in the doorway, danger emanating from him like wind out of the Arctic. He was holding a pistol, leveled directly at Ralph.

In his eyes Gwyneth saw only darkness and a total absence of soul. In his eyes, Gwyneth saw the devil incarnate.

Ralph, his hand still on Gwyneth's throat, edged away from her, but the marquess's satanic gaze never left him. "Release the lady," he ordered in a dangerously soft voice which sent chills racing the length of Gwyneth's spine.

Ralph sneered, and his beefy hand pushed harder against Gwyneth's throat. Panicking, she coughed, hoked, clawed upward, her bulging eyes staring at the marquess as her world began to go dark. Through it she heard Morninghall's sinister command.

"Release her or die. *Now.*"

Ralph began to laugh.

The marquess fired.

His hand never lowered, his eyes never blinked, his mouth never moved as the pistol went off with a crashing bang. Ralph jerked, thrashed, and went still.

The scent of gunpowder filled the cabin as the guard's dead hand slid from Gwyneth's throat with terrible slowness. Gwyneth's eyes fell shut and she felt a thick, numbing haze stealing mercifully over her, enfolding her in an envelope of fuzziness. Through it came no thought, no feeling, no emotion. Her hand went to her bruised throat, and numbly she crawled away from the guard, huddling in a corner and drawing her legs up beneath her as she coughed and wheezed and tried to get her breath.

"Await me outside," she heard Morninghall say to the other guard, who cowered against the door, whimpering. Without a word the man fled, leaving Gwyneth at the mercy of the devil himself—a devil who advanced on her with purpose and magnificent rage, a devil who reached down and wordlessly caught her elbow.

His touch penetrated the blessed numbness, obliterating it.

"Don't touch me!" she cried, pushing herself further into the corner and kicking savagely out at him. Tears stung her eyes, began to spill down her cheeks, and she covered her face with her hands, ashamed. "Don't touch me. I cannot take anymore. Please—"

She was no match for his strength, no match for his determination, no match for the man who pulled her to her feet only to gather her stiffly, protectively, to his hard chest when her knees would have given out beneath her.

She wept into her hands, feeling his heartbeat against her knuckles. She looked up into his chiseled, satanic face and saw, for the briefest moment, something hugely tender and unguarded there, before he jerked his head up and stared unseeingly at the grimy wall opposite him.

His heart was thundering beneath her ear.

"You have suffered much at the hands of others today," he said hoarsely. With one quick movement he swept her up and into his arms. "Come. I shall see you home."

"Switching clothes with an imposter sentry? It will never work."

"It *will* work."

The Reverend Peter Milford slowly paced the *Kestrel*'s small cabin, his hands clasped behind his back, his eyes worried, the lantern light painting crescents of gold atop his fair curls. He was restless tonight, and with good reason. "It will never work, I tell you, because the guards are wise to us, Connor. You said so yourself. They'll notice a new sentry in their midst and be suspicious."

His two companions sat watching him. A lantern swung gently above their heads, sputtering and flaring in the moist, salty night breeze which wafted in through the stern windows. Outside, the sea hissed and sighed, a great, black vista stretching away into the night. Far, far in the distance, beyond the slit of the drawn curtains, the lights of Portsmouth lay like fireflies on the horizon, winking on and off as the schooner rose and fell atop the waves. But there was no chance that the *Kestrel* herself was equally visible. She carried no lights on her deck, and with her head to the wind, her crew of recently escaped prisoners standing watch in the rigging and on the deck above, there was little likelihood of her being caught by surprise by one of the Royal Navy frigates that patrolled the Channel.

"The guards can be bribed," Connor protested, topping off his ale and carrying his mug to the stern windows, where he leaned casually against the cushions. "I don't know what you're fussing about, Peter. We've used this same ploy before."

"Which is precisely the reason why it should not be used again," the third man said, speaking for the first time since the discussion had turned from the plight of Merrick's cousins to the plan for getting them off the prison hulk.

The others looked at him, Connor with frustration and distrust, the chaplain with something like relief. "See?" Peter said, as though these words had decided the matter. "I told you, Connor, it's too dangerous."

Connor impatiently ran his hand through his chestnut hair, the strain of worry showing clearly on his face. He looked at the man who had spoken. "Fine. You're now the brains behind this venture," he conceded, a bit heatedly. "What do you suggest?"

Ignoring Connor's taunt, the man leaned back and crossed his arms behind his head, causing his chair to creak and groan with protest. At two inches over six feet, he was a formidable man, lean, hard-muscled, and emanating the deadly grace of a duelist. His coat was perfectly tailored to his powerful shoulders; his boots, crossed lazily at the ankles, mirrored the lantern light. That same golden glow carved planes and shadows from his face, emphasized the bold cut of his nose and firmness of his mouth, and gleamed from eyes that burned with intelligence. Even relaxed, he exuded moody, predatory danger; even seated, he made the schooner's cabin seem ridiculously small.

"The sentries aboard the prison hulk will be on the alert tonight," he murmured, his low, deep-timbred voice calm with self-assurance. "There was the incident with Lady Gwyneth Evans Simms this afternoon to rouse them, and another hole was discovered in the ship's hull just aft of the entry port, beneath the guards' scaffolding. An unfortunate occurrence, I'm afraid."

"Who discovered the hole?" Connor demanded, setting down his ale and frowning.

"Radley, of course."

"Radley must be dealt with."

"Radley cannot be dealt with without arousing suspicion."

"Why not?"

"Think, man," their leader murmured, gazing patiently at Connor. "There's been a rash of escapes from the *Surrey*. Should they continue, there is bound to be a full investigation as to why security does not seem to be tighter than it is. There is also the possibility that a change in officers aboard the hulk will be instituted, and that we cannot afford. Radley is fanatical in his quest to root out would-be escapers, but he is a stupid man and easily made to do my bidding. We need him as an example of . . . authority, if nothing else."

"And Morninghall?" Connor drawled, raising one eyebrow.

"Ah, Morninghall"—the man smiled darkly—"seems quite preoccupied with his own problems of late, does he not?"

"Far too preoccupied to concern himself with prisoners who have no wish but to escape," Peter added, rejoining the discussion and shooting a quick glance at their leader.

"Poor Morninghall," Connor said with false sympathy, affecting a great, exaggerated sigh. "A sad lot, his! But you're right, we need him aboard that prison ship. Without him the Black Wolf would be all but helpless."

"Yes, well . . . of course." Their leader did not laugh. "Tonight's rescue, gentlemen. It is off. Tomorrow night, I think, would suit us better. Peter, as tomorrow is the Sabbath, I expect you can devise a . . . moonlight service of some sort?"

The chaplain picked up his own mug, his eyes gleaming conspiratorially. "Such as a candlelight vigil for the souls of the recently departed prisoners?"

"That would be appropriate. And it will not arouse suspicion. Include the guard that was shot today, if you will."

"Good thinking—his friends shall want to attend the service. The more that do, the scantier the watch shall be."

Connor watched them over the top of his mug. "Of course, Morninghall will have to give them all leave to attend."

"He will," their leader said.

"So, tomorrow then?"

There was a light knock on the cabin door.

"Yes?" Connor called.

It opened and Orla, her dark hair loose around her shoulders and her cheeks flushed from the night wind, came in. She shut the door behind her, turned—

—and stopped.

There was a crash. All eyes turned to Peter, who had dropped his mug and was now staring at the lovely woman whose blue eyes were locked with his.

Connor's grin was wicked. "Yes, Orla?"

His second in command tore her gaze from the boyishly handsome chaplain, who was emitting hasty apologies as he bent to wipe up the spill, his rounded cheeks bright with color. She looked at her captain. "I thought you'd want to know that Jenkins has spotted a vessel a league or so off to the north. Probably a frigate, by what we can see of her."

"Thank you, Orla. Our friends will want to be off shortly then."

Orla, with a shy, stolen glance at the discomfitted chaplain, nodded and went out.

"You were saying, Peter, old boy?" their leader murmured, smiling as the chaplain hastily set his mug back on the table, only to knock it over again with his sleeve.

"Damn! Oh—dear God—*damn!*"

His two friends exchanged amused glances. Then their leader got to his feet, dwarfing the cabin with his height as he pulled the poor chaplain up with him. Peter's face was scarlet, his hands fluttering nervously. "I'm so sorry, Connor," he twittered, shoving his curls off his suddenly damp brow. "What a mess I've made—"

Connor waved his hand in airy dismissal, his mouth quivering with suppressed laughter. "Never mind, Peter." He winked. "Go now, and Orla and I *both* will see you tomorrow."

As the chaplain sputtered a protest, his companion dragged him to the door. "Till tomorrow, then, Merrick." He paused, his hand on the latch, a little smile creeping over his stern mouth. "In the meantime do take pains to guard yourself well."

The American regarded him suspiciously, quizzically.

"Rumor has it that Admiral Falconer's wife is on a quest to get her ship back," he explained. Then he smiled with real humor, his eyes gleaming. "Your sister has a formidable reputation, Connor."

"*Shit,*" Connor said.

The door closed behind them.

"Really, Gwyn, you have been dreadfully silent all day," Rhiannon said, as she sat in a chair in the back garden, a novel open on her lap and Mattie snoozing in the grass at her feet. "In fact, you've not been yourself since you returned from the prison ship yesterday afternoon." Gwyneth, abnormally quiet, was on her hands and knees pulling weeds out of the stones that framed her bed of purple Aubrietia. "It's Morninghall, isn't it?"

Gwyneth's head dipped lower, the straw hat she wore shielding her face from Rhiannon's inquisitive gaze. "I don't want to talk about it."

Rhiannon kicked off a shoe and rubbed her bare toes through Mattie's warm, sunlit fur. The dog stretched and groaned in delight. "You shouldn't let yourself get all hot and bothered just because he took it upon himself to steal a simple kiss. Why, I think it's all rather romantic, don't you? Besides, if His Lordship were to learn he's upset you so, he would no doubt consider it a great victory."

The weeds that dared to sprout among Gwyneth's flowers had no chance against her sudden anger; up they came, roots and all, to land ingloriously in the wooden bucket. "Perhaps His Lordship *has* gained a victory," she conceded, averting her flushed face as she attacked the weeds, "but that victory will pale when he is faced with the consequences of my first *attack.*"

"Ah yes, the petition," Rhiannon said, referring to the signatures that she, her sister, and the Ladies Committee on Prisoner Welfare had spent the morning gathering after Gwyneth had called them all together and regaled them with tales of conditions aboard the prison hulk.

"Among other things. Morninghall may ignore *my*

pleas for compassion on the part of those prisoners—
for now—but there is no way he can ignore the pleas
of several *hundred*."

"You said, 'Among other things.' What *other* things
are you planning, Gwyn?"

The weeds came out with increased speed. "I have
already sent another letter to Richard in the Transport Office, and tomorrow I shall start investigating
the bills, records, and receipts of the contractors who
supply food and clothing to the prisoners, as I have a
suspicion they are as corrupt as the day is long. No
doubt they're using inferior or insufficient provisions
and pocketing the extra, at the prisoners' expense."

"And Morninghall?"

"Morninghall shall be dealt with."

"He's going to be a difficult man, Gwyn. And if he
is as disaffected and bitter as you say he is . . ."

"I don't care what his feelings are in the matter.
They are not the issue."

"Really, Gwyn, such anger toward the man! And all
over a simple kiss!"

Gwyneth kept her head down, using the brim of her
hat to shield her face from her sister, lest Rhiannon
guess Morninghall had given her more than just a
"simple kiss." She had no desire for her younger sister
to know what had *really* happened. What sort of
example would *that* set?

Rhiannon, after all, was only seventeen years old.

As Gwyneth fancied herself a role model, something of a mother figure, she would not confide the
truth in Rhiannon. And she did not want to admit—
even to herself—that for the first time in her life she
had misjudged an adversary, that this time she was in
waters over her head. The Marquess of Morninghall
was no cowardly mine owner, no corrupt minister, no
easily threatened manager of an orphanage. He was a
powerful, intelligent, and exceedingly dangerous
man, and the memory alone of what he had done to
her, of what he had reduced her to, was enough to
make Gwyneth's cheeks blaze with heat. The mortifi-

cation of it all . . . She bent her hot brow to her sleeve, unable to even stomach the thought of facing that wretched brute again, after what had happened between them.

And yet, for the sake of those poor souls aboard the hulk, she would *have* to face him, would *have* to endure those diabolical eyes, that mocking mouth, those insensitive and ungallant comments, the knowledge that she was attracted to him and both of them knew it. And she would have to hope, against that horrid, wanton part of her that had enjoyed every minute of it, she would be strong the next time he launched his sensual attack on her confused senses.

In the meantime she would keep herself as busy as she possibly could. She would focus her energies on the prisoners and her passionate plight to ease their hard lot. She would collect signatures from the people of Portsmouth, she would drive the Transport Office mad with her requests and suggestions, she would spread the word about the appalling conditions aboard the hulk among her many friends and acquaintances, and she would launch a campaign to collect food, clothing, and monetary donations for the needy unfortunates. She would *not* think about Morninghall and how he had made her writhe and moan— *oh, wretched humiliation!*—beneath his touch; she would not think about how she had urged him on with her impassioned pleas; she would not think about the triumph in his wicked, hard-as-slate eyes, the skill in his beautiful hands, the gushiness that had wafted through her as she felt his mouth upon her lips, her breasts, her—her secret areas. *Oh, God.* William had never done such things. William had not even made her a woman because he had preferred to worship her as a virgin, a package forever unopened and caught in a state of maidenly innocence, as though keeping her that way would halt his own inevitable aging.

Damn William for leaving out that vital part of her education, which would have prepared her for dealing with and dispatching a devil of Morninghall's ilk!

And then, from out of nowhere, it came: the memory of Morninghall's unguarded compassion after the guards had molested her, the gentleness in his embrace as he'd gathered her protectively against his chest.

No, she had imagined it surely. Men like Morninghall did not feel compassion for others.

Rhiannon's voice intruded upon her thoughts. "Do you want to know what *I* think?"

"What?"

"*I* think you ought to search out the Black Wolf and join forces with *him* against Morninghall."

Gwyneth turned a deep crimson. "Really, Rhiannon!"

"Why, Gwyn, you're blushing."

Jerking the hat brim back down over her eyes, Gwyneth turned her attention to the flower beds once more, this time with a renewed vengeance. "I knew I should never have told you about running into the fellow on the pier."

"I know. There are a lot of things you shouldn't tell me, Gwyn. And even more that you should. Such as, what it felt like when you came to your senses in Lord Morninghall's bed."

"Stop it, Rhiannon."

"Or what it felt like when he kissed you."

"Rhiannon, I'm warning you."

Her sister giggled. "Or why—"

"Lady Simms?"

Sophie's hesitant voice interrupted them. Looking up, Gwyneth saw the maid standing in the doorway that led from the back garden into the house, her face as white as the late-afternoon clouds that drifted lazily overhead. Her eyes were huge, and she was wringing a dust rag as though it were the neck of a chicken destined for the supper pot.

"What is it, Sophie?"

"There's a . . . gentleman 'ere to see you." The girl sucked her lip between her teeth and darted an anxious glance behind her. "'E says 'is name is L-Lord Morninghall."

Gwyneth froze. A clump of weeds slid through her fingers. For a moment she could only stare at the maid, her stomach bouncing right from her abdomen to her throat. *Morninghall!* She was in no mood for another confrontation with him, not when she was dressed like a common peasant, not when she was still shaken from the encounter she'd had with him the previous day, not when her innocent little sister would be subject to his carnal innuendos and the possible truth about what he had done to her, not when her blood became all warm and tingly at the very thought of those fascinating eyes.

Rhiannon, her eyes glinting, a conniving smile playing across her lips, lazily turned her head to address the maid. "Oh, do show the marquess in, Sophie. And stop acting like a silly rabbit, will you? He's only a man—"

"Oh, no, ma'am, 'e's Lucifer himself, 'e is. Those eyes, they're colder than a January frost, they burn right through a body, they do. Beggin' yer pardon, ma'am, I don't think 'e ought to be allowed into the 'ouse, 'e's the very devil, 'e is!"

"That will be enough, Sophie," Gwyneth said sternly.

The maid stared at her, her eyes swallowing up her white face. "So what shall I tell 'im, my lady?"

Aware of her sister's challenging grin, Gwyneth willed her queasy stomach to calmness and drove her spade into the dirt. She had a sudden burning wish that that moist earth was Lord Morninghall's heart.

"My lady?"

"Why, do show him in, Sophie. It is rude to keep a *guest* waiting, is it not?"

Chapter 9

He did not know why he had come.

Damon stood on the stone steps just outside the door of the tidy brick house, arms crossed loosely over his chest, weight slung on one hip, eyes surly and annoyed. To all appearances he was a bored aristocrat, yet only he knew his heart was pounding, his every instinct telling him to bolt before *she* could humiliate him by turning him away. He stared gloomily at the tubs of pink and red flowers set on the edge of each step. He stared at his hat, which he'd politely taken off when the terrified maid had answered the door. He stared at a spider dropping from a silken thread beneath a flower box at the nearest window, stared at his watch, stared at—

The door opened.

The maid stood there, almost holding herself up by the door latch as she gazed up at him in horrified fascination. "Lady Simms will s-see you now, my lord."

His stomach turned over. He had not expected her to invite him in, had not really thought she'd receive him. He was not prepared for this; he didn't know what he'd say, didn't know what he'd do—

Christ, just drop the damned notebook off and be done with it.

The maid was holding the door open wide, using it as a barrier and all but hiding behind it. Despite the turmoil in his heart, Damon's face remained remote. His hat in his hand, he stepped inside the house. It

took a moment for his eyes to adjust to its cool
shadows after the bright sunlight outside, and as the
dancing spots faded, he saw he was standing in an
elegant little receiving room, the walls painted in
warm shades of peach and hung with watercolors of
songbirds and wildflowers. *Charming.* There was a
collection of porcelain birds in a china cabinet, a vase
of white and mauve lilacs on a low table, a delicate
doily beneath it. A gentle breeze wafted through the
house, heady with the scent of lilacs and making
the gauzy white curtains whisper and curl at the
windows.

How bloody charming. He felt the old anger, then a
sense of being left out, alone, standing on the fringe of
a circle of firelight, the rest of the world gathered there
together while he was left to shiver in the cold beyond,
a lone and hungry wolf.

"R—right this way, m' lord. 'Er Ladyship is out in
the garden, she is."

He inclined his head, allowing the girl to lead the
way and thanking God no one could hear the mad
racing of his heart. He gazed about as he walked,
conveying an air of faint disinterest, his hands behind
his back and still holding the hat, his footsteps
echoing loudly on the polished hardwood floor. He
felt like a bull in a china shop: out of place, uncomfortable, on edge. He shouldn't have come. He didn't
know *why* he'd come. He was a damned fool for
coming, and now there was no way out of it.

The maid disappeared around a corner, glancing
nervously over her shoulder to be sure he was following. Her timid behavior was starting to irritate him.
But, then, it was typical. Women found him frightening, and he'd long since given up trying to be anything
but what the world thought him to be: a devil, a
scoundrel, a monster. After all, his own mother had
taught him he was something to be feared and
loathed. She'd been terrified of him.

In his mind's eye he saw again the wine bottle
hurled through the air at him, slamming into his back,

*saw again the telescope and Lady Simms's out-
stretched hand—*

A rush of damp heat broke out beneath his clothes.
His heart started to pound and he suddenly felt short
of breath, slightly dizzy, as if someone had just
punched him, hard, in the head. Still, he managed to
keep his gaze perfectly impassive and fixed straight
ahead.

The maid opened another door and, cowering back
against it, indicated a colorful garden walled with
brick, where the cheerful warbling of a blackbird was
the only sound.

Flowers were the first thing Damon noticed. Purple
Aubrietia, covering the earth like the bedclothes of a
royal. Pots of carved stone, bursting with red and
white tulips, heather, and some pinkish flower whose
name he didn't know. The first blooms of azalea and
rhododendron, the last blooms of yellow forsythia,
their dead and dying flowers intertwined with sprays
of brilliant green leaves. Rose bushes threading their
thorny way up a wooden lattice, ivy crawling the wall
and sunning itself on the mossy, age-worn top, lilacs
waving in the mild breeze and pale purple wisteria
draping the side of the house above his head. Brilliant
red flowers in the window boxes, and in the rectangu-
lar patch of lawn in the center of this dazzling display,
daisies scattered like stars and here and there the
sunny head of a dandelion.

"I take it you are either unsociable, my lord, or you
have never seen a garden before."

He froze, then turned and saw her.

"Lady Simms," he murmured with an icy smile.
But beneath his chilly exterior his insides were in
turmoil.

She looked very ill at ease. "Lord Morninghall."

He let his gaze rake insinuatingly over the gentle
swell of her breasts and was rewarded with a wash of
scarlet that blazed across her cheeks. Aaah, she remembered, and remembered well. "It is indeed a . . .
pleasure."

"Spare me your sarcasm, Morninghall. What do you want?"

She was near a bed of Aubrietia, her legs folded beneath her, her spine stiff as whalebone, a trowel clenched in one lily-white hand, which she was tapping against her knee, as though she wanted to murder him with it. Her eyes were wary and uncertain, and a straw hat ringed with a plum-colored ribbon threw her face into shadow. Her pale hair was a shining riot of curls down her back, reflecting the sunlight like a sparkling waterfall, and smudges of earth and grass stained her simple muslin dress. He felt hardness beginning to tighten his loins. God, she looked sensual, desirable, charming, earthy, delicious, angry.

And, he thought maliciously, perhaps a little nervous.

Another voice, faintly amused, came from nearby. "Really, Gwyneth, that's no way to treat a guest."

He turned his head. A lovely young woman, half-hidden by a lilac bush and accompanied by a sleepy-looking dog, reclined in a chair, watching him. She had soft, ginger hair arranged in a loosely braided coronet atop her head, a laughing mouth, and the same elegant neck, classic shoulders, and grace of movement displayed by Lady Simms. She smiled at Damon, innocently unaware that he could slay her with one glance from his devil's eyes, and offered her small, fragile white hand. "I fear I must introduce myself to you, as my sister will not." Her eyes sparkled. "I am Rhiannon Evans."

Gwyneth snapped, "He does not deserve the honor of an introduction, Rhiannon."

Damon ignored the waspish comment. "I see that beauty runs in your family, Miss Evans," he said chivalrously, bowing low over the girl's hand and brushing it with his lips. He looked wickedly out through his lashes at her, and was rewarded with a swift wash of color across her cheeks—and a sparkle in her eye which was not horror but excitement and delight. As he straightened up, he saw the protective, angry look that tightened Lady Simms's mouth, and secretly gloated. "It is a pleasure to meet you, Miss Evans," he murmured and lowered her hand.

"And you, my lord. My sister lacks for male companionship, so it is indeed an honor to have you here. I do so hope you'll stay for tea."

"Rhiannon!"

"In fact, I shall go put the kettle on now, so that the two of you may . . . talk. Up, Mattie!" she chirped, calling the arthritic old dog up off the grass and moving toward the door. "Time to go inside!"

"Lord Morninghall will *not* be staying," Gwyneth said sharply.

"Oh, but I think I will," Damon countered smoothly. He directed his most charming grin at the girl. "Tea would be lovely, Miss Evans. Thank you."

Eyes sparkling, Rhiannon slipped into the house, and Damon was alone with the object of his torment.

Awareness of the previous day's intimacy was paramount in both of them. Damon's memory burned with it, and he could see the dark flush in her cheeks, the embarrassed evasiveness in her eyes. Here among her flowers, the sun slanting down through the leafy green branches of a chestnut tree and dappling her straw hat, her tumbledown curls, the lemony muslin of her simple gown, she was earthy and girlishly sensual—a far cry from the militant woman who was doing her damnedest to turn his life upside down and the Transport Office on its ear. He had a mad urge to throw her down in those daisies and dandelions and finish what he had started.

Instead, he looked at her and waited for her to speak.

She turned her face away and pushed freshly turned earth against a rock, her trowel scraping against tiny pebbles in the dirt.

"And you accuse *me* of rudeness," he said softly with the faintest trace of amusement.

She did not look up at him. "My sister is a born

matchmaker. Worse, she does not know trouble when she sees it."

"Surely she is wasting her efforts if she thinks to push *us* together."

"Indeed. I cannot imagine anyone more heinous, horrible, and rude to be paired with than you, Morninghall."

"Spare your poor imagination the effort, then, as I have an equal abhorrence of being strapped to someone who makes Boadicea seem like a daisy-faced angel."

"Thank God for small miracles."

"Indeed."

She kept her head down, intent on her task, her trowel flashing and chunking in the dirt as she mutilated the leaves and roots of a dandelion plant which had dared venture into the sacred boundaries of her flower bed. But he could just see her mouth beneath the wide brim of the hat, and it was turned up at the corners in a reluctant smile, as though she were enjoying this little exchange despite herself.

Oddly that pleased him. He was enjoying it too, though he'd be damned if he'd ever admit it. On an impulse he reached up and pulled a springy branch of white lilac down to his nose. She was still digging in the dirt, a little faster now. He eyed her, wondering what she would do if he broke off a blossom and offered to her, how he would feel if she rejected it.

He released the branch as though it had burned his hand. It bounced violently back to its rightful position, and something twisted angrily in his gut.

"So, was your first husband as wretched as you find me?" he asked, more tauntingly than he had intended.

She raised her head, a disappointed look in her eyes. "I should've known that a pleasant conversation with you was doomed to a premature end. But since you ask, Morninghall, William wouldn't have known 'wretched' if it up and bit him on the nose."

"Ah, so he was a model husband then."

"He was a good man."

"Perfect, I suppose. I cannot imagine *you* settling for anything less."

"He was far from perfect. And do you have to inject anger into what might otherwise be a civil, if not enjoyable, conversation?

"Forgive me." A wary smile flitted across his face, then was gone. "I shall inject vanity instead and ask you how he compares to me."

"Why, Morninghall, I *do* believe that forbidding demeanor of yours has cracked in a smile. Such interest you have in my late husband! But if you must know, William was old, feeble, decidedly unpassionate." *Unlike you with your sensual mouth, your devil's eyes, your sinister, dangerous charm, your lethal hands, your face like a fallen angel's* . . . She tilted her head, watching him. "He was as different from you as a kitten is from a leopard. You challenge me. He coddled me. You infuriate me. He calmed me. He was easy to figure out. You're impossible. But enough of that, because I'm sure you did not come here to talk about my dead husband."

"You're absolutely correct, I did not." Letting her veiled query hang between them, he flashed a cunning look at her from beneath his lashes and bent at the waist to sniff a tiny, delicate rosebud.

"Then why *did* you come here?"

He straightened up, brows raised, his dispassionate, unsettling gaze moving over her. "Why, to return something that is yours." He reached into his pocket and, to her horror, withdrew her little notebook, the binder of which was stained and warped from its dunking in the prison ship's brine. "Here."

She snatched it away, her cheeks growing hot all over again. "I must have dropped it when I swooned."

"Yes."

"I suppose you've read it."

"Of course."

She thinned her lips. "And?"

"Interesting observations." He struck a thoughtful pose, head tilted, finger tapping his mouth, eyes fastened intently, unnervingly on her. "I rather liked the one about me. 'The Marquess of Morninghall is a man with a diabolical, exceedingly handsome countenance and no shortage of vanity.' *'Exceedingly handsome.'* That rather makes up for the abuse you've hurled at me over the short span of our acquaintance, does it not?"

"You had no business reading my notes."

"They were confiscated property. I especially applaud the one you wrote to yourself. Something about checking the contractors' records against the naval ones to ensure the prisoners are not being cheated. How magnanimous of you, my lady, to start investigating the problems at their source instead of laying them all at my door."

"You *agree?*"

"Of course. Though you'd be wise to have me accompany you when you visit the contractor from whom we purchase the prisoners' clothing."

"Why?"

He sat down on a low bench, one arm draped lazily over the top, hat dangling from his fingers as he challenged her with his unflinching gaze. "Radley says he is not to be trusted around women."

"And you are."

"I am not in a position to be . . . objective."

He smiled, just the briefest, tiniest reflection of genuine amusement, and in it she saw the man he could be, the man that perhaps, in a kinder, more innocent time, he had been.

Her heart tripped, missing a beat.

His gaze remained on hers, penetrating, amused. Gwyneth, to her chagrin, could not hold that gaze. Lips pursed, face growing hot all over again, she bent her head and attacked a blade of grass springing up between the rocks. "Very well then, I shall expect your company tomorrow afternoon, as that is when I intend to check those records."

"My pleasure. Be on the pier at two o'clock, and I shall meet you there."

"But my appointment with Mr. Rothschild is at three!"

"So? Change it."

"You are impossible, Morninghall."

"I know." He was grinning, a bit more bravely now. "Damned infuriating, aren't I?"

"Yes, you are. But as you have asked such a personal question of me, I now find I have one for you. Tell me, Morninghall. You once had a promising career. Now you hate the navy, hate Bolton, and apparently hate yourself." Sitting back, she cocked her head and gave him a speculative look. "Why is it that Bolton put you—not only a nobleman but a promising young officer—in charge of a prison hulk? Why did he demote you when he could've just thrown you out of the navy?"

He jerked his head, indicating her notebook. "You tell me."

"It's something to do with that duel, isn't it?"

"The duel was the culmination of everything that had gone before it. And yes, the reason Bolton put me in charge of a prison hulk. It was his way of avenging that sniveling brat he called his son."

"There's got to be more to it than that."

He shrugged, set his mouth, and looked away, as though the whole thing were no longer worth taking about. "It was simple, really. Adam Bolton and I were rivals from the day we first met each other as lieutenants on the same ship. He hated me because I was higher born than he, and I hated him because he was a swaggering braggart, not above using his father's influence to excuse his failings, his ineptitude, and his cowardice." He looked away, his eyes now hard with remembrance, his body taut and defensive. "When promotion time came, I was passed over and the post of commodore was given to Adam—though I was the one with more seniority and, if I may be so bold, more laurels. But what did that matter? Adam was the son of an admiral, and I lacked such a weighty sponsor."

Gwyneth sat back on her heels, quietly listening.

"Needless to say, Adam Bolton took great delight in ordering me around, giving me the most ignoble assignments, and spreading slander about me throughout the fleet. Naturally I got resentful, but he was spoiling for a fight. So was I. One day he went too far and I took a swing at him."

"Ah. So this must've been the reason for the court-martial."

"Precisely. But the cocksure little bastard didn't stop there. When he chose a naval gathering to accuse me publicly of slandering his father to the First Lord of the Admiralty—a ridiculous accusation as I'd never even met the fellow—I challenged him to a duel. You know the rest."

"Yes, it becomes very clear now. The Boltons effectively ruined your naval career, pulled the rug right out from under you, didn't they?"

He turned away, a muscle ticking in his jaw.

"Why didn't you resign, Morninghall? Why suffer the indignities they've heaped upon your head?"

"I have my reasons. And you've already gone tit for tat as regards our questions. I've answered yours, as you answered mine."

"I see. Enough for one day, eh?"

"You could say that."

Gwyneth went back to her weeding, surprised and oddly happy she'd got even this much out of him. "Fair enough. We could discuss our forthcoming visit to the contractor instead."

"We could."

"I mean, I *am* grateful for your gesture of concern on behalf of the prisoners."

That smile—fleeting, wary, hesitant—came back to his stern and unforgiving lips. "Do not delude yourself, Lady Simms. The concern is not for them . . . but for you."

She jerked her head up, but at that moment the door opened and Rhiannon swept out, looking from one to the other like a hen overseeing her chicks. She held a tray in her hands; a teapot, cups and saucers, and a plate of scones competed for space atop it.

The concern is not for them . . . but for you.

Such words, delivered in that low, deep voice, were enough to send a wave of heat through every vein in Gwyneth's body. Standing up, she shook the weeds from her skirts and shot him an equally wary look. The marquess was watching her, still smiling, still dangling his hat from his hand with negligent abandon.

"Cream and sugar, Lord Morninghall?" Rhiannon called, pouring steaming tea into little china cups and interrupting the fragile moment.

"Please," he said, turning his all-too-considerable charm on her innocent sister. "Three sugars, if you will."

Rhiannon's head jerked up. "*Three sugars,* my lord?"

"I'm sure His Lordship needs all the *sweetness* he can get," Gwyneth put in, wryly.

"Indeed," he responded with a hot, private glance at Gwyneth's breasts that left her feeling as though he could see right through her bodice. He took his cup and a plate from Rhiannon and, as though to prove his words, slathered so much honey on his scone that it required a supreme balancing act on his part to keep it from dribbling onto his fine white shirt.

Gwyneth watched as he lifted the scone to his mouth, his tongue slicing out to catch drops of the honey as it oozed from the top of the crumbly pastry. Then, slowly licking the sweet syrup from his lips, he gave her a wicked, sidelong glance from under his lashes that said all the things his mouth didn't.

It made her recall the words he'd spoken just the day before, when she'd been flat on her back on his mattress, keening under that very same tongue:

Ah, madam, you are sweeter than this honey I lick from you. My God . . . I want you . . . all of you . . . now.

Gwyneth choked on her tea.

He merely lifted an eyebrow, a mocking smile touching one corner of his mouth.

"I do so love . . . *honey*," he murmured knowingly.

Gwyneth's cup began vibrating madly against her saucer. She set them both down on the grass.

"Are you well, Gwyn?" her sister asked, cocking her head and looking at her with concern.

"Yes—yes, the tea is just a bit hot, that's all."

Morninghall lifted his cup, his eyes wicked behind the rim. "Yes. Very hot," he said, still watching her.

Rhiannon was oblivious to this silent communication. She buttered a scone and lifted it to her lips, her eyes dancing with excitement. "So, my lord. Gwyn tells me you gave her a tour of your ship yesterday."

"Yes. At gunpoint, I am afraid."

"My sister can be very persuasive when she wants to be," Rhiannon chirped, slipping a piece of her scone to the dog that waited patiently at her feet. "But you have to admit, she gets the job done. And what do you think of her dress, my lord? Doesn't she look pretty today?"

"Rhiannon," Gwyneth warned.

Morninghall's eyes warmed, and if she did not know him better, Gwyneth would've sworn there was a teasing twinkle in those arresting depths. "I would like to say the yellow suits her and she looks quite charming. I would like to say she looks gentle and sweet, fairer than any of these flowers that surround her in this garden, but since her fingers are tightening around her spoon, and I already know what damage she can do with flying projectiles, I think I shall refrain from making any comment whatsoever."

"But my lord!" Rhiannon cried happily as Gwyneth went as red as her flowers, "You have just *made* your comment! What a clever man you are. Don't you think he's clever, Gwyn?"

"I think I'm still gripping that 'flying projectile,' Rhia, and that you have as much cause to beware it as does our esteemed *guest*."

"Don't listen to her, my lord," Rhiannon said, airily waving a hand. "She hates it when I play matchmaker."

"And do you do so often?"

"Oh, no. Gwyneth does not have time to think about finding a new husband. She never speaks of anyone—well, she didn't until you came along, that is—and very seldom allows gentlemen to call on her or take her out. You're the first one she's taken this much of an interest in since William died, and a fine choice she's made"—the girl giggled shyly—"I mean, Gwyneth told me you were handsome, my lord, but I had no idea you were *this* handsome, and Gwyneth *could* do much worse than to chose a marquess for her next husband—"

The tea Damon had just sipped exited his mouth in a violent expulsion. He grabbed for his napkin, choking.

"Rhiannon!" Gwyneth cried, mortified. "His Lordship and I barely know how to be nice to each other. I can assure you that marriage, of all things, is the very *last* thing on either of our minds."

"Yes, your sister and I were just discussing how much we abhor each other's company," Morninghall added, recovering himself.

"Detest it."

"Loathe it."

"Simply cannot tolerate it."

Rhiannon sipped her tea, unfazed. "Funny," she said, "for two people who profess to hate each other, you both have awfully big smiles on your faces."

Morninghall's disappeared immediately.

Gwyneth looked down at her half-eaten scone, her face blazing.

Rhiannon giggled nervously.

It was Morninghall who finally broke the awkward silence. He got to his feet, setting his teacup down on the table. "Duty calls. I'm afraid I have business in town that cannot wait. Thank you for tea. Good day, Miss Evans. Lady Simms."

He turned his back and all but ran to the door.

"I shall expect to see you tomorrow afternoon, my lord," Gwyneth called, cupping a hand to the side of her mouth. "We have that date with the clothing contractor, remember?"

"Of course. Two o'clock."

"Three."

"Two or not at all," he snapped, and with that he moved past a cowering Sophie and disappeared into the house. Moments later a door slammed in the front of the house, and the garden was quiet once more.

In the lingering stillness Rhiannon shut her eyes and settled back in her chair. Gwyneth, still looking at the door through which the marquess had passed, let out her pent-up breath. She looked at her sister, not knowing whether to throttle or praise her.

"Rhiannon—"

The girl blushed. "You were right, Gwyn. He was positively . . . *magnificent*."

Chapter 10

Toby Ashton sat listlessly on the lower deck, his Transport Office clothing hanging in sweaty tatters off his bones. The air was so hot and soupy it cost him precious energy just to draw it into his lungs. He did not know what day it was. He did not know what time it was. Neither mattered anymore, for Nathan was back in the Hole, Connor was gone, and their steely determination had been all that had kept him going. Now all he had left were his memories of home and the miniature of his mother that hung from a grimy chain around his neck.

And gnawing hunger.

Even hope had deserted him. He drew his knees up to his chest and leaned his head against the curve of the hull, too weak, too tired to do anything but wish for the only thing he *could* wish for and expect to receive: death.

The sounds of everyday life aboard the prison ship surrounded him. Most of the prisoners—some of the *Raffalés* excepted—occupied their time and minds with various professions and trades, charging one sou for an hour-long lesson in dancing, fencing, math, or languages. Their more noisy compatriots marched up and down the battery like a pack of gypsies at a village fair, trying to sell the clothing off their backs, even the space where they slung their hammocks, for money to spend on gambling. Fifteen feet away a group of Frenchmen were singing bawdily in a language Toby didn't even care to understand, and through this melee he caught the endless back-and-forth tread of the guards' feet on the deck above. He stared sightlessly into the gloom. The ceaseless din of the ship was as much a part of his existence as the constant hunger, the heat, the stench of hundreds of unwashed bodies, the vaporous fumes that passed for air.

Closing his eyes, he put his hand to his throat and gently stroked the miniature's surface, quiet tears of grief slipping down his wan and sunken cheeks.

He hoped the French prisoners wouldn't notice. They were an ill-mannered lot, as cruel and vicious as a pack of childhood bullies, and if they saw him crying . . . Toby wiped his face on his sleeve as inconspicuously as possible. Without Connor and Nathan to defend him, the bullies had resorted to ridiculing him about his weight, his meekness, and for not eating the rats they laughingly tried to cram down his throat. Although the American prisoners had tried to defend him, their energies were usually spent in devising a new method of escape, and they could not be everywhere at once.

If only Nathan were out of the Hole. If only Connor would come and rescue them.

Toby choked back a little sob and huddled into a ball, the miniature hidden in his hand lest one of the French prisoners see it and rip it right off his neck. So miserable was he that he didn't even notice the commotion near the hatch, until the mass of milling, shouting prisoners began to shove backward, coming in his direction.

He dragged his head up, shoving the cracked spectacles back up his nose. Yes, it was definitely coming his way, the excited chatter of French voices growing louder and louder.

Had someone been released?

Had that someone been Nathan?

He thrust the miniature down beneath his shirt and half-rose, peering through the milling bodies, steadying himself on a knife-carved bench and hoping against hope. He shoved a greasy swatch of hair out of his eyes and stared desperately. Survivors of the Black Hole always got a hero's welcome back among the other prisoners. Could it be Nathan, released prematurely? *Oh God, please, let it be Nathan!*

He got to his feet just as Jack Clayton, one of the guards, thrust through the milling throng, a lantern held high and his eyes sweeping the gloomy depths.

"Toby Ashton? I'm lookin' for Toby Ashton!" Clayton, a murky form in the acrid gloom, was stooped nearly double, swinging his head this way and that like a giant, lumbering bear. "Ye down here, lad?"

Hope fled, and fear tingled through Toby's blood like tiny ice crystals.

Something had happened to Nathan.

One of the Frenchmen bullied his way to the forefront of the oncoming crowd.

"There he is, hiding in ze corner! I'll get him for you!"

It was Armand, one of Toby's most virulent tormenters. He grabbed Jack Clayton's sleeve, his narrow, beady, black eyes dancing excitedly, his mad grin showing a mouthful of broken teeth, most of which had been lost in the fights he and his kind staged nearly every night in order to have something on which to bet.

Toby shrank back against the hull but there was no escape. Armand lunged forward and yanked him brutally toward the guard, snapping his neck and making his teeth slam together. A piece of the filthy old shirt tore off with a dull shriek. Laughing, Armand tossed the scrap aside as Toby jerked the torn shirt up to cover his chest—and the miniature that was now frightfully exposed to Armand's greedy eyes. But Armand had not seen it. He grabbed Toby's arm, his bony fingers sinking like claws into his flesh, and shoved him violently toward the guard.

Toby tripped and landed in a heap at the guard's boots. His chin smashed painfully against the damp

deck, knocking the breath out of him and sending his
spectacles skidding across the deck.

A large, beefy hand caught him beneath his shoulder and hauled him to his feet. Wiping the sudden
flow of warm blood from his chin, Toby looked up,
chin quivering in the effort to contain his tears.

"Come with me," Clayton growled, retrieving
Toby's spectacles and pushing him toward the hatch.

Dread coursed through him. "My brother—"

"Move."

Toby shot a fearful glance at the guard and began to
walk. The planking was sticky and hot beneath his
bare feet, and the overhead deck pressed down,
adding to the feeling of suffocation. Sweat broke out
of every grimy pore, trickled down his back. The
filthy, sweat-caked rags clung to him, scraping against
the inside of his thighs and skinny arms. He forced his
head up, staring straight ahead and clutching the
tattered shirt at his throat to hide the tiny painting of
his mother. Leering faces filled his view, swimming
out of the gloom. Taunts and inhuman screeches met
his ears, and someone stuck a foot out, trying to trip
him, before falling back, laughing.

Jack Clayton wheezed in the acrid gloom just
behind him, hurrying him along.

The hatch to the upper deck loomed just ahead,
hazy with the light coming down from above. Toby
stopped, looking fearfully around at the guard.

"Go on up."

Swallowing a thick lump of terror—*why have they
summoned me? Nathan, Nathan, please God, let him
be all right!*—Toby scampered up the filthy ladder,
one hand still holding his shirt closed and the other
clutching each step to keep his balance. By degrees the
cloying heat of below began to slacken and cool, fresh
air, alien to his starved senses, swept against his face.
He looked up at the rectangle of light above him and
saw wispy, feathery clouds moving across a pastel-
blue sky.

Then the awful premonition hit him.

He froze, unable to take those final steps onto the deck to confront the terrible scene he knew he would find. Connor had come to rescue Nathan and had failed, and both were lying dead on the mudflats. The Black Wolf was no more, and the final hope was gone. And now the guard was forcing him up to make him look—

Whimpering, Toby couldn't move.

Clayton's knee thumped into his arse, hard, spilling Toby out onto the deck and breaking the moment of paralyzed horror. He landed on his hands and knees, slivers of the deck impaling his palms, and looked up to see stumpy masts rising dizzily above him, a line of laundry fluttering between them. Clayton's musket prodded him in the backside, and gasping, Toby scampered to his feet.

He ran to the rail before anybody could stop him.

"Nathan!"

He stopped, clutching the rail, the wind ruffling his grubby hair.

Beyond the harbor the mudflats stretched before him, a flat, marshy ribbon on which only a few gulls picked, their heads bobbing as they trod the grime and filth that rimmed the high-tide line.

There were no bloated bodies on those flats.

No Connor, no Nathan.

Nothing but seabirds and rippled sand scored by the waves.

Toby fell to his knees and covered his face, sobbing with relief.

Clayton was behind him. "Get up."

He hauled himself to his feet, gulping in great draughts of the fresh, sweet air, the very strangeness of it making him want to wretch. It was too much, too soon. He clutched his stomach and, eyes watering in the hazy sunshine, stared up at the guard.

"My brother—"

"In the Hole." The guard reached out and yanked Toby away from the rail.

"Then why was I brought . . ."

"His Lordship wants t' see ye."

Toby had no idea who "His Lordship" was, but the look on the guard's face and the severe tone of his voice boded ill. Bravely he tried to smooth his repellent clothing, determined to conduct himself in a way that would make his brothers and father proud . . . until he realized the guard was shoving him aft, toward the captain's cabin.

"Oh no, ye don't," the big man growled, blocking Toby's escape route with his musket. "I've had about all I can take from the likes of ye, boy. Now get yer arse moving, and don't stop 'til yer beyond that door, ye hear me?"

Cold terror washed through Toby. He had heard stories about the new captain, how he was so terrible he'd made the pretty English lady faint when she came aboard the ship yesterday, that he was so ruthless some men were faking illnesses so they'd get transferred off HMS *Surrey* and onto the port's hospital ship.

And he had heard that Armand and his friends were already plotting to murder him if the prisoners' beer rations were not increased.

"But why does he want to see *me?*"

They were beneath the shadow of the poop deck now, and the captain's door loomed ahead like the door to a mausoleum.

"Damned if I know." Clayton knocked on the door, once, twice, and then, hauling it open with an ominous creak of its hinges, seized Toby's arm and shoved him inside.

The door shut behind him with a crash like a coffin being sealed.

Alone, Toby stumbled to his feet, sealing his arms protectively over his chest to contain his pounding heart. He curled his toes into the rug beneath his bare and grimy feet, afraid to move, afraid to breathe, afraid even to look up.

"Sit down," a deep-timbred, cultured voice ordered. "I do not bite."

Slowly Toby dragged his head up and looked about him. The cabin was dim, shadowed, lit by only a wedge of gray light through the partly opened curtains at the stern windows. That light touched the rich maroon leather of a swivel chair, the gleaming surface of a table set with a bottle of port and a single placement of china.

It did not touch the figure who stood in the shadows, leaning negligently against the edge of the window seat.

"Come forward then, so I might see you." This time the voice was a shade gentler, as though its owner had sensed Toby's terror and was sparked by pity and compassion.

Slowly Tony crept forward, into that wedge of light. He felt hideously dirty and malodorous. He hung his head, ashamed.

"What has become of your clothes, boy?"

"They got torn," Toby mumbled, still staring at his toes.

"Look at me when I'm talking to you."

Toby raised his head. He shoved his cracked spectacles up his nose and peered through the grime that hazed them. The figure was still in the shadows, unmoving, and the gloom made it impossible to discern any details of the face.

"I said, sir, they got torn."

"I am a marquess. You do not address me as 'sir.' You address me as *my lord*."

Such an imperious command was enough to infuse Toby with some of the Yankee spirit he thought he'd lost. He stiffened his spine and, raising his chin, regarded that shadowy figure. "And I am an American. You are no lord of mine, and I will address you the same as I would any other man."

Slowly, like some deadly panther uncoiling itself after a nap, the marquess straightened up. He was tall, taller than Toby's father, taller than his uncle Brendan, taller even than Connor. He came melting out of the shadows as though he had been born to them, lethal, leonine power in his every movement, malice wreathing the air that dared to surround him. A glass of spirits dangled from one elegant, relaxed hand, and rich whorls of dark hair framed a flawlessly chiseled face of stone. The mouth was hard, the nose as bold as the blade of a knife. Only the eyes gave the impression of any warmth—the satanic variety, Toby thought fearfully—and these were fierce and glittering with a cunning intelligence that made Toby's blood run cold.

"*Touché*," the marquess said softly.

With the wineglass hanging loosely from his hand, he walked a slow circle around Toby, that hooded, malevolent gaze taking in his greasy hair, his grimy face, his tattered clothes, his raw and ulcered feet. Toby swallowed hard. At last the man stopped, looking at him the way he might regard a dead rat.

"Your condition is disgusting."

The anger in those four sharp words only fueled Toby's indignation. "My condition is not something I have control over . . . *sir*."

"Indeed."

They stared at each other for a long tense moment, the boy in rags, the aristocrat in all his lordly splendor. At last Morninghall turned away, head high and nostrils flaring, as though he could not bear the sight—or smell—of him.

Toby relaxed, sinking down on his heels.

Without warning, the marquess whirled, his hand lashing out to seize Toby's jaw. He forced Toby's chin up, scrutinizing the bloody scrape on its underside, his eyes hardening like ice. Toby fought, trying to jerk away.

"Hold still, damn it!"

His jaw caught in that iron grip, Toby obeyed, eyeing his tormenter with mulish pride even as the marquess inspected the cut. Tears of shame pooled behind his lashes.

"Who did this to you?"

"I fell."

Morninghall released him. "I hear that those

damned Frenchmen have been abusing you. Is it true?"

"Who told you that?"

"Answer the bloody question."

Toby rubbed his jaw with his palm, trying to wipe away the enemy touch. "Aye, it's true," he said sullenly, "but I can take care of myself. You don't concern yourself with anyone else on this reeking tub, there ain't no need to concern yourself with *me*."

"I am concerned about your brother, and he was the one who told me."

Toby froze. Morninghall stalked silently away from him, moving into the bar of light and extinguishing it in a slow and eerie eclipse.

"M—my brother?"

Slowly the marquess turned his head and looked at Toby from over his shoulder. "You do have one, do you not?"

"Aye—he's in the Black Hole." Toby drew himself up. "If you're so 'concerned' about him, then why's he still in there?"

"He tried to escape. He must be punished. If punishment were not meted out to those who try to escape, then chaos would run rampant on this ship, would it not?"

Toby balled his fists. "Have you ever *been* in the Black Hole—*sir?*"

The marquess put his goblet on the table very carefully. "No, Mr. Ashton. I confess, I have not."

"Then I guess you can't know what it's like then, can you?"

Morninghall stared at him for a long uncomfortable moment, then picked up the bottle on the table and topped off his glass. "You are wise beyond your years, young man. How old are you?"

"Thirteen," Toby said sullenly.

A slow, studied nod of the marquess's head was his only answer. Strange shadows flickered across his eyes and he looked briefly preoccupied. Human.

Almost.

Toby crossed his hands over his chest, humiliatingly aware of the raw, nauseating stench of himself. "You . . . you talked to my brother, sir?"

Morninghall seemed to come back to himself. "I did."

"Is he—"

"He is well. As well as one can be, given his present predicament."

"Will you shorten his time in the Hole, sir?"

"I cannot."

"But—"

"I *cannot*," the marquess repeated firmly. As Toby stared imploringly into that stark and unfeeling face, he saw something like compassion there before the ice moved back in to veil what had surely been only an illusion anyhow.

It was too much. Toby, feeling the tears springing up, pivoted on his heel and turned to go before he could disgrace himself—and his country.

"I have not dismissed you."

Something in that low, authoritative voice stopped him dead in his tracks. Swallowing hard and fiercely blinking back the tears, he turned around. Morninghall had not moved.

"I called you up here, young man, to offer you a job," he said quietly. He flicked an aristocratic hand. "Something to get you away from those damned Frenchmen and out of the unhealthy fumes below these decks."

"What, burying dead bodies?" Toby challenged, wiping his nose with the back of his wrist.

Morninghall seemed oblivious to his tears, the disgrace he was making of himself. "No. I need someone to clean my cabin and bring me my meals." He frowned, gazing into his glass, a hint of a smile playing across his mouth. "My last servant was sent to another ship. Complained to the admiral about me, said I was too much of a bastard to work for."

He raised an eyebrow and shot Toby a sidelong look from beneath his lashes, as though daring him to dispute the fact.

Or accept the offer.

Toby stood, confused. He didn't know whether to be enraged, insulted, or grateful that he, of all people, had been plucked from the flames below by the devil himself. Yet there was something about the nobleman's sudden humility, something about the kindness he was showing when just about everyone below treated him no better than they did the rats, that was vastly appealing. He bit his lip, sucked it between his teeth, and kicked at the rug upon which he stood. It was a tough choice: continue suffering the abuse below or work for his English enemy.

Morninghall put down his wineglass and lifted his hand, idly studying his thumbnail. He looked askance at Toby. "The job is not without pay."

"I don't want it," Toby muttered, sniffling.

"You shall eat the same meals I do."

"No," Toby repeated, less forcefully than before.

"You will have regular baths, decent clothing, and—given your good behavior, of course—the chance to escort me ashore when duty and pleasure take me there."

The chance to escort me ashore . . .

Toby's head came up. He blinked away the tears and gaped at the marquess, disbelieving what he'd just heard. God and country forgive him, he had no wish to work for this English aristocrat and he could care less about the money, but decent, warm food in his belly was a far cry from maggots, and if he had the chance to leave the ship, perhaps he could pass information on to Connor. His heart leapt as the idea took hold. Connor, who everyone knew was the Black Wolf anyway, would find a way to rescue him and Nat!

"Well?"

Morninghall's patience was running out.

"Aye, I'll take it," Toby said, looking down at his grimy toes and trying not to sound too eager. Then he glanced up, mutinously. "But that don't mean I gotta like it."

The marquess smiled thinly. "No, I expect you won't. But then, I cannot imagine most of us *do* enjoy our jobs, do we?" he added cryptically and, turning away from Toby, pulled the curtains aside to stare out the window.

Toby waited.

"You may go now," Morninghall murmured, still gazing out that grimy window. "I shall expect you first thing tomorrow morning."

The feathery clouds had given way to low, steel-bellied leviathans marching across a harsh field of gray by the time dusk arrived, and with darkness came a light, chilling mist which crept beneath one's clothing and right into the very marrow of the bones.

It was a dreadful night to have a candlelight service, but the Black Wolf couldn't have ordered a finer one.

Of similar opinion, the Reverend Peter Milford stood on the wet and open deck of the prison ship, a tarpaulin coat covering his robes, his hat pulled low over his brow, his Bible in his hand. A raw breeze drove over the water, heavy with the scent of salt and rain, and he turned his back to it, trying to shield the old book from the cold drizzle.

Above, wet clothing flapped on the clothesline, a lonely sound in the night. Peter rocked back on his heels, waiting as a sailor moved around the circle of guards, silently lighting the taper each man carried with all the solemnity the occasion warranted. Peter was nervous, as he always was when a rescue was to take place; nevertheless he managed to adopt an expression of appropriate gravity as he watched the quiet, flickering flame travel to each cold taper of wax, until at last an array of orange tongues tickled the darkness around him, lighting the faces of those who held them.

Behind the guards, mere shadows in the drizzly darkness, several prisoners stood, relatives and friends of the men who had perished this past week alone. Peter tightened his fingers around his Bible. Morninghall had not allowed the poor souls to have candles, fearing they might use them to start an uprising, but at least he had shown *some* compassion by allowing them to attend and grieve for their loved ones.

The sailor had come to the last mourner and was lighting his taper. The flame sputtered and flared to life, swaying drunkenly in the damp breeze, and the scent of burning wax cut through the rainy darkness. It was almost time to begin, and Peter felt the tightening of his nerves, the faint sense of inadequacy that always plagued him before beginning a memorial service.

The sailor handed him the candle; then Peter cleared his throat and looked around him. The guards huddled miserably in their damp clothing, shielding their flames against the wind with their broad hands. Light flickered against their shiny, wet faces, infusing their eyes with a heightened sense of life and feeling, throwing their individual features into sharp relief. Some of them looked distant, weary, perhaps even sad. Some looked bored and miserable in the wet. Some were restless, while a few stood solemnly at attention. Yet Peter knew that to a man, each and every one of them was glad for the respite from their tedious duties, and were not above the pretense of mourning a colleague most of them had disliked— and prisoners they thought of as animals.

The candles flickered in the darkness. The men looked among themselves, waiting. A heavy raindrop tumbled out of the night sky and extinguished one of the tiny flames; the man who held the candle turned to his mate beside him and relit the fizzing wick.

Peter opened the Bible, feeling the reassuring weight of its heavy, worn spine against his palm. It did much to calm his apprehension. He said a silent prayer for the Black Wolf's success and safety. He prayed his friend would start carrying out these daring rescues for the right reasons instead of the wrong ones, and that God would open his eyes to the truth. He thought of the woman who would assist the Wolf tonight, the lovely Orla with the soft Irish brogue and prayed for her safety too. Then, content that his wishes were safely delivered to God, he looked at his watch. The night wasn't going to get any darker, and it was nearly eleven o'clock.

Time.

Loudly clearing his throat, he raised his head, the light from his own taper flickering across the open Bible. He felt a stab of guilt that he held no love for the guard Morninghall had shot, and that his compassion was all on behalf of the deceased prisoners. He sent up a last silent prayer, this time asking God's forgiveness for being so judgmental and preferential. After all, he reminded himself, God had made the guard too—and God did not make rubbish.

"Good people," he began, raising his voice so it would carry throughout the mourners. "We are gathered here tonight to pray for the souls of those who have died aboard this ship during this past week." *Too flat. You can do better than that, Peter.* "We pray for the souls of prisoners of war who have been released from this earthly suffering, and we pray for the soul of Ralph Leach, who perished while engaging in an act for which we ask God's compassion and forgiveness. This we ask in Jesus' name, using the prayer that He taught us: 'Our Father, who art in heaven, hallowed be thy name . . .'"

The chanting chorus was a low baritone in the darkness—solemn, sad, and contained beneath the drizzling mist.

"'. . . on Earth, as it is in heaven. . . . Give us this day our daily bread and forgive us our trespasses . . . And lead us not into temptation . . . thine is the kingdom, the power, and the glory, forever . . .'"

Lieutenant Radley, the marine commander, stood nearby, his narrow face hard, his shoulders stiff against the cold drizzle. He looked nervous, his eyes darting from side to side, as though he expected the prisoners standing quietly behind him to rise up and club him over the head.

Lord Morninghall was nowhere to be found.

"Amen," Peter finished, quietly.

The mist thickened, becoming a light rain which beat softly on the deck. Gazing over the faces of the men who looked to him, Peter thought he could just see a form, darker than the darkness, sliding through the water a stone's throw off the old ship's starboard bow.

He raised his voice, drowning out any sound the boat might make as it moved through the waves, hoping that the few sentries still on duty would be patrolling the stern of the ship.

"We pray for the soul of Richard Morrill, late of the American warship *Merrimack,* who left this life on Friday last after a blessedly short illness. God, be with his family, be with his friends, and be with him. In Jesus' name we pray—"

Some of the guards shuffled nervously. "Amen," a few of them said, without much conviction.

"Lord, we pray for the soul of Ebenezer MacGill, brother of Jake MacGill, who succumbed to the travails of his existence on Thursday last. Please, o Lord, comfort those he leaves behind, and be with his family during their time of suffering and grief. In Jesus' name we pray—"

"Amen," said Jake, who was one of the dark figures behind the guards. His voice was hoarse. Again only two or three of the guards added their own "amens," much to Peter's tense annoyance.

"Lord, we pray for the soul of Etienne LaFleur, whom we speed on his way to heaven after a conflict that we, in our human ignorance, cannot understand"—LaFleur, one of the Frenchmen, had died in a knife fight—"and we ask that you comfort those he leaves behind, and be with them in their hour of grief. In Jesus' name we pray—"

"Amen."

The crowd shifted on their feet, huddling in the light rain.

"And Lord, we pray for the soul of Ralph Leach"— *Thank you, God, the boat is well beneath the bowsprit now*—"and we ask your forgiveness for what he attempted to do, for the flesh is weak, especially when . . . when times are as hard as they are now. We ask that you, o Lord, judge this man on the good deeds he has done, the good deeds that have been in his heart, and God, we ask that you be with his family and friends. In Jesus' name we pray—"

"Amen," chorused the guards.

Peter bent his head, the water trickling from the brim of his hat onto the deck before him. The Bible's pages were damp beneath his fingers, and as he read a few verses from Corinthians, he passionately raised his voice to cover any noise the Black Wolf might make as he effected the rescue of Toby Ashton and Jed Turner—the two Connor wanted off the ship before it was too late.

"O God, we ask for peace in this world! We ask that all wars might end, and that humankind might exist in love and harmony with one another; we ask for understanding among ourselves; and we pray that you will be with our community, our country, our world. We ask that you put an end to all suffering, Lord, and we pray for forgiveness for those acts of sin that we commit, intentionally and unintentionally, against our fellow man. . . . Lord, in your mercy, please hear our prayer!"

Radley looked at his watch and shot Peter an annoyed glance.

"We pray for wisdom for our leaders, Lord, and we pray that you will guide them along the paths of righteousness, mercy, and love. . . . Lord, in your mercy, please hear our prayer. . . ."

The service went on.

And far forward and below, where the waves lapped

against the smoky old bow, a black-cloaked figure slipped out of a boat and into a hole beneath the deserted gallery.

Chapter 11

It was barely a crawl space in which the Black Wolf found himself, a close, stinking cubbyhole in the bows of stagnant brine, mildew, the decaying remains of an old anchor cable, rat excrement. His back was jammed against damp wood, his knees against his chest. Suffocating darkness enclosed him. He heard the distant words of the chaplain's service, smelled the nauseating stench of the prison ship's bowels, sensed the thick, massing swell of hundreds of prisoners just beyond the partition against which his knees were crushed.

Orla O'Shaughnessy waited in the boat just outside, but that woman had nerves of steel and did not command any worry on her behalf. Cool mist drifted into the hole by which the Wolf had entered this tiny space, but still the air around him was dank and hot. He wished he could see in the choking darkness, wished he could've brought a light, but such a risk was not worth taking. Instead he waited for his senses to accustom themselves to his surroundings and concentrated on getting his bearings by touch. Then he pushed himself forward, twisting his body and thrusting his head through the crude latticework of wood his exploring hand had managed to locate.

"Clayton." His voice was no more than a whisper.

"I'm here, sir," the guard answered, ten British pounds the richer for his assistance.

"Have you the two American lads?"

161

"I got Jed with me," came the answer, a foot away in the darkness, "but I couldn't get Toby Ashton. He won't come, says he won't leave his brother behind."

"I told you not to fail me in this, Clayton."

"I tried, sir, told him the Wolf was comin' for him, but he said he won't leave unless he can get his brother out 'o the Hole an' bring him too. Said that if he escapes without him that bastard Morninghall will get his revenge by making the brother pay."

The Black Wolf crouched motionless, head bent and knuckles against his brow as he cursed savagely. Bloody hell. He hadn't counted on *this*.

"Send Jed up to me then. Quickly!"

Harsh gasps cut the darkness, then the desperate scratching of fingernails against wood, the grunt of the guard, the frightened whimpers of the boy. The Black Wolf squeezed himself into the tiny space between the latticework, his strong hands reaching out in the darkness to seize the youngster's thin, bony ones, squeezing them reassuringly for a brief moment before hauling him up into the tiny space in which he was crushed. His back grinding into the wood behind him, he shifted and shimmied, dragging the youth up through the crawl space and directing him toward the ragged hole in the ship's hull.

"Easy now, lad. My friend Orla out there in the boat will help you."

Too frightened to reply, too terrified of being caught, the youngster pushed his head and shoulders through the hole as the Black Wolf held his ankles to steady him. Moments later the Wolf felt the tug signifying that Orla had him in her arms.

"Got him, sir!" she whispered.

He let go. *One left.*

"Clayton!" he whispered fiercely. "Get Toby Ashton whether he wants to come or not, and be quick about it!"

There was a rustle of fabric, then Clayton was gone. The seconds crept by as the Black Wolf waited, lodged in the tiny, airless crawl space, his heart thundering in his ears, his breathing sounding loud in the darkness. He buried his mouth against his arm, trying to mask it, though the sound was unlikely to be heard. He pictured Peter up there, drawing out the service as long as possible, raising his passionate voice on the wind and doing all he could to play his part in this latest rescue. He sensed Orla several feet away, already spreading a black tarp over the lad, thought of the schooner *Kestrel,* poised for flight and silently cruising the waters just beyond the big anchored men-of-war. Thank God for the misty night, the drifting fog, the gentle whisper of rain and tide.

There was a noise outside the hull, a faint tapping against the old oak.

"Captain!"

His knees crushed against his chest, the Wolf pivoted in the tiny space and thrust his head out of the hole through which he had just passed Jed. Rain pattered softly against his nape, his damp hair, and around him; the night was breezy and dark, so dark it was impossible to tell where the harbor ended and the night sky began. Tendrils of mist and fog crept across the water, enveloping the lights of the men-of-war, the hospital ship, and another prison hulk.

Orla's face, smeared with charcoal, was barely visible in the darkness. "I've got to push off a bit— there's a guard coming around the scaffolding, he'll be on us within the next minute!"

"Right, then. Go."

Impatiently the Black Wolf waved her off, ducking back inside the ship as she put an oar against the rotting old hull and pushed off into the darkness, the swirling rush of water following her. He sat, tense, waiting, and damp, the scent of rain and sea air wafting into his tiny space.

Where was that damned Clayton?

He'd no sooner had the thought when he heard the measured footsteps of the sentry Orla had warned him about, just outside on the scaffolding not two feet away. The Wolf held his breath. The wooden walkway creaked beneath the sentry's weight as he approached and passed.

At that moment Clayton's urgent whisper cut the darkness.

"Sir, I can't find him!"

The Wolf froze. Outside, the footsteps stopped.

Heavy creaks sounded on the scaffolding, and he sensed the sentry leaning down.

Damnation!

Clayton, unaware of the sentry's presence and thinking the Wolf had not heard him the first time, raised his voice. "Sir, the Ashton boy, he's not in his hammock. I don't know where he is!"

Too late. Outside, the guard was on his knees, peering beneath the scaffolding, lowering his lantern and silently running his hand over the curve of the hull. The Black Wolf, trapped, flattened himself against the damp wood at his back as lantern light filled the night beyond the hole, moving this way, moving that, stopping, blinding him—

"What the hell? *Alarm! Alarm! We 'ave us an escape attempt!*"

With all his strength, the Wolf kicked savagely out at the lantern, the arm, as the sentry, howling, tumbled into the harbor and the ship burst into chaos. A bell began clanging wildly, muskets cracked above, footsteps were pounding overhead, the prisoners beyond the latticework were yelling—

And the Black Wolf was gathering himself for a mighty leap to freedom.

He threw himself headfirst out of the hole and into the night.

His body knifed through the darkness and downward. There was a whistle of air past his ears, then nothing but the gut-wrenching shock as he hit the water, its icy embrace ripping his breath away, momentarily paralyzing him, closing over his head and instantly cutting off the ringing alarm from above. He let himself sink a few numbing feet, the heavy folds of his cloak brushing like cobwebs around his face, bubbles hissing and whispering around him. He heard dull thuds, distant pops, the "plop-plop-plop" of musket balls slamming into the surface above.

He doubled his body and dove deep, striking blindly out toward the harbor's entrance and where he knew Orla already would be heading swiftly. The cloak swirled around him, dragging him backward and impeding his progress. Kicking upward as his air began to wane, he groped for his knife, cut the thing off, and left it writhing and sinking in the depths behind him. He broke the surface only long enough to get his bearings, the rain beating against his cold brow. Eighty feet behind him the prison ship was ablaze with light, silhouetted figures running along her foc's'le and poop deck, shots cracking out in the night as tongues of blue-orange fire.

A musket ball plowed the water six inches from his ear.

"Captain! Over here!"

Orla's voice was barely a whisper, but it was enough to guide him. He filled his lungs and dove deep, seeing the dull gleam of light on the surface above him, the inky blackness of the depths beneath. His limbs tingled with the cold, and the current rushed over his head and along his body with the speed at which he drove himself through it. Almost there . . . hold on . . . and then something brushed his fingers. Relieved, he knew it was the rope Orla had tossed to him. He wrapped it around his hand and held on tight, kicking hard so as not to slow her progress, rapidly catching up to the struggling boat.

She backed water, allowing him precious seconds to haul himself up over the gunwales. Then, gasping and dripping, he grabbed both oars, his powerful muscles sending the boat knifing across the harbor and toward the safety of the *Kestrel*.

She grinned at him, her teeth white in the darkness. "Cutting it a bit close, aren't you?"

He looked at her and did not smile.

It was hard to think with the damned noise outside.

Another prisoner had escaped the night before. The morning newspapers were ablaze with the news, the ship was in turmoil, and even now the prisoners, roused to fever pitch by yet another Black Wolf raid, were cheering and yelling loud enough to wake the dead, making the very timbers of the ship throb with their uproar.

Damon had no wish to deal with it. He assigned Lieutenant Radley to the task and shut himself in his cabin, picking at his breakfast of fried pork and black coffee as he went, with no small degree of annoyance and disinterest, through the untidy pile of paperwork and ledgers left by his predecessor. He could think of a hundred things he'd rather be doing, but he wanted to be prepared for his meeting with *her*—even if it was so that he wouldn't appear as apathetic as he felt. There were receipts for food, receipts for clothing, receipts for this, receipts for that, and here a note from the Transport Board. It was stained with tea and he had found it shoved up inside the corner of a desk drawer:

I am directed by the Board to desire that you will immediately forward to this office by coach a loaf taken indiscriminately from the bread issued to the prisoners on the day you receive this letter. . . .

He tossed it aside. So, the navy had been "testing" the bread, making an effort—at least on paper—to see that the prisoners were being fed something edible. Damon wondered, contemptuously, how many times the "indiscriminate" sample had been pronounced unfit to eat. He wondered how many times action had been taken to make what was supposed to be bread "made of whole wheaten meal actually and bona fide dressed through an eleven shilling cloth" consumable. He wondered what had prompted the government even to look into the matter, and wondered why the hell he was sitting here on a bright, breezy morning, troubling himself about something in which he had no interest, about which he could do nothing anyhow, when he could be out petitioning the Powers That Be to give him a command he deserved.

Now, Lady Simms . . . *she* was something in which he most definitely had an interest. And a prurient one at that.

Pain shot through his skull. The headache had started when he got up, and at the thought of the hellcat, it forked out from his temples and stretched pain across his forehead. Cursing, Damon closed his eyes and cradled his head in his hands. He pressed his knuckles against his temples, hard, wishing he could just push the bones together until they met in the middle, thereby putting a quick end to the agony.

Outside and belowdecks, the noise continued.

Leaning on his elbow and propping his brow in the cradle of thumb and forefinger, he turned several more old, yellowed pages, his gaze skimming over notes made by his predecessor, his mind a million miles away. What he wouldn't give to be out on the sea right now, commanding a dashing frigate, a man-of-war, even a little sloop. Anything but a *prison hulk,* for God's sake.

Angrily he turned another page and came across an advertisement to contractors regarding victualing on prison ships:

Sunday.	*1½ lbs. bread*
Monday.	*½ lb. fresh beef*
Tuesday.	*½ lb. cabbage or turnips*
Wednesday.	*1½ lbs. bread, 1 lb. good sound herrings, 1 lb. good sound potatoes*

Thursday.	*1 oz. Scotch barley*
Friday.	*1½ lbs. bread, 1 lb. good sound cod, 1 lb. potatoes*
Saturday.	*⅓ oz. salt*
	¼ lb. onions

The rations seemed adequate enough. *So why, then, are the prisoners so damned thin?*

Gambling away their food? Rejecting it as some sort of damned protest? Disease from within? What then?

The contractors.

The headache was getting worse, beginning to pound against the inside of his skull like a carpenter's hammer, and the noise coming from outside made him want to bang his head against the table until he knocked himself senseless. The fact that he had to meet the hellcat at two o'clock for their scheduled visit to the clothing contractor did nothing to relieve the pain.

With a muttered curse he shoved the whole mess aside. He did not want to deal with Lady Gwyneth Evans Simms, he did not want to deal with this mountain of records, orders, and receipts, and he did not want to deal with those cheating scoundrels who supplied clothing and food to the prison ships. At the moment he didn't want to deal with *anything*. His palm pressed to his forehead as though to hold in his aching brain, he pulled out the bottle of pills the ship's doctor had prescribed for his headaches. He tossed two of them down his throat and chased them with a swallow of black coffee. It was lukewarm now, disgusting. He threw the cup against the bulkhead, coffee and all. A whiff of stench drifted in from the decks below, and a wave of nausea slithered up his throat.

He looked down at his hands; they were shaking.

Get the Peterson's.

He was just heading toward his bookcase to retrieve the tome when a knock came at the door.

So much for seeing whether he was going to live or die.

Unexplainably feeling guilty, Damon snatched his hand back and straightened up, locking his fingers together behind his back.

"Enter," he commanded tensely.

Young Toby Ashton came in. He had been bathed—the rinse water requiring three changes, so Radley had complained, before finally it had run clear—issued a fresh set of clothing, and given a healthy portion of the same food that was now growing cold on Damon's plate. His ginger hair was neatly combed and parted, new shoes gleamed on his feet, and he had been given a fresh pair of spectacles to replace his cracked ones. Yet the frame from which those clean clothes hung was barely more than a skeleton, and no amount of soap and water could wash away the despair and grief in those haunted brown eyes.

Raw guilt sliced Damon's heart like a knife. Peter Milford had told him the boy had been the object of much abuse belowdecks, with the French prisoners stealing his food and making sport of his meekness, his size, his propensity for tears. Given his own personal experiences with an abusive mother, Oxford undergraduates, and unfair naval politics, Damon knew damned well what sort of ostracism and pain the boy must be feeling. He felt what little heart he had going out to him.

Damn it to hell.

It had been so much easier when he'd been ignorant of what really went on belowdecks, when he'd been able to think of the prisoners as *the enemy* and hadn't spared them a second thought. But it was hard to remain detached when you could smell the truth wafting in through the open window. It was hard to ignore the things you'd been forced to face when they repeated themselves in your nightmares. And it was hard to think of the prisoners as a cold and calculating enemy when one of them, a pitifully starved and sickly little thirteen-year-old, was standing there in front of you, his eyes dark with suffering, pride, and grief.

It was all Lady Gwyneth Evans Simms's fault. She'd been the one to bring him face-to-face with reality, with guilt and pain and regret. He'd been fine until she'd come into his life and forced him to look at things he was better off ignoring. Now he had pain and guilt. He hadn't had any of this when his heart had been successfully hardened, when he'd walled himself in with ignorance, anger, and self-pity. But those walls were unsteady, and now the mortar was beginning to crumble.

There was something getting inside them now, something called *feeling*.

And it frightened him.

Frightened him beyond his mother, beyond the reality that he was going to die unloved and unappreciated, beyond anything that ever had haunted that huge ancestral bedroom at Morninghall.

Who are you to complain about your lot in life, your failure to find glory and admiration and affection, when there are people beneath your feet who are dying every day from malnutrition and disease?

Damon felt sick, angry, and violent, especially toward Lady Gwyneth Evans Simms, who had forced him to go belowdecks and witness those unspeakable horrors for himself.

The innocent brown eyes before him were waiting silently, dark with suffering, all the worse because those eyes were those of a child.

Damon sat down heavily and put his head in his hands. "What is it, Toby?"

"Radley told me to tell ye to expect company."

"Who?"

The boy's gaze slid toward the window. "An officer."

"Shit." Damon sent his chair crashing back and ran to the stern windows. Sure enough, there was a boat heading toward them, and in it was Bolton, his iron-gray hair blowing in straggly wisps around his stark face, his gaunt frame stiff as a spike and looking as though it had been driven straight down into the seat with a giant hammer from above.

Oh, joy, he was in trouble this time, but suddenly he didn't care.

He began to laugh—richly, helplessly, insanely.

"Lord Morninghall?"

Damon turned from the window, the image of that boat knifing through the sparkling water still emblazoned across his brain. That a reprimand was coming, he had no doubt. That Bolton was furious that the Black Wolf had humiliated the navy once again, he did not care. Let Bolton and his damned high-ranking friends gnash their teeth and make eternal public vows about how they would soon snare the elusive thief of the night. Let them threaten him with a court-martial, a firing squad, whatever they damned well pleased as punishment for his incompetence and insubordination. It was all quite amusing really. After all, the navy had let him down, hadn't it? The navy had stripped him of *his* pride, swept him conveniently under the rug, and humiliated him by putting him in charge of this disgusting hulk. It was about time the shoe went on the other foot and the navy got a taste of what it so enjoyed meting out.

Oh, yes, damned amusing. Damon laughed and laughed while poor Toby eyed his enigmatic benefactor with dubiousness and distrust, thinking he'd surely come unhinged.

He backed toward the door. "Will there, uh, be anything else, sir?"

Morninghall threw himself into his swivel chair with boyish abandon and poured a generous measure of amber liquor into a glass. He looked at Toby, his lips still twitching, his eyes gleaming with private amusement. Then he raised the glass, his elegant, long fingers wrapped almost lovingly around its base.

"Anything else?" Another short burst of laughter, then he turned his profile toward the window, the glass still raised in his hand. "Oh, yes. To our friend the Black Wolf. May he continue to humiliate men like Bolton, and may he never get caught!"

Yes, definitely unhinged, Toby thought, eyeing him distrustfully. Or foxed.

He backed out of the door and silently shut it behind him, the marquess's evil laughter following him down the short corridor to the deck beyond.

Bolton's mood was as foul as the stench that came creeping across the waves from the prison hulk. He sat rigidly upright, lips pulled back in a severe line, raw fury burning through his breast.

Damn that blasted Morninghall, the incompetent son of a bitch! He had made a laughingstock out of him *and* the navy one too many times with his inability to contain his lot of war wretches. Something had to be done. Bolton had had it up to his epaulets with this Black Wolf nonsense and Morninghall's dismal failure to put an end to it.

He stared up at the prison hulk before him. He could just see Morninghall on the deck, looming over a cowering midshipman. *Foyle.* Bolton lifted his telescope for a better look. From what he could tell, the bastard wasn't just talking to Foyle, he was giving him a damned good dressing-down. He couldn't see the marquess's face, but he could see the poor midshipman's, and it was tight-lipped with fear and resentment—as most people's are who find themselves the recipients of an unfair and unwarranted attack.

Still picking fights with people, the surly son of a bitch. *I see you haven't learned a thing, have you. I'll get you for being so damned arrogant.*

Adam's dear face rose up in his memory. Adam, his

beloved son, lured to his death and murdered by that very bastard who was even now reprimanding Foyle. It had been a duel, an old-fashioned, cold-blooded, pistols-at-dawn duel. Two shots, one from each man, and Adam had fallen to the dewy grass, dead. Morninghall had calmly lowered his pistol, wrapped a handkerchief around his arm, and walked away. That had been the end of it—and the end of Adam.

"You may have escaped justice from the courts for killing my son, Morninghall, but you'll not escape it from me. I'll get you. You just see if I don't." Bolton ground his fist into his palm as the smoky hull of the prison ship reared up out of the harbor before him. "You knew my Adam never had a chance, you privileged, arrogant bastard. If you were to drop dead before my eyes, I'd laugh. I'd bloody *laugh*."

He froze, the words ringing in his brain like the last peal of a bell. *If you were to drop dead . . . drop dead . . . drop dead . . .*

The idea was too horrible, too wonderful, even to consider.

His heart began to pound with excitement.

Payment, justice, an eye for an eye. Adam had not deserved to die, and Morninghall would pay. Bolton would see to it. He'd pay with humiliation, with disgrace, and ultimately with death. But Bolton, who could not afford to get his own hands dirty, had to find a way to bring it about.

He saw Morninghall striding to the rail to receive him.

And Foyle staring hatefully after him, his eyes burning with resentment.

Foyle.

Foyle would know every prisoner aboard the hulk. Foyle would have no trouble finding some wretch right beneath Morninghall's aristocratic nose whose hatred of the marquess was every bit as virulent as Bolton's own. Foyle was young and ambitious; Foyle would do anything to get promoted; Foyle wouldn't dare question an admiral.

Best of all, Foyle would also hate Morninghall.

For the first time since Adam's death, Bolton felt alive—wonderfully, gloriously *alive*. Assassination via a prisoner would never be traceable to him. He balled his hands into fists beneath his cloak, and looked up at the cabin windows above.

His voice was raw with emotion. "An eye for an eye, *my lord,* and then we'll be even."

Oh, yes, Morninghall would pay.

And he would pay dearly.

Chapter 12

unctual as ever, Gwyneth arrived at the pier just before two o'clock, her face shaded by the brim of a smart green hat, her hair coiled and pinned to the back of her head, her parasol, which matched her gown of pine-green bombazine trimmed in black lace, rapping an impatient tattoo against the weathered gray planking on which she stood.

Morninghall was late. She was willing to bet he had no intention of meeting her at all, and was sitting in his cabin with a telescope trained on her at this very moment. She easily could picture him leaning back in his swivel chair, feet propped against the window seat, laughing as he watched her make a fool of herself.

And only a fool would trust Morninghall.

She would have been better off doing as Rhiannon had suggested: seeking out the Black Wolf and soliciting *his* help instead!

She gazed across the sparkling waves toward the prison ship. A breeze, rich with the scent of the marshes, played over the water, ruffling the black ribbon just beneath her breasts. The sunlight was warm against her face as she looked up to where a pair of gulls wheeled, white against blue, their harsh cries echoing over the harbor. It was peaceful here, pleasant, yet she could not help thinking about the last time she'd been on this wharf, when she'd encountered the enigmatic Black Wolf himself.

Gwyneth's heart fluttered and she put a gloved

hand to her breast, feeling a bit foolish. And yet female hearts were fluttering all over Portsmouth, and feminine tongues were wagging with speculation about who the Black Wolf really was. Rumors abounded that he was an escaped American prisoner of war—but his being American didn't detract at all from his status as a hero. The English government might not be lifting a finger to ease the plight of the prisoners of war, but if the overwhelming outrage Gwyneth had witnessed when she had described the conditions in which they were kept—and the subsequent eagerness of the people of Portsmouth to sign her petition—was any indication, there was much to be proud of when it came to the generosity and compassion of the English people in general.

Involuntarily she looked behind her, but the pier was empty. The faint flutter became an involuntary ripple of pleasure, skating across her flesh and centering between her legs. How well she remembered that intrepid figure, his cloak swirling around him and making him seem a phantom straight out of the depths of the night. How well she remembered his enigmatic, whispery voice, his powerful charisma, his passionate, dizzying kiss.

And how easy it would be to stand here and fantasize about him, if it weren't for the Marquess of Morninghall and her equally wanton response to *his* kisses.

Gwyneth shivered despite the warmth of the day. Something must be wrong with her. It must be those two years of deprivation she'd spent with William. After all, women like herself did not fall in lust with devils like Morninghall. Women like herself did not fantasize about dark avengers from out of the night. For heaven's sake, she was starting to act just like a heroine out of one of Rhiannon's silly novels!

You're only human, Gwyn. There's nothing wrong with you. You are not the first woman to find the marquess dangerously attractive, nor will you be the last. And as far as the Black Wolf goes . . .

She thought of the ladies of Portsmouth.

Yes, only human.

A sudden movement from the prison ship caught her eye. Shading her eyes with her hand, Gwyneth saw a boat putting off from the ancient, charred leviathan with three figures sitting in it. Two of them were sailors. The other, stiff and commanding, wore blue, the color matching the deep azure of the harbor.

Morninghall.

Well, la-dee-da, he was keeping his word.

Of course, he was only doing so to unnerve and annoy her, she thought, to put her off guard. Of course, he wanted only to rape her with his gaze, to plunder her senses with his very nearness. Hell would freeze over before his motives for helping her had anything to do with compassion for those poor prisoners.

She shut her eyes. God help her, of all the hulks in England, why had she chosen this one?

The boat was making good speed, the oars rising and falling on either beam and flashing in the sunlight. The marquess sat in the stern, looking neither left nor right, his grimly carved face in shadow and only his mouth painted with a slash of sunlight. Behind him Gwyneth could see the huge mass of the prison ship, where hundreds of arms were thrusting and gesturing—quite obscenely, she noted—from its iron-barred gun ports. Raucous jeers and taunts rolled across the water on the breeze, and a sudden stab of pity assailed her. She didn't envy a prison-hulk captain his life—or his command.

The boat was close enough now that she could see the buttons on the marquess's coat, the arrogant blade of his nose, the dark whorls of his gloriously rakish hair. Obviously the distance between the pier on which she stood and the ship whence he'd come was misleading, for the journey seemed to be taking forever. She began to fidget, feeling like a fool standing here on the pier, waiting, conspicuous, open to observation. She should've arrived late and made *him* wait. As it was, she could feel that malevolent gaze upon her, and she wondered what he was thinking . . . plotting.

Remembering.

Her face blazed with sudden heat. She had a sudden wanton image of herself, lying on her back with her legs open, his head buried between her thighs.

Oh, God . . .

The boat was still approaching, that motionless figure in blue as intimidating as the figurehead of a Viking ship.

Gwyneth wanted to flee, or at the very least to turn her back and stride slowly up and down the pier as she waited for the boat to arrive—anything to avoid standing here like an actress onstage. Instead she forced herself to remain exactly where she was, her posture spike straight, her wrist poised elegantly atop the parasol, her chin high, and her gaze nailed to the approaching boat. Two could play the intimidation game. He needn't know she could not wait to see him, that her blood was singing with excitement. She would stand right where she was, as resolute as he. See how she liked it!

She watched as the boat came alongside the pier, bumping hollowly against the slimy old poles that supported it. Moments later Morninghall, a leather satchel tucked under his arm, was climbing up the small ladder.

Gwyneth's heart began to race, and her hands went damp within her gloves. She clenched them over the parasol and waited, nearly snapping the ivory handle.

He reached the pier and gave her a long, simmering glance that could've burned the crust off a piece of toast. "Good afternoon, Lady Simms. You are look-ing"—his soulless gaze raked the length of her body, burning holes through the suddenly too-hot bomba-zine as he caught and lifted her hand—"deliciously lovely today."

Gwyneth stiffened and yanked her hand from his. "We are here together on business, Morninghall, and do not forget it."

"Ah, but I can wish that it were *another* sort of business, can I not, my lady?"

Turning his back on her heated reply, he tugged his smart naval coat off and, with casual disdain, tossed it into the boat. It landed in the puddle of water that sloshed in the bottom, there to lay in a sad, inglorious heap of blue. Gwyneth's mouth fell open. Even the oarsman and the young lad on the other seat looked at His Lordship with horror and confusion, respectively, but Morninghall seemed not to care. "Await me here, Roberts," he said to the former and, taking off his hat, tossed it the way of the coat. It landed with a soft thump.

"That's Rogers, sir."

"Of course. Rogers. I shall be back in about two hours. Let the boy out of your sight and it'll be your damned head."

"Young Mr. Ashton is safe with me, sir."

"Be sure of it—or else."

He turned, the breeze ruffling his bright white shirt, and wordlessly offered his elbow to Gwyneth. But she had caught sight of the skeletal waif sitting forlornly beside the oarsman, and her forehead was pleating in a frown.

"Really, Morninghall, must you starve your servants as you do your prisoners?" she accused, impaling him with an angry look.

He took her hand and shoved it in the crook of his elbow, covering it with his own. "Toby *is* one of the prisoners. I took pity on him and rescued him from the masses." He arched an eyebrow at her, but his eyes glittered with defensive anger. "Why, I thought you would've looked kindly on my action . . . not condemn it."

"Oh," she said lamely, "I . . . see."

"Do you? Then let's go," he snapped, all but dragging her down the pier. "I haven't got all bloody day."

Her shoes skidded on the bleached planking. "I want a word with young Toby."

"Later."

"You can't just leave him sitting in the hot sunlight for two hours, that's cruel!"

"Don't jump to conclusions you have no business making in the first place. Rogers—Roberts— whatever the devil his name is—will take him off to the George for a pint and a hot meal."

"A hot meal?!"

"Yes, what of it?"

She made her feet move, lest she be dragged the length of the pier. God help her, he was magnificent in his *badness!* She tilted her head to the side and looked up at him as she all but ran alongside. "You know, my lord, I am beginning to wonder about you. Taking pity on a prisoner. Bringing him on boat rides across the harbor. Hot meals out. Careful, lest I begin to think you have a heart after all."

His jaw hardened. "Only fools make mistakes like that, Lady Simms. You do not strike me as a fool."

"And you don't strike me as the soulless serpent you try so hard to emulate," she retorted. And then, more softly: "At least—not always."

He glanced down at her. Something confused and fearful shadowed his eyes, and for the briefest moment the harsh lines of his profile softened. Then, scowling once more, he yanked her along as though he wanted to get away from her perceptive words. Anger and annoyance was stamped on every line of his face.

Gwyneth was relentless. "Why, Morninghall? Why these sudden kindnesses?"

"None of your business."

"No, it *is* my business. I want to know why you suddenly seem to care about someone other than yourself."

"I felt guilty," he growled, eyes straight ahead as he guided her between the seedy buildings that hugged the waterfront and up a narrow, cobbled side street. "Guilt and compassion are two different things."

"If guilt spawns compassion, then I have no complaint with you, Morninghall."

He set his jaw and went silent after that, veiling his expression and giving no clues about what he was thinking. But despite his stony facade, the tangible anger that emanated from him, Gwyneth sensed there was great unrest behind those devil's eyes of his, and that she had set something quite wonderful—and powerful—in motion.

Did Satan have a heart after all?

All too soon they arrived at a small, unkempt brick building within sight of the waterfront. The marquess raised his hand and grasped the iron knocker, nearly cracking the peeling wood of the door with the force of his blows.

"We're an hour early, Morninghall!" Gwyneth hissed in fierce protest.

"Good."

"Mr. Rothschild is unlikely to be expecting us!"

"I know."

The door swung open, and a wizened old man stood there, his expression surprised, then indignant. His shiny pate was as bald as an egg, speckled with liver spots and ringed by a fringe of yellow-white hair limp with grease. Spectacles perched on his bulbous red-veined nose, and his clothing was businesslike and well made. He might've looked benign, perhaps even grandfatherly, if not for the suspicious, trapped gleam in his cunning black eyes.

"M—my lord! I did not expect you 'til three—"

"Of course you didn't. Surprise, surprise, Roth-schild. Step aside or be knocked aside, it makes no damned difference to me."

"Morninghall!" Gwyneth gasped, shocked.

Ignoring her, he grasped her elbow and dragged her past the little man, who trailed them in high indignation.

"Really, my lord, I must protest! I object to this high-handed treatment! I am right in the middle of my lunch, the books aren't finished, I—I haven't finished adding up all the figures—"

"You mean, doctoring them? Pray, Rothschild, I

shall see them as they are. *Now.* And as for your lunch, finish it in the other room with my blessings. I'll call if I have need of you, which, by the way, I doubt."

"Sir, I *must* protest!"

"Protest all you like. In the meantime bring me the damned books, starting with January of this year, and be quick about it."

Bristling, his fists clenched with helpless rage, the contractor scurried off into another room. Gwyneth, shocked and embarrassed, turned her head to stare at the marquess. He had already taken a seat and was pulling a thick, black ledger out of his satchel. He looked up and caught her gaze.

She saw the impatience there, the unspoken challenge for her to protest. She sat down slowly. "I must say, Morninghall, I don't think much of your methods, but they most certainly yield results."

He merely opened his book and began flipping through the pages with businesslike efficiency. "Rothschild's reputation is as a cheat, a liar, and a knave. Soon, perhaps, you'll see why I wished to surprise him with our untimely arrival. Men like him need to be caught off guard."

He found the page he wanted, leaned back in his chair, and looked at her from across the table, his gaze flat as a viper's and just as unsettling. She found the quiet scrutiny unbearable.

"Must you gaze at me like that, Morninghall?"

"I'm just looking."

"It is *the manner* with which you're looking that I find most uncomfortable. If you're going to intimidate anyone, intimidate Rothschild, not me."

"Do I intimidate you?"

"I am not going to answer that."

He merely smiled, knowingly, and let his gaze slide heatedly down her throat . . . over her collarbone . . . to her breasts, which were tingling with fire beneath their bombazine shield.

"I mean it, Morninghall."

"Really, Lady Simms. Do you think I'm going to leap out of this chair and—" he lifted one wicked eyebrow *"ravish"* you?"

The very thought made her heart pound. She bent her head, her face hot as she fumbled through her reticule for her notebook. "I don't know what to think anymore, Morninghall. You're a man of many facades—and surprises." She remembered his strange wariness, his anger, when she had accused him of having a heart, and slapping her notebook on the table and leaning forward, she pressed her own attack to deflect his. *"I'm* still wondering about this sudden display of compassion on behalf of that boy."

He looked down at the ledger, casually flipping a page. "I told you, it was guilt, not compassion."

"You're not nearly as hard-hearted as you think you are. That boy proves it."

"Yes, and Satan was able to charm Eve before he brought about man's downfall too."

"Satan was once an angel of God."

"I am no angel."

"No, but you took pity on that boy, took him into your care, and here you sit, going through these tedious records and digging through pages of figures, and for what reason? Your conscience? This heart you say you don't have?"

"To get you out of my life," he snapped, growing angry.

"Try again, Morninghall. I don't believe you for a moment. I see a spark of goodness in you, and I'm going to do everything I can to fan it into a flame that consumes everything in its path."

She sat back, smiling with triumph, her arms folded smugly across her chest, her eyes bright beneath her prim little hat.

Damon looked up slowly, his hand stilled where he had been turning another page. He did not say a word, merely stared at her until her confident smile began to wane, her color faded, and she straightened up in the chair, wary now, her hands lowering to her lap as though she were poised to flee.

"What did you say?" he asked softly.

"I . . . I said that there is goodness in you and that—"

"*There* is *no good in me,*" he ground out with such malevolence that her eyes widened and she leaned backward, paling.

There isn't, he thought savagely, releasing her from his gaze and angrily turning the page. The very idea that there was made him feel uneasy, defenseless, afraid. Goodness drew people to you, made them want to see inside your soul, *be* inside your soul—an intimacy that sent threads of terror straight out to his fingertips. Intimacy made you vulnerable, and if you were vulnerable, people took advantage of you, humiliated you, hurt you. It was better to be diabolical and wicked and keep people at arm's length, and best to be so damned intimidating that no one would ever challenge you.

"Morninghall, I didn't mean to—"

"*I said, 'There is no damned good in me!'*" he snarled, furious now. He flipped another page, nearly ripping it from the binding. "There's nothing admirable, worthy, or lovable about me! My own damned mother knew it; she turned on me every time I wanted a hug, hurled wine bottles at me when I persisted! Every time people have been nice to me, they've turned on me, and despite that *pleasant* exchange in your garden, I know you're no different from any of the rest!"

She stared at him in shock. He didn't care. He realized he was breathing hard and fast, and he didn't care about that either. Another page nearly ripped as he turned it with violent force. How dare she assume he was something he was not? She could not see, could not *feel,* his darkness! She did not live in his devil's body with its charred, black heart, its constant yearnings for something to which he could not put a name, its paralyzing sense of despair, envy, fury, and self-hatred. She was light and he was dark. She was good and he was evil. The dark hated the light, hid from it, and there was nothing she could do to change that . . . nothing! Stupid female, she ought to flee, run as far and fast as she damn well could before it was too late for her!

She's getting too close, isn't she, old boy?

Fear rippled through him, cold and dark. He began to feel hot, shaky, sick.

Too close to what? He didn't know, didn't want to know. The core of him, probably. The darkness. Why else did he feel this unexplainable fury, just because she'd proclaimed him *good?* Fury, just because Billy had brought him some daffodils? It was the same violent anger he felt every time he saw the nauseating love and tenderness between a mother and her child, a pair of lovers, a boy and his dog, the same thing he felt every time he regarded something delicate and pretty and fragile: impotent rage. He didn't know what spawned it, but whatever it was, it was dark and ugly, and he was afraid to look at it too closely.

And if Lady Gwyneth Evans Simms ever figured out what it was—some deficiency within himself that Damon could not, would not, examine—he knew he'd be as vulnerable as a snake freshly shed of its skin.

Too late, he realized he was sweating, trembling, breathing too fast. Too late, he realized an attack was upon him, that he couldn't get enough air, and oh, God, there was the terrible gray tunnel, lingering on the perimeter of his vision. Dread coursed through him and, with it, nausea. *Oh, shit!* Not now, not with *her* here to witness his ultimate humiliation!

He jumped to his feet, gasping, his chair crashing back as he wiped his damp brow. Christ, he had to get out of here before the attack hit.

"Morninghall?"

"I've got to get outside—"

She caught his hand and held it down on the table,

misinterpreting the source of his agitation. "The depth of your self-hatred knows no bottom, does it, my lord?" she asked softly.

Shivering with flashes of heat and cold, suffocating and short of breath, Damon wanted only to run, to flee, before it was too late. A drop of sweat rolled down his temple, and beneath her cool palm he made a fist, trying desperately to regain control before everything exploded. There was the humming in his ears now, getting louder by the second, the fatal racing of his heart—

He raised his head and turned the full force of his stare on her in a last effort to save himself.

"Kindly remove your hand from mine, Lady Simms, or I will not be responsible for what I shall do to you."

She only looked at him—and did not let go.

Too late. The roaring crashed into his ears, cold sweat burst from every pore, and he saw the dizzying rush of the gray tunnel imploding on his vision.

God help me.

The attack struck.

Chapter 13

❦

"**M**y lord?"

He tore free of her and lunged blindly across the room, the panic chasing him, a thousand demons shrieking in his ears, strangling him, dimming his vision, yanking his soul from his body and spinning it round and round above his head. *I'm going mad!* he thought. He saw Lady Simms's horrified face, Rothschild running from the back room, sunlight and shadows, the door. *I must reach the door!*

He never made it. He collapsed, the floor smashing into his hip, the plastered wall against his shoulder and cheek. As he lay there, propped against the wall, gasping, shaking, dying, he heard Lady Simms come running across the room, smelled peaches as she fell to her knees beside him.

"Get out of here, Rothschild! Fetch a doctor!"

Her hand gripped Damon's shoulder.

"It's all right, Morninghall," she said firmly, her face close to his, her voice sounding as though it came from a hundred miles away. He made a strangled noise, unable to breathe, his body shaking violently. Her hand was cool against his brow, smoothing his hair, and through the thundering pound of his heartbeat, through his half-closed, staring eyes, he saw her green dress and knew it was the last thing on earth his eyes would ever behold.

"I'm dying"—*gasp*—"I'm dying"—*gasp*—"help me, I'm dying—dying—dying...." He heard only

his own rapid panting, felt only terror as death came
whooshing in from all sides, reducing him to a
whimpering, helpless animal cowering against the
wall. Shuddering convulsively, he shut his eyes and
pressed himself against the plaster, each deafening thump of his racing heart, each gulping breath
of air surely his last. Oh, God, he couldn't breathe.
Help me—

"Please, hold me," he wheezed, too terrified to be
ashamed. "Please . . . I'm dying. . . . Hold me."

"You're going to be all right." Her voice came in
undulating waves from far away, scared, shaky, desperate. *"Don't just stand there, Rothschild, get a
doctor!"*

"Hold me." His breath was roaring through his
lungs, yet still he couldn't get air. *"Please . . ."*

White with horror, Gwyneth knelt close to the
stricken marquess and, without hesitation, put her
arms around his heaving shoulders. The violent tem-
po of his breathing bounced her up and down. Great,
rippling shudders racked his powerful frame, and his
shirt was hot and damp beneath her cheek. She
looked up at his head resting against the plaster wall,
the beads of sweat rolling down his flushed brow. His
eyes were half shut, and through the veil of his lashes,
she saw they were wild and glassy.

"Why now . . . why now, of all places? . . ." he
murmured.

She sat down on the floor with him, managing to
pull him away from the wall and up against her body.
He turned his face into her chest, his hot breath
blasting the swell of her breasts, the violent shuddering tearing through his body with merciless cruelty as
she held him close.

"Damon." Her voice was gentle yet firm.

He turned his face to the side, his ear against her
breastbone, trying to draw breath. "Hold me,
madam—please—don't leave me. Oh, *damnation,*
this is so bloody humiliating—so—so—"

"Calm down," she said, stroking his hair and holding him close against her breast. "You're not dying. You're *not dying,* Damon. Do you hear me? You're not dying! Now take deep breaths. Slow, deep breaths, in through your nose, out through your mouth."

"I can't—can't breathe—dying—"

"Deep breaths, Damon. I have you. You're not going to die."

He tried, but his lungs were already starved for air, pumping madly, and he could only gasp helplessly. Then, on a last, defeated exhalation, he sagged in her arms, his weight nearly sending her over backward.

For one terrible moment Gwyneth thought he was dead—until she realized he was still breathing, softly and calmly. The short, rapid gasps had leveled out and returned to normal.

It hit her then. *Just like Morganna.*

The door opened and Rothschild was there. She hadn't even heard him run out.

He came sheepishly forward. "I couldn't find a doctor, m'lady."

"Never mind. I think he's going to be all right now."

"What's wrong with him?"

"I don't know."

"Too damned highbred, if you ask me. High-strung. All that inbreeding and blue blood, no wonder he had a fit."

"I don't think it was a fit, Mr. Rothschild." It occurred to Gwyneth that it was quite improper to be sitting here on the floor with the prone body of the Marquess of Morninghall in her arms, but she didn't care, for her memory was reaching back over the years . . . reaching back to her little sister. Morganna had been terrified of thunderstorms, and whenever one had rolled in over the hills, she had displayed the same behavior just exhibited by the marquess. The sweating, the shakes, the blind terror, the utter conviction that they were dying, the out-of-control breathing until unconsciousness restored everything to normal—yes, the symptoms were exactly the same.

"What do you think it was then?" Rothschild asked, squatting well away from Morninghall, as though he feared contamination.

Gwyneth smiled and stroked the marquess's hair, caught up in those long-ago memories.

"My little sister used to get them," she said softly. "The doctor never did figure out where they came from." A long moment went by, the ticking of a shelf clock the only sound. "But I did."

Consciousness came back to him by degrees, nudging his brain awake with a varied offering of scents: the sweetness of fresh peaches . . . beeswax . . . the faint pungency of his own sweat . . . the damp mustiness of an old room. He became aware of the floor beneath his thigh and legs, of fabric and warm flesh against his cheek, a heartbeat beneath his ear, and somebody's arms wrapped around his shoulders.

His heart was no longer racing. He could breathe.

Slowly, dazedly, Damon opened his eyes.

The first thing he saw was Rothschild, squatting on his heels, staring at him. The second thing he saw was a green bombazine sleeve two inches from his nose—and suddenly he knew just who was holding him.

Lady Gwyneth Evans Simms.

Mortification blazed through him. He remembered his shameless, childish pleas just before he had passed out, remembered how pitifully he had begged to be held. God help him, he had never been so embarrassed, so utterly, crushingly *humiliated* in all his cursed life.

Realizing he was awake, she relaxed her hold on him. "Are you all right now, Morninghall?"

Her voice was full of pity, compassion, feeling, tenderness—enough to send him fleeing from it and straight into another attack.

"Christ. Bloody hell. *Damnation.*" He pushed her

arm aside and shoved himself out of her embrace, driving his fists into his eye sockets as if to obliterate the memory of what had just happened to him—and how he had reacted. He could not look at her, could not face her, after the attack had reduced him to a groveling, terrified child. Gone was the image she might have had of him, of a man of strength, intelligence, sanity. She had seen him for what he was: a lunatic, a madman, a coward.

He lurched to his feet, pushing a fist against his clammy brow, and on unsteady legs reeled his way back to the table. The ledger lay just as he had left it. A stack of leather-bound books, which Rothschild must've dumped there as the attack had struck, made a haphazard pile beside it. He threw himself down in the chair, his brow bent and resting in one palm, his eyes on the page so that he wouldn't have to look at either of them.

The expectant silence was unbearable. Neither one of them had moved, and he could feel them both staring at him.

Hold me . . . please . . . I'm dying.

Christ, he wanted to die, wished he *had* died, if only to escape this humiliation.

Go ahead, laugh at me. Laugh at me for my weakness. Ridicule me, I dare you!

But she wasn't laughing. She hadn't laughed at all.

He turned the page, blind to the writing before him. A moment went by, then he heard the rustle of her skirts as she got to her feet and moved across the room, toward him. She pulled out her chair. It made a faint scraping noise, a sound amplified a hundred times in the awkward silence. He stared down at the page with what he hoped was calm insouciance, his face burning.

And Rothschild, that miserable wretch—Damon jerked his head up and saw the contractor standing in a corner, his expression a mixture of scorn, malice, and fear.

"Go on, get the hell out of here!" he roared, lunging

half out of his chair and shooing the contractor off with a violent motion of his hands.

The old man fled.

Damon sank back down into the chair and raked his hands down his face. Lady Simms sat quietly across from him, not saying a word. Unable to stand it any longer, he looked up and impaled her with a stare hot enough to melt rock. "I suppose you think me a raving madman now, don't you?"

She only sat looking at him quietly. There was no mockery in her eyes, no ridicule, no fear, nothing but tenderness. For some reason that was more frightening, more awful, than any emotion that soft violet gaze might've conveyed.

She took a great, bracing sigh. Then, as though the incident had never happened, she pulled one of Rothschild's books toward her and calmly opened it. "Right. Shall we start with January?"

Midshipman Foyle didn't get any respect. He didn't get it from the prisoners, he didn't get it from the other midshipmen who served on Portsmouth's *real* naval ships, he certainly didn't get it from that fire-breathing bastard of a captain, Morninghall.

Earlier in the week Morninghall had found out that he and Radley had been lying to him about the conditions below, and the marquess's rage had been of the sort that Foyle never wished to experience ever again. He dreaded to think what would happen if the captain found out that he, in partnership with Radley, was stealing food and clothes from the shipments meant for the prisoners and selling them back to the contractors for a profit.

His eyes swept contemptuously over a group of prisoners scrubbing the deck. He didn't see why the captain suddenly had decided to care so much about them. They were only prisoners; they didn't count for anything, except as something on which to take out one's anger. Oh, yes, they were definitely good for that. Who would know if he withheld the food of some wretch who'd given him a dirty look? Who'd know if he cracked a rib with his musket because one of them had failed to get out of his way? Not Morninghall, and it was all the better when that arrogant tyrant was off the ship, because then he could bully and threaten to his heart's content, swaggering up and down the quarterdeck, hands behind his back, chest puffed out against his uniform as he surveyed his command.

In Morninghall's absence his word was law among these wretched masses.

Except this morning, Morninghall—who had never bothered to go belowdecks before—had caught him tormenting one of the French prisoners, an old man with a peg leg who'd needed to be shown who was boss.

Given Morninghall's apathy toward the prisoners, Foyle hadn't expected to be punished, but Morninghall had shown no sympathy. Grabbing Foyle by the ear, he had marched him topside, and there, in front of all the other midshipmen, the marines, the sailors, and, yes, even the prisoners, given him such a fierce dressing-down that Foyle's ears were still ringing.

Foyle directed a baleful glance at the empty cabin. His Lordship had gone ashore, and it was no secret he was checking Rothschild's records against the ship's. Foyle dreaded his return, because if he found the discrepancies, heads were going to roll.

And two of those heads would be his and Radley's.

Cold sweat ran down his back, but at least he now had an ally, Admiral Bolton. Fit to be tied, the port admiral had come aboard first thing that morning, marching straight to Morninghall's cabin, shutting himself inside, and hopefully giving the bloody nob the lecture he so richly deserved. Five minutes had passed. Ten. Then the door had banged open and Admiral Bolton, red-faced and furious, had emerged. Immediately spying Foyle, he had called him aside.

"Ah, Mr. Foyle." Admiral Bolton had beckoned him with a fatherly arm. "Walk with me for a moment, will you?"

"Yes, sir," Foyle had murmured, awed and flattered. "Of course."

The admiral had drawn him well away from everyone. It had taken a few minutes for his color to return to normal, but when he spoke, his voice was calm and friendly. "I couldn't help noticing that your captain gave you a good drubbing this morning, Foyle. What was that all about?"

Foyle had swallowed nervously. "I was late for my watch, sir," he'd lied. "But it wasn't *my* fault. The captain had me scrubbing latrines and nobody told me what time it was—"

"Scrubbing *latrines?* That's a pretty damned humiliating task for a young and promising officer like yourself, isn't it?"

"Yes sir. *Very* humiliating." That part of it was true at least. Morninghall *had* forced him to clean the prisoners' toilets, probably as punishment for letting them get so bad in the first place.

"And reprimanding you in front of your peers. I can just imagine how embarrassed and angry that must've made you feel."

"Yes, especially as I didn't deserve to be punished in the first place. But I'm always getting blamed for things that aren't my fault, sir, things I didn't do."

"It's terrible when you find yourself with a cruel son of a bitch for a captain, isn't it? I bet you'd just love to be transferred off this miserable hulk, away from that tyrant and onto a *real* ship."

"A frigate, sir?" he'd asked hopefully.

"Hell, why not?" The admiral had rested his arm on Foyle's suddenly proud and eager shoulders, just as a father or best friend might've done, and guided him to the rail. The fact that all the other midshipmen had been watching from some distance away, green with envy over the attention he was getting from one so powerful, had done much to take the sting and humiliation out of Morninghall's earlier dressing-down. At last the admiral had spoken, his eyes fixed on a distant point somewhere in the harbor. "You know, Mr. Foyle, there could be some . . . *financial reward,* let alone that transfer for you, if you play your cards right. Only thing standing in your way, my boy, is that damned Morninghall."

Foyle had swallowed hard, not daring to speak.

Bolton had still been gazing over the harbor. "What happened to that last captain? Ah, yes, prisoner uprising. Got to watch those prisoners. One spark and they go off like a keg of gunpowder."

"Yes, sir . . . we have several wretches aboard who are all too ready to start trouble," Foyle had said, fidgeting with sudden understanding and excitement.

"Hate Morninghall as much as you do, do they?"

"Yes, sir, just as much."

"Well, boy, only you know what you want out of life. Transfer, that frigate, a bit of money on the side . . . ah, never mind. Just the ravings of an old man, pay them no heed. . . ."

Pay them no heed, but the look in the admiral's eyes had bade him to do just the opposite.

Admiral Bolton—for reasons most likely connected to the outcome of a recent duel, Foyle thought wryly—very clearly wanted the Marquess of Morninghall dead, and was willing to pay highly to ensure the deed got done. Foyle knew well how to accomplish what the old man wanted, in a way that could never be traced to either the admiral or himself.

Now, as he made another stately turn about the deck, Foyle paused and, inclining his head, motioned to one of the guards.

"Wilson?"

"Sir?"

"Bring me that Frog prisoner, Armand Moret, up from below. The one who's been making all the trouble. I understand he's been inciting the savages, and it's time someone of authority had a *word* with him."

Wilson brightened. None of them liked Moret.

"Aye, sir!" he said, his boots echoing on the deck as he hurried off to find the Frenchman.

Foyle turned and resumed his slow pacing of the deck, smiling.

If he closed his eyes, he could almost see that frigate Bolton had promised.

Chapter 14

⌒⟨᥆᥆⟩⌒

The next two hours passed in uncomfortable silence, with Gwyneth taking notes and Morninghall, the ship's ledger at his left hand, Rothschild's records at his right, saying no more than he had to as he waded through five months of figures.

His face was as hard as a wall of flint, his eyes glittering with shame and anger. It was obvious his attack had severely compromised his pride, and Gwyneth knew that only a fool would open her mouth and make mention of it. To do so would be fatal—and she happened to value her life.

Instead she put on a businesslike face and made a note of each discrepancy His Lordship found, wishing she could fix her mind on her task instead of on the way his hair tumbled over his brow, sticking up through his splayed fingers as he rested his forehead in his hand. All through this silent scrutiny a niggling little voice was making itself known in her mind. Morninghall was not such an evil man after all. A baffling one, yes. A potentially violent one, yes. An arrogant, intimidating, enigmatic, moody one, yes. But not evil. No man who took pity on a suffering child was evil.

She silently watched his finger moving down a column of figures. What a lot she had learned about him this afternoon. . . .

She'd learned that he did indeed have both a heart

and a soul and, for some strange reason, was fiercely
reluctant to admit he had either.

She'd learned that, when he felt threatened, he had
the same kind of reaction Morganna used to get when
frightened by thunderstorms.

And she'd finally admitted to herself that she was
madly in lust with him, maybe even starting to *like*
him.

For despite everything, he seemed to value her
brain as much as he professed to want her body.
These ledgers alone were proof of that. Since the two
of them had been sitting here, he'd asked her opinions, trusted and encouraged her input. William
never would have let her help like this; William, dear
as he was, simply would have indulged her, patted her
on the head, and, with a smile, told her to leave such
things to him.

Gwyneth swallowed, feeling a sudden pang. Although the very air cracked and simmered around
him, she wanted nothing more than to get up, go
behind his chair, and thank him for treating her as an
equal. She wanted to put her arms around him, tell
him he had no need to be embarrassed or ashamed
about the attack, no need to hide behind a facade of
ice or to think she was so cruel she would ridicule
him.

But he would not thank her for doing such a thing.
He was a man—magnificent and, yes, dangerous—
and men did, after all, have their pride. It was
better—and safer—to keep silent . . . for now.

Still, it was all becoming clear. She'd been fooled—
at first—by that satanic face, that malevolent arrogance, that sinister, lethal grace that defined his every
move. Now she was beginning to suspect the reasons
Morninghall behaved as he did, the reasons he kept
everyone at a safe distance. She thought about what
he'd said about his mother, how she'd hurt him, let
him down. She thought about how the navy had done
very much the same thing. Who could blame the man
for refusing to let anyone near him, when everyone

and everything he'd tried to trust in his life had failed him?

Not an evil man, after all.

Rothschild, however, was not so perceptive. His waxy face was a study in dread as he cowered in a nearby chair, understandably terrified of Morninghall. As well he ought to be, Gwyneth thought on a note of private glee, as she saw the marquess slowly straighten up, his dark brows drawing together and his lips going tight once more.

"Rothschild," he said in a hard, flat voice without looking up.

"M—my lord?"

"It seems that a shipment of clothing was sent to the hulk on the twenty-first of February. Your records also show you were paid for this shipment in full. Correct me if I am wrong."

"That is so," the contractor said nervously.

Morninghall turned another page but still did not look up. "Then why is it," he murmured with frightening calm, "that when I consult the records in *my* possession, it becomes apparent that this order was never, in fact, delivered?"

Cold, slate-blue eyes lifted and locked on the contractor's, and Gwyneth suppressed a shiver of admiration.

"Are you daring to suggest that I—that I cheated the navy, sir, and kept the money for myself?"

"I am." The flat, lethal stare did not waver.

Rothschild went red under that malevolent scrutiny. He leaned forward, his knuckles whitening on the arms of his chair. "S-surely there must be a mistake. Perhaps *your* records are incorrect, my lord, as I distinctly recall making that shipment. In fact, I remember it as well as I remember what I ate for breakfast yesterday."

Morninghall only fixed the cowering man with an icy glare and, circling something with his pencil, continued on.

"Interesting, how a whole shipment of clothing

could just . . . disappear," he murmured, his left fore-finger whispering down a column of the hulk's figures, his right hand holding a quill pen and matching each entry against Rothschild's. Gwyneth watched his eyes moving beneath his long lashes as he worked, noted the banked anger that was creeping into the previously flat tone of his voice and his misleadingly detached expression. "Isn't it, Rothschild?"

The contractor's brow beaded with sweat; his Adam's apple shot out of his cravat. He gripped the arms of his chair, looking as though he were about to flee.

Finally the marquess let out a controlled, ominous sigh, carefully laid the quill down on the table, and idly studied his perfectly manicured fingernails.

"It would seem that you have sent clothing to the prison ship that never arrived—"

Rothschild leaped to his feet. "There was a mistake in the bookkeeping. I'd never do such a thing!"

"—sent other shipments that were not only partials, and of inferior quality—"

"I'm telling you, my lord, there *must* be some mistake!"

"—and here, on the twenty-third of April, even sent an entire order of shoes to the prison hulk, all of which were one size and all of which"—the marquess lost interest in his hand and, looking up, turned his glacial stare on the cowering contractor—"were designed to fit the *left foot only.*"

Rothschild's face drained of color and his eyes darted from side to side, like a cornered animal. He looked to Gwyneth for help, but she only shook her head and gazed at him with sadness and accusation.

Morninghall was relentless. "I'm sure they were a most *comfortable* fit, weren't they, Rothschild?" His tone was dangerously soft, crackling with undercurrents of threat and violence.

Rothschild's face contorted. He made to back away, but the marquess was slowly getting to his feet, his great height towering over the wizened old buzzard, his eyes completely devoid of soul, pity, or mercy.

Rothschild shrank backward, cowering against the wall and staring up at the marquess as he advanced.

"Damon?"

Gwyneth's voice broke the spell, and slowly he turned to look at her. His eyes burned with fury; his stance was rigid with rage. He was angry— beautifully, wonderfully, magnificently angry—*and it was about time.*

"Don't," she said quietly.

His nostrils flared, and she saw the gold flecks glittering in his wintry irises.

"I need you, Damon," she murmured, again using his Christian name and intently holding his gaze. "The prisoners need you. If they put you in gaol for murder, neither of us will accomplish anything."

Her quiet, steady voice seemed to have the right effect. The marquess stared flatly at Rothschild for another long moment; then, a blood vessel throbbing in his temple, he turned, gathered up all of the ledgers, and pulled Gwyneth up from her chair.

"Let's go."

Rothschild exploded in outrage. "You can't take those! Those are *my* property!"

Desperate, the contractor threw himself in front of the door. Without missing a beat, Morninghall bore down on him, crunched his lapels in his fist, and tossed the man aside like so much garbage.

"Find yourself a solicitor, Rothschild, because you're damned well going to need one."

Gwyneth, hot on his heels, was hard pressed to contain her unladylike whoop of triumph. She knew that Morninghall's tightly coiled anger had been building since his attack, and she could only hope the fury that made the air crackle around him was not simply because he'd found a release for that anger, but because she had finally awakened him, truly *awakened* him, to the treachery and horror the prisoners under his care were forced to endure. Was he fueled by guilt over all that he hadn't seen before? Had the tour belowdecks, the suffering in Toby Ashton's eyes, and, now, blatant evidence of the corruption that permeated the contractors' community finally turned that malevolent energy that was so much a part of him toward something noble and good?

God help them all: the devil was out for blood. Things would be happening at last.

It was nearly dark by the time Damon, with Lady Simms still in tow, managed to track down Bolton at a gathering of senior naval officers at the George Inn—where he rudely upset the assembly and made a formal complaint about the discrepancies he had found between the contractor's and the ship's records. Then, leaving the smoky room in an uproar, he dragged Lady Simms back out into the street and blindly made his way toward the waterfront.

"You were magnificent, Morninghall," she was saying happily. "I knew you'd come around to the right way of thinking, if only your eyes were opened."

Something exploded inside of him. "Spare me the hero worship, madam, and don't deceive yourself into thinking I'm anything I'm not. I'm doing this only to get you out of my hair, out of my life."

"Of course you are, my lord."

Her blithe tone made him all the more furious. How dare she try to paint him as some angel! He was savage and awful, and he didn't give a damn about anything except getting back to his cabin, slamming the door shut, and drinking himself into oblivion.

Why am I so goddamned angry?

It was the attack; it had to be. It hung between them like a gangrenous stench, and *she* was either too polite or—more likely—too scared to bring it up. And he sure as hell wouldn't. But his secret was out now, and as he'd spent these past hours waiting for her to open her mouth and mention it, to confirm that he was indeed as barking mad as his mother before him, he had felt the tension and the fury building.

And building.

But she hadn't said a word.

Christ, he still wanted to—to ravage her, to destroy her before she could destroy him.

He glanced down at her, walking so trustingly beside him, and hated her all the more for her blind faith that he wouldn't lay a finger on her. He hated himself too. She thought him compassionate, did she? She thought he had a heart? If only she knew that, at this very moment, he was one step away from throwing her into some shadowy doorway, ripping the clothes off her back, and driving his seed home just to prove he wasn't as damned compassionate as she thought. Kind and good, eh? She'd be singing a different tune, indeed, when he was finished with her.

But that was the problem, wasn't it? Despite his fury, his so-called hatred for her, he didn't *want* to finish with her. For here it was, ten o'clock and nearly dark, and the last thing on earth Damon wanted to do was bring her back to her little house in town, part company with her, and once again be left standing outside in the dark.

Alone.

The very word sent a current of anxiety humming through his blood. It was as if there was something awful living in his body and he was trapped inside his own skin with it, with no way out. He told himself his sudden jitters had nothing to do with fear. They had everything to do with loneliness and that he suddenly found the idea of parting from her . . .

Painful.

"My lord?" She jolted him from his thoughts.

He looked about him, temporarily disoriented. They stood on a quiet street in the dark, lantern light spilling from a window overhead, a gentle breeze fluttering the sleeves of her gown and carrying with it the sound of laughter and revelry from a distant tavern. Out in the harbor, just visible through an alleyway, anchored ships threw dancing patterns of light upon the black water. When had it grown so dark? How the devil had they gotten here? He had no idea what route their feet had taken, no recollection of so much time passing, nothing.

"It's late, Morninghall," she said, squeezing her arms over her chest in the chill night air. "My sister will be worried about me."

He looked away, selfishly reluctant to let her go, hating himself for this sudden—*dependence* on her. Still, the attack lay heavily between them, and he knew he needed to say something about it, maybe even thank her for—*oh, God*—holding him. But he couldn't, so instead he set his jaw and stood there, kicking at a loose cobblestone, delaying the inevitable.

"Any gentleman would walk me home, you know."

"If you're looking for a gentleman, you've made a damned poor choice." He kicked harder at the stone, trying to contain the writhing knot of emotion within his chest. "I'm hardly a suitable escort."

"You're not a madman, Damon. Stop tormenting yourself."

"No? Then what the hell is wrong with me?" he shouted. "You stand there and tell me I'm not going to end up in a damned asylum just like my mother, you tell me my mind isn't coming unhinged, you tell me there's nothing mortally wrong with my brain—"

"It's late, Damon. And I'll tell you no such thing, because I don't believe any of it. Let's go."

Maddened by her quiet patience, he seized her elbow and leaned down into her face, preventing her escape. "If only you knew what I want to do to you right now. If only you knew how I want to throw you down, right here in the street, and drive myself into you until you're screaming for mercy—"

She only looked at him, unfazed, unconcerned, infuriatingly unworried. Such a reaction shook him to the core and he saw red, wanting only to shake her until her teeth fell out, to crush her against the brick building behind her and slam himself into her again and again until he roused some iota of respect for his anger, some smattering of fear, loathing, *anything*—

He spun away, driving the heel of his hand against his brow, baring his teeth, and clenching his eyes shut with the effort it took to control his violent impulses. He turned his face heavenward, his chest rising and falling as he tried to steady his breathing.

A moment went by, then he felt her hand, that achingly sweet little hand, tucking itself into the crook of his elbow. "Come, let us walk," she said gently.

He exhaled sharply and, with a curse, allowed her to lead him along. God, his head felt as if it were going to explode. He didn't want her to talk about his attack, yet he was furious that she wouldn't. He hated her, yet he wanted her more than he'd ever wanted anything in his life. He feared her, desired her, thought he'd very well kill any man who dared look twice at her, and here she was, expecting him to walk her home, as though he were a—a goddamned *gentleman* or something. Didn't she know the only one from whom she needed protection was *him?*

They walked in silence, neither speaking, their footsteps echoing against the buildings on either side of the street. For Damon every step was an exercise in control. It took everything he had to will his face into its comfortable facade of stone, all his strength to calm the frenzied emotion that was spinning inside his head. Eventually he began to notice the kiss of the night wind on his cheek, the coolness of the air, the faint scent that still clung to the woman who walked so trustingly beside him. Fresh peaches: he wondered if it was perfume or bath soap. He wondered if she knew he was homing in on it as a bee to a flower. He wondered what she would look like in the bath, that creamy, peachy bar sliding over her wet and glistening body, oozing great frothy bubbles down her arms, her legs, between her generous breasts, as candlelight played over her silken, dripping skin. . . .

"You are not safe with me," he said at last, his voice hoarse with strain.

"Really? I beg to differ, Morninghall, for you have brought me home safely. See? There is my house just ahead. Truly you have proved yourself to be a most admirable escort."

And she was right. There were her stairs with their wrought-iron railing, their pots of pretty flowers, shining softly beneath the glow of an upstairs lamp.

It was time to let her go.

His heart started tripping in his breast.

They stood together for a long, awkward moment, neither saying a word. He looked at her, looked away, didn't want the evening to end. Finally she sighed and pulled her fingers from his elbow.

The night was deadly quiet around them.

"My little sister, Morganna, used to have attacks just like yours whenever a thunderstorm hit," she said softly, almost to herself. "She used to run screaming from the room, fall into the sweats and shakes, and hide under the bed until it passed."

Damon swallowed hard and looked down at the light pooling across the cobblestones. "And . . . did *she* end up in a madhouse?"

"No, she ended up married to a wonderful man who loves her and worships the ground she walks on. And do you know something, Morninghall?"

"What?"

She paused, a little smile of encouragement on her lips, her voice dropping to a secretive whisper. "She's no longer afraid of thunderstorms."

He glanced up at her. Stray light made tiny stars in her eyes, and her mouth was curved in a shy smile. There was nothing severe or militant in that open face. It was girlish, charming, and tilted in that coy angle most women adopted when they wanted to be kissed.

Absurd, of course. She hated him.

Annoyed at the ridiculous wanderings of his mind, he caught his hands behind his back so that he couldn't touch her.

"Good night, Lady Simms."

The smile faltered. "Good night, Lord Morning-hall."

He turned abruptly and stalked off into the darkness, painfully alone, a shadow that cleaved itself to the night and was soon gone. He never knew that she stood out there in the quiet street for a long time, the lonely breeze ruffling her skirts, her heart aching with longing as she stared into the darkness after him.

And he never knew he had misinterpreted the hopeful tilt of her cheek, after all.

Her heart heavy, Gwyneth picked up her skirts and went into the house.

Chapter 15

"Nathan Ashton. It has to be Nathan next, no
question about it."

The three men and the woman disguised as a man
sat in a corner of the Thirsty Whale Tavern, well away
from the massive stone fireplace around which most
of the hard-drinking sailors, soldiers, and other row-
dies were carousing. It was quieter here, less smoky,
and although the sort who frequented the Whale were
not officers—and thus were less likely to care very
much about the four who kept to themselves in the
corner—it was still best to practice caution, especially where Connor Merrick was concerned. Recog-
nition could be fatal for him.

A lantern, its glass globe hazed with grease and
smoke, stood on the table before them, glowing orange against their faces. An ale sat before the Reverend Peter Milford; Connor Merrick and Orla
O'Shaughnessy were both drinking rum; and a glass of
very expensive port—or what was left of it, that is—
was beside the wrist of their leader, subtly resplendent
in a loose white shirt tucked into snug-fitting
breeches. At the moment his fingers were drumming
an agitated tattoo on the table. The decision that
Nathan had to be the next one out was unanimous,
but how the rescue would be performed was, as it
frequently was, the cause of much debate.

"I don't know, man, the idea sounds awfully
damned bold," Connor was saying, shaking his head

and pouring more rum into his mug. "I still think we ought to smuggle him out in a water cask."

"I agree," Peter said stubbornly. "It's far safer."

Orla shot a glance to their leader, who was unconvinced.

"The devil take it, we're talking about life or death rescues!" he said fiercely, pushing his hair off his brow in exasperation. He leaned forward, nailing each of them in turn with his gaze. "None of this is *safe*."

Silence followed, despite the noisy din across the room. Peter was troubled, reluctant to try anything so unorthodox. Orla's winged eyebrows were drawn in a slight frown, as though she needed a bit more convincing. Only Connor, possessed of a recklessness that knew no limits, was willing to hear the plan out. He pulled his felt hat down low to conceal his chestnut curls and leaned over the table. "All right then, I'm all ears."

"Peter?"

The chaplain was shooting discreet glances at Orla and needed to be jarred back to attention. "Yes, yes, do go on. I'm listening too."

"Orla?"

She made the pretense of adjusting her chair, unobtrusively moving it a few inches closer to the chaplain's. "Aye, I'm game for anything."

"Right." Their leader sipped his port and, casting a quick glance over his shoulder, leaned forward over the table, looking to each person in turn. His companions leaned close as well. "Here are the details," he murmured and briefly outlined the rescue plan. A few bribed guards, a short talk with the prisoner, a bit of deception, and, as he told them, it couldn't fail.

"I think it's damned brilliant," Connor said, his eyes gleaming.

"I think it's rather amusing," Orla added, looking to the chaplain.

"I think it'd be cruel to the boy."

"Oh, for God's sake, Peter!"

"This'll kill him. I cannot condone this, I'm sorry."

Their leader, frustrated, shot another glance over his shoulder and leaned low over the table, his face dark and intent. "That boy won't leave the hulk until his brother is either dead or escapes. Do you have a better idea?"

Peter swallowed hard, but his jaw was stubbornly set. He looked away, struggling with his conscience.

A tense silence ensued. Finally Orla reached out and very slowly laid her fingers over the chaplain's wrist. He turned his face to hers, his eyes filled with pain, indecision, and—as he glanced down at that fine hand—the beginnings of gentle love.

"The boy will be fine," she murmured, squeezing his hand and giving an encouraging little smile. "We'll tell him of the deception as soon as we've rescued him as well, and it's therefore safe to do so. Right, Con?"

The captain grinned. "Right."

On the second week of his employment for the Marquess of Morninghall, Toby entered that man's cabin to clear his breakfast away and was stopped by the nobleman's cold words before he could even begin the task.

"Sit down."

Instantly suspicious, Toby did so, gazing warily across the table at his superior and keeping his hands steepled between his knees.

"Have some toast, Toby."

"I'm not hungry, sir."

"Have it anyhow."

"I don't want any. Besides, I don't see *you* eating it."

The marquess thinned his mouth and shot him an irate glare, but said no more on the subject. He had been tense and in a visibly savage mood ever since the Black Wolf—*Connor!*, Toby reminded himself on a note of secret pride—had rescued Jed, and Bolton's subsequent visit had not helped matters one bit. Somewhat nervously, Toby sat waiting for what was to follow.

The marquess shoved his unfinished plate away, the

eggs cold in their thin, buttery juice, the fried pork hacked to uneaten shreds, only the toast and marmalade sampled and the latter, Toby noted, quite generously. The pot had been full when he'd brought it in with the breakfast tray a half hour ago; now it was nearly empty, and Toby wondered idly if Morninghall had just dipped his spoon into the stuff and eaten it like candy.

He didn't have time to wonder any longer, for the marquess cleared his throat and got straight down to business.

"I have decided to . . . relax your brother's incarceration in the Black Hole," he announced flatly, his tone inviting neither curiosity nor gratitude. A note had come for him earlier, which Toby had brought in with his breakfast, and it lay folded beside his right hand. Morninghall looked at it as he might a spider that had crawled across his plate, then picked it up and began to tap it with faint agitation against the table linen before finally tossing it aside and impaling Toby with his devil's stare. "You will not say a word about this to the other prisoners, lest they see this as an example of laxity and I am paid for my . . . *generosity* with a damned mutiny. Is that understood?"

Toby was reeling from the marquess's words. He leaned forward, his hands pressed between his knees, afraid even to hope. "But—you mean—you're actually going to let Nathan out of the Hole?"

"I am. You may visit him this afternoon, immediately following his release. After that time he will be sent to the hospital ship, as his condition will no doubt require medical attention."

Confused and ignoring the warning in those flat, soulless eyes, Toby blurted, "Why are you doing this?"

"Because it pleases me."

"But—"

"I *said,* 'Because it pleases me.' Hold your tongue lest I change my mind."

Tony shrank back behind the vase of purple lilacs he'd brought in with breakfast and bowed his head. He squirmed and fidgeted, so excited he couldn't keep still.

"You're kinder than your reputation allows, sir."

"A pity," the marquess said acidly, "because kindness has nothing to do with it." He watched Toby for a moment from beneath hooded lids, the silent, unnerving scrutiny making Toby feel like a sapling stripped of its bark. Then, wordlessly, Morninghall got to his feet, moved in that fluid, sinister grace of his across his cabin, and, pulling out a desk drawer, produced a small leather bag. He tossed it onto the table.

"Your wages for the week."

Toby picked up the bag and held it tightly against his chest, thinking only of how it might aid Nathan. "Thanks," he murmured, his eyes downcast.

"Don't thank me. You bloody well earned it. Now go, and take these damned plates with you. My appetite is shot to hell this morning."

Grateful to escape the marquess's moody presence, Toby swiftly gathered up the plates, the condiments, the silverware, piling them onto the tray with a faint clatter. But when he reached for the vase of flowers Radley had told him he must always bring to the captain, Morninghall's hand struck like a cobra, seizing Toby's wrist in a hard, punishing grip.

Toby froze.

"Leave them," the marquess said tightly—and released him.

Toby stared up at him. Then, rubbing his wrist, he grabbed the tray and rushed from the room.

Damon sank back into his chair with a pent-up sigh, his heart pounding in his ears, his nerves buzzing. He opened his eyes and found himself staring at the lilacs, sitting innocently in the vase within striking distance of his fist. Then, like the workings of some great piece of machinery that has finally called it quits for the day, he felt the endless churning inside of him come grinding to a halt.

Silence.

Deep, throbbing silence.

Nothing but him—and the flowers.

He swallowed hard and stared at the fragile little blossoms, each one an individual, each one exquisitely formed, each one wreathed in scent. He stared at the soft, cloudy masses of color. He stared at the crisp, waxy leaves.

He waited for the rage to come, that blind, overwhelming rage that hated beauty and loathed fragility, that frenzied rage that would make him smash the flowers beneath his fist until he'd obliterated them into a sad pile of nothingness.

But the rage didn't come.

Nothing came except this—this—sudden overwhelming *emotion,* this sense of raw sentiment expanding in his breast, shattering the paralysis there until he thought his heart would burst with the intensity of it.

Christ, what was happening to him? Confused and shaken, the wicked, diabolical Marquess of Morninghall put his head in his hands and, for the first time since he was a child locked into a bedchamber that terrified him, wept—without knowing why.

Toby held his breath for as long as he could as he descended into the choking gloom belowdecks. Morninghall had forbidden him to say a word about Nathan's release to the other prisoners, but he hadn't said he couldn't tell Nathan! He managed to hold his breath until he reached the orlop deck; there it finally burst from his lungs, and the subsequent inhalation of pungent fumes nearly made him vomit.

He steadied himself, got his bearings, and, pressing a hand to his pocket to ensure that his little bag of wages was still there, darted through the milling masses.

They spotted him instantly.

"Ah, look, if it isn't *le capitaine*'s favorite! Run, run, little *garcon,* before we spit on you!"

"We'll do more than spit on him, eh?"

A fist flashed toward his face, but he ducked and evaded the blow. A chorus of cheers and guffaws went up, and frightened, Toby made a mad lunge for the last hatch. He had nearly reached it when someone grabbed his shoulder and spun him brutally around, ripping his new shirt.

He gasped and looked up. One of the Frenchmen stood there, arms crossed over his chest and legs planted in a formidable stance. He was dressed in nothing but his trousers, and these were pasted with excrement, sweat, and pus that leaked from a rack of crusted knife wounds across his sunken belly. Shivering, feverish, and skeletally thin, his eyes staring out of his skull like twin frenzied lights, he grinned and stared down at Toby.

Fear darted up Toby's spine, and he looked desperately about for a familiar American face, but only French ones looked back at him, grinning, shifting, and malicious, as they began closing in around him.

"Where from?" the bony one asked, letting his awful gaze rake over Toby's cowering form. It settled on his pocket, where the little money bag was hidden.

Toby swallowed, aware of the press of bodies closing in on him. He tried to back up but came against a hard, stinking stomach. "Newburyport."

"Newburyport?"

"Near Boston."

"Ah! Boston fine town, very pretty!" The Frenchman grinned and patted Toby's shoulder, his arm, his pocket, his eyes lighting with a predatory gleam when he felt the pouch there. "General Washington, *très grand homme!* General Madison, *brave homme!* You my friend, Toby! Americans brave men—fight like Frenchmen!"

"Like hell they do," Toby said proudly, despite his fear.

"Ah, you brave lad, brave like Madison, no? Americans very brave! Very brave!" The Frenchman's grin then immediately vanished and he struck like an adder, his hand snaring Toby's wrist and nearly breaking it. Toby planted his heels, but it was no use. The man hauled him through the cloying, crowded gloom, through the masses of prisoners, all of whom were yelling abuse and taunts, until they came to Armand Moret, who was sitting on a bench surrounded by his cohorts. "Come, show us how much you be my friend, Toby! Friends go to dice table, eh, Toby!"

"You're no damned friend of mine," Toby protested, angrily trying to shake loose. "Let me go!"

Armand looked up, his lips splitting in a dingy smile. "Or what, you'll call your aristo friend down on us?" he broke in. "You sniveling little traitor. . . . Sit down."

Toby choked down his fear and tried to back up. Bodies pressed against his spine, and someone pushed him forward. He fell and was caught by strong hands that shoved him mercilessly at Armand.

"Leave us, Paget," Armand said to the man who had brought Toby to him. "I'm sure my *friend* Toby here has much he wishes to tell me."

Paget went red, his gaze flashing to Toby's pocket. "He's my friend, my friend!" he cried possessively and, yanking a knife from his trousers, lunged for Armand.

Immediately the deck exploded in screams and shouts of excitement which drowned out all other sound. Toby leaped backward and tried to run, but the men behind hemmed him in. Someone caught him and forced him to watch the fight, and in the melee he saw Armand deflect Paget's knife and strike a lightning blow to the side of his head. Paget stumbled and fell to one knee, gasping.

"Get up, get up!" cried the other prisoners, kicking at Paget in their frenzy to see the fight continued. "Get up!"

Paget was crying. The noise level rising to fever pitch around him, he got up and girlishly slapped Armand in the chops with the side of his hand. Armand hit him back, and again Paget fell. He sat there, sobbing, his head in his hands as Armand reached down to help him up.

"Friends, Paget?"

"Friends, Armand, we friends, you my friend," the man blubbered, tears streaming down his face.

Sniffling, he reached up to accept Armand's help, and it was the last movement he ever made. The dagger that suddenly appeared in Armand's fist plunged straight into Paget's throat, all the way to the hilt.

Toby's scream was drowned in the outburst of cheers as Paget thrashed and died on the deck in a gurgle of blood.

Then Armand looked up, jerked the dripping blade from the dead man's throat, and advanced on Toby.

"You work for the aristo, you stinking little louse," he spat, venom dripping from every word. "The aristo, who lives in luxury while we noble Frenchmen starve to death! You work for him, and you're going to tell Armand here each and every detail of his schedule so that we can"—he pantomimed the blade passing across his own throat and made an ugly, awful grimace—"balance the scales, eh?"

"No!" Toby cried as Armand's bloody hand lashed out and spun him around, instantly pinning his spine against the Frenchman's stomach. He felt a tug as Armand ripped the little bag from his pocket. Then there was only that horrible blade of death against his own throat, Armand's fetid breath in his face, and those vicious eyes leaning over his shoulder, blazing into his.

"You *will*," the Frenchman hissed into his ear, pressing harder on the blade, "and you're going to start now."

* * *

The Ladies' Committee on Prisoner Welfare—
organized by Gwyneth and now proving to be her
greatest source of exasperation—sat around a delicate wrought-iron table in her sunny garden, sipping
tea, remarking on the fine weather, and exclaiming
over her lilacs and prize beds of Aubrietia. But at the
moment Gwyneth didn't give a fig about the scent of
her lilacs, the beauty of her Aubrietia, or the likelihood of how nice her roses were going to look next
month. She had called the group together to discuss
ways of helping the prisoners aboard the hulks, but
from the moment Lord Morninghall's name had been
mentioned, there had been talk of nothing else.

"Really, Gwyneth, I am completely baffled," the
Countess of Hinney murmured, setting her cup down
in its saucer and peering at Gwyneth from beneath an
elaborate bonnet trimmed with pearl-colored ostrich
feathers. "Why you continue to defend that demonic
Morninghall, when all of the *haut ton* know he is
nothing but a disreputable monster, is beyond me.
The man is dangerous, a devil with no hope of
redemption, so for your own safety—not to mention
reputation—I advise you to stay well away from
him."

"Lady Hinney," Gwyneth said firmly, "I did not
call us together to discuss Lord Morninghall, but to
organize a drive to collect food and clothing for the
hulk prisoners."

"Really, my dear, if you *truly* want to help them,
why not concentrate your efforts on the Black Wolf
instead?" She lowered her voice to a conspiratory
tone, aware that Lady Falconer, who had arrived the
day before from Surrey and had gone out to her coach
to retrieve a shawl, would return at any moment.
"Now *there* is a man who is *doing* something for the
prisoners. Imagine, rescuing them in the dead of
night, right out from under the nose of your lord, time
and time again!" She clapped a hand to her bosom
and rolled her eyes back in delight. "How dashing!
How brave! How utterly romantic!"

"I do think it best if we abstain from talk about the Black Wolf in Lady Falconer's presence," Gwyneth said dryly, looking at the door where she expected her friend Maeve to reappear at any moment. "Given that the Wolf is reputed to be her brother, and here she is, American and married to the most celebrated British admiral this side of Nelson, she's caught in the middle and such talk can only be distressing to her."

"But the Wolf is positively gallant!" piped up Miss Claudia Dalrymple, seizing the chance to join in the conversation.

"Which is more than one can say for Lord Morninghall!"

"Yes, Morninghall wouldn't know the meaning of *gallant* if it up and bit him on the nose," chirped Miss Mary Chivers, daughter of the influential Lord Sands. "Why, *I* heard that when he stabbed Bolton's son through the heart in that duel, he was actually *laughing*," she added with a dramatic shiver.

Rhiannon, sitting in a nearby chair with Mattie dozing at her feet, drawled, "I *do* believe the duel was fought with pistols, Mary."

"Nevertheless, he should not have laughed. That just goes to show how dreadful a person he really is, doesn't it? And why you invited him to our committee meeting is simply beyond the pale, Gwyneth!" She put a hand to her white bosom, which had begun to heave with practiced emotion. "As Lady Hinney has already said, the man is a monster!"

Gwyneth set her teacup down with a loud bang. "The man is a naval commander, and I have invited him so that he may advise us of the things we might do to aid our cause. Such information can only help the prisoners."

"Yes, I can imagine it would—*if* Morninghall shows. But he won't, and you and I both know it."

"He will show," Gwyneth said adamantly.

"I would not be so sure," Lady Hinney murmured, cutting a piece of frothy lemon cake with her knife and holding it artfully poised in her hand. "It is half-four, and he still has not arrived."

"And he really can't expect us to wait all day for him."

Lady Hinney gave an amused snort. "I'm sure that is *exactly* what he expects, Mary."

"He will *be* here," Gwyneth said tightly, even though her own confidence in Morninghall was beginning to wane. Had she misinterpreted the look in his eyes outside her house in the darkness? Had she only imagined the softening in him, the quick glimpse of vulnerability and warmth before he had pulled the dark drapes of himself shut once more? No, he would be here. Her skin was prickling with anticipation at the very thought of his diabolically beautiful form darkening her doorway like the devil conjured up from hell, his gaze sweeping over her little gathering with satanic disdain. She'd already bet Rhiannon a crown that Lady Hinney would faint dead away at her first sight of him. Rhiannon had upped the bet to a guinea, saying Mary Chivers would too.

Damn you, Morninghall, where are you?!

Trying to maintain her confident, businesslike composure, Gwyneth opened her notebook. She froze as she heard hoofbeats approaching in the street beyond the wall, and her pulse quickened—but the hoofbeats continued on. Her heart fell, and she hoped her face did not give away her disappointment as she shot what had to be her fiftieth surreptitious glance toward the doorway in a third as many minutes.

She didn't bother trying to fool herself. She hadn't invited Morninghall here just to gain his professional input—she'd invited him because she desperately wanted to see him again.

She ached to see him again.

And here it was, half-four, and he had not arrived.

"You sound dreadfully certain of something I doubt we shall see, Gwyneth," Lady Hinney was saying, dabbing her lips with her napkin. "If Morninghall was going to come, he would have been here by now."

"He accepted my invitation," Gwyneth snapped, flipping the pages of her notebook with unnecessary force. "He was probably detained. Now, shall we get on with this meeting?"

The older woman, resembling a giant tomato in her loud, poppy-colored silk gown, merely smiled and reached for another piece of cake. "Detained, my dear?" She gave a little snort and dismissed Gwyneth's hopes with an imperious wave of her hand. "More likely he just tossed your invitation into the sea and promptly forgot about it. After all, the man has a well-earned reputation as a knave, a blackguard, a monster—"

"Really, have the lot of you nothing better to do than gossip about the character of this damned Morninghall fellow?"

All heads turned as Maeve, Lady Falconer, sailed out of the house with her parasol clutched in her right hand like a sword. Her outburst stunned Lady Hinney into silence and bug-eyed shock.

"Well, I never . . ." the stout old matron began, before the angry look in Lady Falconer's eye silenced her. The group fell silent, nervous in the presence of Admiral Sir Graham Falconer's fearsome wife, who wore a necklace of sharks' teeth around her neck and—it was rumored—a dagger strapped to the outside of her ankle. Maeve had once been the Pirate Queen of the Caribbean, and though she was gowned in amethyst silks and her hair was swept up in a crown of fire atop her head, neither did a thing to bring a genteel and ladylike quality to the woman who had terrorized the West Indies, snared herself the most eligible bachelor in the Royal Navy, and—as it was well known—allied herself to Lord Nelson just before the Battle of Trafalgar.

Maeve was not known for her patience, and of

course all this talk about her escaped brother being
the Black Wolf must be very trying for her, Gwyneth
thought. Mixed loyalties were never easy.

"Thank you, Maeve," Gwyneth said with tightly
reined anger. She noted the day's date in her notebook and then the names of the present committee members. "Perhaps we can begin our meeting
now?"

Lady Falconer opened her parasol with a violent
snap. "It's about time. Had I known this *meeting*
was going to be nothing more than a boring tearoom
gossip session aimed at assassinating a man's character, I damn well would've stayed home."

Lady Hinney jerked her chin up, then looked away,
angry and humiliated.

"Well, where *is* His Lordship, then?" piped up Miss
Dalrymple, smiling faintly as she gazed at each committee member. "We've been sitting here waiting for
him to arrive for the past hour."

"Perhaps he's trying to think up a way to capture
the Black Wolf," Miss Chivers said, giggling. Her eyes
widened. "Papa tells me that if he does not, the
Admiralty is going to have his head!"

"Better his than the Black Wolf's," Lady Hinney
slid in. She paled as she saw sparks lighting Maeve's
tiger eyes and drew back, her hands fluttering. "But
Gwyneth is right. Morninghall is beyond gossip—and
redemption." She laid her hand on Gwyneth's, keenly
aware of Maeve's fearsome stare from across the
table. "So, dear child. What would you have us do for
these poor prisoners?"

Thankful that they were finally getting down to
business, Gwyneth began outlining her idea to collect
food and clothing from among the good people of
Portsmouth. But her words were detached from her
seething thoughts, and as the minutes passed to an
hour, the excited hope that had lit her spirit and
tightened her jittery heart turned to ashes in her
breast.

I won't let you get away with this, Morninghall, she vowed, already anticipating a confrontation. *So help me God, I won't!*

Chapter 16

~~~⟨C⟩~~~

"This is not the way, Damon. It's too dangerous, and cruel-spirited besides. For pity's
sake, where is your heart?"

"You mean to tell me you finally acknowledge that I
lack one?" Damon said faintly. "I daresay, it took you
long enough, Peter."

"To attempt such a thing as this—"

"It shall not be an *attempt,* but a success."

"There has to be another way!"

"There isn't."

With that Damon began to descend the hatch,
leaving the sunlit upper deck behind.

Peter had no choice: he either could let Damon go
about this business alone, or he could follow along to
pick up the pieces. "May God be with us all, then," he
said defeatedly.

The two men swiftly made their way down into the
depths of the ship. If the lower deck was hot, the orlop
deck was a humid, stifling hell. Nothing had changed
since the last visit he'd made to this wretched place,
Damon thought sourly. The heat, the stench, the
stygian gloom—it was all here. Bent nearly double to
fit beneath the overhead beams, he pressed his arm
against his nose, trying to strain the foul air through
his shirt sleeve. It did little good.

The prisoners milled around them, trailing them
like bubbles after a passing ship. Damon brushed past
them and tried to ignore the nagging press of his own

conscience, which had been damnably active lately.
Yes, he'd deliberately shunned Lady Simms's silly
party after he'd accepted her invitation; yes, what he
was about to do was going to hurt Toby. But he could
not jeopardize things—the least of which was his
life—on what trust he dared place in Toby Ashton.
Peter was a godly man but, at times, hopelessly naive,
and Damon had learned long ago that to survive in
this rotten world, you couldn't be naive—nor trusting. Be that way, and you'd damn well end up dead.

Out of the corner of his eye he saw scores of
prisoners, their faces gaunt, their bodies thin and
hunched beneath the overhead deck. He tried to shut
his mind to their suffering, but such escape was no
longer possible. The emotion that had swelled his
heart, brought tears to his eyes when he'd found
himself staring at the lilacs, struck him now: a col-
lapse of defenses, a frightening propensity toward
softness, vulnerability, feeling, compassion. Something that made his heart hurt.

I truly am *going mad.*

They descended the last ladder and reached the
hold. Peter lifted his lantern. Around them the black,
dripping planking swung into orange focus, curving
upward to meet the hulking old beams of the orlop
deck above. Pools of stagnant brine sloshed at their
feet, and the steady drip of water echoed through the
vast space with an eerie constancy, like the slow
ticking of a clock. And there, tucked against the hull,
was the Black Hole, outside of which the guard
Damon had sent down five minutes earlier waited
with his own meager light.

Damon thought of the last time he'd been down
here, of how he'd caught Lady Simms during her
faint. He remembered how she'd felt like a sack of
feathers in his arms, how her silken hair had tumbled
over his wrist, how the swell of her breasts had
tempted his eyes, his mouth.

His loins tingled. She was going to be furious with

him for not showing up at her little party after he'd accepted her invitation, but he was still embarrassed about the attack. Besides, she'd made him feel raw with real fear the other night, out there in the darkness in front of her house. She'd gotten under his defenses, and he had no intention of letting her do so again. For the briefest moment he'd fancied she could be a friend; she had not laughed at him, had showed him compassion and understanding, and for a short, wary while—especially when she'd told him about her sister's fear of thunderstorms—he'd felt a rush of warmth and trust in her. That rush of warmth and trust frightened him. It was too close to intimacy, and he didn't want to feel intimacy with her or anyone else. To hell with her silly party.

There it was, that twinge from his conscience again. "Damon?"

Peter was waiting, his eyes silently condemning. Ignoring that pleading gaze, Damon took the lantern from him and picked his way over the massive timbers of the keel and ribs. His shoe squished in stagnant water, and despite the low din of prisoners on the decks above, the sound seemed to echo in the gloom. A handful of them had trailed down the hatch after them, and he could hear their muted whispers, their harsh, heavy breathing as they too tried to draw breath from this stinking air.

The Black Hole reared out of the shadows, tall and forbidding.

In his mind's eye he saw little Toby, hopeful, excited, naive in his belief that Damon was going to release his brother. If only he could have told him the truth.

Impossible, of course.

The guard, Clayton, was waiting.

"Open it up," Damon snapped irritably.

A sense of doom hung in the air, silencing even the prisoners poised on the ladder behind them. The lantern sputtered and hissed; water dripped steadily from somewhere. The Black Hole looked down at them, charred, evil, deathly silent, like a coffin standing on end.

Producing a key, Clayton bent and unlocked its door. Then, his hand on his pistol, he seized the latch and yanked it open, hard.

Nothing.

Peter Milford, standing beside the silent, stone-faced marquess, felt his heart catch in his throat as Clayton shone his lantern into the hole.

"Shit," the guard muttered and, crouching down, reached into the dark opening.

A foul stench issued forth, and nausea hit Peter full in the stomach.

"What is it?" Morninghall snapped, already moving impatiently forward.

The guard looked up, his strapping bulk shielding Nathan Ashton's body from the marquess, the chaplain, and the crowd of men gathered on the ladder behind them.

"I think he's dead, sir."

It was not easy for Gwyneth to find anyone ready and willing to take her out to the prison hulk, but in the end she found a fisherman repairing his nets near the pier who—for the right price—finally complied.

Now she sat in his small boat, her feet placed carefully to the side of the sloshing puddle in the hull, her gloved hands buried in her skirts as he rowed the small craft through the harbor's light chop. Beneath her rigid exterior Gwyneth was seething. She'd already gone through every delightfully torturous method she could think of with regards to killing Morninghall. After she had dared to trust him, after she had deceived herself into thinking he really did have a soul after all, he had left her high, dry, and humiliated in front of the most influential women in Portsmouth.

It was simply not acceptable.

Strangulation. Ah, yes, that would do quite nicely. Her hands curled into claws.

Overhead, low, heavy clouds were moving in from the northwest, drawing over the sun like curtains and stealing the brightness of the day. With them came a breeze that ruffled the water and topped each wave with a tiny whitecap. The harbor had been a deep, hard blue; now it faded to gray, and the day was suddenly cold.

Gwyneth shivered, drawing her arms around herself, and when she looked up, she saw, beyond the fisherman's brawny shoulder, a boat heading toward them. It had come from the direction of HMS *Surrey,* and a single sailor pulled at its oars.

She frowned.

The fisherman twisted around in his seat to see what had caught her attention. "Ah, yes, another one," he said noncommittally, facing her once again as the two craft approached each other. "Came from the prison hulk ye be wantin' t' visit, it did."

Gwyneth was watching the other boat as it began to pass them just to starboard. "Another one?"

In answer the fisherman just grinned—and watched her face in mild amusement.

Gwyneth's mouth fell open in horror.

No. It can't be.

But it was: a corpse, lying in the bottom of the boat, a strip of sailcloth thrown over the torso and face, the feet poking up above the gunwales.

"Dead body," the fisherman grunted, putting his muscle into another stroke of the oars that pushed them ever closer to the prison ship from which the other boat had come. "Take 'em out of here every day, they do. Die like flies, especially once the weather starts getting hot."

Gwyneth felt sick. She stared, horrified, at those bare feet sticking above the other boat's gunwales— and then she looked up and caught the eye of the sailor who was rowing it.

He leaned on his oars and let the momentum carry his boat along as he looked across the water at her. Sea-seasoned and lean as a nail, he was gazing at her with blatant appreciation, and she wasn't so far away from him that she couldn't see his dazzling grin, the laughing charm of his green eyes, and feel affected by both.

"Morning, ma'am!" he called, gathering his oars in one hand and touching two fingers to his temple in mock salute. He appeared tall and handsome in a rakish sort of way, with rich, chestnut hair caught carelessly at his nape and a day's growth of beard cloaking an angular jaw.

To think that anyone could smile while performing such a grim task as transporting dead bodies for burial—

Gwyneth jerked her chin up and stared straight ahead, refusing to acknowledge him. A moment later the two boats were well past each other.

"I hope ye've got the stomach for this," the fisherman mused, watching the other craft moving further and further away from them. "They's bound to be more where that one came from."

"Yes, I'm sure there *will* be." Gwyneth muttered, her steely gaze on the approaching hulk.

The fisherman merely gave her a thoughtful look, but Gwyneth wasn't thinking about the prisoners.

She was thinking of a certain marquess named Morninghall—and enjoying every moment of his impending demise.

Damon stood in his cabin at the windows, his hands clasped behind his back as he watched the boat that carried the body of Nathan Ashton moving further and further away. He felt anxious inside, unsettled, but he merely gripped his hands tighter in a futile attempt to ignore it, never relaxing his rigid stance nor allowing the barest flicker of emotion to cross his face.

Behind him he heard approaching footsteps, then the creak of the door as Peter Milford came in with the boy.

His kept his back toward them. He was dreading this with every beat of his heart.

What heart? he asked himself on a wave of self-loathing, but even as he thought it, he knew he must have one, for it was burning a hole right through his breast with all the kindness of acid.

He heard the door click shut behind him, the rustling of clothes, the boy's nervous breathing, Peter clearing his throat.

Damon turned slowly, his hands still knotted behind his back, his eyes veiled and expressionless. What pleasure he had found in watching little Toby eat the hearty meals he'd given him, what pleasure he'd found in restoring some of the boy's human dignity by ensuring he had baths and clean clothes—pleasures that even a few short weeks ago Damon would've been too busy licking his wounds and nursing his anger to care, let alone think, about. How nice it had felt to know that he had been able to do something good for somebody, something kind. He'd forgotten how good that felt inside, and now he was about to destroy it all.

He cleared his throat.

Toby stood in front of Peter, never looking so young and frail as he did now, framed as he was by the chaplain's lanky height. His eyes were frightened behind his spectacles, and his shirt—torn and grubby—was fiercely buttoned at his throat. Damon's eyes narrowed dangerously.

"What happened to your shirt, Toby?" he asked, frowning.

The boy didn't respond, but only looked down at his toes, his hair hanging over his spectacles and his throat working as he battled with some inner torment. "The other prisoners, sir. They . . . they don't like me much 'cause I'm working for you."

"Of course they don't. That is why I gave you a berth in the guards' quarters, and why I have advised you not to go belowdecks."

Toby looked up, biting his lip. "They're plotting to kill you, you know."

Damon's sigh was a world-weary one. "Yes, such aspirations do keep their minds occupied in the face of explicit boredom. Hardly worrying, I daresay. But I told you not to consort with them, Toby." His made his voice gentler. "Must you learn things the hard way?"

As I did, he thought on a note of bitter disgust.

"Damon—" Peter began warningly.

"Answer me, Toby."

Toby looked near to tears. "I wanted to tell my brother he was going to be released," he blurted, his eyes defiant.

Damon took a deep, steadying breath. His gaze flashed to Peter's, just above that ginger head, but there was no help from that quarter. "Sit down, Toby," he said gently.

The boy must've seen something in his face, or caught something in his tone, for suddenly his eyes widened with fear, and he twisted around to glance worriedly up at Peter. From his angle he could not see that the chaplain's face was tight with condemnation as he met Damon's gaze. When neither man said anything, Toby slowly pulled out a chair.

Damon sat down beside him and leaned his elbows on the table. He raked a hand through his hair. He wasn't good at this sort of thing; he really wasn't. Damn Peter for not doing this for him—after all, he was a clergyman, well used to this sort of thing. But no, Peter had wanted nothing to do with it, had refused to participate in this part of Damon's scheme. Just like friends, always deserting you when you need them most, Damon thought with acid satisfaction. He was better off without them.

Mentally steeling himself, he reached out and laid his hand over Toby's. The boy pulled away, but not before Damon felt the thinness of that pitiful little wrist. The bones there were like two dowels beneath his fingers, and the thought made him feel sick.

"Toby," he said gently, refusing to meet Peter's angry gaze, "there is something I must tell you about your brother."

The boy's eyes filled up and his lower lip began to quiver. "You've changed your mind?"

"No, Toby, I have not." Damon took a deep breath, feeling sadly inept, loathsome, vile. "Your brother is . . . dead."

Toby only stared at him. Not a muscle moved in his gaunt little face, and he seemed to forget to draw breath. Behind him Peter looked down at Damon and slowly shook his head, condemning him, before placing a steadying hand on the boy's shoulder.

"H—he . . . he can't be dead," Toby said, blinking. He shook his head, denying the words. "Connor was supposed to . . . No. I won't believe you, he can't be dead!"

Again Damon reached out to cover the boy's hand. "We opened the Black Hole to take him out, and . . . he was gone. I'm sorry, Toby." He looked up helplessly at Peter, who was still standing behind the boy and glaring. "Really, I am."

Toby stared at him. Then something broke inside of him and his face crumpled, his shaggy ginger head falling into his hands as his sobs burst forth. Feeling the anguish that emanated from him, Damon gently touched his shoulder.

The boy exploded beneath him.

"Don't you touch me, you wretched English bastard, you—you *murderer!*" he cried, leaping to his feet and sending the chair toppling over backward. "If you hadn't put him in there, he wouldn't be dead! If you hadn't waited so long to free him, he'd be alive today! It's all your fault, and I hate you with all my heart!"

"Toby, I—"

"Murderer!"

Sobbing bitterly, the boy raced from the cabin. Damon gazed at the door, then raked his hand through his hair and gave a weary sigh. He looked up, only to find Peter's condemning gaze leveled upon him.

"I hope you're satisfied," the chaplain said quietly, and strode swiftly from the cabin after the boy.

Damon, clenching his fists, turned back toward the window.

And saw the boat carrying Lady Gwyneth Evans Simms heading his way.

Chapter 17

Gwyneth was in a fine temper by the time the fisherman—dramatically holding his nose and making exaggerated choking, gasping noises—brought the boat up against HMS *Surrey*'s black and smoky hull. Radley stood at the top of the rickety stairs, staring down at her. She got the feeling he'd been standing there for some time, waiting.

"Fine day, Lady Simms!"

"I have come to see his Lordship."

Radley smiled and, taking off his hat, passed his wrist across his brow. His hair was thinning, and his oily scalp glistened between the sparse strands. "Lord Morninghall is not receiving any visitors to the ship, madam."

"Is he aboard?"

"Aye."

"Is he ill?"

"Nay."

"Is he meeting with superiors, inferiors, or anyone else?"

"Don't think so, ma'am."

"Then why won't he receive visitors, Mr. Radley?"

"Specifically put, ma'am, he doesn't wish to receive . . . *you*."

"Very well, then." She gave Radley her sweetest—most threatening—smile, then turned her attention on the fisherman. He had been watching this exchange silently with high amusement; now something in Gwyneth's stare wiped the grin off his face, though the sparkle in his rheumy old eyes remained. "Would you mind rowing me to just beneath the captain's cabin?" she asked, her tone poisonously sweet.

The grin came back. "Not at all, ma'am."

He took up the oars, pushed off from the huge hull, and maneuvered the boat around. No doubt he was anticipating fireworks, and no doubt he was going to get them.

The boat moved aft, toward the stern. The blackened, peeling hull slid past on Gwyneth's right like a giant wall, close enough to touch. She kept her head up and her gaze straight ahead, but out of the corner of her eye, she could see the dim faces of the prisoners behind the barred gun ports just above. A few started yelling in French and broken English, and the sound caught hold until the whole ship reverberated with the uproar.

The captain's cabin was an outcropping of grimy windows and rotted old woodwork that protruded at the stern end of the ship. There, just beneath those high, out-thrust windows, the fisherman brought the little craft to a halt and eased the dripping oars out of the water. Whirlpools twirled off like miniature cyclones across the oily surface, as though fervently searching for the retrieved blades.

Gwyneth sat for a moment, surveying her situation and tuning out the low roar of the prisoners. The sea sucked and gurgled around the old ship's rudder, where moss and slime grew several inches thick and the water was greenish black in the shadow cast from the cabin above. Slowly, thoughtfully, she tilted her head back, scrutinizing the wooden scrollwork that decorated the man-of-war's windows. Once resplendent in gold, red, and blue, the scrollwork was now charred and smoky, chipped and faded with age. The ship's name, once so proud, was now all but illegible beneath a layer of grease and grime, and far above, her colors fluttered weakly in the light breeze.

Staring up at that blank array of windows, Gwyneth cupped her hands to her mouth. "Morninghall!"

Nothing.

She waited a moment, then tried again, louder this time, in a militant tone that would've done a general proud.

"Morninghall!"

The windows remained shut, the reflection of the clouds above sliding over their grimy surfaces. She thought she saw movement behind one of them, but she wasn't sure. But the prisoners' yelling was getting louder, and just above them, leaning over the railing that framed the poop deck, several guards had gathered, gazing down at her in amusement.

Damn him. *"MORNINGHALL!"*

A ripple of laughter passed through the guards, and she heard their whistles, calls, and lewd comments over the uproar of the hundreds of prisoners contained behind the barred-up gun ports.

Her face perfectly composed, Gwyneth turned to the fisherman, who was regarding her with a smirk. "Give me your oar," she shouted over the rising din—and rose perilously to her feet in the little boat.

Raising an eyebrow, he passed the oar to her.

Then, without further ado, Gwyneth drew back and hurled it, harpoon-like, straight through Morninghall's window. There was a crashing explosion, and bits and pieces of glass and woodwork rained down in the water about them.

"For God's sake, lady!" the fisherman cried, shielding himself with an arm over his head.

Gwyneth brushed the glass from her seat, sat back down, and arranged her skirts with perfect nonchalance, seemingly oblivious to the prisoners' cheering and yelling, the whooping laughter of the guards above as she looked up at her handiwork.

She didn't have long to wait. Sure enough, there was movement behind the dark, jagged hole where the oar had gone. It was the marquess. He casually flicked a

spear of broken glass aside and then, his face dangerously composed, leaned out the window, directing the
full effect of his below-freezing stare on Gwyneth.

"Well, well. If it isn't Lady Gwyneth Evans Simms.
I should have known."

"You *did* know. You knew when you accepted my
invitation and then failed to honor it."

"Ah, so that's what this is all about." His smile
was mocking, amused, infuriatingly condescending.
Brushing aside broken glass, he propped his elbows
on the sill and thoughtfully rested his chin in the heel
of his hand, his gaze never leaving hers. "Obviously I
changed my mind. Fancy little tea parties are not my
favored mode of entertainment, you understand."

"You *said* you would come, Morninghall."

"I guess you cannot trust my word, then, can you?"

"Don't play that game with me, you scoundrel. You
deliberately set out to make me angry, no doubt
hoping I'd return to my original opinion about how
very awful you are."

"Did I?" he murmured faintly, even while his smile
seemed to falter. "Really, my dear, you should count
your blessings that I *didn't* show up. How horrified
your twittering, gently bred friends would've been to
have Satan himself darkening their charming little
affair! But never mind that. I'm more intrigued by
your calling card." He faded into the gloom for a
moment and reappeared with the damp oar, which he
casually handed down to the grinning fisherman.
"Quite an unusual one for a—ahem—*lady,* is it not?"

She fisted her hands, the soft kid of the gloves
threatening to split atop her knuckles. "Are you quite
finished?"

The marquess only laughed, one short, amused
bark ending in a rumbling chuckle that sent chills
creeping up Gwyneth's spine. "Ah, Lady Simms," he
said expansively, with a darkly charming smile. "If
you are so determined to come aboard, then by all
means do so. Either way, you lose."

"Do I?" she purred.

"But of course. Leave now and we shall consider it my victory for having scared you off. Come aboard and confront me, and the whole ship will speculate about just what sort of *transactions* will be going on inside my cabin."

"You're despicable."

"I know."

"And to think I believe you have a smack of decency in you."

"You should know by now I do not." He smiled again, a gesture of courtly charm, but behind it she saw lethal, predatory intent, not unlike a grinning wolf. "Which shall it be, *dearest?*"

"Why, Morninghall, I shouldn't wish to disappoint you. Have Radley await me on deck. I'm coming aboard."

For the briefest moment his face went blank, and Gwyneth felt a wave of triumph, a delicious confidence that his rudeness was just what she suspected it to be: carefully crafted armor designed to keep her, and anyone else who ventured too close to the *real* Lord Morninghall, well at bay.

She would greatly enjoy piercing it.

The prisoners' cheering, yelling, and pleas for mercy all merged into one overwhelming uproar as Gwyneth, her skirts in one hand, carefully climbed the stairs built into the side of the hull. With faint uneasiness she saw their grimy arms reaching madly through the gun ports around and below her, even as the clamor they made pushed all thought from her head. Up she climbed, higher and higher, the wooden bannister beneath her hand vibrating with that awful, maddening din. She felt the prisoners' crazed hatred, rage, and excitement, and she moved quickly, wanting only to reach the deck and escape those thrusting, claw-like hands that stretched toward her. These were dangerous men, as all men were when caged, maltreated, and deprived of the most basic human freedoms and dignity. Flutters of fear rose in her throat,

but they were nothing when compared to what she felt
at the thought of confronting that diabolical lord who
waited for her in his cabin.

Except he wasn't waiting for her in his cabin; he
was waiting at the top of the stairs, a lean, malevolent
figure silhouetted against a lowering gray sky.

He reached out, gallantly taking her gloved hand to
steady her as she stepped onto the tiny platform. She
could feel the heat of him right through the soft kid,
could see the lethal strength in every long, well-bred
finger that tightened around her hand.

"Lady Simms."

"Lord Morninghall."

"It will be such a . . . *pleasure* to have you aboard."

Then, with a mocking grin, he turned, presenting
his elbow.

She glared at him but had no choice but to take it.
Moments later they were in his cabin, where at last
she pulled free of him and moved a safe distance
away.

Clutching her parasol, she turned to face him. He
was leaning negligently against the edge of his table,
arms crossed over his chest, his unsettling gaze raking
over her with a slow, simmering heat. She could see
him taking in every detail of her attire, no doubt
stripping away every shred of it in his imagination.
She had donned a long-sleeved, high-necked walking
dress of rose muslin, totally devoid of ruffles, lacing,
and frills in order to discourage just such a pursuit on
his part; the only bit of delicate femininity it allowed
was the green-and-gold embroidery that edged the
bodice and meandered in twin trails down the front.
A gray cottage mantle, also clasped at the throat, and
a smart straw hat with a round brim gave her what
she'd hoped was a stern and businesslike demeanor,
but Morninghall's devil stare seemed to burn right
through the gray ribbon that tied just beneath her
breasts, and already she could feel her nipples beginning to tingle with response.

"You don't learn, do you?" he murmured faintly.

A tingle of fear raced through her. *Remember that flash of alarm in his eyes when you said you were coming aboard. Remember his compassion to the boy, no matter what he called it. Remember his magnificent rage in the contractor's office. Remember that lost look in his eyes out there in the darkness in front of the house. He is compassionate and vulnerable, and the idea that he is either is scaring him half to death.*

"Oh, I've learned a lot," she returned, refusing to be cowed by that flat, diabolical stare.

"Have you?" he asked, tucking his chin between thumb and forefinger and rubbing it slowly in a manner that made him seem all the more menacing and frightening. He still leaned against the table, yet every muscle in his body radiated power, every nuance and shadow that moved across his eyes danger. "Why don't you be a good girl and tell me exactly what it is you've learned?"

"Don't patronize me. Besides, you won't like any of it."

"Really? Try me, madam. I can be painfully tolerant."

"Somehow I doubt that."

He merely smiled. The message that gesture conveyed was more effective, more awful than anything he might've said.

Steeling herself, Gwyneth moved to his swivel chair and sat down on the edge of its seat, her back unbending. She planted her parasol in front of her, its point stabbing the deck, and crossed her hands atop the handle as she leaned forward and met that waiting stare. "I have learned, Morninghall, that you are a master of deception, and that you are not as evil as you would have others believe."

"Oh, this is rich," he murmured, but a cold, wary glitter came into his eyes and his smile wasn't quite so self-assured.

"You never had any intention of coming to our committee meeting, but accepted my invitation so that your failure to show could only restore your reputation—at least in *my* eyes—as a black-hearted scoundrel."

The barest flicker of something—admiration? alarm?—moved across that iridescent stare. He smiled chillingly, then slowly lowered his hand, his head tilted a little to one side.

"And why would I do that?" he asked silkily.

"Because I am getting a little too close to the core of whomever Damon, Lord Morninghall, is."

He uncrossed his arms, then straightened up, so tall that his great height seemed to lower the deck above by several inches. He filled the cabin, and every inch of him was throbbing with rage. With slow, menacing grace, he moved forward.

Toward her.

"Too close, eh?" he murmured dangerously.

Gwyneth had seen that look in his eyes before, the one where his lids came down to half-shutter fiery, glittering intelligence, anger, and, yes, desire. No, not desire. That was too mild a word for a man like this one. What she saw there was a craving, a hunger, an obsession as lethal to him as it was to her. She knew what was coming, and her skin began to prickle with warning, with hope, with wanton, screaming excitement.

She straightened up, holding her ground in the face of his advance. "Yes, too close, and you don't like it, do you, my lord?"

"You have no idea what I like, and you have no idea who the real Damon, Lord Morninghall is," he said softly and, reaching out, tilted her chin up with the tip of his finger.

She remained stiff and unresponsive, though her nostrils flared with delicious fear as she stared up at him. "Oh, but I think I do—Damon."

He released her. She thought he would come back with a cold retort, but instead he moved slowly behind her chair, his fingers whispering along its arm as he passed. She sensed him standing just behind her, over her, staring down at the top of her head: a magnificent, angry force she could sense but could not see, could feel but could not face. She shivered uncontrollably, yet she refused to turn around and give him the satisfaction of knowing he was unnerving her. She refused to flinch, even when his dangerously warm fingers, came down to rest lightly on her shoulder.

God, help me.

The seconds crept by, crackling with tension. Every beat of her heart was louder than the one before it, every nerve in her body began to scream. She heard his slow, measured breathing. She felt his hand burning through the muslin to her shoulder. And now his fingers were pushing into the delicate flesh just beneath her collarbone . . . questing . . . seeking. She stared fixedly at the opposite bulkhead, hardly daring to breathe.

Then, with one quick, savage movement, he tore her hat off—and sent it flying across the room.

Gwyneth's mouth went dry.

She felt his fingers in her hair, slowly splaying through the heavy masses and sending pins tinkling to the deck.

She shut her eyes, praying for strength.

But what she got was desire, and he was a master at inducing it. She felt it skating in husky waves over her flesh as his hand moved toward the swell of her breast. She felt it tightening her chest, deepening her breathing. She felt it in the warm flood of moisture now pooling between her thighs, in the wild, erotic images her mind played out before her eyes of the last time she had dueled with this man—and lost.

But he is not so terrible, not such a monster as he wants you to believe! She had *seen* that glimpse of goodness in him, God help her, she had!, that spark of humanity he kept brutally locked within himself, and the tiny flame of hope it gave her was all that kept her frozen in the chair, hardly daring to breathe, when

every primitive survival instinct was shrieking at her
to run for her very life. Light and dark, good and evil,
it all faded and she knew only that dark and masterful
hand, combing out her hair, pulling the rich waves of
silk down around her shoulders, the slow, skillful
fingers catching in a tangle, gently tugging it free . . .
now moving downward to linger on the clasp of her
mantle, thumbing suggestively over it before moving
with scorching slowness back up her neck—

"You want me, don't you, Lady Simms?"

His voice was a dark angel's, wickedly soft, seduc-
tive, and husky. He was leaning down over her, so
close that the low words stirred the wispy hair at her
temple, so close that she could feel the quivering
anger that made every word he uttered something
dark and threatening and deadly. She swallowed hard,
but there was not a drop of saliva left in her mouth.
She felt the heat of him looming around her. She felt
the untamed power that emanated from him. Now his
knuckles were grazing the side of her neck, his palm
and fingers opening to cup the fragile, white column
of her throat and encompass it totally, only the thumb
moving as it tested her frantically beating pulse. That
hand was hot, hard, terrifyingly powerful, the long
fingers deadly. He could kill her with one quick
movement and she was powerless to stop him. She
knew it. He knew it.

She began to shudder.

"Did you hear me, Lady Simms? I'll bet that when I
spread those clamped legs of yours, I'll find you hot,
wet, and wanting."

She didn't answer, only staring straight in front of
her. The pressure on her throat tightened. His hot,
male scent, deliciously spicy with the taint of sandalwood, infiltrated her senses. Then he slowly released
the pressure, letting his fingers drag across her wind-
pipe before moving down the swan-like column of her
neck, skimming the sensitive skin there until coming
to rest on the fastening of her mantle. She felt the

barest tug, a loosening; then, with a faint whisper, the cape-like garment slid from her neck and he was pulling it up and off, letting it fall to the deck behind her.

"I'll bet your sweet honey is flowing like a river down there, isn't it? Just waiting for me to"—his lips were warm against the side of her neck, and she shut her eyes on a shiver of delight—"lap it up greedily. . . ."

Her insides went hot and wobbly; her hands were sweating inside her gloves. Gwyneth tightened them around the handle of the parasol, staring straight ahead and trying to hold onto herself, her cause, her reason.

Then she realized what she had to do: gain the upper hand, throw him off balance.

"As a matter of fact, it is."

He paused. "What?"

"I'm not going to bother denying that I find you dangerously attractive, that my body aches for yours, that there are things I've never done before but would find wildly exciting to do with you. There, I've admitted it, Morninghall. I've admitted that I desire you, would like to get to know you better. But can you admit the same? Do you have the strength to say you can't resist *me?*"

He laughed. "I cannot resist you, my dearest Lady Simms."

"Well, there's a start. The last time we went about this business, I let you have the upper hand. Now it's my turn."

He chuckled softly, his lips still moving over her neck. "*Let* me?"

"Yes, *let* you. And I'll only *let* you carry on like this if you let *me* tell you some things you'll not want to hear, Morninghall."

"Please, call me Damon. We are . . ." his lips nuzzled her ear, brushed her nape, ". . . past the hand-holding stage, are we not?"

"Give me your answer."

"I don't care what you want to tell me. You know as well as I that it will fall on deaf ears. . . ."

"Go ahead then, proceed. Let's have this out once and for all."

These were brave words, but Gwyneth, breathing as though every inhalation might crack lungs gone suddenly to glass, knew the exact moment his fingers found the top button of her dress, just above the knobby bit of bone at the base of her neck.

God help me.

He began to undo it.

"Go on then," he murmured, close to her ear. "Tell me what you think."

He had the first button undone. She could feel the sweep of cool air against her nape, the grazing kiss of those hot, skilled fingers. He found the second, a half inch lower than the first.

"Well?" he taunted, already moving to the third button.

She swallowed hard, tiny beads of dew sheening her brow, and plunged ahead before he rendered her completely mindless. "I think that beneath that hard, diabolical armor in which you wrap yourself, you are a very sensitive and caring individual."

"You're correct, I don't want to hear this."

"No, my lord, you're *going* to hear it or I'll get up and walk out of here, whether you like it or not."

A fourth button slid through a tiny hole. His fingers were between her shoulder blades now, brushing against her skin as he worked, dragging shivers of exquisite feeling from every pore as they moved lower.

And lower.

"All right then. Carry on."

She swallowed hard, desperately trying to hold onto her resolve, her purpose, her mind before she lost them altogether. "I think that you have been"—*oh, God, he's making me melt, please give me strength and courage*—"cruelly misused, scarred even, and that there is something beautiful worth saving in your soul."

"The lady needs spectacles," he murmured, but the slow, purposeful descent of his fingers faltered just the same.

Then continued.

"And I think the reason you have these—these attacks, Damon, is because there is something dark and wounded inside of you, something afraid, something that needs to be confronted, to be—healed." She shut her eyes, glad that he could not see her fear. "But you won't confront it, because the idea of doing so . . . terrifies you."

His fingers went deathly still. His breathing stopped. There was no sound behind her, just a stunned tension, like that awful moment between a close bolt of lightning and the terrible crack of thunder that always follows. Gwyneth held her breath and shut her eyes, waiting for that thunder, a blow against the side of her head that would break her neck and knock her sprawling from her chair, never to get up again.

No blow came, no words came, only the cool breeze whispering in through the broken window, swirling around her exposed shoulders, down her damp spine, into the delicate, curved middle of her back.

And *him*.

"You're mad," he said without rancor. "Bloody crazy, in fact."

"I'm not crazy and you know it. Something threatens to get too close to you, and you have an attack. Something starts to penetrate those walls of apathy, anger, and self-pity you've erected to protect yourself, and you have an attack. You're afraid of intimacy, Damon, of anyone getting too close to you."

"Tell me then," he murmured, his fingers grazing the side of her neck, "if it is fear of intimacy that incites these strange attacks, then why did I have one just after I met you for the very first time? That would seem to dispute your ridiculous theories."

"Maybe your soul knew something your conscious mind did not: that I was going to be the woman to penetrate those defenses and find out your secrets."

She heard the whisper of fabric behind her as he straightened up, and then there were only his fingers sliding down, over her collarbone and beneath her gaping bodice to scald the trembling white flesh of her bosom.

Gooseflesh began to rise on her arms, and she knew that, for her, it was all over.

She had pushed him too far, and now he was going to make her pay.

"How very interesting," he murmured from somewhere just above her ear. His dark fingers smoothed the swell of her right breast and moved slowly toward the nipple. "And do you want to know what *I* think, Lady Simms?"

"I suppose fair is fair."

"I think that your theories are a load of bollocks. Codswollop. The ramblings of an insane mind."

She swallowed, overcome with heat as the raspy pad of his forefinger reached her areola, tracing it, circling it. It was all she could do not to lean her cheek into the cool, crisp fabric of his sleeve and moan in defeat.

"I am not insane, and you know it," she said, still staring rigidly at the opposite bulkhead as all feeling moved out of her bones and drained into that wet conflagration between her thighs.

"No, but you think I am, do you not?"

"Another misconception only you suffer. You are not insane, just—wounded."

"Wounded," he murmured darkly. His hand was fully beneath her breast now, cupping it, weighing it, his thumb skating over her hardened nipple with exquisite and torturous repetition. She shut her eyes, sighing with pleasure.

He continued to stroke her, maddeningly, until she could no longer maintain her rigidity. She began to squirm, pinned between the hard bar of his arm and the stuffing of the chair's back. He pushed the gown off her shoulder, complete with chemise, exposing the rounded white flesh of her shoulder, her breast.

Gwyneth sank her teeth into her bottom lip to contain a helpless moan.

"And what do you think might *heal* this so-called *wound,* madam?"

"Understanding . . . and love."

He let out a snort of laughter and pushed his thumb into her hard nipple, driving a tiny cry of pleasure from her. "Love and understanding. Dear God, that's rich."

"Everyone needs love and understanding. Especially you, Damon. Your soul begs for it. Your body begs for it, and yet you push it away—"

"My body begs for only one thing," he said with a bitter blitheness that tore at her heart, "and so does yours. Quite shamelessly, I might add. Look down at your nipple, my dear Lady Simms, and you will see that it blushes like a new rosebud. It wants to be suckled."

"Stop it."

He was grinning, hiding now behind amusement. "It wants to be . . . *understood.*"

"Damn you, do not mock me!"

"It wants to be *loved.*"

He caught the hard, engorged bud between his thumb and finger and began to pinch and roll it gently. She gasped, sinking down into the chair as he flicked his thumb over it, sending bolts of lightning sizzling through her belly and into that tingling, burning place beneath her skirts.

Hot waves of feeling washed through her. Her head rolled from side to side against the chair's back, her cheek finally falling against his sleeve. Now his palm was rubbing her nipple, and tiny kittenish sounds clogged the back of her throat.

He flicked his thumb across the tight raindrop of

flesh and leaned over her left shoulder to brush warm, drugging kisses against her collarbone and the swell of her breast.

"Are we now through with this ridiculous exchange?" he asked, challenging her.

"Only if you're prepared to step back and let me walk out of here. Don't forget, *I'm* holding the cards now."

"You hold them because I allow you to," he growled, his breath warm against her flesh. "I could have you right here, right now."

"Such rage that fuels you! I know that it goes beyond the navy and has its origins in something much deeper."

"I could have you in this chair, with your skirts tossed up over your face and your wrists tied behind its back."

"I know that your threats and your words and all your attempts at intimidation are only to keep me away from the *real* man beneath that cold and unfeeling demeanor."

"And *I* know I will have you. Today. *Now.* And I also know that you think this silly babbling of yours will distract you enough to keep you from succumbing to me. But for how long can you keep it up, my dear?" he murmured against the side of her neck, as his right hand came down alongside her head, dipping into her bodice and seeking the opposite breast.

"How long do you think I *want* to keep it up? What on earth makes you think I don't want to succumb to you, and the sooner the better? I'm mad for you, I told you that."

"Good, then let's dispense with this nonsense and get down to business."

"I am not finished. . . ."

"Neither am I."

He bent over her left shoulder, his weight pressing her down into the chair, his warm, spicy scent filling her senses. Through half-open eyes she saw the glorious waves of his dark hair, the faint shadow that

cloaked his jaw, the long sweep of his lashes and the
devil's eyes that glittered beneath them. She moaned
as his lips grazed her neck . . . her collarbone . . . the
swell of her breast. He cupped it in his hand, then
lifted it up toward his mouth like an offering.

She was trapped, pinned effectively between him
and the chair.

"Now isn't this much more fun than telling me
things I don't want to hear? Now tell me something I
do want to hear."

His lips breezed over her hot flesh, seeking her
puckered, waiting aerola. He circled it lazily with his
tongue, avoiding the aching nipple, and Gwyneth's
moans became helpless gasps. The nipple thrust
shamelessly toward him, tight and hard and pink, and
he continued with this exquisite torture for another
long moment before finally giving it the attention it
craved. His mouth closed over that swelling tissue,
pulling it into its hot, liquid warmth. She felt the first
rasp of his tongue, the first questing, flicking taste he
took of her. Her eyes fell shut, and only his other arm,
hooked firmly against her rib cage, kept her from
sliding bonelessly out of the chair. "I cannot resist
you, Damon. Is that what you want to hear?"

"I suppose I should admire you for admitting it."

"Make me admire you equally, then, and admit
that what I've said to you is the truth. Admit it, and
stop hiding behind your fear."

"Dare you call me a coward?"

"You are no coward, merely an intimidating,
manipulative, magnificent devil of a man who is
afraid to face his own demons."

"Ah. And you have appointed yourself as the one
who will make me face them."

"I think you are worth saving."

He merely laughed, his teeth grazing her nipple and
setting it on fire. Gwyneth's head lolled against the
velvet upholstery of the chair back. Dimly, she heard
a clatter as the parasol fell from her loose fingers and
hit the floor.

"I think you are worth . . . understanding," she persisted, faintly.

Against her nipple he mumbled, "Ah—but am I worth *loving?*"

The defiance, the fragile, guarded hope—it was all there.

"Yes," she breathed. "You are well worth loving, Damon. God help me, you are. Now prove it—to yourself as well as to me. Prove it by carrying me to that bed and letting us make love with tenderness and feeling, not with fighting and fury and the desire to conquer. I challenge you. Can you do that?"

He merely pulled her nipple up between his teeth, drawing it in and out of his mouth, his hand shaping her breast as he went. Her senses, her reason deserted her, and she felt that hot, pooling warmth between her thighs growing, spreading, flaring out in all directions to consume her.

Then his hand skimmed down her stomach, gathering her skirts at the knee and dragging them back up her thigh.

"Don't disappoint me, Damon," Gwyneth panted, as first her right cheek, then her left crashed against the chair's velvet padding. "Don't, I beg of you."

And he didn't. Damon felt her squirming, sighing delight, smelled her musky desire and the damp heat that emanated from her, and knew that this war between himself and her, himself and the truth of what she'd said, could not go on. With a growl of impatience, he crushed both skirts and petticoats in his hand and yanked them up to her hips, exposing her long, slender legs from foot to thigh.

There, before him, were stockings and garters, pale white thighs, and her silken mound of dark-gold curls.

Breathing hard, he cupped it in his hot hand.

You're mad, Lady Simms. Utterly, barking mad. But you challenged me, and so I'll challenge you. I'll give you what you want. Then we'll see if you let me down as everyone else has in my life.

He pressed down on her mound, grinding his palm

and the heel of his hand against her until she moaned softly.

Let's see if you really are as different as I so desperately want you to be.

And then, dipping his head once more to savor the sweet bud of her breast, he drove the blade of his hand between her already parted thighs.

She arced back against the chair. "For heaven's sake, Damon, *prove it!*"

It was enough.

Damn her—and himself—to hell.

Still suckling her breast, he slid his fingers through those damp curls, parted the slick petals of her hot woman's flesh, and then, rubbing the hard bud of her clitoris with his thumb, shoved his middle finger deep inside of her, all the way to the knuckle.

She screamed and bucked, and he felt her hot climax contracting the flesh all around his hand.

This is just the start of it.

With a savage growl, he swept her up and carried her to the bed.

Chapter 18

Triumph.

Gwyneth was dimly aware of a sinking sensation, a feeling of falling into and then being embraced by thick, silken pillows and a bed as soft as clouds; tousled sheets and then Morninghall's crushing weight, his darkly beautiful face, as he lowered himself atop her. She felt his powerful length covering her, felt their clothes crumpling between their straining bodies. His hand skimmed down her ribs and hips, untying one garter, then the other. As he peeled her filmy stockings down her knees, her calves, her ankles, she was deliciously afraid, wondrously excited, unable to think of anything but this dark and beautiful lord. Her slippers were already gone, though she did not know when she had lost them; her body was still throbbing from that exquisite pleasure-pain he had brought her to, begging shamelessly for more and already thrusting upward, toward him, of its own accord. She looped her arms around his neck, met his hungry kisses, and closed her eyes as his tongue hungrily, desperately invaded her mouth.

Somewhere, maybe in the back of her imagination, maybe deep within some previously untouched part of her soul, Gwyneth heard a low, rising, rumbling sound, like a gathering of mighty force.

But no, it was only Damon's hand on her breast, Damon's fingers squeezing, stroking, massaging her flesh, Damon's hard mouth grinding against hers, Damon's heady, suddenly gentle and teasing kisses.

"Wait!" she gasped, giggling. "There is something I must tell you—"

"No more of your prattle, woman, or I swear I'll go mad!"

Laughing, she put her arms around his shoulders and pulled his head down to hers. She kissed the side of his jaw, then raised herself up to nuzzle his ear. "Deep in your heart, you know you're really a kind and gentle man, and you're going to prove it to me," she whispered.

He tossed back his head and made a noise of high amusement.

She pulled his head back down. Amused he might have been, but he could not hide the fact that he was intrigued and listening avidly. She put her tongue in his ear, swirling around the folds of flesh until he groaned with delight. "You must admit it, Damon, because if you can, I'll tell you a little secret of my own."

"Anything you say, my lady. I admit it."

"Good. Because, you see, I am a virgin, and I wouldn't want anyone but a kind and gentle man to make me a woman."

"A *what?*" he cried, pushing back and away from her.

"A virgin."

"But—but you were a married woman!"

"Married, but untouched. I trust you'll be gentle."

He was pulling back, shaking his head, his face going white with appalled horror. "Oh, no. This changes things entirely. I'm not making love to a virgin, no way in hell, no matter what you want of me."

"Damon!"

"For God's sake, I'll probably *break* something—"

"Isn't that the idea?"

He merely stared at her, stunned and shocked, his

eyes unguarded, confused, and disbelieving. Then she saw something else coming into them: respect. For in backing off and refusing to touch her, he had just proved to her—and, more importantly, to himself— that he was indeed not the wretched beast he believed himself to be.

She stretched her arms up toward him in silent invitation but saw the indecision warring with want in his eyes, the tortured look on his face. He swallowed hard, then lowered himself back down, refusing to seduce her, wanting only to hold her.

In that stunned and wondrous moment they both heard the roaring noise Gwyneth had thought she'd imagined just moments before. Except now it was punctured by a gunshot, a shout, a rising cacophony of yelling voices. Gwyneth felt only the spring of the mattress as Lord Morninghall leaped off her with a violent curse. Then when he grabbed her hand and yanked her from the bed, she felt terror as he dove for the pistol on his table at the very moment the door crashed open on its hinges and a crowd of dirty, rage-maddened men burst into the room, all screaming like madmen.

There were at least thirty, maybe forty of them, with several hundred more shoving from behind.

Gwyneth screamed.

"Get back, Gwyneth!" the marquess roared, leaping in front of her and squeezing off a shot. One of the grinning men at the forefront of the pack stumbled and fell sprawling. The man's demise did not deter his companions, though, and those nearest to him trampled straight over his body, rushing into the cabin, screaming like a legion of demons straight out of hell. Gwyneth saw it all in flashes that would haunt her worst nightmares for years to come: the tide of crazed, murderous men storming into the cabin, the deck beyond them a blur of movement and streaks of scarlet as the guards tried desperately to contain the prisoner uprising; gunfire all around; the wild clangor of bells some place, screams, shouts. And Lord Morn-

inghall, his pistol spent, his last noble act to shove her
desperately toward the window before the mob fell on
him, pulling him down, burying him beneath their
leaping bodies and flashing fists, their savage, kicking
feet and unholy shouts of triumph and rage. She
screamed and tried to race past the frenzied tangle for
help, all the while listening to the sound of fists
against flesh, against bone. She saw one of Morninghall's glossy boots kicking out beneath the clamoring
horde, just the boot and nothing else, heard their
enraged curses and yells, saw their flailing fists, saw
that glossy boot relax and go still. Hands grabbed at
her as she tried to run past, and she was jerked up
against a filthy chest, smelling tooth rot as a mouth
crashed over hers. She heard her own screams, felt her
arm nearly ripped from its socket, then saw Lieutenant Radley's wild face as he hauled her out of the
melee and out of the cabin, across the deck and to the
rail. She screamed Damon's name, felt a bullet whiz
past her head, heard gunfire at close range—

And then only empty space as she tumbled over and
over again before hitting the shocking icy water of the
harbor.

The impact drove the breath out of her. Hissing
bubbles of silence enclosed her and she felt herself
sinking, the loose curtain of her hair swirling about
her face and blinding her, the weight of her skirts
dragging her down . . . down . . . down into the cold,
black depths. Blissful, terrifying silence. Raw, aching
cold. *Give it up and die.* Then fingers snared her
upthrust hand and she was yanked forcefully toward
the surface, which she broke sputtering, coughing,
and crying. Something hard stabbed her in the ribs
and wood smashed against her cheek before she
realized she'd been tossed into a boat. She opened her
eyes and found herself staring up into the handsome
face of the seaman who'd been rowing the dead body
ashore.

The body was gone and she lay in its place.

"Get down, woman, things have gone mad," the

man said urgently, picking up his oars as the angry pops of gunfire broke the air above.

"I can't leave! I must go back! Lord Morninghall, he tried to save me, the prisoners overwhelmed the ship, they'll kill him, for God's sake, take me back!"

Her rescuer flung down his oars and grabbed her upper arms, his fingers digging into her flesh to calm her hysteria. He stared hard into her eyes. *"There is nothing you can do!"* Then, wasting no time, he began rowing with all his strength toward shore, sending a wake of ripples fanning out from astern. Shots rang out from the prison hulk, and Gwyneth heard the agonized screams of dying men and splashes as bodies were hurled off the ship.

"You can't just leave him to their mercy!" she cried in anguish. *"They'll kill him!"*

The sailor kept rowing, desperate to get them away from the hulk.

"Damn you, *take me back!*"

He ignored her until he was satisfied they were well clear of the danger. Then he paused in his vigorous rowing, and as the sea streamed past the boat and the sounds of gunfire echoed across the water, his jade eyes met hers. They were wise, those eyes, too wise for such a youthful face, and in them was a deep and sympathetic sadness. Very quietly he said, "If they haven't killed him yet, they will certainly have done so by the time any of us can get to him." He reached out and gently touched her shoulder. "It is too late, my lady."

It is too late.

Gwyneth stared at him for a moment, the truth breaking over her in harsh, crushing waves of pain; then she bent her head to her hands and sobbed.

Jack Clayton roared and bashed his way through the howling mob that was bottlenecking outside the captain's quarters in his desperation to get inside. Blows fell on his head and on his beefy shoulders, but he did not feel the pain, only a blinding, crazed need to get to the marquess. Trained to respect his betters, unswerving in his loyalty to those he served, he gripped the stock of his musket in both hands and used the weapon like a pike, driving it into a spine here, the back of a skull there, making halting but steady progress toward the cabin. His face was grim and his movements automatic, for the bodies that fell beneath his stabbing, swinging blows were no longer individuals, no longer human, just part of a surging, bloodthirsty mass of moving faces, writhing arms, screaming voices, crazed eyes. His friend Al Cavendish was back to back with him, and together the two guards, now joined by their mates as they too barreled their way through the fracas, fought their way toward that broken, open door.

Out of the corner of his eye, Clayton caught a glimpse of that sniveling coward Radley, his face contorted not so much with terror but with crazed excitement as he ran back from the rail where he'd thrown Lady Simms overboard.

"Watch it, Jack!" yelled Cavendish, and Clayton hurled himself sideways, colliding with an enraged prisoner who came at him with a bloody knife. He jerked the musket savagely up, clipping the wretch under the jaw and instantly breaking his neck, and the fellow slid bonelessly to the deck, there to be trampled by hundreds of running feet.

"Get back, you sons of bitches!" Clayton roared, driving the butt of his musket into the shoulders of the men who blocked the door as he fought his way forward. "Get the hell back!"

Just off to his right he saw the young marine Paul Mattson clinging to a nearby shroud and aiming a blunderbuss at the knot of prisoners who pushed and shoved at the cabin door as they cheered on whatever grisly horror was going on within. Flames shot from the weapon in one deafening explosion, and the prisoners fell like a row of dominoes.

Howling in rage and viciously swinging his musket, Clayton vaulted over their bodies and into the cabin. Men stampeded toward and past him in a wave of humanity gone mad, desperate now only to escape the cabin, the ship. Somewhere outside, the blunderbuss roared again, screams filling the air. Clayton chopped and clubbed his way through the advancing mob, through which he could just see glimpses of Lord Morninghall's overturned table and chairs, the rug, and there, on the deck, a hand, a boot, a white shirt covered in blood,—*oh, shit*—before the sight was blocked once more by the massive exodus.

Almost there, he thought, and as the last of the prisoners tried to charge past him, he saw that one of them was the troublemaker Armand Moret, his hands stained with blood, his mouth an insane grin of triumph in his bony skull. Without pity, thought, or care, Clayton brought his musket to full cock, jerked the weapon up, and, aiming it point-blank at the Frenchman's chest, fired.

The explosion rocked the cabin, obliterating the sickening thud of Armand's body hitting the deck, the sound of china crashing from a nearby cupboard, the maelstrom just outside. For a brief, awful moment the cabin went as still as a tomb. Then, as the smoke cleared, Clayton, coughing, tossed down his musket and charged forward, knowing he was already too late.

He saw the upended legs of the table, the overturned swivel chair, a lost boot, and there, lying facedown in a widening pool of bright red blood—

Lord Morninghall.

The marquess was completely still, and there was a dagger sticking out of his back.

Clayton turned away with a pent-up exhalation of defeat. He passed a shaky hand over his face, wiping away the sweat and the grime and the sight of the carnage before him, and met Cavendish's horrified eyes.

"Oh, *shit,*" he said again.

* * *

The bedroom was dark and quiet as a tomb, shadows reaching into the very corners. Only the window and the cushioned seat below were illuminated by the faint moonlight sifting down through the heavy, fast-moving clouds that filed in from the sea. No candle burned on the bedside table; only embers glowed in the hearth. A cool breeze moved through the room, sighing in from the window like the breath of a spirit, lifting the gossamer white curtains on an invisible hand then letting them drift down over the bent head of the woman who sat huddled on the seat below them.

An untouched cup of tea had gone cold on the sill beside her, and her still-damp hair was caught at the nape of her neck in a black velvet ribbon. Her knees were drawn up under her chin, her arms anchored about them. Through tragic eyes Gwyneth gazed out the window at the distant harbor, silent and still beneath the clouds, where she could see the prison ship lit up in a blaze of light.

It hurt to look at it, yet she could not look away. Out there in the distance, beyond the dark shapes of the hedges beneath her window, beyond the newly budding roses and the crowded brick houses that fell away toward the black vista of the harbor, she could see the lights of boats carrying various naval officials to and from the prison hulk.

She wondered which boat had carried Morninghall's broken body away from the carnage, and pressed a damp handkerchief to her nose, the back of her throat aching with tears.

She swallowed hard, choking on a lump of grief.

Her rescuer—his name escaped her, though she thought it was something like Kiernan or Connor, something like that, something Irish, it didn't matter really—had landed her safely on shore, then promptly disappeared into the frantic press of rushing naval officers and seamen, all running to and fro in their haste to respond to the alarm out in the harbor. No one had paid her any attention. No one could help her. No one had answered her pleas to be taken out to the prison ship, to Damon. She had finally been escorted to some room in some naval office, questioned, interviewed, and told to wait. She had sat dazedly on a bench for God knew how long before a gentle hand had touched her shoulder and she had looked up to see the compassionate face of Maeve, Lady Falconer. Her friend had promptly ushered her out of the crowded building, into her own private carriage, and, as the sun began to sink from the sky and the clouds to sweep in from the sea, brought her home.

The rest of the evening had passed in a dull, throbbing haze of numbness. Brief vignettes of it hung suspended in her mind. She remembered Maeve murmuring something to her sister as they'd entered the little house; she remembered Rhiannon enfolding her in her arms, leading her up the stairs and to the hot bath the maid was already drawing; she remembered the hot tears slipping down her cheeks and pattering softly upon the carpet as Rhiannon quietly stripped the wet clothes from her trembling body.

"He was worth saving, Rhiannon," she'd cried brokenly as she'd sat in the warm tub and bent her head to her hands in grief. Her little sister had said nothing, only squeezing warm, peach-scented bubbles out of a sponge and over her back. "I saw the goodness in him, Rhiannon, the compassion, saw it at last, and now it is too late and I can't see anything but his boot, kicking out, falling still, over and over and over again. . . ."

"I know," Rhiannon had whispered. The water had sounded sad and lonely as it trickled back into the tub.

"He didn't even have a chance . . . no, he had only *one* chance, and he *gave it to me*."

"Hush, Gwyn. It will be all right."

"He's dead, Rhiannon. It's not all right."

Rhiannon had retreated into silence. Nothing had remained but the broken trickle of the water, sluicing back into the tub.

Dead.

Now the curtains lifted in the breeze once more, whispering over Gwyneth's face and the back of her neck. She wondered if Morninghall's spirit was in the wind, if this was his way of coming to say good-bye.

Her eyes filled once more, and she shut them on a great, trembling breath. The tears leaked silently from her eyes, ran brokenly down her cheeks.

Damon.

She wanted the numbness back, all of it, not these flashes of agony.

She remembered stepping out of the bath, Rhiannon placing a thick, plush wrapper around her shuddering body and leading her toward the dull glow of the fire. She remembered sitting there on the stone hearth, staring into the embers as the last light faded into gray beyond her window. And as the day died, and the night out there went black, Gwyneth realized it was absolutely silly to be sitting here sobbing over the death of someone she didn't love, but in the rest of that thought she answered herself that she had indeed loved Morninghall, loved him quite passionately, and it was her deepest and most agonizing regret that she had not had the chance to tell him so. He would've given his dark, mocking laugh, of course, he might've wanted to do something rude and impossible to try to convince her there was nothing about him worth loving, but there would've been that brief flash of vulnerability across his cold gaze, that sudden, fleeting proof that he was indeed worthy of, and desperate for, that which he deserved no less than any other.

Love.

And now it was too late.

Dead.

Gwyneth sniffled and rested her brow in her hands, her hair splaying around her fingertips. Outside, the stars made milky pinpricks of light in the gaps of moving cloud cover, here one moment, gone the next. Wind rustled through the lilac bushes, through the tops of the nearby trees: a lonely, mournful, empty sound that tore at her heart. From downstairs came the low murmur of Maeve's and Rhiannon's voices, the faint scents of cooking meat and freshly baked bread; from somewhere out in the night came the distant, approaching clatter of a horse's hoofbeats. The fire popped in the hearth, dying, and again the wind came, keening through the night and the trees, making them bend and sigh and whisper.

Gwyneth sat motionless, staring with empty eyes across the still and darkened harbor.

"Damon."

The wind pushed harder, making the treetops scrape against the low clouds.

"Oh, my magnificent, wonderful Damon," she whispered, crumpling the damp handkerchief in her hand. "How hard you fought against the sunlight in yourself, the goodness." She leaned the side of her head against the windowsill, already damp with her tears. "God will have seen that goodness, Damon. If I saw it, certainly He, who knows the secrets in all our hearts, will have seen it too. You may believe otherwise, but I know He'll take you into heaven. I know He will keep you safe and sound until someday—" A bitter, choking sob rose up in her throat, and she pressed the handkerchief to her face to contain it.

The tears were flowing freely now. Out in the night, the lonely traveler was closer now, the rattle and squeak of a carriage, the sound of shod hooves against cobblestone passing by on the street outside the house. The world went on as usual, heedless of the life that had ended only hours before, a life that had been cut short before it ever had had the chance to know itself, to realize its full and powerful potential, to laugh and love and be loved in turn.

When she came up for air, she couldn't hear the horse and carriage anymore. She realized that they must have stopped just outside her house, and as she raised her head and brought the wet hankie from her face, she heard the rumble of a deep, male voice downstairs.

Two male voices, interspersed with Maeve's and her sister's.

They have come to tell me he is dead. I cannot go down there; I cannot face this. Please, God, give me strength as I pray you gave it to Damon during those last, awful moments.

And the strength did not fail her. It never had, and it did not now. With an almost mechanical resolution, Gwyneth wiped the last tears away, forced her chin up, and was just changing into a simple, dark dress when she heard her sister's light tread coming up the stairs. There was a soft, hesitant knock on the door.

"Gwyn?"

"It's open."

The door opened slowly, revealing first a blinding bar of light in the bright hall beyond, then Rhiannon's willowy silhouette. Gwyneth blinked against the sudden brightness and turned away. She bent her head so that her sister would not see she had been crying.

Rhiannon came forward quietly and took her sister's cold hands.

"Gwyn, Admiral Sir Graham Falconer and the Reverend Peter Milford are downstairs. They wish to speak with you."

For a long moment Gwyneth could not move. The final confirmation was here at last. An admiral and a pastor, the pallbearers of death. One the representative of the navy, the other of God. She took a deep, steadying breath, straightened her shoulders, and, nodding once, followed her sister down the stairs.

It was the longest, and hardest, walk she ever took in her life.

Chapter 19

Blinking in the light, Gwyneth composed herself and walked quietly into the parlor.

The heavy drapes were drawn at the windows. A fire flickered in the hearth, snapping and crackling quietly. She saw Mattie, sprawled on his side before it, and then, a circle of people sitting in chairs, all engaged in sober conversation, their tones low and respectful.

So softly had Gwyneth come into the room that no one yet noticed her. Maeve sat in one of the velvet-upholstered chairs, her hair glowing red in the firelight like a rich and expensive wine. In profile beside her sat her magnificent husband, Sir Graham, who, despite his fine naval uniform with its tasseled epaulets and rows of gleaming gold buttons, and the commanding air he wore as easily as his wife did the sharks' teeth that ringed her throat, looked like nothing less than some dark and ruthless pirate straight from a Caribbean plundering spree. A hoop of gold pierced his ear, and though he was in the middle of his fourth decade, his handsome face had yet to show signs of age and his midnight black hair was still rich, flowing, and devoid of any threads of gray. Gwyneth felt a flood of pain just looking at him. Like Morninghall, the admiral filled the room with his charisma and presence. Like Morninghall, he was a study in masculine power, beauty, and grace. But where Morninghall had been remote and enigmatic, Sir Graham

was relaxed and open. Now, as she silently watched
him, he leaned close to his wife, one broad, darkly
tanned hand resting on the arm of her chair and
covering her own.

Their fingers, she noted with a pang of sadness and
envy, were loosely entwined.

To think that someday she and Morninghall might
have shared the same enduring love.

Too late.

The chaplain, in contrast, was fair-skinned and
slightly built. His hazel eyes were kind, compassionate, far too serious for one so young in years; his hair
reflected the dancing light of the fire in a mass of curls
any cherub would envy. Yet despite his overwhelm-
ingly gentle demeanor, Gwyneth sensed an iron core
in him. Both men looked up as she moved into the
room and rose immediately to their feet.

"Lady Simms," the admiral said in his deep, commanding voice, moving forward to take and bow over
her hand.

"Lady Simms," the chaplain echoed in his softer,
gentler one.

Maeve only looked up, an unreadable expression in
her lovely golden eyes.

Gwyneth returned their greetings and then, her
heart beating a lengthening crack against her breastbone, sank into a chair beside Rhiannon with quiet
words that the men should do the same.

Chairs scraped and clothing rustled. An air of
expectancy filled the room. Gwyneth steepled her
hands between her knees and pressed against them,
hard, to brace herself for what she knew was coming.
She forced her head up, determined to be brave. "You
wished to speak to me, Sir Graham, Reverend Milford."

The admiral leaned back in his chair and cleared
his throat. "I understand that you have undergone
considerable trauma this afternoon while trying to
bring reform to our prison ships. A deplorable and
shameful lot the hulks are, and may I first offer you

my warmest gratitude for undertaking a task that most, even in our own navy, would prefer to turn a blind eye to."

"He's dead, isn't he?" Gwyneth said flatly. She stared unblinkingly into the admiral's azure gaze.

He raised one dark, piratical eyebrow, and the Reverend Milford cleared his throat.

"Lady Simms—"

"No, no, do be straightforward and tell me. I have prepared myself. There is nothing more that can happen this day to make it worse than it already has been. Just please tell me it was over quickly and that he died with a minimum of suffering."

The admiral frowned and looked at his wife, but before he could speak the chaplain's gentle voice broke the hush of the moment.

"Sir Graham will tell you no such thing," he said quietly. "Lord Morninghall survived."

"Oh, Gwyn!" Rhiannon shrieked, quickly slapping a hand over her mouth.

Gwyneth grasped the arms of her chair and leaned forward. "Do not jest with me, Reverend. I saw him go down beneath the prisoners, I saw the murder and hatred in their faces. They beat and kicked him. I saw it all with my own eyes—"

"The reverend is quite right, Lady Simms," the admiral interrupted, his deep, masculine voice filling the room. "Lord Morninghall is gravely ill and lying in hospital as we speak, but he is not dead."

The room tilted and Gwyneth felt deep, wracking shudders pass through her body. She could not sustain another shock.

"Not dead," she whispered shakily.

"Not dead," the admiral confirmed. "Though damned close to it, I might add."

Gwyneth took a deep, steadying breath and tightened her hands around the arms of the chair. Her heart pounded against the flood of sudden hope, and her eyes filled with fresh, stinging mist. She leaned her head back against the chair, took a deep breath, and, composed once more, looked at the admiral. "I'm sorry," she whispered with a fragile smile. "This is all too much for me to take in, too much to . . . to hope for." She shook her head, still dazed by the revelation that Damon was alive. "I—I don't understand why you're here then . . . you being an admiral and all . . . I mean, I thought you'd come to tell me he was dead. . . ."

The admiral gallantly ignored her confusion. "Forgive me, Lady Simms. I've distressed you unnecessarily." His thumb caressed the back of his wife's hand, faintly agitated. "I must confess that this sort of thing is not my strength, and I'd be far more useful back at sea, where my foe is one who can be vanquished with stratagem, shrewdness, and cannon strength."

Maeve smiled wryly. "What my husband means is, he does not care for the political end of his duties and would rather be out blowing up ships and fleets."

"I see," said Gwyneth, though she did not see at all.

"Allow me to be blunt, Lady Simms," the admiral said. "Morninghall's superiors and a committee of officers of which I am thankfully not a part have suspended him from his duties until such time that a decision can be made concerning his fitness to command a prison hulk. It has yet to be decided whether or not that suspension will be a permanent one." He took a sip of tea. "Apparently his ship has been the target of numerous successful escape attempts, and the navy has had its fill of the subsequent embarrassment. Furthermore, Morninghall has not, shall we say, made himself at all favorable to his superiors, and his recent record speaks of insubordination and contempt for them. He has been warned by his commanding officer to tighten security, but still the escapes have continued, and today's events have finally broken the patience of that officer and others."

Maeve was gazing down at her husband's hand, her face flushed. She looked decidedly uncomfortable—no surprise, considering the fact that her brother, also escaped from the prison hulk *Surrey,* was reputed to be the Black Wolf. What a difficult position Sir Graham was in—and how diplomatically he was handling it, Gwyneth thought in admiration. She was willing to bet he couldn't wait to get back to his post in the West Indies, away from this whole business.

Nodding, Gwyneth met the admiral's gaze. "So what do you ask of me, Sir Graham?"

He glanced at his companion. "Reverend Milford here tells me that Morninghall has no family. He also claims the marquess is something of a lone wolf who is not on a friendly, intimate basis with anyone. However, we have come to you for help because we don't know who else to turn to."

"What do you mean?"

Sir Graham looked directly at Gwyneth. "Lord Morninghall is semiconscious and out of his head." Then, softly: "But it's your name he's calling."

Gwyneth's mouth fell open and she felt a direct lance of pain to her heart, so intense she was forced to put her hand over it. In confusion she looked from the admiral to the chaplain. "My name?"

"Yes, over and over again. He will not stop."

Gwyneth sat back in her chair and closed her eyes, assailed by such a wave of feeling she could not speak. Beside her, Rhiannon reached out and took her hand.

"What sort of injuries has His Lordship sustained?" Rhiannon asked quietly, seeing that her sister was too choked up to answer.

"He was beaten senseless and took a knife in the back. The doctor thinks it missed the vital organs, but I warn you not to get your hopes up too high. His Lordship is falling in and out of consciousness, and it is impossible at this stage to gauge the extent of damage to body and brain."

Gwyneth found her voice. "You're saying he may die."

"He will most certainly die if he is not allowed to recover in an environment of total peace, quiet, and devoted attention."

Gwyneth's spine tingled with a mixture of hope and horror. She closed her eyes, silently squeezing and relaxing her hold on the arms of her chair.

It's your name he's calling.

"So what is it you want of me?" she whispered.

"Since it is you the marquess seems to want, we're hoping you can have some effect on his recovery. He's been brought aboard the hospital ship *Perseus,* but, as you may imagine, it is a crowded, excitable place, and the surgeon there has many to look after besides him." Sir Graham leveled his stare on her with quiet entreaty. "I would like you to take him out of Portsmouth, away from the navy, and into an environment as I've just described."

"You cannot be serious, Sir Graham! I cannot nurse an injured man here in my house. It is utterly unthinkable."

"The admiral did not say you must bring Morninghall here," Reverend Milford put in gently.

"Most assuredly not," Sir Graham agreed. "People would talk. Your own reputation would be damaged beyond repair. No, my lady, the reverend and I have discussed the matter at length, and we have come to the conclusion that Lord Morninghall's recovery would be best brought about if he were to be taken home, and you were to go with him."

"And home is?"

"His ancestral seat in the Cotswolds, Morninghall Abbey."

Gwyneth sat very still in her chair. She looked down at her hands, so white against the darkness of her dress, and felt the weighty silence around her, the expectant gazes of her companions.

"We have already arranged for a carriage to convey you, should you decide to go," the chaplain added gently.

"And if I do not?"

There was a long, expectant silence, with only the flames popping and cracking in the hearth. Reverend

Milford pushed his hand through his curls, and when he met her gaze, his face looked suddenly weary, pained, and sad.

"If you do not go then Morninghall will not be the first naval officer to die aboard a hospital ship."

Gwyneth bent her head to her hand. Raw emotion pushed beneath her eyelids, and she could already feel the tears beginning to trickle down her cheeks. Guilt pummeled her heart, for if she hadn't distracted him, Damon would've heard the prisoners in time to save them both. But no, he had chosen to save *her* life, not his own, and the very least she owed him was that same selflessness in return. If she could pull him through this, God only knew what they might find together. Maybe the two of them *could* have what Maeve and Sir Graham had.

Ah—but am I worth loving?

God help her, he was.

Rhiannon could no longer contain herself. "He's calling for you, Gwyn. You *have* to go."

Gwyneth gave a little smile and looked into the flames. "There is no need for any of you to go to any lengths to convince me," she said quietly. "I shall be ready to leave just as soon as you have the carriage brought round."

Chapter 20

Gwyneth felt as though she'd spent the last two
days at sea after the endless rocking and jounc-
ing of the coach. The vehicle, escorted by two sailors
on horseback, was comfortable and well sprung, but
nevertheless it had been a tedious, painful journey,
with frequent stops along the way. Now the Thames
Valley with its pastoral fields, rich clay soil, and
farmhouses of gray stone and flint was behind them,
as were the ancient spires of Oxford. As she gazed
anxiously out the window, the scene that met her eyes
was the spectacular beauty of the Cotswolds.

It was breathtaking countryside, rising in dramatic,
undulating hills planted with acres of feathery barley,
grassy pastures, and young wheat which waved end-
lessly in the wind. Occasionally the varying plots of
green were broken by a freshly tilled field, creating a
patchwork effect divided by a hedgerow here, a ram-
bling wall of yellow Cotswold stone there. Clumps of
elm, beech, and oak were plunked down at random,
lone, plumed sentinels in a countryside that rolled
and yawed and stretched for as far as the eye could
see. Above, thick, white clouds moved across a sky as
blue as flax, dragging their shadows across the windswept fields with them. Looking down at this magnificent vista, Gwyneth felt like some great, soaring eagle
wheeling above it, a spirit released from her body.

If only her companion could see it.

Opposite her the marquess lay moaning in pain and

delirium, his blanketed body propped against pillows and strapped securely to the small seat so that the endless bouncing would not spill him to the floor. Heavily bandaged, he looked no better than he had the evening—was it two nights ago? three?—the two seamen, sternly supervised by Sir Graham and a worried Reverend Milford, had lifted his inert, broken body out of the little boat that had brought him from the hospital ship and carried him swiftly to the waiting coach. Gwyneth had nearly swooned when she'd first seen him, for the bandages wound about his head, the sling that supported his arm, and the purple, bruised flesh of his cheek and jaw—had all been quite shocking. Now he was feverish as well, his hands hot and a film of sweat glistening at the base of his throat. Thank God a messenger had been sent ahead, and a doctor would be waiting for them at Morninghall.

"I will take care of you, Damon," she murmured, lightly touching his face through the hot bandages. "So help me, God, I will see you out of this, and I will see you better, even if it kills me. I *will not let you down.*"

A gust of wind buffeted the coach, and a growing part of her fought against the premonition that she was bringing the Marquess of Morninghall home not to heal—but to die.

The coach bumped over a rut in the road and began to slow as the horses labored up yet another hill. Anxiously, Gwyneth stared out once more, hoping for her first glance of Morninghall Abbey, but there was nothing out there but an occasional farmhouse tucked into a valley, the clouds moving like great ships across the blue sky, and wide, rolling fields, the grasses randomly sprinkled with dandelions and tiny white daisies.

Even as she thought it, she knew she was wrong. There *was* something different now. A coolness in the air perhaps. A darkening as some of those massive clouds began to slide across the sun. A sense of uneasiness, maybe even expectancy, as though this ancient land knew its lord had finally come home, and it was preparing the scene for his arrival. Gwyneth shivered, feeling it in her very bones, and on the seat across from her the marquess murmured something in his opium-induced stupor and tried to raise his bandaged head.

She took his hand in both of her own, squeezing the long, hot fingers.

"It's all right, Damon. I am here."

"No . . . not here . . . Gwyneth, where are you? Gwyneth. . . . *Gwyneth*—"

"Easy, Damon, we're almost home."

Her words seemed only to agitate him further, and he began to thrash like a child. He got one of his arms free of the strap and began tearing at his bandages.

"Do hurry, Edwards!" Gwyneth called up to the driver.

"Get on with ye!" the man yelled, trying to coax more speed from the flagging horses.

Gwyneth leaned forward and put her arms around the marquess, trying to hold down his struggling body with her own. She did not know if he recognized her, did not know if the damage he'd sustained had reduced his keen intelligence to that of an infant, but her nearness seemed to calm him and he went still, moaning in pain, sobbing, the sweat gleaming on his throat and his chest rising and falling with his rasping, quickening respiration.

Outside, the clouds were definitely growing thicker, gathering like a massing army and blotting out more and more of the blue sky. As the wind gusted again, she could feel the heavy threat of rain in the air.

"Almost there, my lady," came the driver's voice from above. "Another half a mile at most."

Thank God.

Damon lay back against the seat, shaking and making horrible keening noises of pain and fear.

Her own heart pounding, Gwyneth took his hand in her own, trying frantically to calm him. Now the road was leading into a great tree-lined drive, curving gently as it followed the crown of this highest, noblest hill.

Damon clutched her hand in a death grip, his harsh, rapid breathing filling the coach.

Her fingers began to throb and she tried to free her hand, but his grip became desperate, savage.

Greenish darkness and a cool, eerie silence came as they passed beneath a low, heavy canopy of oaks. Sounds were amplified. The horse's hooves crunched against the gravel; the squeak and rattle of the coach echoed against the wall of huge trees on either side. A drop of rain splashed into the coach, followed by another. And there, looming up out of the shadowy depths ahead, was a huge pair of iron gates which barred the drive from this point on. A massive, eight-foot-high wall draped with ivy ran out from either side of them, the stone no longer yellow but a dull tan beneath the heavy trees and the sudden retreat of the sun.

The coach came to a lurching stop. Gwyneth looked out and saw, perched high atop pedestals on either side of the gates, two ancient sentinels of black stone—mighty, life-sized wolves, warning her away with baleful, staring eyes.

She swallowed hard and, as Damon's grip on her fingers became crushing, looked through the gates.

Beyond them was a long, flat drive laid out like carpet for royalty.

And there, clouds of gray framing its majestic, forbidding splendor, stood the great house itself, Morninghall Abbey.

"We're here, my lady!"

The clouds moved across the sky, and the last of the sunlight fell off.

The Marquess of Morninghall's hand slipped from hers as he collapsed in a dead faint.

* * *

"Hurry, we must get him inside!" Gwyneth cried, leaping down from the coach before it even had come to a stop and impatiently holding the door wide as two bewigged and liveried footmen hurried forward.

The steps of the great house were lined with servants, the men elegantly dressed and powdered, the women watching with fearful eyes. Gwyneth had no time to take in the arrayed magnificence, no time to greet the elderly, arthritic butler who introduced himself as Britwell, no time to wonder about the nervous looks passing between the twin ranks of servants.

She impatiently waved a footman toward the open door of the coach, biting her lip, fidgeting with worry. The servant, a huge, strapping country lad, leaned into the carriage and brought the marquess out. Holding his master like a babe in his arms, he looked silently to Gwyneth for direction.

They hurried toward the house.

"I trust you got Admiral Sir Graham's missive?" Gwyneth asked as Britwell rushed along beside her.

"Yes, my lady. It arrived yesterday. The doctor is waiting in His Lordship's bedroom."

The marquess stirred, began to moan, and, as the footman carried him past the twin rows of servants and up the stairs, started fighting against the arms that held him, thrashing and crying out with pain.

"Right this way, my lady," Britwell urged, hurrying the little party into a magnificent receiving hall, down a corridor, up a sweeping flight of stairs, and down another corridor lined with books, portraits, busts, and antiquities. He was moving fast, nearly running, so Gwyneth grabbed up her skirts and began to run too, trying to keep up.

"No . . . NO!" Damon was mumbling, as the footman rushed him down the hall. "Gwyneth, no . . . don't let them bring me in there, please—"

At the far end of the long corridor, a man emerged from a room and hurried toward them.

"I'm Dr. MacDowell," he puffed, staring anxiously at the man thrashing in the footman's arms. He quickly ushered them all into the bedroom, dashed to the bed, and began turning down the sheets.

"Set him right here, man——"

Damon's fist was flailing, swinging into empty space. "Gwyneth, no . . . not here. . . ."

"He doesn't want to be in here!" Gwyneth cried, trying unsuccessfully to prevent the footman from putting the struggling marquess on the bed.

"He has to be in here, it's the only room we have prepared for him," the doctor snapped. "Footman, close the door, pull those drapes——"

"Gwyneth! . . . Help me . . . the wolf . . . going to bite me," Damon was mumbling. "*Don't let him bite me* . . . Mama's in here . . . she'll hurt me—— *Gwyneth!*"

"It's all right, my love," she said soothingly, leaning over the bed and taking his hand. "Nothing is going to hurt you."

"Don't listen to him, he's delirious," the doctor said gruffly, pushing her out of the way as he took Damon's arm, shoved up the sleeve of his nightshirt, and felt around for a vein. "It's just nonsense he's spouting, nothing more."

"Wolves, Gwyneth," the marquess whispered, his head thrashing from side to side on the pillow. "Don't let them bite me . . . don't let them bite me. . . ."

Desperate, Gwyneth spun to look around the room—and saw what he could not see but obviously remembered well.

"Get *rid* of that hideous thing!" she cried, spotting the great pelt of black fur that hung above the massive stone fireplace.

Britwell protested, "But my lady, that wolf hide has been there since the first marquess killed it with his bare hands back in——"

"I don't care how long it's been there, get rid of it, it's frightening him!" She whirled and saw a huge portrait, directly opposite the bed, of a formidable-looking woman in court dress and jewels. "And who is that?"

"It's his mother, the late marchioness—"

She waved another footman toward the painting. "Get that *witch* off the wall and out of here too!"

"But my lady, it's his *mother*—"

"Get her out of here!"

The footman ran toward the painting. Britwell, speechless, stood back with a little smile of admiration on his face. Down went the wolf pelt, and out the door. Down came the painting, and out the door. There were two pedestals on either side of the huge, carved bed, and on them sat two more wolves, these of black marble; without hesitation Gwyneth grabbed up a spare sheet, tore it in two, and threw it over each baleful, staring head.

On the bed the marquess had curled into a pitiful ball, his arms over his head and covering his bandaged face. He was sweating and trembling convulsively, and as the doctor tried to come near him, he struck out with a fist that, even directionless, was potentially lethal.

Unafraid, Gwyneth went to him, sat down on the bed, and snared the white-knuckled hand. She held it to her cheek tenderly.

"It's all right now, Damon. Those stupid wolves are gone. Your mother's gone. *I'm* here, and I'm not going to let anyone hurt you."

As he curled himself around her fist, sobbing, she looked up at the doctor. A shocked stillness hung over the room, and everyone in it was staring at her with a mixture of fear and respect, as though she were some general just in from a war.

The doctor swallowed hard.

"You may come near him now," she said firmly. "He'll give you no more trouble."

Later that evening, many miles away on a windy stretch of the Channel, Connor Merrick stood at the helm of the schooner *Kestrel* and watched the random lights of the English coast sliding in and out of the mists just off to starboard.

They were close-hauled on the starboard tack, the schooner sailing so close to the wind that Connor's face was damp with salt water, his hair wet with spray. Wind hummed through stays and shrouds, and the black, endless waves angled out of the night toward them, breaking against the *Kestrel*'s rapier-sharp bows and parading beneath her hull in great, sweeping swells of mighty power and hissing foam.

"See anything yet, Orla?" he called to the woman who sat far out astride the bowsprit, watching.

"Not yet."

Not yet. A signal, three short, hooded blinks of a lantern, wasn't much to ask. Had Milford been detained? Where the hell was he?

He stared grimly at Orla's slim figure, a dark smudge against the charcoal night and darkened sea. With her piratical past she was priceless, he thought, as sharp and keen as a well-honed knife. He was sure going to hate losing her, but he did not love her, not in the way she wanted to be loved. He could give her a place on the *Kestrel,* he could give her friendship and adventure and a reason to exist—but he could not give her love.

He thought of the one man who could—and smiled wryly. It was doubtful the Reverend Milford, once he asked for Orla's hand, would take kindly to her roving the seas and smuggling prisoners of war off the hulks any more than his brother-in-law Sir Graham Falconer had to his sister Maeve's desire to continue terrorizing the West Indies as the formidable Pirate Queen of the Caribbean.

Poor Maeve.

Poor Maeve, my arse.

His ribs were *still* sore.

He wiped the spray from his face, remembering. No sooner had he left Nathan's body hidden beneath a tarp in the marshes when alarms had sounded from the prison hulk, and he'd rowed frantically back toward the stricken ship just in time to see Lady Gwyneth Evans Simms take what surely would've been a fatal tumble into the harbor had he not been there to fish her out. Her hysterically babbled news about Morninghall had been like a fist to the gut, and in that moment Connor had known it was the beginning of the end. Without the marquess aboard the prison hulk, all was lost.

And young Toby had yet to be rescued.

Not that he'd had time to do the deed himself. He'd barely brought Lady Simms to shore and watched her disappear into the crowds when a figure had dropped lightly down into his boat like something out of a boarding party. He'd looked up to see his sister, elegant in silk and sharks' teeth, smiling that ominous smile of hers and calmly holding the point of her dagger against his ribs. People had been rushing about like chickens with their heads cut off—rushing to shore, rushing to boats, rushing to piers, yelling, shouting, giving orders—but none of them had taken notice of the ex–pirate queen, and *she* had been equally oblivious to them.

I want my ship back. Now. And Orla.

It had taken all of Connor's significant powers of persuasion to convince her to let him keep the *Kestrel.* After all, Maeve might've married an Englishman, but her heart was still American, and even she could not argue that the *Kestrel* was best kept in the service of the country that had built her. With a promise to sway her powerful husband to abandon the hunt for the missing schooner, Maeve had finally set her lips and ordered—*ordered!,* Connor thought with a little chuckle—him to "just return the *Kestrel* to our home in Barbados when you're damn well finished with her, *or else.*"

The "or else" was not worth considering, he thought, grinning and massaging his ribs.

Ah, well. By now she and Sir Graham and their growing brood were on their way back to the West Indies, and trouble from *that* quarter was—for the moment at least—diverted. As for returning the *Kestrel*—

Orla's voice broke in.

"Captain! There, just a point off to starboard, the signal! Again! Do you see it?"

He turned his head and, yes, he did see it, the last, fuzzy blink of gold piercing the gloom like an eye out there in the darkness. He shoved the tiller hard, and the schooner turned into the wind, there to lay shuddering and rolling as the waves drove beneath her.

The crew—some French, some American, all snatched from the prison ship *Surrey* by the Black Wolf himself—ran to their stations. Connor grinned to himself. That crew was about to increase by one, and tonight he was the happiest soul on earth.

The boat came melting out of the gloom like a craft from the netherworld, the oars rising and dipping with steady purpose. Moments later Connor heard it bumping lightly against the *Kestrel*'s hull, then the voices of greeting as those gathered at the rail reached down to help the newcomers aboard.

At last, he thought, on a wave of relief.

Having a prisoner fake his own death had been the most clever, the most brilliant, the most daring of the Black Wolf's rescues. It was also, Connor thought grimly, the last, and there was still little Toby to get out. Toby, alone and defenseless and at the mercy of the other prisoners and those bastards Foyle and Radley. Toby, who had lost his fearless protector—

"Welcome aboard, Reverend Milford," he heard Gerard, one of the Frenchmen, say warmly. At the same time that gentle cleric stepped onto the *Kestrel*'s shiny, wet deck, Connor saw Orla running toward him, her hair flying about her excited face. The chaplain's countenance broke into a happy grin at the sight of her.

Connor looked on with a paternal smile as the two embraced.

And finally came that voice he had waited so long

to hear, that of the man the Black Wolf had risked life and limb to rescue.

Connor walked forward, smiling, and there were real tears in his handsome eyes.

"Nathan," he said, extending his hand and heartily pulling his cousin up onto the salt-sprayed deck. The two embraced each other warmly. "It is good to have you back at last."

Chapter 21

∞

Damon knew he was dreaming; he could see the Black Hole awash in liquid flame and rearing horribly out of the darkness as he approached it. He thought of the person locked inside, a person with thoughts and fears and feelings just like himself, suffering, hungry, lonely, and in pain, and he began to hurry, the oily brine igniting into flames now, licking at his calves, clawing at his legs, his stomach, his chest. Fear and desperation drove him, sweat drenched his body, but there was no turning back, no salvation for him unless he could reach that horrible box and free the man inside—

Hurry up, damn it!

He was running now. He had to run because that man was himself.

The unholy roar started on the decks above. He knew instantly what it was: the prisoners, hundreds of them, coming down through the decks, down the ladder for him, and there, leading them, was his mother.

He screamed as they came, yelling like savages, at him. *I pray to God the flames get me before you do, Mama!* Burn, burn, *burn*—

She reached for him, fingers cold as a tomb against his burning flesh.

"Damon—Damon it's me, Gwyneth!"

No, no, no, you're not Gwyneth, you're my mother. Hurry, flames, take me, burn me. I'm horrible, I'm not worthy, I don't deserve to live after what I know lurks down here in this floating hell, after this suffering I have seen. God forgive me, I did try to help them. Yes, Peter, I know my reasons were all wrong. It was because I hate the navy. I see now they were wrong, and if I live I'll do it for all the right reasons, I swear I will, just get her away from me—

"Damon!"

Her icy hand seized his wrist, and with an inhuman howl of terror he lunged away, trying to escape, clawing at the wrappings they'd put around his head and over his eyes. But it was too late. He was in his cabin now and the prisoners had him, pulling him down once more, punching him, kicking him, grabbing him by the hair and slamming his head against the deck over and over again, raining blows against his elbows, his legs, his ribs. *Run, Gwyneth, RUN!* And now a great whooshing, violent, sucking noise, and he was, *oh God, no, please, God, NO-O-O-o-o-o-o-o!,* hurtling through a tunnel, arms flailing, and at its end was Morninghall Abbey, and he was flung into that massive sixteenth-century bed. It was dark, the spirits were coming, Mama was coming, he could hear the door creaking open, *You are a very bad boy, Damon,* it was she, she, SHE!

Everything crashed to a stop.

Dead.

No sound, no sight, no . . . anything. Just hot, ringing silence.

He lay curled on his side, wrapped in sheets damp with his own sweat. He heard himself panting, the sound close and loud and stifling against the pillow. Beyond the stillness that cloaked him, beyond his own desperate breaths, he heard the patter of rain falling against glass and gutter and stone and grass. *Morninghall.* Shudders racked his body, and from deep in his throat came a primitive, frightened whimper.

I am awake. This is real. And, God help me—I am at Morninghall.

He tried to open his eyes but saw only darkness.

He curled closer into himself, blind and trembling and afraid. Damp heat enveloped his face from the nose up. Dull pain throbbed in his lower back, clouded the side of his cheek, his skull, his jaw.

He was in The Bedroom.

And he was in the dark.

Alone.

No, not alone. Someone else was here, someone whose breathing he now could hear, someone whose hand was gently stroking his shoulder and telling him that everything was going to be all right, that he was safe, that she would look after him. Her soft hair tickled his jaw, and he could smell her light, elusive fragrance.

His heart began to beat in that strange, rushed way it always did before an attack, and he began to shake. He didn't know who was leaning over him, didn't trust those words, didn't know what she was going to do to him.

The woman's voice was close to his ear. He could feel its warmth on his neck.

"Damon."

He wished he could stop shaking.

"Damon, you're going to be all right. It's me, Gwyneth. Can you hear me?"

Gwyneth? Gwyneth who?

That gentle hand caressed his shoulder. Her fingers, sliding into his loosely curled fist, remained there. The scent of peaches—

Lady Gwyneth Evans Simms.

A bomb exploded in his chest, shattering the last of the delirium that was far preferable to what he knew to be true—the truth being that he was indeed at Morninghall, and Lady Gwyneth Evans Simms was here with him, seeing him in all of his vulnerability, all of his weakness, all of his *insanity.*

He parted his lips, and the voice that rasped against the pillow was a soft, hissing whisper from a mouth as dry as sand. "Lady Simms?"

"Yes, it's me, Damon. *Gwyneth.*"

Gwyneth. She was leaning far too close to him, too close to his soul, and the panic began to feed off of it.

"You . . . survived," he whispered.

"Yes. Radley threw me overboard."

"Tell me . . . you're not hurt. I was so afraid that they . . . got you too. . . . So afraid."

"I'm all right, Damon. Be still now. I want you to rest, not to think about what happened."

"We never . . . got to finish what we . . . started."

"We will, my lord. When you're better."

But he was blind, and he could feel the sickness inside of him, could feel the powerful effect of gravity, of death, on every cell in his body. He wasn't going to get better. He was dying, this time for certain.

"I'm not . . . going . . . to get better," he whispered.

"Don't talk like that."

"'Tis true. You should not see me like this. . . ."

Her fingers burrowed even farther into his loose fist, and in that awful quiet he shared only with his own heartbeat, he prayed to God she would *not* go away; he wanted her to pull him up against her sweet, cool body and hold him, just hold him, because he was dying and he was scared.

"If you think I'm going to leave you, after all the worry you've put me through, I beg you to think again, my lord."

She pulled her fingers from his and put her arms around him, one against his back, the other sliding beneath his neck and his throbbing, bandaged head. Her embrace, heartbreakingly sweet, tender, and loving, brought with it the panic, which came howling down at him like a storm out of the Arctic.

No one had ever hugged him before. *No one.*

He froze, stiff and scared and blind and unmoving, his heart pounding in his chest. The panic screamed and clawed for a hold, making his body break out in fresh sweat, his stomach to fill with nausea, before sliding defeatedly back down into the well from which it had risen. In time Damon became aware that his heart was no longer beating so hard, that the rasping, panting gasps that were his breathing had calmed, and that *she* was still leaning over him, her arms wrapped safely around him.

The attack had passed. He had looked it in the face, stood his ground, and it had gone away. *It had gone away.*

Jesus . . .

He relaxed, just a little bit. Maybe being held wasn't so bad after all. In fact, when she pulled back and held his hand once again, he missed her closeness.

"I'm hurt badly," he whispered into the hot, smothering blindness, the words not as much a statement as a question.

"Yes, Damon. You are."

"How . . . badly?"

"Only time will tell."

"No. I wish to know . . . now."

"Later."

He thinned his mouth, feeling like a child denied a piece of candy. Anger and frustration made him curl his fingers around hers, crushing her hand in his fist.

"You're hurting me, Damon."

Embarrassed, he immediately loosened his grip but dared not release her. If he let her go, she'd leave him just as he'd asked her to, for he had never been kind to her and she had no reason to remain with him. In fact, he couldn't understand why she was here now with him at all. Had she been there all the time he'd lain ill? He had a vague sense of elapsed time, a hazy memory . . . something about wolves. Still he didn't want to be alone. He needed her. He wanted her close by, but he didn't dare tell her that. And he didn't dare tell her he rather liked being hugged as well.

"I'm sorry," he whispered against the pillow, and he meant it.

"I know."

"I never . . . wanted to hurt you."

"I know that too. Rest now. Get better."

Outside, the rain fell softly, peacefully. He could smell the damp earth, the fresh-washed pastures that rolled out into forever, the mustiness of this ancient room in which he lay—and the light fragrance of the woman who sat beside him. He wondered if she knew he liked being held and hugged. He wondered if she knew how much he needed her. He wondered if the lilacs were still in bloom, and what she would have done if he really *had* broken one off that day in her garden and given it to her, and suddenly wished with all his heart that he had.

He wondered if she knew that he loved her.

There: that powerful knot of emotion squeezing his heart, the same one that had struck him when he'd gazed upon those lilacs in their vase and seen them for what they were, and he was suddenly glad she could not see his eyes—for in them were tears.

Her voice came close beside his ear. "Can you take something to drink, Damon?"

He nodded, not trusting himself to speak, the back of his throat aching.

Slowly she pulled her fingers from his fist. It took all of his will not to tighten his hand around hers and trap her there with him, and as she got up, he squeezed his fist together and curled it under his jaw, trying to contain her warmth, her essence, that little bit of *her*.

He could hear liquid gurgling from a pitcher to a glass, the rustle of her skirts, the quiet thump of the pitcher as she set it back down on a table. Her arm slid beneath his head once more, and he felt the cold rim of the glass against his lips. She lifted his head, and the slight movement was enough to send nausea swimming through his belly and needles of fire shooting through his brain. They must've cracked his skull in twenty pieces, he thought, and suddenly he wished he had his *Peterson's* so that he could see what it had to say about skull fractures. Christ, he felt awful.

"My head hurts," he said faintly.

"As well it should. Drink, Damon. Please."

She was no *Peterson's*. She wasn't going to tell him *anything*. Too ill to be annoyed, he sighed in defeat, let the side of his head rest heavily against her arm, and opened his mouth. It was wine, thinned with water, cool and sweet and delicious. He took a swallow and felt it trickle all the way down to his stomach; there it sat heavily and waged a war with itself as to whether it wanted to stay there or come back up the same way it had gone down.

"You've drugged it," he murmured.

"Yes. Laudanum. It will make you sleep."

He was too sick to fight with her, and he didn't mind sleep, as long as *she* stayed with him and Mama didn't seek him out in his nightmares and he woke to find this woman sitting here beside him all over again, hugging him. He took another sip and listened to the rain outside and her quiet breathing as she sat beside him, and he felt a deep, languorous peace stealing over him.

Nice, he thought.

Peace. Stillness. How strange it felt after living so much of his life in a state of twisting emotion. How blessedly wonderful.

Finally she took the glass away and picked up his loose fist once more, wrapping her little hands around it. She remained silent, and he wondered if she were quietly waiting for the laudanum to take effect, to drag him back down into that place where everything was nothing and nothing was everything and neither everything nor nothing mattered.

"Lady Simms?" he whispered.

"Yes?"

He swallowed hard, gathering the courage to say what he must. "You . . . you won't leave me, will you?"

She squeezed his fist within her hands, as though she knew how much it had cost him to ask her that. Then she lifted his hand to her lips, and he felt the fragile bones of her face beneath his knuckles, the cool silk of her skin, the feathery graze of her hair.

"Not if you don't want me to."

The laudanum was already washing in a fog over his senses, dulling them, muddying them, darkening them. He had a crazy vision of his skull, cracked and broken, and the laudanum leaching into his brain from all the little fissures, extinguishing it, extinguishing *him*.

Tell her before it's too late.

"*Do* you wish me to leave, Damon?"

Her voice came from far, far away. His body was leaden, and someone was lowering him on a great, swinging cot, down, down . . . down.

"Damon?"

"No," he whispered. "I don't . . . want . . . you to go."

He fell asleep with his knuckles still pressed against her cheek.

"Toby Ashton! You in here? Come on out, damn your eyes, I'm sick to death of chasin' ye around!"

The door of the forward garrison opened, admitting a sliver of light. Toby crouched miserably in a corner, staring fixedly at that widening slit. Since the prisoner uprising he'd managed to stay out of the way of the sentries who'd paced the deck and gallery, managed to stay out of Foyle's and Radley's way, managed to make himself as insignificant as he felt. The ship was charged with watchful tension, and the guards, whose capacity for abuse seemed to have increased markedly since the revolt, were not inclined to be kind to a skinny, starving American, the sight of whom seemed only to disgust and annoy them all the more. They were not above laying their muskets across his arse if he didn't get out of the way fast enough—but still, working up here for Jack Clayton and doing an odd job or two was a better fate than returning to the hell belowdecks, which was the only other one open to him.

The door was opening further. "Toby? Bloody hell, you in there?"

He thought the voice was Clayton's, but he wasn't sure, and because he wasn't sure, he wasn't going to risk leaving his hiding place. Besides, the English all sounded alike. Well, all of them except for the dead marquess, whose speech had been polished, articulate, cultured, a bit more nasal than that of the lower-class guards who had served him. Poor Lord Morninghall. Despite that last, angry scene with him, Toby could not help but feel responsible for his death. After all, *he'd* been the one to tell Armand—admittedly, under duress—the details of Morninghall's schedule. He should've warned the marquess what they'd been plotting.

But I did warn him! he reminded himself fiercely. *I did warn him, and he would not listen!*

And now the marquess, his savior, the monster who had taken pity on him, was dead.

Toby had no doubt about *that*. After the guards finally had contained the revolt, he'd watched them remove Lord Morninghall's body from the cabin. He'd seen his swollen, bloody face, the knife sticking out of his back, the huge crimson stain on his snowy shirt, the slow drip, drip, drip of the blood across the deck as they'd carried him off the ship. Toby knew a dead body when he saw one, and if that wasn't confirmation enough, Foyle's satisfied smile as he watched this sad sight would have been, because everyone knew Foyle had despised the marquess. And the trail of blood was still there on the deck, now a deep, rusty color, like paint that had dripped from some huge and awful brush and left to dry.

It was ridiculous to think that anyone would have cleaned it up. Lord Morninghall had been a fastidious and, when the mood took him, compassionate man, and had at least made an effort to make things better than they might've been. In hindsight Toby remembered how he'd had the decks scrubbed and doused with vinegar every day; how he'd set the windsails above to try to direct the breeze down into the dank and stinking hold; how he'd discovered that cheating contractor and might've exposed God knew how many more, had he only lived. And, Toby thought with trembling lip, *how he tried to help me.* Midshipman Foyle, however, in temporary command until Bolton could appoint another, was cut from an entirely different cloth than his elegant, well-bred predecessor. Since he'd been in control, Foyle had been lording it over the hulk like a bantam in a barnyard, bullying, swaggering, posing, and threatening. Punishment and abuse were highest on his list of priorities.

"Toby Ashton? Where the hell are you?"

Yes, it *was* Jack Clayton after all. Toby sighed with relief. The big guard had been like a watchdog, so devoted had he been to Lord Morninghall, and though he was stern, intimidating, and unwashed, there was a kind streak in him that Toby inherently sensed and trusted. He relaxed and moved hesitantly out of the shadows.

Clayton immediately seized his elbow and pushed him back into the corner.

"Now listen up, an' listen up good," he whispered fiercely, with a quick glance over his shoulder. "I got a message for you from the Black Wolf, but you tell anybody I gave it to you and I'll come back from the grave after they kill me an' murder ye with me bare hands."

"The Black Wolf?" Toby's eyes widened in disbelief. "But how do you know about . . ."

"Never mind, that don't make no difference an' I ain't got time to be explainin'. He's comin' for ye on Saturday, in a fortnight, and it'll be yer only chance to escape. Got that?"

"Yes, sir. But why so long?"

"He's waitin' for the ship to calm down. Radley's got eagle eyes, y'know."

"I know. But how does he plan to get me out? I can't swim!"

"Ye're goin' out in an empty water barrel when we send 'em ashore for refillin'. Broad daylight. Mind barrels, kid?"

Toby shook his head slowly. "No, Mr. Clayton . . .
I don't mind barrels."

"Good." The guard straightened up, spat a wad of
spit on the filthy deck, and nodded back toward the
shadows. "Get on with ye then and stay out o' trouble,
and don't let me hear another word about it, ye hear?"

The door closed behind him, and all was dark in the
room once more. Toby sighed and felt tears leaking
out of his eyes. Nathan was dead, Morninghall was
dead, most of his shipmates had escaped—or were
dead.

But Connor was alive.

Brave, wonderful Connor.

And Connor was coming for him.

Chapter 22

⟨✦⟩

Dour and bespectacled, Dr. Phineas MacDowell was about as cheerful as the Scottish climate that had bred him, with a grizzled head of hair that still showed traces of fiery red in its wildly curling locks. Now, with the help of Britwell, the gloomy Scot heaved and struggled and managed to slide the Marquess of Morninghall's sweat-drenched body as close to the edge of the big bed as it could be moved without his tumbling off. There he turned him onto his left side so that his right arm hung over the edge.

Bloodletting was a daily ritual, and Britwell's face mirrored his distaste for it. He looked down at his master, who was feverish and semiconscious.

"Are you certain that bleeding him is not doing more harm than good?" he asked as the doctor retrieved the pewter bowl he used for the treatment. "You know how Her Ladyship feels about it."

"Her Ladyship is not a doctor," MacDowell grunted, pulling his lancet from his bag. "This is the only way to remove excesses and irritability from the blood, and I can't think of a better way to restore your lord to health. Now get me that bucket of hot water and stop questioning my skills."

Sighing, Britwell did as he was asked and placed the pail on a chair next to the bed. The doctor reached for Lord Morninghall's arm; His Lordship swore weakly and tried to pull it away. But sick and helpless as he was, he was no match for the Scot, who was now forcing the arm downward and pushing the hand and wrist into the bucket of hot water to swell the veins. Fervently, Britwell prayed for Lady Simms to come back. She'd gone out to the garden to gather a bunch of fresh flowers, and she was the only one who'd been able to intimidate the doctor out of performing this ghastly treatment.

"Hold him down," MacDowell growled. "I can't do two things at once."

His face tight with protest, Britwell steadied Lord Morninghall's shoulder as the doctor pulled his hand from the bucket. The fingers were still dripping water. MacDowell tied a tape around the wrist at the pulse, flexed the fingers back and forth a few times, and finally pulled them all the way back, exposing a vein at the underside of the wrist.

"I really think——"

"I don't want to hear it, Britwell. Can't you see your master's running a fever? Do you want him to die? Besides, he can't feel a damned thing anyhow; he's out of his head."

And with that MacDowell touched the scalpel to the vein.

Damon, who was drifting in and out of the blanketing effect of laudanum, felt it immediately. He flinched and tried to jerk away, but it was no use. The doctor held him tight, and he could not fight the man's strength. He tried not to listen to the sound of his blood, trickling down his palm and into the pewter bowl. It was an alarming, awful sensation, as though his life itself were draining out of him, and he could already feel anxiety creeping in from the farthest corners of his foggy brain.

"Stop," he whispered, but MacDowell, still chastising Britwell for interfering, did not hear him. "Please . . ."

The anxiety was getting worse, beginning to affect his breathing now.

"Please stop . . ."

Footsteps were coming down the hall.

It was his savior, and he knew it the moment *she* was in the room.

"Dr. MacDowell!" Her voice sliced through the room like a thunderclap. Damon smiled in relief as he heard her move angrily across the floor to the other side of the bed. "I'll thank you to stop that beastly exercise this very moment!"

"Under the circumstances it's advisable, my lady—"

"God gave us each a certain amount of blood, and if he didn't want us to have that much he never would've been so generous with it in the first place! Pick his hand up now, and stop the bleeding at once."

Fight, my little tigress, fight!

"But—"

"Do it!"

Swearing under his breath, the doctor raised Damon's arm. Damon felt the man's fingers biting angrily into his wrist, felt the warm blood trickling down his skin and into the inside of his elbow. His head felt suddenly faint, and he must've passed out, for the next thing he knew, there was only stillness, warm arms embracing him, and the sound of quiet weeping.

It was Gwyneth, and she was crying over him.

Just as he'd never had anyone hug him before, he'd never had anyone cry over him either.

He weakly moved his head on the pillow, trying to let her know he was there.

"Oh, Damon . . . If I'd known that bloodthirsty *wretch* was going to do such a thing the minute I turned my back, I never would have left you. Oh, please forgive me, my darling. . . ." She broke down in more tears, their warm moisture spreading over his neck and chest. "I'm so sorry. . . ."

"Nothing . . . to forgive," he whispered into the darkness that cloaked him, and tried to raise his other arm to rest it across her shoulders. But he hadn't the strength to do even that.

"He hurt you. That's it, Damon, I don't care if he

has served your family nearly as long as Britwell, I'm sending straight to the village for someone else."

He merely smiled weakly, for it took all his strength to move even the muscles of his face. "You're . . . the first champion . . . I've ever had," he whispered. And then, with what he hoped was light humor, he added, "Glad I don't . . . have to face the doctors . . . alone."

"Never, Damon. I swear it."

She held him for a long time. Presently the warmth of her body, combined with such a resolute promise, brought him a feeling of peaceful security, and he let go of consciousness and allowed himself to sink back into darkness.

The new doctor didn't even try to bleed the marquess, having already heard tales from the villagers, who'd heard them from the servants, of Lady Gwyneth Evans Simms's ferocity. He came twice a day to change the dressings on his patient's back, advise ways to keep the fever—which came and went with alarming regularity—down, and make guarded, hesitant predictions with regards to his patient's prognosis. The knife he'd taken in the back may have nicked a kidney, the doctor thought, which was why His Lordship was so gravely ill. The knife may have hit nerves, which could cause partial paralysis, but of course that was impossible to tell until His Lordship had regained some of his strength. Those two horrors aside, the doctor made no bones about the fact that he found Lord Morninghall's fever a matter of grave concern. Such a concern was not easy to discount, as Damon's fever burned the sheets beneath him, indeed, the very air that surrounded his body, and pus soaked the wrappings that girded his lower back and made the room stink of imminent death.

But Gwyneth was determined that this dark and diabolical angel, this remote but magnificent lord she loved, would not die. With the help of old Britwell, whose grave face reflected the anguish he shared with

her at seeing his master in such a state, she stripped
the damp sheets from the bed, threw the windows
open wide to invite the sweeping Cotswold breezes
inside the gloomy room, bathed Damon's feverish
body with cool water, and sent one of the staff to
Burford to procure a large bag of dried lavender from
a local shop. This she sewed into pouches she placed
beneath Damon's pillow, atop the gilt-encrusted table
at the foot of the ancient bed, and even at the feet of
the two wolves who guarded their ill lord so fiercely.

At the beginning of the second week, Damon's fever
broke. He stirred from his heavy, death-like sleep, not
saying a word but weakly nodding when Gwyneth
asked him if he could take some chicken broth, which
heartened her to no end—especially as he trustingly
rested his hand in the crook of her elbow as she
spooned it to him, and managed a weak smile before
lying back against the pillows and drifting away from
her once more.

The following day he took some oatmeal for breakfast, managed to stay awake until lunch, and woke
early in the afternoon, complaining irritably that he
was starving to death. And as Gwyneth sent a servant
down to the kitchen to bring up some more broth, it
was all she could do not to throw open the windows
and shout with glee and triumph.

Lord Morninghall was on his way back to the land
of the living, at last.

The Reverend Milford, together with Jack Clayton,
came for Toby just before dawn and hustled him
quickly out on deck.

Toby had a sense of foreboding, which was reflected
in the tense faces of his companions. But despite the
loud hammering of his heart, he willingly went with
them, trusting them—and Connor, who was supposed to be piloting the water boat—to know what
they were doing.

On the still-darkened deck the water barrels stood
in neat, shadowy rows, ready to be loaded onto the

boat that would take them to shore for refilling. Working quickly and in hushed whispers, the chaplain quickly pried the top off one, and Jack just as quickly lifted Toby straight up and put him down inside. Several feet away stood another guard, his back toward them, and Toby suspected he'd been bribed to see and hear nothing.

"Get down in there, good an' tight!" Jack whispered, taking the lid from the chaplain, and as Toby crouched down, his knees against his chest, the hard, slimy wood against his spine, the lid came down over his head, blocking off the faint moonlight.

"Further!" Jack hissed. "I gots to get this lid on!"

His body crunched in half, Toby bent his head and tucked it against his knees. He felt the rough lid pressing down against the knobby nape of his neck and shoulders, heard the dreadful sound of it being tightened down over him. Reverend Milford had bored a coin-sized hole in the lid for him to breathe through, and through it Toby heard the chaplain's kind voice.

"You all right in there, Toby?"

"Cramped, sir, but I reckon I'll be just fine."

"Very well, then. Can you stay that way for another two or three hours?"

He had no choice really. "Yes, sir. I'll manage."

"Good, then. Not a sound from you, or all shall be lost. May God be with you, Toby."

He heard the two men walking away, then he was all alone in the close, stifling darkness. He huddled in the barrel, terrified of moving, of breathing, of being. *In another few hours Connor will be here. Nothing to worry about. You'll be all right. Think about how many others Connor has rescued. . . .*

Time passed. The air inside the barrel became hot, stuffy, and humid with his respiration and body heat. The sweat began to roll down his chest and back, and a tiny pinprick of light came through his airhole and touched the damp wood a half inch from his nose as the day began to dawn. Scared, Toby squeezed the miniature of his mother, still hanging from a chain around his throat, and it brought him some small measure of reassurance.

Outside he heard men talking and smelled the thick smoke from the galley. He knew the ship was awakening.

He dug his elbows down against his ribs and hips. He heard heavy footsteps moving about, the tramping trudge of prisoners as they were brought topside to perform menial deck tasks, Radley's cruel voice shouting at someone. People were passing just a few feet from where he crouched, so he huddled closer against himself, hardly daring to breathe in the close darkness.

"Fine day this morn, eh, Jack?"

"No finer than any other, if ye ask me. We'll see rain by noon."

"Aye. Cloudin' up already, ain't it?"

Toby shifted slightly in the barrel, his back and neck on fire from being stuck so long in his cramped position. He squeezed the miniature harder, until he could feel the strokes of paint beneath his thumb. The pinprick of light was growing brighter, and the sounds were more numerous now: the tread of passing sentries, gulls screaming overhead, distant splashes as a bucket was emptied over the side. And now someone was hailing the prison hulk in a thick Irish brogue that gave no hint of its owner's true accent, an American one, and Toby, near tears in the barrel, knew that Connor had come for him at last.

"All right, get those damned barrels off the deck and loaded, and be quick about it!"

It was Radley, impatient and angry as always.

Toby swallowed hard and waited.

From nearby he heard footsteps and grunts as men lifted something heavy.

They're moving the barrels now. The boat is here, and Connor must be watching. God, I'm scared.

They were picking up a barrel near his now. Toby braced himself, knowing that if his body rolled at all within the barrel, he'd be discovered. Then he heard the voices, close and just overhead, the hands on the wood that enclosed him, the grunts and curses of the men who lifted it.

"Geez, this one's heavy!"

"Shut up an' quit complaining."

"Ye'd think the bloody thing was never emptied, for God's sake. . . ."

Toby clenched his teeth, trying not to cry out as his head and nape bumped painfully against the lid. He felt a sudden drifting sensation, and knew they were hoisting the barrel to a block and tackle and swinging it out to the water boat. He shut his eyes, terrified, and prayed to God the rope wouldn't break.

He could not know that, back on the prison hulk's deck, Foyle was standing with his hands on his hips, head thrown back and watching.

He could not know that Foyle had suddenly frowned and was pulling out his spyglass, training it on Toby's barrel.

And he could not know that Foyle had spied the small breathing hole the chaplain had cut in the lid.

Foyle's loud bark rang out suddenly. "Hold it up there, I say!"

Toby braced himself, his barrel swinging wildly in the air as those on the water boat tried frantically to get it aboard.

"Damn you, I said *halt!*"

He heard Connor's swift curse.

Then all hell broke loose.

Chapter 23

The Marquess of Morninghall awoke to the same hot sheets beneath his body, the same clinging darkness that banded his eyes, the same dull ache in his lower back, and the same twittering of chaffinches just outside his window that had been his lot every time he'd managed to thrust himself above the surface of unconsciousness over the past two weeks. But on this early June morning something was different.

He knew he wasn't going to die.

He was ravenously hungry, his head was clear, and he was thoroughly sick of being in this confounded bed. Somewhere during the course of his illness the bed had ceased to terrify him, and he wanted nothing more than a huge breakfast, mobility, and Lady Gwyneth Evans Simms—and not necessarily in that order.

"Gwyneth!" he roared.

Silence.

He waited impatiently, sitting up in bed and gripping the edge of the mattress. He couldn't see a thing through the bandages that wreathed his face, but the scent of lavender hung in the air, and he dimly remembered Gwyneth's telling him she'd put it beneath his pillow and around the room to freshen the ancient chamber. He could also smell the sunshine outside, and the roses, their scent wafting up from the gardens far beneath his windows. Some, he knew, would be a blushing crimson, others a pale salmon or yellow or white, some the size of soup bowls and others the size of teacups. He took a deep breath of their gentle perfume and found it pleasant. If the roses were out, then the gentle hand of summer would be grooming the fields of wheat, barley, and oats that rolled away in all magnificent directions beyond his windows—

"Gwyneth!"

Reaching blindly behind him, he yanked his pillows up against the great arcaded panels of the headboard, lay back, and gingerly touched his face through the bandages. Damn these infernal wrappings! He wanted them off.

Now.

What the hell had they done to him?

He was just sliding his forefinger beneath the gap the bandages made as they rose to cover his nose when he heard hurried footsteps echoing toward him down the corridor.

He lowered his hand and let it rest beside him, drumming his fingers against the sheet.

The steps came into the room and stopped.

"Damon?"

"Good morning, my dear Lady Simms." He raised his hand and blindly, aristocratically bade her to enter. "Do come in."

"Awake, I see."

"Yes, and damned hungry as well. Bloody starving, in fact. And I'd like these confounded bandages off at once."

He heard her soft laughter as she approached, caught the scent of peaches, and felt her hands on his face, soft and warm and gentle through the bandages. Behind her came more footsteps, and her hands stilled for a moment as she turned and spoke. "Janie? Bring me a pair of shears and a bowl of warm water. Your lord is awake."

"And *annoyed,*" Damon finished darkly.

"Stop it. The staff are already scared to death of you."

Small wonder, he thought, as most of them had never met him and probably believed all the stories that had been Mama's legacy. Then his irascibility fled as *she* sat down on the bed beside him, her body close to his, her warmth so very near, her scent, that delicious, sweet scent of peaches, soap, femininity, *Gwyneth,* infiltrating his senses. As she explored his face through the bandages, testing for sore spots, he realized he wanted nothing more than her hands on his flesh, wanted nothing more than to touch her. Just . . . touch her. He wondered what she was wearing, if her breasts were pushing against a soft, silken bodice, if her hair was scraped back in that damned bun, if she was looking at him with tenderness or anger or patience. Once, in a time far removed from the one in which he now knew himself to be, he would've hoped for the anger and the confrontation it would've bred.

But not now. Now he wanted the tenderness.

"So." His tone came out as a mixture of sugar and vinegar, for tenderness was something he'd never experienced before meeting her, and reaching out and asking for it, in any manner, was difficult for him. "Whose brilliant idea was it to bring me here to Morninghall, of all places?"

He stretched a hand toward where he thought her thigh must be. Was she in silks? Bombazine?

Velvet. She was wearing velvet.

His fingers sank into the lush fabric, feeling her leg beneath. He waited, tensely, for her to remove his hand.

She did not.

"Reverend Milton's and Admiral Falconer's."

"Why the hell should Falconer care about *me?* He's one of *them.*"

"One of whom?"

"One of the navy's favorites. *Them.*"

Damn. He couldn't keep the anger out of his voice, even now.

"Really? I found him to be a charming, noble-hearted man who seemed every bit the hero he is proclaimed to be. Really, Damon, he acted out of your best interest."

"*No one* acts out of my best interest."

"If that is so, then why do you think *I'm* here?"

Her challenge brought him up short. He didn't know the answer to that, wasn't sure he wanted to know, and the examination of the question filled him with agitation, confusion, and despair.

"I don't know," he muttered, mulishly setting his mouth and feeling that thick and emotional *something* pushing against the vault of his chest. "Obviously, though, you do. Why don't you tell me?"

"No, Damon. You know why I'm here, and I'm not going to do the work for you when the answer lies within *you*. I ask you again: why do *you* think I'm here?"

"They probably paid you."

"Try again."

"You wanted to torment me."

"Really, I expect better from you than that," she said chidingly.

Her tone was infectious. Some of his crossness subsided. "Uh . . . because you have a guilty conscience?"

She let out a great, audible sigh, but he could sense her smiling patiently down at him. "What *am* I going to do with you?"

He could think of a few things. Dear God, could he . . .

"You could take these confounded bandages off my face to begin with," he murmured, his fingers stroking her thigh through the velvet skirts. "And then, perhaps, we could discuss some of the things *we* can do. . . ."

He expected her to reprimand him.

Instead she giggled.

"You find that amusing?" he asked, trying to make his mouth look fierce.

"I find it—encouraging. Now sit still while I put you to rights again."

He heard the maid return with the shears and bowl, then her hurried retreat. Gwyneth's hands were on his face once more, gently thumbing his cheekbones and touching his brow, his jaw, his temples through the bandages. It felt good, relaxing. He lay back against the pillows, smiling and hoping she would never stop touching him.

Maybe insanity wasn't so bad after all.

But on a sudden note of dread, Damon knew he wasn't insane. He was enjoying this, enjoying *intimacy,* and he was a hundred percent right in the head.

He swallowed.

"Does that hurt?"

"No."

"Does this?"

"No."

"Good. Be still, then, while I cut these wrappings off." Her thumb slipped between the bandages and the gap at the base of his nose, and he tensed as he felt the cold point of the shears sliding beneath, snipping, cutting, moving up, up, up toward his eye. He froze, barely daring to breathe, and had a sudden, awful fear that when the bandages came off he still wouldn't be able to see, that he would be forever blind, crippled, helpless. He squeezed his eyes shut as she peeled the warm, damp wrappings away from his face. A kiss of cool air swept in against his cheeks, brow, and bared eyes.

An expectant stillness hung in the air.

"You may open your eyes now, my lord."

His guts seized up, for the truth was, he was afraid to open his eyes, afraid he would be blind, and he didn't want her to know he was such a coward.

"You have not told me why you're here at Morninghall," he persisted, trying to buy time, "and I've run out of guesses."

But he knew why she was here. He knew, and that truth was so fragile, so frightening, yet so very much to hope for, he dared not give voice to it.

"Open your eyes, and I shall tell you."

"I cannot."

"Yes, you can."

Anger and frustration swept through him. Sweat broke out beneath his spine and his heartbeat quickened with agitation, but he did not open his eyes.

Her voice was gentle and patient.

"Open them, Damon. Please."

His fist tightened in fear. If one of his eyes was missing, he wouldn't be able to see her. If he had brain damage, he wouldn't be able to see her. If, during the beating, something had broken inside his head, and he was forever impaired, he wouldn't be able to see her, and not being able to see her was something he wasn't ready to contemplate—

"I have something very important to tell you, Damon, but I will not do so unless you open your eyes."

There was such raw, aching tenderness in her voice that it made him suddenly want to bawl like a baby. He wanted to hate that tenderness, tried to hate it as he'd always hated pretty flowers and fragile porcelain, but there was something so beauteous and sweet about it, something so loving and warm, that he could not. And where there had once been rage and fury and black, twisted wrath, he felt only a huge, choking knot of emotion constricting his chest, leaching out of that knotted ball of feeling there and crawling up the back of his throat until it tightened and closed painfully and he could not even swallow.

I have something very important to tell you, Damon, but I will not do so unless you open your eyes.

Up his throat that emotion went, into his nose and beneath his squeezed-shut eyelids, and Damon had no choice in the matter. The emotion floated them open.

He saw watery, blurry colors: the darkness of the wall paneling, the gilt and white of the ceiling, and *her* face, wavering above him as though it were mirrored on a rippled pond, the detail not quite clear but hinted at, soft, ethereal, a pastel study in peach and rose, framed in gold. He blinked and the ripples stilled, her face swinging into focus now so that he could see her soft hair gathered in a ribbon and the mass of it, loose, hanging over one lovely shoulder, her face serene, her eyes gazing down at him. There was no anger, no impatience in that girlishly sweet face, those shining, violet eyes. Only softness and compassion.

And something else.

You know what it is, Damon.

No. It couldn't be, he didn't deserve it—

But it was.

He felt the mist filling his eyes and threatening to spill into tears, felt the emotion cracking open his chest, welling up in his nose and the back of his throat. "I *have* opened them, Gwyneth," he whispered, taking her hand. "I *have* opened my eyes."

She touched the side of his cheek, her smile serene as she gazed down at him. "So you have, Damon."

He swallowed painfully, still holding her gaze. "And that which you wish to tell me?"

Her smile deepened, so heartbreakingly beautiful, so angelic in its warmth and purity that the ugly black thing inside of him fought for a last foothold in his aching chest, then leaped free of that raw, gaping crack and fled forever. As it fled, his chest caved in and everything broke inside of him, and the tears that had been there for so many years finally came, rolling down his cheeks and quietly wetting the pillow beneath his head.

He knew what she was going to say, even before she uttered those simple words that would change his life forever.

"That which I wish to tell you, Damon . . . *is that I love you.*"

He drew her to him, unable to contain himself any longer.

"I love you too, Gwyneth. God help me, I do."

He felt her arms go around his broken body, pulling him up and into her embrace, and as his head fell against her shoulder and the great, hitching sobs claimed him, the light shone upon him at last.

The Marquess of Morninghall's recovery was a rapid one, for in his case *im*patience was a virtue. By eight o'clock he was out of bed and on his feet, by nine he was wolfing down a breakfast of bacon, eggs, and toast while footmen stood silently behind his chair, and by eleven he was sitting in a huge tub, enjoying his first real bath in weeks.

That which I wish to tell you, Damon . . . is that I love you.

Oh, his nerves were still buzzing, his heart pounding, but this time excitement, not anxiety, was the cause. He felt as though he had emerged from a thick and gloomy cocoon, strong, eager to experience life for the first time, *invincible*. His past life, his years in the navy, even the terrible injuries that had brought about his return to Morninghall—all was behind him now, and in his heart, in his future, there was only Gwyneth.

His head hurt only mildly, and when his new valet, Robin, helped him from the bath and held a dressing gown for him, he felt like a new man. Clearing the steam from the mirror with his sleeve, he saw that his nose was not broken, his teeth were all there. It was amazing. So was the fool's grin that seemed permanently affixed to his mouth now, bringing devilish warmth to eyes that no longer looked empty, flat, and soulless. Oh, there was still some faint bruising around one cheekbone, and he got dizzy if he turned his head too quickly, but it occurred to him that he was oddly unafraid now of his own body and any attempts it might make to sabotage his health.

Why had the fear left him? Was it because he had lain so close to death, faced it, and emerged triumphant? Had something happened to him while he'd slept the sleep of the dead? He smiled. Surely his new joie de vivre and the fact that the lady had told him she loved him had more to do with his current state of serenity than anything else.

Oh, he could not wait to begin this day, to begin his *life!*

He turned from the mirror. Robin was waiting with his clothes, which Damon recognized from his wardrobe aboard the prison ship. "Sorry, my lord," the young man explained at Damon's questioning look, "Lady Simms had them brought up from Portsmouth with her. She thought you'd be needing them."

"She is correct. And where is the lady, Robin?"

"Waiting for you in the Yellow Room, my lord."

"Leave me now and go fetch her."

"But I am here to assist you—"

Damon smiled. "You can assist me best by *fetching the lady.*"

The lady arrived five minutes later, and her violet eyes sparkled when she spotted Damon up and about and garbed in a loose white shirt and breeches, his hair still damp and tousled from his bath. She put a finger to her lips, grinning behind it in delight, pink roses staining her cheeks.

He cocked an eyebrow at her. "Would you confess your thoughts, my dear Gwyneth?"

"I would, my lord, but they are too wicked for words."

"But not, perhaps, for actions?" he murmured, giving her a heated look.

"Such actions shall ensue when you are sufficiently recovered."

"I do think I shall be the judge of my recovery, dear nurse."

She blushed fiercely, but boldly held his gaze. His stared back, his blood heating. Didn't she know he felt as strong as Atlas? Didn't she know the very sight of her, in that pale rose dress with the embroidered trim, was making him mad with desire for her?

"We shall see," she conceded at last.

"Yes . . . so we shall," he murmured, his voice

holding a deep note of promise. He moved forward and took her hand, raising it to his lips. Desire immediately darkened her eyes. "In the meantime there is something I must do. It has been well over a decade since I last walked the halls of my own house." His gaze softened as he stared lovingly down into her sweet, upturned face. "It would please me, my lady, if you would accompany me."

"It would be an honor . . . my lord."

He turned slightly and offered his elbow, and he felt her little hand slip into its crook. Then, side by side with the woman who had—in more ways than one—brought him back from the very brink of death, the Marquess of Morninghall began the journey that had awaited him for a lifetime. How many times in his dreams, his nightmares, had he made this very same walk! How many times had the very thought of doing it filled him with anxiety and dread! But now, as he moved slowly through the long, echoing corridors, the silent rooms, gazing upon each ancient bust, each magnificent old painting and tapestry, each spectacular window view with an almost boyish wonder, he felt nothing but excitement, pride, and rebirth. This was Morninghall Abbey, his house. *His* house!

And he had come home.

He all but raced her through the east wing in his excitement to show his lady all. "There in that state room is where I played hide-and-seek with my nanny! There, on that very window seat, is where I used to sit reading Plato and Aristotle! And here, in this very corridor, is where I used to race my cousins, and whoever got to the pillasters at the end first won—"

He froze. His smile faded and the color drained from his face.

They were in the Lord's Corridor, and there, an arm's length away, was the portrait of Mama.

Staring down at him.

"I—" he began, faltering. Taking a deep breath, he raked his hand through his damp hair and glanced away, his smile wan. "My—my mother."

Gwyneth moved closer to him, almost protectively. "I know. I had her moved out of the bedroom. Don't you remember?"

The past fortnight was still a jumble of strange dreams, pain, and fog, and he didn't know what had been real and what had been the result of fever and delirium. But he could well remember Gwyneth, his tigress, defending him against the doctor—and shouting for the removal of this very painting.

He looked down at her, his love for her shining in his eyes. "I will never forget," he said softly—and touched his lips to her brow.

She slipped her hand in his, and they stood together silently.

"You must think me a coward for staying away all these years," he said at length.

"No, my love." Her voice was gentle, understanding. "I don't think you're a coward at all . . . but a survivor."

His heart filled with emotion, and he could only squeeze her hand, not trusting himself to speak. *She always says the right thing. Dear God, can this love truly be happening to me? Can it?*

He stared up at the portrait of his long-dead mother, and gradually that face ceased to be the one that had haunted and terrified him all these years. It became only a collage of paint and brush strokes, powerless now, a testament to a past that was long gone and never would be again. Another monster faced and conquered. Another memory put safely to eternal rest. Slowly the clouds moved out of his heart and sunlight broke upon it once again, strong now, gathering heat and light and brightness. And as the fear associated with his mother died a final death, so too did her hold upon him. He glanced around him at the vast, echoing corridor, at the paintings, at the magnificent gilt ceiling above. No longer did Mama's presence haunt the shadows and every darkened corner of this magnificent house. No longer did the great walls seem as if they were about to fall in around his ears, crushing him beneath tons and tons of stone in an attempt to murder the devil child he had been before he could gain maturity. Now Morninghall Abbey was just a house, and a very grand one at that, and there was only one thing this house needed to become a home.

He placed his hand over Gwyneth's and continued his walk.

A marchioness.

Chapter 24

Damon felt well enough to exercise his intentions the following afternoon.

He secretly ordered Britwell to have a picnic lunch made up and brought, together with a thick, woolen blanket, to the edge of what he'd heard Gwyneth refer to as the Poppy Field. He spent the morning closeted in his mother's bedchamber, putting the last ghosts to rest and going through the ancestral jewelry until he found what he was looking for. Then, feeling boyishly excited, nervous, and optimistic, he went looking for Gwyneth.

He wasn't surprised to find her outside in the rose garden, surrounded by blossoms and hard at work with a pair of pruning shears. He leaned against the warm, yellow stone of the house, a lazy smile flitting across his face as he silently observed her. She wore a flounced muslin walking dress of pale lilac, and a small, round straw hat, tied under her chin with a violet ribbon, shaded her face from the sun. She was humming, and she was happy. The sight of her, with her shining curls trailing down her back, was enough to set his blood to simmering.

She looked up and her face immediately brightened.

"Why good morning, my lord."

"Greetings, madam."

"You should be in bed, resting!"

"You're absolutely correct. I *should* be in bed." He

plucked a stray piece of grass and chewed absently on the stem, his gaze never leaving hers. "But not resting."

She snapped to her full height and tried to glare at him, but laughter played in her eyes and around her mouth.

"Really, my lord, you should not be exerting yourself so."

"I can assure you, dear lady, that the efforts at control that currently plague me are far more *exerting* than what I have in mind," he murmured, arching an eyebrow at her.

Roses bloomed in her cheeks, and she tried to purse her traitorous lips.

"You are a very wicked man, Lord Morninghall."

"Yes, wicked at heart. Tell me you would have me any other way."

"I would not."

"Hold your tongue then, madam. I have a surprise for you, and I shan't have it spoiled."

She made a helpless noise, grinned, and placed her shears in a nearby basket. "Look at me! Here I've been intimate with you, silently dreamed of you in the private darkness of my bedroom, and nursed you through a life-threatening injury—you'd think I could stop blushing," she said, obviously embarrassed with herself.

"Pray, don't," he returned, straightening up and tossing the grass aside. He came forward and stretched out his hand toward her. "I find it most charming. Come. I have something to show you."

Mindful of her skirts, she stepped free of the rose bushes and grinned up at him. Her hand was small and warm in his, and he felt a fierce protectiveness toward her which was alien and wonderful all at once as he escorted her across the emerald expanse of manicured lawn and out past the stables, empty save for a few workhorses and an aged hunter. He moved slowly, still a bit painfully, content to enjoy the moment, the anticipation, the hazy sunshine, the company of this woman beside him. He noted the tenseness with which she gripped his hand, the faint pucker of her brow, the question in her lovely eyes. She was anxious, expectant, and faintly nervous, and he felt those same sensations within himself. But, oh, he knew something she didn't! *He* had a surprise, and he was enjoying every moment of the anticipation of giving it to her!

Out over the fields they walked, where daisies, dandelions, and clover grew in wild abandon among the grasses. Some of the dandelions had gone to seed, their fuzzy heads scattered, their empty, balding stumps long since ravaged by the wind. To Damon the day smelled like childhood memories: fresh, sun-scented, and alive. The sky above was a milky blue and the air pleasantly warm, cloaking the surrounding hills of the magnificent Cotswolds in a pearly haze.

"How lovely it is out here," Gwyneth said, pausing. "You can see for miles and miles and miles in nearly every direction."

He looked down at her face and saw the same serene, heady exultation he felt reflected in her shining eyes, her wind-kissed cheeks, her smiling lips.

Yes. She will make a wonderful marchioness.

He grinned, bursting inside with the anticipation of what he would soon ask her.

She lifted her face to the breeze. "I can imagine you standing here as a young boy, looking out over this magnificent vista and knowing it would all belong to you someday. . . ."

"Indeed. This is where I used to come to get away from *her*."

She squeezed his hand, but he had said the words with no heat, no resentment, determined never to let Mama and the bad memories interfere in his life again. Wrapping his arm around Gwyneth's waist, he pulled her up close against his side.

"Do you know, I used to sit up here for hours," he

continued with a winsome smile. "I would imagine myself a great, soaring hawk, floating free on the wind high above this land, all-seeing and all-knowing as my shadow fell across the acres of golden wheat and barley below."

She leaned her head against his shoulder. "I imagined that same thing myself when I first saw these hills."

"Did you?"

She tilted her head to gaze up at him. "I did."

He smiled and gently stroked her ribs through the light muslin of her gown before looking out once more over the magnificent rolling vista. "You were right, you know."

"About what?"

"About me. About the things I've kept locked within myself, about my dread of getting close to anyone, about everything. I thought you were talking a load of rubbish, but somewhere, somehow, I ended up looking deep inside myself and found that you spoke the truth. You saw something I didn't. Something I didn't want to see. And you've made me realize that allowing oneself to love and be loved isn't so frightening after all."

"Indeed," she said softly. "It is more frightening *not* to allow yourself to love and be loved." She looked up at him, the sunlight spraying across her nose and making the shadows of her eyelashes fall across her violet irises. "I love you, Damon."

"I know you do." He bent down and, cradling her upturned face in his hands, very gently, very tenderly kissed her brow, letting his lips rest there for a long moment. "And I love you too, Gwyneth."

Hand in hand they stood on the brow of this high hill, gazing out over the miles spread before them. Nothing here had changed over the years, Damon thought. And yet *everything* had changed, because the woman he loved stood beside him, and nothing on earth could've made him appreciate this spectacular beauty more. The distant combed pastures, with their fringes of trees, hedgerows and yellow stone, had never looked so beautiful; the ripening fields of barley, oats, and wheat, the perfect brown rectangles of freshly tilled earth bordering the emerald and silver-green ones had never looked so brilliant. He closed his eyes and inhaled the clean wind.

And this hill on which he stood had never felt higher.

He had sacrificed so much to fear, resentment, and vengeance. But, oh, had they been worth sacrificing *this*?

No. Never.

The self-imposed exile, the hatred and envy, his vendetta against Bolton and the navy—he was through with all of it.

"Come," he said and led her along the brow of the hill toward the sun-bleached wooden fence that bordered the far edge of the east field. There, beside a post, the wicker lunch basket sat atop a folded blanket, just as he'd instructed. He picked them both up, feigning surprise.

"Well, well. Would you look at this!"

"Oh, Damon, you've planned a picnic! What a lovely surprise!"

Smiling in anticipation of his *real* surprise, he merely laid a finger across her lips and opened the gate. There, spread in glorious color before them, was the Poppy Field.

Her eyes filled up at sight of it, and his heart sang inside his chest.

Thousands of the scarlet-orange flowers nodded and bobbed in the wind around them. Close up they were sparsely scattered among the purple thistles, but further out, across the field and toward its edge, they seemed to grow closer and closer together, until they finally merged into blazing sheets of crimson against a brilliant green backdrop.

He watched her face. "I used to come here too."

She only looked at him, love and understanding in her eyes. Then, still grasping her hand, he moved ahead of her, carefully tramping a path through the thigh-high thistles and poppies so she would not tear her dress.

Deep within the waving field of brilliant flowers, he paused and looked over his shoulder at her.

"Is this a good spot, my dear?"

"It is lovely, Damon."

His skin tingled with excitement. What he had planned was far more than a *picnic*.

He carefully stamped out an area among the tall, waving stalks, and together they spread the blanket over the little clearing. Damon set the lunch basket on the edge of the blanket and sat down, tugging Gwyneth down alongside him. She pulled off her hat and tossed it aside, and together they lay back on the blanket, hand in hand and side by side, the forest of poppies and thistles nodding in the wind several feet above their heads and enclosing them in walls of privacy and beauty.

Gwyneth smiled up at the blue sky. How blissfully happy she felt to be out here amid such tranquil beauty, and with the man she loved besides! She turned her head and looked into the simmering, slate eyes of the marquess.

"Is this your surprise?" she asked.

"Part of it."

Turning on his side, he propped his head on the heel of his hand and gazed lazily at her with those diabolically beautiful eyes. Gwyneth's blood ignited. God help her, every cell in her body melted when he looked at her like that, and she felt her insides oozing right down into the blanket and the hard earth beneath.

"Let me guess the other part. You're going to ravish me."

"I don't think that either of us would consider that a surprise."

"I suppose not. We both know it's going to happen. . . ."

"But it need not happen now, if you do not wish it."

"Of course I wish it." She blushed and tried to smooth a lump in the blanket. "Besides, if you do not ravish me today, when *will* you?"

"Difficult as it would be, I *could* wait until after we are wed."

Gwyneth froze, unsure she'd heard him correctly. Yet the charming, rakish smile was still carved into his darkly handsome face, brighter now if anything, and one wicked eyebrow was lifted in query.

"Well?"

"Is that—a proposal?"

"It is trying to be a proposal. I can rephrase it, if you so desire."

She giggled. "Oh, Damon!"

"Shall I rephrase it? I can bow over your hand like a rakish young buck and say, 'My dear Lady Simms, will you do me the honor of becoming my wife?' That is the dandy's approach. Or—"

She giggled again, drinking him up with her eyes, loving every inch of him, wishing he would hurry up and begin the ravishment.

"—I can do it as a pirate might, by sweeping you off your feet and carrying you straight to the nearest clergyman without giving you any leave to deny me—"

Her giggle became laughter, and she reached out to swat at his shoulder playfully. "Those ways are all well and good, but I want to know how you think the Black Wolf might do it!"

He stared at her, momentarily taken aback. Then, swiftly recovering, he smiled and murmured, "I suppose he would kidnap you and wrap you in his black cape, and adopt much the same method as would our pirate."

"And how do you know he has a black cape?"

"Well, if *I* were the Black Wolf, I'd certainly wear a black cape."

"Oh, Damon, I do so wish you'd ravish me!"

"Consent to be my marchioness, and I shall consider it."

"Damon!"

"Do you worry about your sister? Rhiannon will come to live with us, of course," he explained, with more patience than his racing heart dictated. "So will your dog. Your maid. Your—your flowers, if you want them. I shall give you anything you desire, my beloved Gwyneth. All you must do is ask and I will give it to you."

"What of your naval career?"

"To hell with it. If they have not thrown me out of the service, then I shall hand in my resignation. I don't belong there and never did."

"What of the prisoner, young Toby?"

"I will . . . buy his freedom."

"*Buy* it?"

"Why not? The guards who serve the prison hulk are easily bribed. How do you think the Black Wolf managed so many rescues?"

"My dear Lord Morninghall, you are not only a very wicked man but a powerful one."

"My power is naught without a marchioness. Don't make me beg, woman."

"Perhaps I want to be carried off, Black Wolf-style."

"Perhaps you *will* be, if you don't mind that tongue of yours."

She laughed and, plucking a blade of grass, tickled his nose with its end. But he misinterpreted her teasing as reluctance to accept his offer, and she saw the confidence, and patience beginning to fade from his face. "For God's sake woman!" he said, growing desperate, "you may even continue your charitable work, and with my blessings. I'll even help you. Marry me, Gwyneth."

She tossed the grass aside and leaned toward him, her eyes sparkling. "Very well then, my lord. I will marry you."

With a triumphant laugh, he tumbled her back

down to the blanket, and her giggles were abruptly silenced as his mouth came down hard atop hers. Her eyes fell shut and she made a soft moan of content-ment deep within her throat as his tongue slipped out and slowly caressed her lip, moving back and forth with sensual languor before pressing gently against her teeth. She opened her mouth to admit his en-trance, her head sliding on the waves of her own silken hair as she moved beneath him. His tongue dipped deeply into her mouth and she tasted his hunger for her, his craving need. It awoke a similar craving in her, and moaning softly, she reached up to embrace him, his shoulders so wide she could barely link her hands together atop them. The wind sighed through the forest of poppies and thistles around them, and faintly she heard the cry of a kestrel somewhere in the hazy sky above.

At last he broke the kiss, and as her eyes drifted open, she saw him staring down at her, the little sunbursts of gold in his eyes seeming to draw her up into their very depths. Ever considerate, he had not lowered his weight atop her, but lay alongside her, his powerful body branding the length of hers with its heat.

"My dearest, cherished Gwyneth." He reached out and tenderly cupped her cheek, and his gaze roved over her face as though he were looking at an incom-parable treasure. "You have shown me things I did not know existed, you have sent the ugliness and rage fleeing my heart, you have made me whole again, defended me, and saved my life. I love you with all my heart, and I want nothing more than to prove it to you with my body, with my soul, with every means at my disposal, but . . ."

"But what, my lord?"

His thumb gently caressed the side of her face. "But I must know something. The last time we were about to make love, you told me you had never known a man before."

"That is so."

"But—I am confused. You were married. . . ."

She reached up and traced the curve of his brow with her fingers. "Lord Simms wed me only to rescue me from an unfortunate situation," she said and briefly outlined the life she and her sisters had led at the inn. "He was an old man, far past the call of passion, who was content to worship a wife from afar. He often told me he dared not take my maidenhead because he was afraid it would rob me of my purity, my innocence. We were the fastest of friends, Damon—but we were never lovers."

He stared down at her, slowly shaking his head. "How can any man look upon you and *not* want to possess you, wholly and fully?"

"*You're* looking upon me," she quipped, rising up on her elbows and trying to recapture the lightness of the previous moment, "and I have yet to see you begin the task of possessing me wholly and fully."

Lowering his brow until it touched hers, he gazed fiercely into her eyes. "I know I've been a brute in the past, but I swear to you, Gwyneth, I shall be as gentle, as considerate as you deserve to have me be."

"I know you will." She stared into his eyes and very slowly said, "Now, get on with the ravishing, will you, my lord? My body is on fire and I cannot stand the suspense much longer."

"Oh, you'll stand it," he growled, returning her sly smile, "for I intend to draw this out until I have you mindless with want."

"Then what are you waiting for?"

"Minx!"

He kissed her once more, and she felt his fingers working lightly at the embroidered white bow that tied beneath her waist. Her hand covered his, and she rode its movements as he caught one end of the ribbon between thumb and forefinger and slowly, gently pulled until the bow fell apart and the ribbons lay trailing across her ribs and stomach.

"Aaah, that's better," he murmured, and she sighed in delight as he pushed her backward and bent his dark head to nuzzle the warm valley between her breasts. Liquid warmth pulsed through her, thick and viscous. Her breasts tingled with need and want, eager for the touch of those dark, masterful hands, the branding heat of that searing, sensual mouth.

She drove her hands upward, exploring the warm, hard slabs of his chest through the loose shirt. "My turn," she said huskily and helped him pull the shirt off over his head. Then she lay back, staring up at his splendidly proportioned torso, his powerful chest and shoulders, with admiring eyes.

"That's better," she echoed slyly.

He laughed. She answered him with a shy little giggle. Then he drew her up, laid her across his knee, and slowly unbuttoned her dress all the way down the back, his warm hands palming and smoothing the tingles from her flesh. She shivered as he scooped the fabric from one shoulder and dragged it slowly, enticingly down her arm. By the time he got to the other shoulder, she was a vessel of steaming heat. Moments later the gown was a discarded pile of color beside the picnic basket, and she wore nothing but her chemise, petticoats, and garters, her womanly regions burning with want.

She saw the hard bulge in his breeches, and with studied demureness murmured, "You seem well practiced in the art of undressing a woman, Damon. Might I begin to hone my own respective talents on you?"

He took her hand and gently placed it atop the rock-hard swelling at his groin. "If you delay much longer, my dear fiancée, I shall think you don't want me after all."

A light breeze drove through the forest of poppies and thistles, making her chemise flutter against her skin and setting afire every inch of flesh against which it whispered. She knew the gauzy fabric did little to shield her rosy areolea and taut nipples from his chillingly hot eyes, and she secretly gloried in the fact. Sure enough, the marquess's gaze was drawn helplessly to her bosom, and she could feel him growing even harder, stiffer, larger beneath the straining fabric that lay between him and her hand. Oh, the thought of being *ravished* by such a man filled her with dizzy heat!

He lifted his gaze and let it burn into hers.

Holding it, she pulled off first one of his boots, then the other. Then she sat back and slowly let her palm rove down his splendid chest and hard, flat stomach, down over the dark arrow of hair that led to the closure of his breeches. Her heart hammered in her chest. Her womanly regions burned and ached. And still he watched her, his eyes shimmeringly iridescent with shifting shadows, colors, and nuances of controlled desire. Her thumbs grew clumsy and it was all she could do to thread each button through its hole, but somehow she managed, finally rising up on her knees as she undid the last one, dropping kisses against the warm skin of his chest. His arm circled her back like a wreath of steel, holding her tight against him, and she felt his hand stroking her hair and combing out the thick, silken tresses with his fingers.

"Don't be afraid," he murmured huskily into her hair.

The huge hardness of him filled her hand. "I'm not afraid, Damon. A little shy, but not afraid. How could I be, when I have wanted this since the first time I met you?"

"Wanted this? Forgive me, Gwyn . . . my guilt knows no bounds . . . my memories of how I threatened and bullied you still plague me, terribly."

"Stop torturing yourself," she said. "That is behind us."

She let her fingers slide into the warm bed of hair that lay beneath the loose flap of his breeches, and rested them, light as a butterfly, atop the velvety head of his shaft. He groaned hoarsely, and as she raised her head to look at him, she saw his eyes had glazed with desire. She gently stroked him, feeling the shape of him, the texture, the temperature, the size. He was deliciously rigid, as stiff and hard as a pike, and the knowledge that he would soon fill her made her inner regions tingle and weep with longing.

He caught his breath through gritted teeth as she stroked him reverently, exploring the soft tip, the huge and swollen length of sheathed steel. "By God, Gwyneth, you're going to finish this before it's even started if you keep this up."

"I thought you said you wanted to draw this out," she murmured, reaching lower to cup and handle his testicles.

"And *I* thought *you* were a virgin."

"Virginity and innocence are two different things." She dragged her fingers back up and traced little circles atop the velvety tip of him until he began to shudder with the effort of holding himself back. "Besides, I have married friends, and they *do* talk, you know."

He swore fondly, and she positioned herself so that she was crouched down before him. Around them the poppies blew in the gentle wind, and sunlight bathed them in its warmth. She rained kisses down his mighty chest, past the faint blue bruises that still clung to his ribs, and down into the wiry soft curls from which his manhood sprang. She felt his hands in her hair, gripping it almost savagely, heard the strained inhalations of his breath as he fought to draw air through clenched teeth.

She held his staff between her palms and slowly brushed her cheek against each side of it.

"Gwyneth, stop."

Smiling, she held it again, then used her lips.

"Gwyneth, I'm begging you, please. Stop."

She gripped it a third time and slowly closed her mouth over it.

He swore and, grasping her by the shoulders, pulled her off of him. Laughing, she saw that his face was rigid and strained with the force of his self-control, his eyes blazing with desire, his nostrils flaring like a stallion's.

"Did I nearly undo you?" she asked chidingly.

"Bloody hell—"

"I trust you will pay me back for such an indignity."

"Tenfold, my lady, I swear it!"

And he did. He tumbled her backward until she lay on the blanket once more, his mouth branding hers with savage heat and his hard, ruthless length pressing almost painfully against her belly. His kisses burned her face, her throat, her breasts through the gauzy chemise. Relentlessly, his mouth moved downward, his hands shaping the contour of her ribs, her hips, her thighs. They settled on her ankles and, skimming her long calves and thighs, dragged the hem of the petticoats all the way up to her waist and over her head. She felt his mouth kissing the inside of her ankles, felt the warm touch of his tongue, licking, tasting its way back up her leg, warm upon contact, cool and shivery when the air hit each damp spot.

"Oh, Damon," she said, trembling in delight.

She tried to claw the gauzy skirts off her face so she could see him, but he tossed them back over her eyes once more, covering her face in a light veil of fabric. "Leave them," he commanded, his voice low and husky against the inside of her calf, his hands still vise-like around each ankle. "It shall heighten your pleasure if you can feel, but not see, what I am doing."

"This is—like bondage!"

He chuckled. "Indeed."

And he spoke the truth. She gasped as his mouth grazed her knees now, his tongue swirling around each kneecap, his hand smoothing its way up her thigh and preparing a trail for his mouth. She knew what he was going to do to her. She knew, and her body knew, and already it was hot and wet and beginning to tremble violently.

Whimpering like a mindless animal, she stared up into nothing through the light material covering her face, feeling his hand moving toward her pelvis, his mouth not far behind it. His lips, teeth, tongue were nibbling the inside of her knee now, the sensitive skin inside her right thigh. *Oh* . . . She felt his fingers pushing slowly upward, toward the pool of liquid fire that drenched the junction of her thighs. *Oh, God* . . . She felt him put his hands beneath her boneless legs and drag them as far apart as they would bear, fully exposing her damp flesh to his hungry gaze. Her body tensed and she moaned softly, crushing a fold of the blanket in her fist.

"Damon . . ." she murmured, feeling the cool sweep of the breeze against her hot, exposed flesh, "must you make me wait so long?"

"I fear I must, my dear," he murmured with dark amusement. She heard a light snapping noise, and a moment later something ticklish and soft was grazing her feet, ankles, and calves. She tried to jerk her legs shut, but his ruthless hand and one knee held them open.

"That tickles!"

"Yes. Again, dear lady, it will heighten the pleasure." He chuckled wickedly as he continued to drag whatever it was he held up over her kneecap.

The savage burning in her exposed womanly area, the tickling caress of whatever instrument of torture he held had Gwyneth quaking inside. The center of her, still hungry for his mouth, his tongue, his huge and swollen manhood, burned for him.

The feathery tickle was moving higher up her leg.

"What *are* you doing?" she cried, staring up at the sunny whiteness through the veil of fabric.

"Teasing you."

"With what?"

"A poppy," he said and dragged the fragile blossom along the sensitive inside of her right thigh, over the top of her mound, then down along the inside of her left thigh. Gwyneth made a hitching sob deep in her throat, and her head lashed from side to side beneath the veil of muslin. She felt Damon's hot knee bracing one of her thighs open, his hand holding apart the other, and strained against both. On a low, keening cry, she felt him dragging the poppy back up the inside of her thigh . . . felt him parting the petals of her womanhood with his fingers . . . and then felt him flicking the poppy over her own damp flesh, back and forth, side to side, until noises of keening anguish burst from her tortured throat and she was sobbing, begging, crying for mercy.

She heard his dark laughter, felt him grasp the base of each of her thighs in his big hands and bury his face between her open legs. His hot mouth found and fastened upon the quivering seed of her passion, and she bucked upward on a cry of raw ecstacy, her back arched nearly double, the veil of fabric still obscuring him from her view. He drew her engorged bud of femininity deeply into his mouth, sucking it hard and laving it over and over with his tongue, until the first violent waves of climax rushed over Gwyneth and burst from her throat with a harsh, ripping scream.

"Stop!" she cried, mortified, but he did not end the sucking pressure, and she screamed again as another violent wave of pleasure roared through her, crashing over her senses with such force that she blacked out for a moment. When she came to, limp and stunned, he was gently pulling the veil of skirts down from her face, gazing down at her with love, hunger, and a look of charming, little-boy devilry.

"Do forgive me, my lady," he said innocently, "but you taste *ever* so good. . . ."

As she gazed, panting, up into his mesmerizing, diabolically beautiful eyes, he grinned, and she saw that his manhood rose tall and proud against his stomach and bulged with unspent passion.

"Three times lucky?" he asked wickedly.

"I dare you."

"You should know better," he murmured, raising both brows and gently lowering himself down atop her, supporting his weight with his forearms so as not to crush her. Everything between her legs was still throbbing with fire, and she doubted there was any-thing left in her. But he proved her wrong. As his mouth, sweet and musky with the scent of her, grazed her jaw, her chin, and finally fastened on her lips, as his hands cupped her breast and pushed it upward so that he might suckle the thrusting, peaked nipple, she felt the fire building inside her once again.

"I love you, my dearest Lady Simms," he murmured against her throat, against the soft flesh of her breast, against her heart. "You have made me a very happy man."

She felt his manhood probing her entrance, but she was so slick with moisture down there that, despite his size and her own tightness, she felt little pain, only firm, delicious pressure as he entered her. He groaned as he slid just inside her and cradled her face within his big hands, kissing her brow, her eyelids, her cheekbones.

"I promised to be gentle," he said hoarsely, searching her gaze, "but there is one thing from which I cannot spare you pain."

"Do it," she gasped, swept up in a fire of her own.

He lowered his head, claimed her mouth, and surged upward and forward. Pain ripped inside her. It was brief, a sharp tearing of virginity, then it was over, gone, behind her, and he was surging gently into her, filling her passage, expanding it as he moved deeper and deeper inside her.

This was heaven. This, with the blue sky above, the wind coasting over their hot bodies, the sunlight warming their skin, and the forest of poppies and thistles whispering and nodding all around, this, with Damon making love to her, her wild, magnificent lord—this was heaven at last.

He withdrew slowly, eased himself gently back into her, then began to pick up the pace. As Gwyneth straddled his hips with her long legs and matched his quickening, now pounding rhythm, as his mouth drove desperately into hers, she saw him raise his head in a soundless cry, felt his hot seed filling her womanhood, and felt a third crashing explosion rock through her.

She cried out, sobbing with the anguish of it all, and as their shudders quieted and she once again heard the distant birds, the wind through the poppies, their own matched ragged breathing, she felt as though she were home at last, and this wonderful, windswept place was the one that had waited for her forever.

The marquess raised his head and looked down at her, his iridescent eyes burning with a love so fierce it pierced right through to her heart.

"That surprise I have for you," he murmured and, stretching, reached for the lunch basket.

Still clinging to him, she turned her head and watched as he withdrew a small, silk-wrapped bundle. As the shimmering wrappings fell away, he held up a magnificent ring, a ruby framed in diamonds which winked in the sun and shot prisms of fire into her eyes.

"For you," he said simply, "the future Marchioness of Morninghall."

Chapter 25

Damon was not a patient man. Over the next two weeks he obtained a special license from the archbishop, sent for Rhiannon in Portsmouth, and, in a small, private ceremony within the splendor of Morninghall's own chapel, married his lady. It was a beautiful, almost divine affair, with a glorious morning shining through the chapel's ancient panes of stained glass, bathing them both in light the color of sparkling gems, and only the bride's sister, the loyal Britwell, and the great house's other staff witnessed the solemn event.

For Gwyneth the day passed in a blur. Great tables laid with food were set up on the lawns outside, the neighboring villagers were invited, and the dancing and feasting lasted far into the night. If she did not notice that the staff at Morninghall were gradually warming to their long-absent master, she could not be faulted for it. If she did not notice her sister's cat-in-the-cream smile, it was only because she was wearing one herself. Indeed, the day passed too quickly to recall much of it afterward, but her proud new lord made sure the wedding night that followed was one she would never forget. When at last Gwyneth fell into an exhausted slumber some time in the wee hours of the morning, she felt as though the Marquess of Morninghall had left no inch of her body unloved.

The following day dawned dull and wet. They awoke late and lay long abed, snuggled together beneath the covers and listening to the rain falling outside until at last their growling stomachs demanded attention. Breakfast was brought to them by a blushing maid—a tray of tea, toast, and marmalade which they ate while sitting on the window seat, the misty, rolling countryside spread before them. Afterward, when the pot of tea was empty and nothing but crumbs lay on the silver plate, Gwyneth lay back against Damon's chest and luxuriated in the feel of his arms wrapped securely around her, his chin resting atop her hair. Together they watched the rain streaming down the pane just outside.

Their first full day of marital bliss, however, was destined for interruption. As Gwyneth nestled snugly in her lord's arms, she became aware of the distant tattoo of a galloping horse. She didn't think much of it until the sound grew louder and the horse burst through the long alley of trees, moving steadily toward the house.

Its rider wore a naval uniform.

"Bloody hell," Damon swore, tightening his arms around Gwyneth.

"Shall we go downstairs?"

"We'll go down when we're damn good and ready, Lady Wife," he growled and, kissing the skin just behind her ear, gently pushed her down on the velvet cushions.

Dressed in a loose, white shirt tucked into snug-fitting, dark riding breeches, the Marquess of Morninghall met Britwell at the foot of the stairs and strode into the library just over an hour later. His features were schooled to chilling calm, his manner aloof and relaxed, but inside he was fuming. How dare they interrupt only a day after his wedding! How dare they trouble him in a place where he finally had found peace and refuge! Damn their eyes, every last bloody one of them!

The poor messenger was sitting in a chair near the

fire, trying to dry his clothing and staring up in awe at
the magnificent paintings that looked down at him
from their lordly heights. By the look on his face, it
was obvious he'd never seen such wealth and opu-
lence and was more than a little overwhelmed by it
all. As Damon entered the room, he lunged to his feet
and offered the missive. Impatiently, Damon
snatched it from his hand.

"I understand congratulations are in order, my
lord," the lad croaked, cringing as Damon ripped the
seal open, his brow darkening as he read. "And I trust
you're recovering well from your recent injuries—"

Damon's withering glare instantly quieted him and
he fell silent, hands clasped behind his back and eyes
downcast.

The contents were as Damon expected.

*We are given to understand that you have sufficiently
recovered from your recent injuries; therefore, we have
deemed you fit to command and order you to return to
Portsmouth immediately.*

It was signed simply, "Bolton."

That was it then. Nothing about the Admiralty's
decision regarding his competency to command a
prison hulk, nothing about the state of affairs on
board the *Surrey,* nothing but a cold order to return to
Portsmouth *now.* Damon clenched his jaw, his fists,
his muscles. A familiar coil of rage started within his
breast, but then Gwyneth was there, her hand on his
shoulder, and instantly the rage went away.

"As bad as you expected?" she asked gently.

"Worse."

He shouldn't have expected they'd let him stay up
here forever—away from the prisoners of war, away
from the petty hatreds and jealousies of his superiors,
away from the navy he so detested. He shouldn't have
expected they would have relieved him of his duties.
After all, he was a marquess—they wouldn't dare.
How he hated the irony of it! Well, it was about time
to pull rank. He'd just return to Portsmouth and

tender his resignation. After all, there was no reason he *couldn't* stay up here forever; the decision was his really.

His eyes resolute, he went to his desk. There he penned a quick note to Bolton, folded, and sealed it. The waiting messenger looked at him fearfully. "Stay and warm yourself by the fire," Damon said, handing the note to the lad, "and I'll have Britwell bring you some lunch to sustain you before you go."

He took Gwyneth's arm and led her from the library, never hearing the messenger's words of gratitude.

"Let me guess," she said, looking up at his face as they walked down the long corridor. "You have to go back to Portsmouth."

"Of course. I should've known they weren't through with me yet."

"Will you be long?"

"No. I'll hand in my resignation as I ought to have done years ago, tie up some loose ends, and return to you just as soon as I am able."

"Why Damon! You speak as though you plan to go alone."

"Of course."

She playfully swatted his shoulder. "Think again, dearest husband. *I'm* going with you."

The journey seemed to take forever. With the Marquess and Marchioness of Morninghall traveling in the long-unused but still-gleaming family coach and Rhiannon, Sophie, and Mattie in another that followed behind, they made the slow trip south to the coast. The rain that had started the morning after the wedding continued for several days, and the roads were rutted and muddy all the way to Portsmouth. Certainly the rain did nothing to lift spirits that were already low, and try as she might, Gwyneth could not coax her new lord out of his brooding, melancholy mood.

She couldn't tell whether he was furious about

having his honeymoon interrupted, annoyed about having to deal with a situation and environment he plainly hated, or just wrestling with something private and deep—indeed, she had begun to think it was a combination of all three, with heavy emphasis on the latter. She could not help but notice the preoccupied, faraway look in his iridescent eyes, the lines of tension around his mouth, and last night, as they'd crawled into their bed at a roadside coaching inn, she'd gently asked him what was troubling him so.

"The Black Wolf," was all he'd said, all he *would* say, surprising Gwyneth with the admission. Why on earth was he thinking about the mysterious rescuer, of all things? Of course, it must be due to their growing proximity to Portsmouth. He was probably unhappy about the fact that the man who had caused him such embarrassment would once again become the bane of his pride. Or perhaps he was merely jealous. After all, Gwyneth thought rather shamefully, the Black Wolf had once kissed her, set her blood afire, and she had even unwittingly brought up his name while Damon had been trying to propose in the poppy field.

Obviously it was a sore subject with him, and out of respect for his feelings, Gwyneth decided to say no more about the Black Wolf.

She could not, of course, know that her husband was wrestling with his own conscience, and wanted nothing more than to talk to her about it.

The time just wasn't right.

They arrived in Portsmouth on a dismal, rainy afternoon which hung a ragged cloak of fog and mist over the old city. Damon had the coach brought round to Gwyneth's rented house, where he saw the women safely inside, and then, promising to return to them that evening, he made his way back toward the harbor front to start taking care of those "loose ends."

He stopped at Bolton's office first, and found the admiral out for the afternoon. But there was a sealed envelope for him, and in it were Bolton's orders

forbidding him to take any prisoner away from the
prison hulk—not even the thirteen-year-old American lad, whom he'd heard all about from "certain
parties." Fuming, Damon climbed back into the
coach and ordered the driver to take him to the docks.
Shortly afterward he was in a boat and on his way out
to HMS *Surrey*.

Wrapped in a cloak against the weather, he sat on
the damp seat, quietly watching the old ship rearing
up out of the fog like a long-forgotten ghost. He wasn't
sure what he had expected to feel at his first sight of it
after all that had come to pass. Surprisingly he felt no
tension or fear, despite that last memory of the
prisoners charging into his cabin and bringing him
down with their blows. Certainly there was no nostal-
gia, no liking for the thing, and the only emotion that
stirred his breast was a heavy sense of despair, for he
knew that no matter what he did, no matter how he
had tried to help the poor unfortunates aboard the
hulk, it would never be enough. The suffering would
end only when the war did. It was a sad and simple
truth.

Radley met him on deck, his eyes full of contempt
and dislike. He did not inquire after Damon's health
and Damon, acknowledging him with a cold nod, did
not volunteer any information. He merely strode past
the assembled marines and crew to his cabin and shut
the door.

He stood there in the quiet room, the rain trickling
down the windows. There was his bed, neatly made
up as though he had left it just this morning. There
was the window through which Gwyneth had hurled
the oar, now repaired and spattered with rain. And
there was the spot on the deck where the prisoners
had brought him down, the little knothole in the
wood against which his face had been pressed as
they'd beat him, kicked him, slammed his skull over
and over until all had gone hazy, then gray, then
mercifully black.

He sat down in his swivel chair and looked pensively at the spot. He looked at it and felt no fear, none at all. Nothing, in fact, but a strange, restless emptiness.

I don't belong here. I never did. I just want to finish what I must and go home.

And home was with Gwyneth.

There was a rap on the door. "Damon?"

"Yes, Peter. Come in."

The door swung open, and the chaplain stood there. He looked at Damon for a long moment, his hazel eyes glistening with unshed moisture. Slowly he shut the door behind him, then came forward, his hands outstretched.

"She did it then," he murmured, seizing Damon by the shoulders and looking him up and down as though he were Lazarus raised from the grave. Finally he broke into a wide, uncontainable grin and slapped Damon on the back. "As God is my witness, she did it!"

Damon grinned sheepishly and endured Peter's quick embrace. "Don't tell me you're actually as surprised as you sound?"

"Damon, if you could've seen yourself as I did, as others did, you would know that your return to the land of the living was nothing short of a miracle. As grave as your condition was, both the admiral and I knew that if anyone could save you, it was Lady Simms." He stood back, shaking his head. "I do hope you've shown her suitable gratitude for her efforts!"

"If making her my marchioness displays suitable gratitude, then yes, I have paid my debts."

"You didn't!"

"I damn well did," Damon said proudly as Peter's jaw fell open in stunned disbelief. "In fact, Lady Morninghall is here in Portsmouth with me, and you may ask her yourself."

"Tell me you did it for love," Peter said frowning, "or I shall never forgive you, Damon!"

"What sort of beast do you think I am? Of course I did it for love. Surely you don't think me so honorable as to have done it merely out of a sick sense of *gratitude* for saving my life, do you? The way I'd been feeling, I would've thanked her more if she'd simply stuck a knife in my heart and expedited my end!"

Such a declaration did much to set Peter's mind at rest. Shaking his head, he folded his arms and fell grinning into a chair. "Forgive me, Damon. This is all a bit of a shock, you must realize. Though I must say marriage agrees with you. You seem remarkably changed. Calm. Happy. Relaxed."

"I feel it," Damon said, moving to the wine cupboard and retrieving a bottle of port. He uncorked the bottle and poured them each a glass, handing the first to the chaplain. "I know it sounds addled, but she's changed my life, Peter. I've been separated from her for only an hour, and already I miss her."

The chaplain regarded his glass, a little smirk playing about his mouth. "Ah, but do you miss your *Peterson's* as well?"

"Sorry?"

"Your *Peterson's*. It's still on the table there. You mean you haven't been lost without it?"

Damon turned to stare at the big book, which he had once consulted as regularly as Peter did his Bible. He made a little noise of relief and incredulity. "Actually, come to think about it, I haven't. Perhaps being so close to death robs you of the fear of it. Especially when you realize that such fear is wasted when you're as healthy as I suspect I've probably been all along. Though I did wonder about those heart attacks. . . ."

"Nerves, Damon. Nerves. How many times do I have to tell you that?"

"Yes." He gave a cryptic smile. "I suppose you were right."

A long moment passed between them. From beyond the door and bulkheads came the sounds of the prison ship, the "all's well" of the guards, the cry of a gull outside.

At length Peter said, "I have some news too." He

took another sip of port and stretched his legs out before him, a little smile playing across his mouth as he studied his shoes. "You're not the only one to, uh, deserve congratulations. I asked Orla O'Shaughnessy to become my wife."

"Orla O'Shaughnessy? A former *pirate?!*" Damon laughed and reached over to refill Peter's glass. "Well, what did she say, man?"

The chaplain gave him a sideways grin. "She agreed."

"Congratulations!" Damon said warmly and shook Peter's hand. "She'll make you a wonderful bride, though your gain will certainly be Connor's loss!"

Peter sobered. "That reminds me, Damon. About our . . . activities. I think they should stop. Radley has become suspicious, and I fear he may have planted spies among the guards on this ship."

"Radley has always been suspicious." Damon lifted his glass and studied the depths of his wine. "And I agree with you wholeheartedly, Peter, the activities must stop, but there is still young Toby Ashton to consider. I take it he's still aboard?"

"Yes, but his health is fragile, Damon. Connor tried to get him off, but . . ."

"But what?"

"He failed. Foyle spotted the airhole we'd cut in the barrel for Toby to breathe through as it was being lifted off the ship. Connor barely escaped with his life."

"Bloody *hell.*" Damon put his glass down, his eyes cold and hard. "Is the boy all right?"

"For the moment. He's developed a cough and cannot maintain a decent weight. I'm worried about him, Damon. Clayton's been keeping him out of the way, but if Radley or Foyle finds out the boy's getting special treatment, they'll not go easy on either of them."

"Then they must not find out." Damon got to his feet and moved silently to the windows. For a long moment he stood looking out over the gray harbor, his pose lordly, authoritative, august as he watched the swells parade beneath the rotted rudder, the mists drifting over the water. At last he turned and murmured, "That does it then, we will take young Toby off tonight. Send word to Connor."

"I beg of you, Damon, don't. It's too dangerous—"

"It has always been dangerous, Peter. If there are spies, I dare not bribe the guards, and there is no other way. Besides, I've had enough of this ship, enough of this navy, and enough of trying to make my way in a system I was never meant to inhabit. Tomorrow I hand in my resignation to Bolton. By teatime I shall be on my way back home. Therefore it *must* be done tonight."

He looked at the chaplain for a long moment, and there was an unspoken urgency in that direct, intelligent gaze that articulated Peter's own thoughts. Toby Ashton was dying, and if the Black Wolf did not get him off the ship, his young life would end here—in the stinking bowels of hell itself.

"So be it then," the chaplain said quietly, and even as he murmured the words, he sent up a silent prayer that God would watch over this final act of rescue.

A sense of doom was moving over his heart just as surely as the mists were darkening the sea outside, and he had the awful feeling that this rescue was the one that would go wrong.

Terribly, horribly wrong.

Chapter 26

$\sim\!\!\sim\!\!\circlearrowright$

Darkness had begun to fall over Portsmouth, but in the thick, gray gloom that shrouded both land and sea, it was impossible to discern at what hour day had ended and night begun. Gwyneth, who had spent the day packing up clothes and their most treasured belongings with Rhiannon and Sophie, terminating their lease, and dashing off notes to her former brother-in-law, her friends, and various other contacts, never noticed how much time had passed until she happened to look up from her desk and realize that lamps were already lit in nearby windows and splashing their light upon the wet, darkening street below.

A couple of miles away Damon, attending to various matters of official business and correspondence as he awaited Peter's return, heard the bell on the forecastle announce the evening meal and looked up in faint surprise before hurrying to finish his final tasks as commander of a prison hulk. The schooner *Kestrel,* cruising in the mists that wreathed the Isle of Wight, was running with no lights and her captain was not about to call for any, despite the fact that gloom had now settled over the wet, shining decks and it was all he could do to pick out the ship's bowsprit as it cleaved the mists some ninety feet out from where he stood at the helm. Only Peter Milford, who was with Connor, and young Toby Ashton, still aboard the prison hulk and wrapped in a thin, moth-

341

eaten wool blanket as damp as the night itself, were keenly aware of the time. Hiding in the shadows just outside the forward garrison, the boy sat in total darkness, coughing and trying in vain to muffle the hoarse and phlegmy barks against the blanket so that no one would hear him.

He had no watch, but he knew what the hour was. He'd been on the prison hulk long enough to pinpoint the time just by noting the thickness of the smoke that came from the galley pipe a stone's throw away, or by listening to the clatter of utensils against plates as the guards ate and, later, the merrymaking in which they, and even some of the prisoners, indulged after the meal to try to fool themselves into thinking their lot was any better than it was. But Toby wasn't fooled. His lot was bad and he knew it. He was frail, he was sick, and he was dying. Now, with a defeat borne of illness, he doubted very much he'd make it off the ship alive.

His gallant cousin Connor, however, held an entirely different view on the matter. Tonight the Black Wolf was going to make a last attempt to get Toby off the ship. Toby coughed again and shivered violently, too sick even to contemplate how Connor was going to do it. But do it he would. Reverend Milford had sent word through Jack Clayton: *Be ready at eleven o'clock. Someone will come for you.*

That had been two hours ago. Now the ship was beginning to quiet down. It was half past ten, by Toby's guess. Again he coughed, unable to help himself, hoping no one had heard him as he crouched shivering in the blanket, all the protection he had against the cold drizzle. Seven sentries paced the gallery that ran all around the ship just above the waterline, and a few shadowy figures moved about through the darkness. If he was discovered, they'd haul him before Radley and all would be lost. Toby was past caring if he lived or died, but he didn't want poor Connor to go through all the trouble of rescuing him and then coming up empty-handed.

"Toby?"

The whispered voice came from the darkness several feet away.

Toby held his breath, not daring to move.

"Toby, it's me, Gerry Osley. You know, Jack Clayton's friend. You remember me, don't you? The Black Wolf sent me to come get you."

The night pressed all around, ripe with the scents of wind and salt and rain. A few cold, heavy drops spattered Toby's shoulders, immediately soaking through the thin blanket and chilling his skin. Somewhere aft, in the officers' garrison, laughter and revelry ensued, a lonely sound in the damp and drizzly night. The shadow moved, closer now. Toby squinted and craned his neck, trying to see through the inky gloom, but to no avail. No one but Jack had ever come for him. He kept very still—and then it happened.

He coughed, the violent spasm nearly imploding his tired ribs.

"Aha! There you are!" The whispered voice was vaguely familiar, and now the figure hurried forward, a stealthy shape in the darkness, borne on light, agile feet. Toby curled within the blanket, suddenly afraid. A hand touched his shoulder and he looked up.

The night was dark, but he could see the young, friendly face with its dark eyes and lopsided grin. The guard was not much older than Toby himself, and, yes, he *had* seen him talking to Jack Clayton lately. If Gerry knew about the Black Wolf and the fact that Toby was to be rescued tonight, then certainly Jack— or even Peter Milford—must have sent him. Toby decided the guard could be trusted.

He stood up, his legs shaky and cramped, the movement making him feel dizzy and sick. He balled the blanket and pressed it against his mouth to still another bout of coughing.

"Hurry," Gerry said, steadying him. "The Wolf is waiting."

They moved out onto the open deck. A heavy mist was falling, grainy bits of moisture that dewed Toby's glasses and the shoulders of his blanket, and made his lank hair cling sadly to his scalp. He reached up and clutched the miniature at his throat, shivering.

"You know where I'm supposed to bring you?" Gerry whispered over his shoulder, his face pale and round in the gloom.

"I thought you're supposed to know that."

"They don't tell me anything. Take a guess, Toby. You know if Radley finds us, my arse will be tasting the cat!"

Toby stifled a cough. His knees were knocking with fatigue and cold and he just wanted to lie down someplace and go to sleep. "I was told somethin' about the bow."

"The bow?"

"Figurehead, to be precise."

"Well, then, let's go. We sit out here in the open and we'll be in trouble for sure." Seizing Toby's elbow through the blanket, the young marine steered him down through the decks and forward. Toby ducked as they passed a sentry, but the man pretended not to notice him and Toby suspected Connor had bribed him too. Once, Toby's bare feet slipped on the slimy deck, but Gerry jerked him up before he could go down. Presently they emerged out in the bows, as far forward on the ship as they could go.

Above, the superstructure of the soldiers' garrison blocked out the sky and shielded them from the rain. Beyond the damp, curving railing, Toby could hear the sea moving, and he was suddenly afraid.

All was quiet up there, and he figured the occupants of the garrison must be asleep. But he heard a strange, familiar click from someplace near, and the hair on the back of his neck rose.

"Gerry, I think someone's watchin' us."

"It's your imagination. Trust me, if anyone was watching us, you'd know it. The Black Wolf's already tried for you once, so it stands to reason he'll try again. Anyone sees you sneaking around in the dark, they'll automatically assume he's making another attempt and the alarm will be raised sky-high."

"You sure, Gerry?"

"Of course I am. Now be quiet or someone *will* discover us."

Toby swallowed hard and drew the blanket more tightly around his shoulders. The great figurehead faced the night just before and below them. The floor of the garrison above made him feel closed in, trapped. Far below, waves washed against the stem, the bows, the hull. Moisture dripped from the old wood above, trickling into his hair. He crouched down, miserable, wet, too sick and too uneasy to feel excitement.

Gerry crouched down beside him, his shoulders touching Toby's.

"This Black Wolf fellow, they say he's your cousin. That so, Toby?"

"Aye."

"You must be damnably proud of him."

"Aye."

"Everyone's talking about him, you know. Never heard of so many women fainting and swooning just at the mention of his name. Sure wouldn't mind being the Black Wolf myself."

A noise thudded from somewhere above. Toby whipped his head up, but there was nothing to be seen in the darkness. His uneasiness grew, and his heart began to beat wildly. Something wasn't right.

"I don't think the Wolf's coming for me tonight, Gerry. I want to go back."

"Nonsense. That noise? Just old Hawkins falling out of his bed. Does it every night—"

"No, really, I want to go back—now. I—I don't feel well."

"Don't be so damned lily-livered!" Gerry said with sudden sharpness. "Only babies whine so. You're American, aren't you? We British have respect for you Yanks. You're cut from the same mold as we are, unlike those dancing French monkeys. Now quit whining, and show some mettle, for God's sake!"

Toby gaped at the sudden harshness of Gerry's tone. Sudden dread shot through him. He had to get out of here, now. Something was wrong; this just didn't feel right. He jumped to his feet, turned—

And ran straight into the chest of Lieutenant John Radley.

He had no time to scream. Radley's palm immediately clamped over his mouth, and he was caught in a hold from which there was no escape. "Move and you're dead," his captor snarled, nearly crushing Toby's fragile body with the force of his grip. He dragged Toby back with him against the roundhouse and yanked a pistol out of his coat. "Fine work, Gerry. You'll be richly rewarded for this, I promise you."

"Yes, well it wasn't easy. Jack Clayton wouldn't tell me a bloody thing. Couldn't help but wonder what creature he was harboring when I saw him sneaking into the strangest places with food and coming out empty-handed."

"You're certain the Wolf's going to strike tonight?"

"Damned certain. Clayton wasn't willing to confess, but when I told him what we were going to do to his wife and brats if he didn't, his tongue loosened up a little. Loosened up even more when Hawkins and I took the paring knife to the quicks of his fingernails." Gerry shot a nasty, malicious glance at Toby. "His little *pet* here confirmed everything. The Wolf's coming, sir. Tonight."

"You'd better be correct, Gerry. I've waited too long for the rascal's head on a platter to have it denied me. Damn you, quit your struggling, you wretched bag of bones!" Radley snarled, driving his elbow savagely into Toby's stomach until the boy convulsed, retching.

From above, on the railed walkway built onto the sentries' garrison, Toby heard movement and whispers, and knew that Radley's forces were poised for action.

Training their muskets on the water below.

Waiting for the Black Wolf.

The horrible truth was too much to bear. Gerry had been spying for Radley all along, and had tortured Jack until he'd gleaned the details of tonight's rescue. No wonder the guard had let them pass. No wonder no one had raised the alarm. It all had been a trap. What had they done to Jack? What had they done to the Reverend Milford?

And, oh, God, what would they do to Connor?!

And then each man who stood poised in the wet darkness heard it: the faint splash of muffled oars and the sound of a boat slicing through the water below. From out of the mists came a shape, moving like a phantom through the night, so much a part of the darkness that no one could be sure it was even an earthly craft. In horror Toby watched it disappear beneath the railing, and heard the sounds of the oars backing water. He struggled, trying to make a sound, but Radley cuffed him hard across the temple and, nearly crushing his jaw, dragged his head around to whisper savagely in his ear.

"Make one sound and your cousin's dead the minute he shows his face above that railing, you got it?"

Toby froze. The night pressed down on them, so thick and black that no star, no moon, not even the lights from the nearby ships could penetrate it. He felt the wind pushing the drizzle against his face, the excited thump of Radley's heart against his ear—

And he heard faint scratching noises just below.

Climbing noises.

"Get back," Radley mouthed, signaling wildly with his free hand. Instantly the guards pressed themselves against the roundhouse and headboard, their muskets trained on the rail.

Toby's throat closed with sobs. He heard the scratching noise coming up the deadwood, the main wale, the base of the figurehead, growing closer, growing louder, but still fainter than the whisper of a cat moving along a fence. *Connor.* He heard Radley's tense, measured breathing and that of Gerry and the guards around and above them. *Connor.* Now Radley was quietly bringing his pistol up beneath Toby's chin, its cold muzzle pressing against the soft flesh that spanned the underside of his jaw.

"Toby."

One short, authoritative command.

The Black Wolf.

Again: "Toby!"

Radley held his breath and pressed the pistol hard into Toby's jaw, slowly driving his head back against his shoulder. Toby struggled to see, trembling and looking down the plane of his cheekbones. A hand, gloved in black, reached up slowly and seized the railing. Another did the same. Then, slowly, with more grace than a panther on the hunt, a figure hoisted its head and shoulders up over the rail.

Tension hung in the air.

Not a soul moved.

Radley's hand was shaking as he pushed the pistol deeper into the soft flesh of Toby's jaw. *Come on, my friend,* Radley thought, clenching his teeth, clenching his finger on the pistol's trigger, clenching the boy he held hostage. *A little closer . . .*

The Black Wolf hung there, half over the rail, head raised as he surveyed the darkness for danger. Then, slowly, he swung one long leg over the rail. Radley quivered, and thick saliva filled his mouth. He felt the boy trembling in his grip. He saw the tall, powerfully built figure in black straighten to his full height and look warily around. He was magnificent, deadly, and certainly not a man with whom Radley cared to do business.

He wouldn't have to. In his mind's eye he saw the guards around and above him slowly training their pistols and muskets on his unsuspecting quarry.

Come on, damn you!

His heart began to thump wildly, and the excitement over the hunt, over the kill, had given him a fierce erection.

The Wolf turned back toward the railing, and in the darkness Radley saw Gerry silently bring his pistol up, clenching it in both hands and sighting down it as if he were about to kill some huge, lethal leopard.

"Halt right there or the boy dies."

The Wolf froze in a half-crouch, one hand still stretched toward the railing. Slowly he turned his dark head toward them, and beneath the mask that covered his eyes Radley saw his nostrils flaring with contempt.

Radley stepped from the shadows.

"Give it up, Captain Merrick," he said smoothly, keeping his pistol beneath Toby's chin as he moved forward. "We have you surrounded. Any sudden moves on your part will only make me splatter the brat's head all over the place. You wouldn't want that now, would you?"

Tears leaked from Toby's eyes and streamed down his cheeks. He saw the Wolf's masked face turn slowly toward Radley, saw the quivering tension in every muscle of his tall, powerfully built body. When he spoke, his voice was dark with rage.

"Let the boy go," he whispered savagely. "He is innocent."

"Really, you're in no position to bargain, Captain Merrick."

"I *said,* 'Let him go.'"

The Wolf took a menacing step toward Radley.

"Another step and my men will shoot you dead. And don't think the boy won't follow."

The Wolf did not move. Toby could feel the huge, frightening force of his fury, the magnificent tension that warred within him as he considered Radley's words. He seemed larger than the night, dark, terrible, diabolical.

He towered over Radley, staring down at him with barely leashed menace.

"What do you want?"

"You, Captain Merrick. Preferably alive."

The Wolf glared down at Radley a moment longer. "Let the boy go, and I will freely give myself up to your authority." The dark figure loomed over the both of them. "A trade, Radley. My life for the boy's."

Radley laughed, a low, dark sound of pure evil. "Very well, then. Come here."

"Release the boy."

From above came a clicking sound as someone cocked his musket. The guards shifted, never lowering their weapons. Finally Radley made a noise of derision and shoved Toby toward the Black Wolf, who swept him up into his embrace and laid his cheek against his hair.

Slowly he reached down to retrieve the rope he had brought with him and tied it securely around Toby's waist.

"No sudden moves, Merrick," Radley warned, training his pistol on the Black Wolf's heart.

The figure in black did not answer him, merely taking Toby's shoulders and looking down into his eyes in a final good-bye. "A friend awaits you in the boat below," he murmured for Toby's ears alone. "And your brother and cousin await you aboard the schooner *Kestrel*. Go. And Godspeed."

"My brother and *cousin?* But who . . . what? . . ."

But the Black Wolf only pressed his fingers to Toby's lips, and saw him safely down into the boat that would take him through the mists and back to his family.

Then, slowly, he turned to face his fate.

"Who indeed?" Radley murmured coldly, and as his men leaped forward to restrain the unresisting figure, he ripped the mask off with one vicious yank.

And found himself staring into the ice-cold eyes of Damon Andrew Phillip deWolfe, the sixth Marquess of Morninghall.

Chapter 27

❧❧❧

"Lud, would you look at these newspapers! It took me the better part of the last two hours just to wade through them!"

Rhiannon swept into Gwyneth's bedroom, her arms piled with the papers that had collected during their absence. Casting a swift glance at Gwyneth, who sat scribbling at her desk, she placed the stack on the chest at the foot of the bed.

"Anything interesting happen while we were away?" Gwyneth asked absently without looking up from her letter to Maeve, Lady Falconer, who was on her way to the West Indies.

"I should say so! The Black Wolf has been up to his gallant exploits. Seems he was so bold as to try to take a young American lad off the prison hulk via an empty water barrel!"

"Tried?" Gwyneth asked, still without looking up.

"Someone discovered the plan, and the Wolf was forced to abandon it. He got away, thank heavens! Well, then, I'll leave you to finish your work; I know that time runs short, and your handsome husband shall be home at any time now!"

But Gwyneth need not have rushed so. By ten thirty darkness, hastened by the gloomy weather, was settling over the city, and she was forced to work by the light of a lantern. By eleven o'clock the night was fully black beyond her window, and she was beginning to feel a bit impatient and annoyed at Damon for his tardiness. By midnight, when he still hadn't returned, she was growing worried, and as the clock on her mantle struck one in the morning, she was pacing the parlor, wondering what to do, where to go.

Rhiannon, who had come in earlier to express concern, offered the usual comforting words: perhaps His Lordship had met up with some old shipmates and was drinking away his last night in the navy at some dockside tavern. Perhaps his business with the port admiral or other naval officials was taking longer than expected. Perhaps he too had paperwork to catch up on, and like Gwyneth was hurrying to get it done. Surely he would be home at any time . . .

But poor Rhiannon was yawning and bleary-eyed, and at Gwyneth's urging, she finally went to bed. An hour later so did Gwyneth, but she could not sleep. She lay in the darkness, listening to the rain outside, the shadows moving up and down her walls as the wind moved the trees, and worried.

And imagined terrible things.

Sometime in the wee hours of the night, she must've fallen into a troubled slumber, for when next she woke, a heavy gray daylight filled the room. She lay in bed for a moment, staring at the empty walls, at the furniture whose tops were now bare, at her trunk, pushed into a corner and overflowing with clothing, valuables, and sentimental treasures.

She heard Sophie moving around downstairs; Rhiannon, down in the kitchen, banging on Mattie's food bowl to summon the old dog to breakfast; carriages clattering in the street outside.

Damon.

She leaped out of bed, hastily washed her face, completed her toilet, and, garbed in a simple gown of peach satin trimmed with green embroidery, hurried downstairs.

Rhiannon was just coming around the corner. Her face mirrored the same worry that snaked through Gwyneth's heart. "Gwyn, maybe we ought to go down to the waterfront and see if anyone knows anything."

"Yes, I'm going now. You wait here in case anyone tries to contact us—"

As if her words had summoned it, there was a sudden knock on the door. Gwyneth froze, exchanging a frightened, paralyzed glance with her sister. The knock came again, sharp, hard, and businesslike, bringing Mattie charging out of the kitchen at a dead run, growling and barking, with Sophie right behind him. Gwyneth and Rhiannon leaped to the door.

Gwyneth reached it first and, as Rhiannon grabbed the dog's collar to restrain him, yanked it open.

Her heart flipped over. Two men stood there, one a naval lieutenant, young but well seasoned by duty, the other a scarlet-clad marine. Gwyneth took one look at their grim, emotionless faces, and involuntarily her hand went to her heart.

"Lady Morninghall?"

She swallowed hard against the rising sense of dread. "I am Lady Morninghall," she whispered, nearly cracking the doorknob with the force with which she gripped it. "Has something befallen my husband?"

"May we come in?"

"Yes—yes, by all means."

The two men entered, though neither made any move to make himself comfortable, standing just inside the small foyer and looking vaguely ill at ease. The blue-and-white-clad officer introduced himself as Lieutenant Whymark. "I come on behalf of Admiral Edmund Bolton, commander in chief of His Majesty's forces in the port of Portsmouth," he said, his voice coldly official and lacking any vestige of human emotion. He produced a sheet of paper from his pocket and, holding it out in front of his face, proceeded to read it, head high, his words droning on and on as the three women stared at him in horror.

"In short, Lady Morninghall," he said flatly, "your husband is being held under close arrest and faces charges of espionage, treason, neglect of his duties, and holding communication with an enemy—"

"Treason!" Rhiannon cried angrily, staring from Whymark to her benumbed sister. "This cannot be so!"

"—which are all severe crimes as defined by the Articles of War, specifically those articles pertaining to offenses against the executive power of the king and his government," Whymark continued, as though Rhiannon had never spoken. "There will be a court-martial, of course, which shall convene immediately." He rolled up the paper and returned it to his pocket, his trained, emotionless gaze meeting Gwyneth's. "I should prepare you, my lady, for the inevitable fact that these are all crimes deserving and punishable by nothing less than the death penalty."

Treason . . . espionage . . . holding communication with the enemy . . .

The death penalty.

The color drained from Gwyneth's face and she staggered back. *I will not faint,* she thought, taking deep breaths to calm herself as she met the officer's steady, pitiless gaze. She felt Rhiannon's hand supporting her elbow. *This is not happening!*

Very calmly, she said, "And where is my husband being held?"

"Aboard the port admiral's flagship. Lord Morninghall has sent word that he wishes to see you—"

"I shall go to him now."

"We will wait outside then, until you sort yourself out."

He turned abruptly, the marine following just behind, and began to walk down the steps.

"Wait!"

He paused and looked back at her patiently.

"What has my husband done to have such terrible charges brought upon him?"

Whymark looked at her in disbelief—a disbelief that quickly turned to pity as he realized she truly *was* ignorant of her husband's treasonous doings. "Did you not know?" he murmured, his eyes softening in sudden understanding. "Your husband was caught last night, engaged in the very act for which he has been charged. I am sorry to inform you, my lady, but the Marquess of Morninghall is the elusive Black Wolf."

"Impossible!" Gwyneth said coldly, as Admiral Bolton met her at the entry port of his massive, beautifully turned-out flagship. He looked down at her angry, militant face and flashing eyes with unshakable aplomb. "Utterly impossible! You have the wrong man, I tell you—my husband cannot be the Black Wolf!"

Bolton allowed a cold, patient smile. He took the marchioness's elbow and, nodding to a brace of Royal Marines to follow them, slowly led her aft. "My dear Lady Morninghall," he murmured cavalierly, "your husband is indeed that notorious criminal, and 'twas one of his own officers who apprehended him. There were many witnesses. I am sorry, but our proof is irrefutable."

"I told you before, and *I shall tell you again,*" Her Ladyship returned in a hard, forceful voice that a lesser man might have found intimidating, "my husband is not the man you seek. He *cannot* be, as he has been with me at our home in the Cotswolds for the better part of the last *month* and I happen to know that, in his absence, the Black Wolf struck the prison ship *Surrey* and tried to take off a young American. Even the Black Wolf cannot be in two places at once. My husband was with *me,* and I am *not* sorry, but I too have *irrefutable proof!*"

"I'm sure you do," Bolton allowed condescendingly, "but be that as it may, I can only tell you that the man who surrendered himself to us last night—while engaged in trying to rescue that very same lad, I might add—is the Marquess of Morninghall."

"I will go straight to the top about this, I swear it!"

"My dear lady, I *am* the top."

She flushed and tried to jerk her elbow free of his hand, impaling him with a look that could've melted glass. They stood there, the slight young woman facing down the glittering, all-powerful admiral who ruled over every officer and seaman who served in Portsmouth. "You will not murder my husband," she vowed. "I will stop at nothing, do you hear me, *nothing* in order to save him! The Marquess of Morninghall is innocent!"

"I do believe the court-martial will decide that. In fact, it shall convene tomorrow with my flag captain presiding over a panel of twelve other officers of highest rank, including captains and admirals. It will be a fair trial, Lady Morninghall, but I advise you not to hold out for any hope for a reprieve."

"You cannot do this."

"I *will* do it. And I will see the sentence carried out, quickly and efficiently."

"I will not let you hang my husband!"

"My dear lady, your husband is an officer. We do not hang our officers; we give them the dignity of a firing squad. Now if you'll please follow me . . ."

Seething, she glared at him, her pulse pounding angrily against her temples.

"Come," he was saying, "I have had your husband taken from the wardroom and placed in solitary confinement so that your visit with him might be more private. Let it not be said that Admiral Bolton does not have a heart, hmmm?"

With an arrogant sweep of his hand, he directed her down another ladder, and there, on the deck below, were cabins set in dim, long rows built into either side of the flagship's massive hull. Lanterns were hung from the beams above, but they did little to penetrate the oppressive gloom, which was even thicker within each of those tiny compartments. Bolton, bent nearly double to move beneath the deck above, led her forward, the two marines following at a discreet distance.

There, standing at attention just outside the last, most forward cabin, was another Royal Marine. His stance was ramrod straight, his musket rigidly poised at his side, his eyes staring straight ahead.

"Lady Morninghall has come to visit the accused," Bolton murmured, directing her forward. "See that she does not get into any *trouble*."

"Aye, sir."

One of the other marines moved ahead to unlock the door, then stood back so Gwyneth could enter. She shot Bolton a look of promised battle, but he was already moving back down the corridor, the remaining marine in his wake.

Gwyneth turned and looked into the shadowy depths of the cabin.

"Damon. Oh, my—"

He was sitting on a wooden bench, looking as contrite as a schoolboy caught in some devilish prank, an endearing half-guilty, half-hopeful little smile touching his lips. He rose at the sight of her, every inch a lord despite the fact that they had confined him like an animal, despite the fact that he'd most likely die like one as well. But Bolton had not lied: he was an officer, and they had allowed him every courtesy. His hair was combed, his face shaved, his clothing a clean, white shirt tucked into snug-fitting, white naval breeches. Gwyneth looked at him and thought him too magnificent to die. Too beautiful, too vital, too full of unused years. Her teeth sank into her trembling lower lip, and then with a little cry, she went into his outstretched arms.

"I am sorry, Gwyneth. Indeed I am."

She felt his strong, warm embrace closing about her shoulders, the comforting thump of his heart beneath her ear. "This cannot be happening, Damon. Someone, somewhere, made a mistake, you cannot be the Black Wolf!"

"Gwyneth." His hand was stroking her hair, calming her as he might a frightened young child. "Dear, loyal Gwyneth. Do you not remember what creatures guard the Marquesses of Morninghall as they sleep? Do you not remember what creatures stand watch from the very gates of Morninghall Abbey?" His voice was patient, resolute, resigned. "Think, dearest wife—and then think upon my surname."

"Wolves," she whispered brokenly, remembering now those magnificent creatures. And she knew what his proper surname was, deWolfe, but she refused to believe this. To believe it meant to believe in his mortality, his guilt, and that they could, and would, put him to death no matter how strongly the heart beneath her ear beat, no matter how valiantly she fought for his life. "No! I cannot believe it!"

"Believe it, my love, for it is true. The wrong man was not apprehended and arrested last night. I *am* the Black Wolf, and I have no regrets, except that you must learn of it in such a cruel and shocking way."

"But *why?*" she asked, pulling back to touch his cheek, to gaze beseechingly into his strangely beautiful eyes. "*Why,* Damon?"

He gave a sad, faraway smile. "Revenge mostly," he finally admitted with a guilty little shrug. He pulled her to the bench, made her sit down. As she gazed up at him, her eyes misty with confusion and denial, he told her the truth, starting with how the Black Wolf originally had been Connor Merrick, who, upon his escape from the prison hulk, had adopted the alias as a direct way to mock Damon deWolfe, its apathetic captain. So apathetic was that captain, so full of twisted fury and self-pity and hatred, that he'd knowingly allowed the rescues to go on right beneath his nose.

"But why?" Gwyneth asked, shaking her head and not understanding any of this.

"It gave me great pleasure to witness Bolton getting his just desserts. I loved seeing someone make a laughingstock of him, and as I had no respect for myself, and was so far gone in despair and anger, I didn't care that I too was being humiliated."

"But if Connor's really the Black Wolf . . ."

"Connor is not the Black Wolf. I am. He started it, but after you forced me to see how terrible things were belowdecks, I became ashamed of my apathy and desperate for a way to atone for it. I needed to prove I was worthy of you. That I too could do something brave and good for someone else. You'd done so much for those prisoners that I felt I could do no less."

Gwyneth pursed her lips. "And I suppose that, because it was also a way of gaining your own personal revenge against Bolton, it made playing the Black Wolf all the sweeter, am I right?"

Damon smiled sheepishly. "Well, yes . . ."

"Oh . . ." She stamped her foot hard. "Damn it, Damon!"

He gathered her close, pressing her cheek against his heart and laying his jaw against her hair. "I have no regrets, Gwyneth. I would do it all over again. Bolton aside, had I been able to save only *one* of those wretched, suffering souls, all that I have braved, all that I shall face in the days ahead would be worth it."

"Five more minutes," the marine called flatly from just outside the door.

"You should have told me," Gwyneth spat mutinously. "Damn it, Damon, you should have told me!"

"I could not. I could not take the chance that, if I were caught, you would be brought down with me." He gently grasped her shoulders and set her back, looking deeply into her angry eyes. "Especially as you were so keen on doing things to help the prisoners yourself. You were safer not knowing. Forgive me, Gwyneth, but I love you too much to allow you into the alliance of the Black Wolf."

"I don't know if I *can* forgive you," she said sharply. Her tears had dried, and she was almost glaring at him. His heart filled with admiration for her spirit, her courage. Already she was rallying, his little tigress, refusing to sit helplessly by—though, of course, there was nothing she could do for him.

She raised her chin, brave and determined. "So tell me, what will happen now?"

"There will be a court-martial, of course, to be held here aboard Bolton's flagship and continuing every forenoon until a verdict is reached and a sentence passed." He paused and looked at her solemnly. "It will be the penalty of death, Gwyneth."

The marine outside called, "Three more minutes!"

"I will write to Admiral Falconer! I will write to my former brother-in-law, Lord Simms! I will petition the Regent. I will not stop until you are freed, damn it. *I will not let you die!*"

He shook his head. "Dearest heart," he murmured, looking down into her face. "Admiral Falconer is on his way to the West Indies; by the time a message could be brought to him, it would be too late. Besides, there is nothing he can do, even if he *wished* to help me." He looked deeply into her angry eyes, his own gaze pleading. "I beg of you, Gwyneth, do not torture yourself so. There is nothing you can do. Absolutely nothing."

She got to her feet and faced him, her eyes sparking violet fire. "There is plenty I can do, my lord, plenty I *will* do. They say you're the notorious Black Wolf, do they? Well, then, *you tell me who tried to take that American boy off the hulk while we were at Morninghall!*"

"That is not for me to say."

"Damn it, Damon, the answer might save your life!"

"Nothing can save my life," he answered quietly, "except a supreme act of God. And given His opinion of me, that, my love, is highly unlikely."

The marine was there, unlocking the door. "Time's up," he muttered, beckoning impatiently for Gwyneth. "Let's go."

She swept to the door, eyes blazing defiance. There she stopped, only to turn and point a finger at the man who sat on the bench, watching her. "Very well then," she said tightly, glaring at him, "we shall just have to see what God says about it, won't we?"

And with that she picked up her skirts and stormed out, determined to save the life of the man she loved.

Chapter 28

The court-martial convened the following morning.

For Gwyneth, who was excluded from witnessing it, it was the beginning of a week of hell. With a tireless fervor that eclipsed anything she had ever done before, with a frenzied devotion that overshadowed the combined efforts she had made on behalf of all the other causes she had ever embraced, she threw herself into the task of saving the life of her husband.

On the first day of the trial, she wrote a long, passionately desperate letter to her former brother-in-law, begging him to use his influence in Parliament and in the navy to obtain a pardon for the Marquess of Morninghall. She called together her committee and the wives of Portsmouth's upper naval crust, hoping they could somehow influence their husbands who served on the court-martial to show leniency. She consulted with various naval personnel, she visited with her husband that afternoon, and sometime late in the wee hours she fell into her bed exhausted, depleted from her efforts.

The following morning and for every morning thereafter, she looked down from her window upon that massive flagship sitting out there in the harbor, and willed her wishes upon those she knew were deciding the fate of Lord Morninghall behind the flat, shining panes of its elaborate stern gallery.

To no avail.

The court-martial went into its second day.

Growing more and more desperate, Gwyneth fired off another letter to Lord Simms. She obtained a copy of the navy's Articles of War and brought them to her solicitor, hoping, with no success, that together they could find a loophole. She wrote to members of Parliament, to the prime minister, to the lords of the Admiralty, to everyone of power and influence she knew.

No one could help her—and the court-martial continued.

On the third day she went to London and pleaded with as many of those individuals as she could gain appointments with.

On the fourth day she garbed herself most splendidly and sought an audience with the prince regent, who promptly granted her request and then sat listening to her story with amused patience, all the while discreetly ogling her bosom, making sexual innuendos with his eyes, and letting his gaze rove up and down her trim frame. The ogling continued, as did the amused grin, until Gwyneth finally brought out her heavy guns, the one thing on which she was banking to save Damon: the fact that the Black Wolf had struck the prison hulk while Lord Morninghall wasn't even *in* Portsmouth, but at home in the Cotswolds, gravely injured and near death.

The Regent stared at her for a moment, then kneaded his fleshy chin before promising to give the matter what thought it merited, cutting her audience short with a faint excuse about having a hundred other matters to attend to before teatime.

And Gwyneth felt her hopes running out.

On the sixth day the trial ended, and the thirteen captains and admirals who served on the court-martial came to a unanimous decision that was immediately confirmed by the Admiralty in London:

Lord Morninghall had been found guilty of the crimes with which he was charged, and was sentenced to die. Execution would be carried out at dawn the

following morning by a firing squad of ten Royal
Marines.

That evening, after Gwyneth watched the sun sink
in a bloody ball into the western sky, after the
shadows in her room deepened and finally succumbed
to the darkness, she got down on her knees beside her
bed. Tears streaming down her cheeks, she prayed
with all her heart that God would help her plight, and
in those last, desperate hours before dawn He did.

God came in the form of the Reverend Peter
Milford.

"Lord Morninghall? If you'll come with me,
please."

The night still lay heavily outside the great gallery
of the wardroom, but the mist was not as black as it
had been the previous hour, and Damon knew that
dawn was on its way.

He had not slept at all this night, but then he
supposed that his body somehow knew it would soon
sleep the eternal rest, and was trying to snatch what
few hours of life remained to it, even if those hours
had been long, reflective, and tortured. Raking his
hair back with his fingers, he sat up, wide awake and
resigned to his fate. Simon Wordsworth, the young
lieutenant who had been given the duty of being his
so-called "gaoler," stood quietly and patiently in the
shadows. Around him the other lieutenants still slum-
bered, their rasping snores and sleepy grunts disturbing the quiet of the large cabin.

"It will soon be time, sir," Wordsworth whispered.
"I thought you would like a wash and a shave, uh,
beforehand," he finished lamely.

"And some breakfast too, I hope?" Damon added
with a little smile he hoped would ease the poor
lieutenant's distress.

"Of course, sir. If you'll come with me . . ."

Damon followed the junior officer out of the wardroom. Two armed marines awaited them outside,

quickly taking up the rear of their small procession. To Damon's surprise he found his stride felt sure and confident, his heart light, his head clear. He thought of God and wondered at the thought, until he rationalized that most men who were this close to death probably did the same. Strangely, his impending death brought him no fear. He envisioned the neat row of ten Royal Marines, all dressed in scarlet uniforms with white belts crossing their chests, their boots shining, their faces expressionless, their muskets stiffly at their sides; he could imagine the marine drummer, could imagine someone coughing, could almost hear the commands: *"Ready!"*—the muskets all jerking up as one—*"Aim!"*—all training on his body—

"Fire!"

It would be quick and, with ten bullets ripping into his heart at once, painless. He had a vision of his body jerking and convulsing before finally falling dead to the deck, his chest nothing but a ravaged, gory hole, his eyes staring and his mouth open in a soundless scream.

And still he felt no fear, nothing but a strange, resigned calm.

Perhaps this was God's way of making these last hours easier. Perhaps the attacks of senseless panic he'd had up until so recently had prepared him for the real thing. Perhaps . . .

Who knows, he thought as Wordsworth showed him into a small cabin, where a young servant waited beneath a hanging lantern. On a bench were a plate of food, a bowl, and a pitcher. Wordsworth turned to Damon and nodded, and Damon plunged his hands into the cool water, splashing it over his face and into his hair as the marines waited stiffly outside. He was keenly aware of every sensation, knowing it would be the last time he'd ever experience them: the slippery coolness of the water, the play of light over the bowl and the shadows his head cast across it, the light scent of the soap, the feel of the deck beneath his shoes. He toweled his face and hair and sat down on the bench. The servant boy immediately lathered his face and neck and began to shave him.

Through the cabin's open gun port he could see the dark, clinging mist lightening to charcoal. He glanced at Wordsworth as the boy pulled the razor over his cheek. The lieutenant's hands were clasped tightly behind his back, and he was rocking back and forth, obviously very ill at ease.

He did not meet Damon's gaze.

The lieutenant's distress only brought home the reality of what was happening. Damon shut his eyes and instead of thinking about it, concentrated on the simple pleasure of the razor moving over his skin. He thought of Gwyneth, as he had done for most of the past, endless night, and he thanked God who had sought to comfort him in this, his final hour that she would not have to see his bloody end.

All too soon the shave was finished, the breakfast was eaten, and Lieutenant Wordsworth and the two armed marines were escorting Damon out of the cabin, up through a hatch, and out onto the damp deck, still bathed in early-morning mist, where a contingent of six armed marines waited silently near the launch that would be swung out and over the side.

A mild offshore wind, ripe with the scent of the mudflats, stirred the heavy mists and rippled Damon's white shirt. Above, lines hummed and the admiral's pennant gave a single, half-hearted crack. Somewhere off in the mists to starboard came the splash of oars as a fisherman headed out to sea to ply his nets.

"Ready, sir?"

Damon nodded. Moments later he was sitting in the launch, Lieutenant Wordsworth and the escort of armed marines flanking him on all sides.

"Gonna be a fine day," one of the oarsmen said tactlessly as the breeze pushed through the mists and made the sea ruffle against the launch's hull. Wordsworth shot the sailor a severe look, and shame-faced, the man looked away.

Slowly the launch moved away from the flagship in a swirl of bubbly foam. Damon kept his gaze straight ahead and did not look back. He could well imagine Bolton standing in his cabin, a satisfied smile on his face, watching. Or perhaps Bolton wanted to savor his final act of revenge in person, and already awaited him at the place of execution.

The wash of water beneath the hull became a low hum as the launch gained speed. The mist clung, sticky and damp, to skin and hair, but the breeze was already beginning to make short work of it, scattering the thick, gray skeins and pushing them out toward the sea.

Wordsworth leaned over into Damon's ear. "The sentence will be carried out aboard the *Athena,*" he said quietly. "You—you understand."

Of course, Damon thought. Bolton would not have wanted blood and guts fouling the deck of his precious flagship.

"That is, unless there is a royal reprieve," Wordsworth added lamely. "If one should come, it will be revealed during those moments just before the command to fire is given."

"Aye, they'll want to make ye suffer first," grunted one of the seamen, leaning into his oar.

"I do not entertain any false hopes," Damon said softly. He bestowed an earnest look upon the lieutenant. "And neither should you."

Biting his lip, the young officer looked away, deeply troubled.

The mist was thinning now, and through it the shore appeared in patches, with long, gray-brown docks stretching like stiff fingers out toward them. Off to larboard the hull of a '74 made a seemingly insurmountable wall, its wet wales glinting in the virgin light, its gun ports all open to catch the morning breeze, its anchor chain disappearing into the gray sea. Was it the *Athena?* No. The launch kept moving, a speedy knife through the sleepy harbor, the water rushing against its bows, the oars rising and falling with perfect dripping precision.

Damon looked wistfully at the nearby shore and at the many brick buildings, all fuzzy in the mist. He thought of Gwyneth out there, somewhere. He hoped Rhiannon was with her. He hoped . . .

That she would be all right.

Already the world was awakening. On the shore ahead he could see movement: fishermen loading their nets into weather-beaten craft, a group of seamen stumbling along the beach, still reeling from a night of hard drinking, and there, just ahead, a hoy, one of those dockyard sailing boats that brought stores around the harbor. Its mast stuck up like a pencil into the thinning fog; the tide and current were causing it to jerk and pull against its mooring line, which slackened and snapped taut with every rise and fall of the sea beneath it.

Coming up out of the mist off the starboard bow was the hull of the warship *Athena.*

"Lay on your oars!"

The rush of water beneath the launch lessened in pitch as the crew brought their oars up and feathered them, letting the craft's momentum carry her forward.

It'll be quick, Damon reminded himself, refusing to let the sudden prickles of fear show in his impassive face. He could feel the eyes of the boat crew and the marines on him, no doubt consigning to memory every detail of his face and form so they could someday tell their grandchildren about him, and how they had accompanied the Black Wolf across the harbor to his death. No doubt some were morbidly envisioning what he was going to look like as a corpse, or thinking about the unlikely events that had led him to this inglorious end. Perhaps some of them pitied him, while others secretly admired him. Either way he knew that none of them envied him, and were already seeing him as a dead man.

"Bring her right up there, to the main chains!"

As the boat crew struggled to maneuver the un-wieldy launch, Damon calmly looked up. High above on the quarterdeck of the mighty '74, he could already see the smartly turned-out captain, a portly, balding man surrounded by two lieutenants. Nearby, their scarlet-and-white chests just visible as they moved about the deck, were the Royal Marines; Damon wondered which of them would be in the lineup to execute him. He found the sight vaguely disturbing, and as the launch closed toward the huge hull he looked away, back toward shore.

And saw that the hoy had broken loose from its mooring and was heading straight toward them.

No one else saw it, of course. The escort of armed marines and Lieutenant Wordsworth were watching the boat crew, and the boat crew was busy trying to maneuver the launch into position. The officers and marines on the deck high above were engaged in conversation or running about preparing the deck for the grim scene that was soon to come. Only the Marquess of Morninghall saw the hoy coming straight on, slanting strangely, purposefully across the pull of tide and current, and only he saw the lumpy figures crouched in its hull beneath a tarp.

And I thought I didn't have friends. . . .

With lordly calm and a perfect absence of expression, he raised his head and gazed out to sea.

Just as one of the officers on the *Athena*'s deck above saw the onrushing hazard.

"Mind the boat!"

Too late.

Damon threw himself out of the launch just as the hoy slammed into it with all the force of a battering ram. He heard the grinding, splintering crash, the surprised screams of marines and oarsmen alike as the launch capsized, spilling them all into the sea. But that was all he heard, because in the next moment the sea closed over his own head and he was swimming underwater with fierce, mighty strokes toward the hoy's retreating stern as though his life depended on it.

As well it did.

He heard the muffled pop of muskets from the warship, their bullets sprinkling the water all around; he heard muted shouts and screams and violent splashing as the occupants of the late launch, most of whom could not swim, thrashed about in panic. Above was the oblong underside of the hoy's hull, swirling with bubbles and confusion and wreckage, and then it was moving swiftly away, its crew returning the fire of those aboard the warship as it fled toward the open sea.

Still underwater, Damon struck out after it.

A rope trailed over the side, leaving a streaming V in the watery gray-white ceiling above his head, and without breaking the surface he caught it, knotted it once around his wrist, and let himself be carried along behind the hoy. Air had never been so precious and he fought to stay conscious, his lungs beginning to constrict, the blood beating in his ears, his brain—

Hold on, damn it, hold on!

His vision went speckly, and his teeth clenched against an involuntary inhalation.

No more.

The air burst from his lungs, and with all his strength he hauled himself to the surface, breaking it only long enough to catch a gulp of air before letting himself be yanked back down beneath the slapping waves. But that brief moment had provided him with a sure glimpse of his rescuers: Orla, a musket braced against her shoulder as she returned the fire of the *Athena*'s men; Nathan Ashton, hauling the sail up with desperate speed; and Connor at the tiller, maneuvering the boat so the sail could best catch the rising wind. Damon shut his eyes and held tightly to the rope, arms outstretched before him, the cold water streaming past and around his body like the current of a spring river. The hoy was moving fast, dragging him along with it, and as he broke the surface for air a second time, he looked over his shoulder and saw the flashes of musket fire from the *Athena,* the cutter dropping from her stern to begin pursuit, and heard the enraged shouts of those who had been denied their bloody spectacle.

No sooner had he dropped below the slapping surface once more when his rescuers were hauling on his rope with violent tugs. As they wrestled him up and into the hoy, his body limp and dripping, the breath roaring through his starved lungs in great, sucking gasps, he saw that a helpful God had already blown the mists back in over the warship, and that their hoy was well on its way out into the Solent.

Orla, pretty, daring, piratical Orla whom Peter so loved, turned to him with a grin on her spritely face. "Please get down there beneath the tarp, my lord. We'd like to keep you safe and hidden until we can get you back to the *Kestrel,* where Reverend Milford and your *wife* await you." Then, just before throwing the tarp over Damon, she snatched up her musket and pointed it aft, her wild, exultant laughter ringing over the waves.

"Would you look at that!"

Everyone in the little boat turned. The mists had parted behind them, but only long enough for them to see the confusion in the water that surrounded the now-distant *Athena.* Sailors were diving into the churning sea, men were shouting back and forth, and the cutter was not in pursuit, but moving about, plucking people out of the water.

"Fools!" Connor cried, laughing. "They're obviously searching for the drowned body of the Marquess of Morninghall!"

Then the fog closed over the fading scene once more, and the little hoy was alone in the mists, heading further and further into the Solent.

"There she is," Connor said, his voice soft with emotion, and as Nathan pulled the tarp off Damon so that he too could see, a reverent hush fell over them all.

Even the Marquess of Morninghall's eyes filled with moisture.

For there, her rail awash, her sails catching the first light of dawn, and her long, plunging bowsprit trained on them like a compass, was the schooner *Kestrel*.

Epilogue

It hadn't changed.

Just as it had for centuries, Morninghall Abbey stood atop its emerald-green throne, commanding a sweeping, unbroken view of the magnificent Cotswolds that surrounded it. When its lord and lady had left, poppies had been strewn everywhere in wild abandon; now they were long gone, apples lay on the ground around the trees, and the wheat had been harvested, leaving the fields shorn and bleached. Blackberries were fat on the vines that climbed the walls of yellow stone, the wild grasses were heavy and bent, and there was a decided crispness in the air, a tense expectancy.

For the lord of Morninghall was finally coming home.

The schooner *Kestrel* had caught up to Sir Graham's mighty flagship *Orion* on her journey back to the West Indies, and as brother and sister had fought over ownership of the little ship, the admiral had calmly welcomed Lord and Lady Morninghall into his cabin. Ignoring the fierce battle raging just outside, and treating his guests to a bottle of his finest port, he'd read them the news a fast-sailing messenger had brought him not seven hours before: the Prince Regent had granted a reprieve to the Marquess of Morninghall, only to have the lord snatched right out from under the guns of the warship on which he'd been sentenced to die.

As darkness fell an hour later, Connor—who'd won a blind eye from Sir Graham and grudging (albeit temporary) ownership of the schooner from his sister—was heading triumphantly off to the east, and the massive, hundred-gun warship *Orion* was coming about, setting a course back to England.

Now the end of Lord Morninghall's long journey was nearing. As the coach, fresh from London where the marquess had met with the Prince Regent, slowed going up that last, noblest hill, the setting sun broke from the clouds and spread a bath of orange glory over the vast rolling hills. It was an omen of the finest sort, and inside the coach the marchioness smiled and exchanged glances with her husband. She wore an elegant gown of turquoise watered silk, and its high empire waist did much to conceal the fact that her belly was already beginning to swell with child. Not that she was trying to conceal it. Her husband's hand rested possessively on her rounded stomach, and as they turned up the road that led to the massive gates of Morninghall, she saw that he too was smiling.

He had never looked handsomer, she thought, studying his aristocratic profile, his virile form, nor lordlier. She thought about their brief time with Sir Graham. The admiral had treated him with the deferential respect due a marquess, and indeed, for the first time in many a month, Damon had been at ease with a naval superior. But perhaps that was because Sir Graham was no longer his naval superior, nor was anyone else in the Royal Navy. Damon had wasted no time in officially handing in his resignation to the unsurprised admiral, and as he'd done so, Gwyneth had seen his proud shoulders going back, as though a great weight finally had been lifted from them.

It was the right, the only decision, and she loved him for it.

Now he was staring out the window, boyishly eager for his first view of the magnificent house he thought he'd never see again, and as he sensed her gaze upon him, he turned. His eyes were cool, but fire simmered in their depths, and she knew that that fire was for her.

She thought of that huge, curtained bed in the ancient chamber and smiled to herself.

"And what amuses you so, my lovely wife?"

"Oh, I was just thinking."

"About?"

"Making love in our own bed tonight."

Damon chuckled darkly and leaned over to graze her neck with his lips. "Great minds must think alike, for I confess I was thinking the very same thing."

"Were you?"

"I was."

They both laughed, staring lovingly into each other's eyes as the coach drew up to the gates. The massive black wolves looked down on them, their marble eyes seeming to gleam with approval; then the attendant swung those iron portals wide, and the coach moved down the shadowy, stately drive.

Toward the magnificent house that waited at its end.

Toward the servants, already gathered on the great stairs in an exultant, cheering array.

And, for Lord and Lady Morninghall, toward a lifetime of bright tomorrows.